For Theresa,

it — t
you — del Re,
all the best.
Un abbraccio,

[signature]

Rivanazzano
06/04/2014

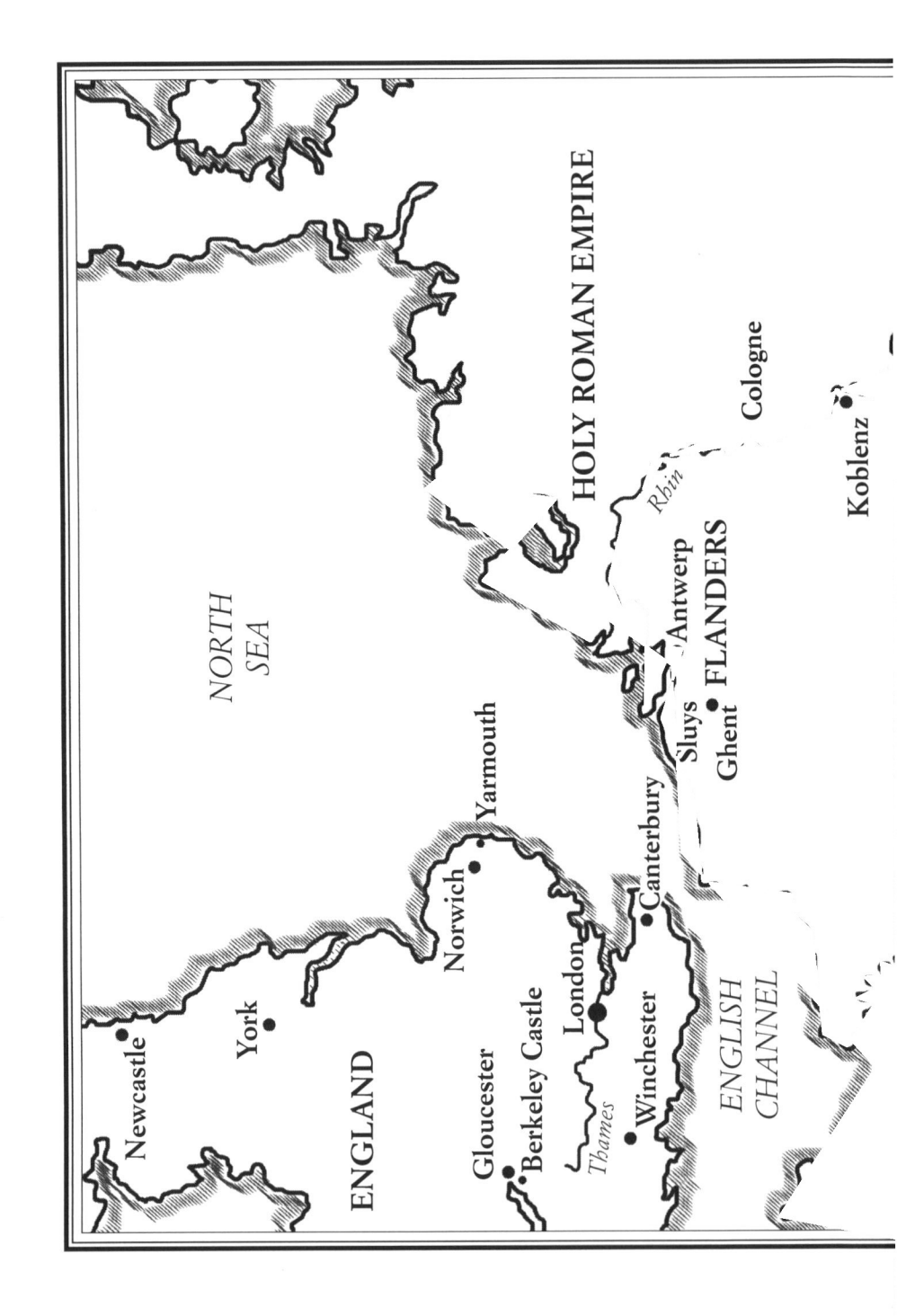

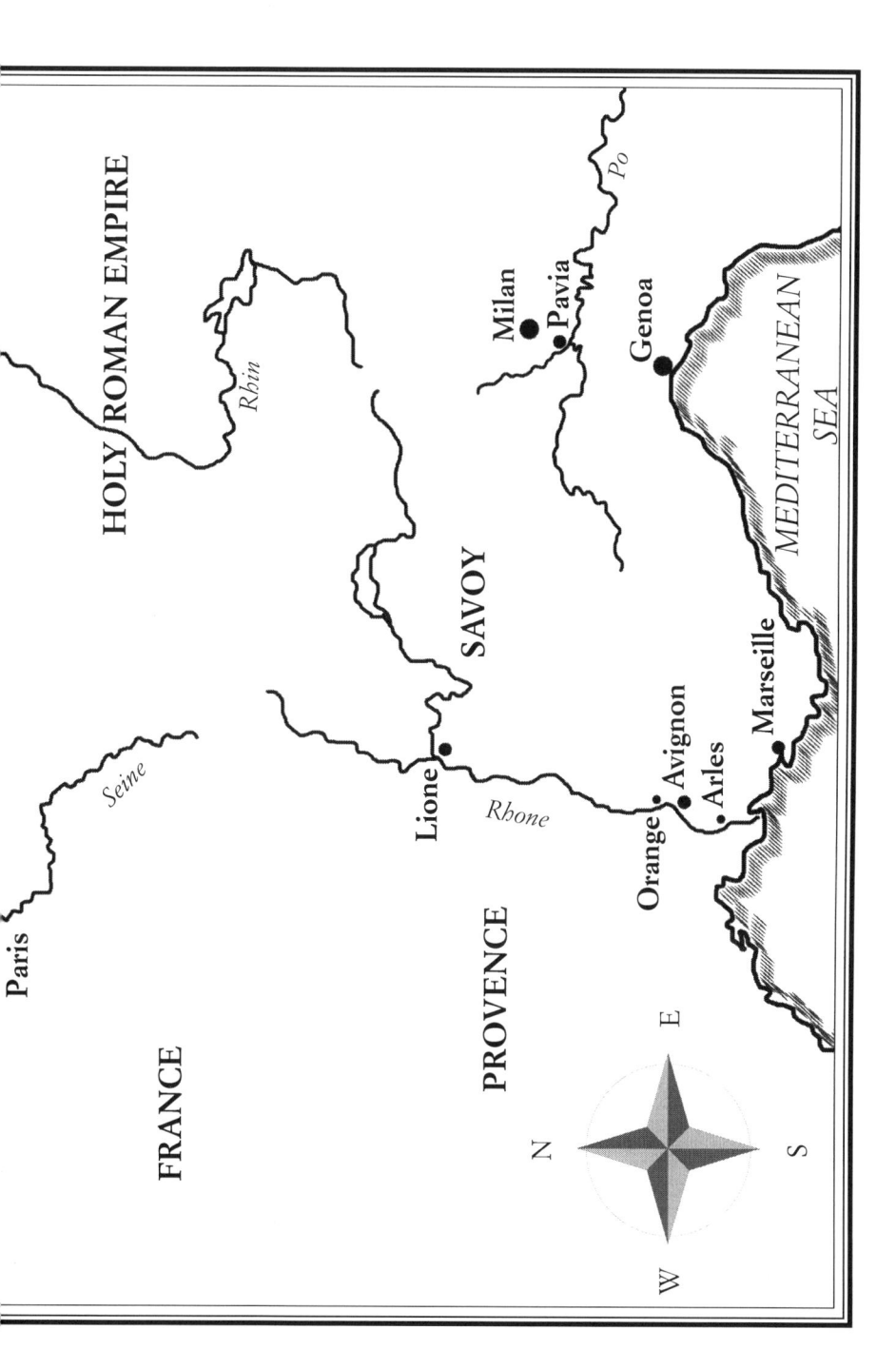

Ivan Fowler
AURAMALA
The King Lives

All rights reserved

© 2013 Ivan Fowler
for Associazione Culturale Il Mondo di TELS/The World of TELS, Pavia (Italy)
First edition January 2013
Second edition November 2013

ISBN 978-88-908336-4-9

Editing: Il Mondo di TELS/The World of TELS and Imogheena Farandel

Cover illustration: Oramala Castle (Pavia, Italy)
from a photograph by Fabrizio Capecchi
Cover graphics by Betty Cominotti

Cartography by Betty Cominotti and Simone Bertelegni

Layout by Simone Bertelegni

Printed by Galli Thierry Stampa, Milan (Italy)

www.auramala.com
theauramalaproject.wordpress.com

O, hadst thou ever been a king, thy heart,
Pierc'd deeply with sense of my distress,
Could not but take compassion of my state!
Stately and proud in riches and in train,
Whilom I was, powerful and full of pomp:
But what is he whom rule and empery
Have not in life or death made miserable?

--

O, that I might this life in quiet lead!

Christopher Marlowe, *Edward II*
Act IV, Scene 6

For our children, and theirs

Acknowledgements

Five years ago *Auramala* began as an ambitious idea of Il Mondo di TELS/The World of TELS, a cultural association of Pavia. I became the designated author almost by accident, thanks to one 'yes' too many, riding on a wave of enthusiasm and healthy, uncontrollable folly. However, right from the start I knew I was a part of a team of formidable professionals. In unison and individually, each in their own way, the people of the association made my work easier and better. Mariarosa Gatti, Elena Giacomotti, Alice Galbiati, Betty Cominotti, Giacomo Sardelli and Simone Bertelegni were joined over the course of the work by many teachers, students and other members of TELS who gave me their precious time, implacable criticisms, topsy-turvy world views, affection and encouragement. On the other side of the Channel, our pro-Berkeley friends offset the TELS virus with their common sense, skepticism and irony.

I wish to thank my family, my mother Hilary, my siblings Kylie, Imogheena and Simon, and above all my wife Enza, and my sons Niccolò and Dario, who have shared their house for five years with the ghosts of a distant past. *Grazie!*

And finally, my thanks go to Jeremy and Kerry. Without you, this novel would have had no heart.

Auramala

Fabulae personae

*Invented characters

The Welshman
Lay-brother (conversus) at the Abbey of Sant'Alberto di Butrio in the Apennines of Pavia.

Brother Demetrio*   (deh-MEH-tree-oh)
Benedictine Brother at the Abbey of Sant'Alberto di Butrio. He is a healer.

Gilio*   (JEE-lee-oh)
Benedictine Novice and pupil of Brother Demetrio.

Don Rogerio*   (don ro-JEH-ree-oh)
Head of a peasant family of Pizzocorno, a village in the territory of Sant'Alberto di Butrio.

Natalino (senior)*   (nah-tah-LEE-noh)
Don Rogerio's father, who sailed the high seas on Genoese galleys in his youth.

Maria*   (mah-REE-ah)
The mother of Don Rogerio's now-deceased wife.

Natalino (junior)*   (nah-tah-LEE-noh)
Don Rogerio's youngest son.

Silva* (SEEl-vah)
A wise-woman who lives in the woods and practices healing and magic.

John de Ulgham*
Agent of the King of England's secret business. Descendent of Saxon thanes of Northumberland, and one-time wandering university student.

William de Tels*
John de Ulgham's pupil and assistant in the art of secret business. Younger son of Sir Henry de Tels.

Sir Henry de Tels*
Knight of Norwich, he fought on many occasions against the Scots and Irish under both Edward I and Edward II.

Sir Thomas de Aldcliffe*
Knight of Lancaster and loyal servant of Henry de Grosmont, heir to the Earldom of Lancaster.

King Edward III
King of England, son of Edward II.

Henry de Grosmont
Heir to the Earldom of Lancaster, the most powerful nobleman in England after his cousin, King Edward III.

William de Montague
Earl of Salisbury and one-time mentor to King Edward III.

Richard de Bury
Bishop of Durham, mentor to King Edward III and chief overseer of the King's secret business. All agents of said business are bound to his service.

William Bateman
Auditor lawyer from Norwich, attached to the Papal Court of Avignon, but loyal to the King of England.

Henry Tideswell
A merchant captain and a smuggler.

Ubaldo de Fénis   (oo-BAHL-doh deh FEH-neess)
Knight of the Dukedom of Savoy. He is temporarily in the service of the House of Fieschi of Genoa.

Niccolò Fieschi   (neek-koh-LOH fee-EH-skee)
Genoese merchant prince of the House of Fieschi. His uncle, Cardinal Luca Fieschi, has recently died and Niccolò has taken control of the fortunes of his family. The House of Fieschi is aligned with the Guelph (Papal) faction.

Francesco Forzetti   (frahn-CHEH-skoh fort-SET-ti)
Lombard mercenary and chief agent of the secret business of the House of Fieschi.

Wiligelmo da Campione*   (wil-ee-GEHL-moh dah cahm-pee-OH-neh)
Apprentice marble sculptor from Campione, in northern Lombardy, who lives with his father and sister in Avignon.

Pietro da Campione*   (pee-EH-troh dah cahm-pee-OH-neh)
Master marble sculptor from Campione in the north of Lombardy, father of Wiligelmo e Alehandra.

Alehandra da Campione*   (ah-leh-HAHN-drah dah cahm-pee-OH-neh)
Daughter of Pietro da Campione and younger sister of Wiligelmo.

Miquel and Rotbert*   (MEE-kwehl ROT-behrt)
Ecclesiastical scribes working in various departments of the papacy in Avignon.

Opicino de Canistris   (oh-pee-CHEE-noh deh cah-NEE-striss)
Priest, scholar and map-maker from Pavia, Lombardy, now living in Avignon. He was once the tutor of the daughters of Filippone Langosco, Palatine Count of Pavia. Canistris is aligned with the Guelph (Papal) faction, and is attached to the Papal Court of Avignon.

Gherardo Spinola   (geh-RAHR-doh SPEE-noh-lah)
Merchant prince of the House of Spinola of Genoa, Marshal of Robert of Anjou, King of Naples, rival of the House of Fieschi and ally of the House of Doria. Both the House of Spinola and the House of Doria are

traditionally aligned with the Ghibelline (Imperial) faction, although at the time of the narrative they are nominally in the service of the Guelph (Papist) King of Naples.

Bianca Bottigella*   (bee-AHN-ka bot-tee-JELL-ah)
Daughter of Matteo Bottigella, noble woad merchant of Calvignano, near Pavia, and of Filippina Langosco, one-time pupil of Opicino de Canistris. Both the Bottigella and the Langosco families are aligned with the Guelph (Papal) faction.

Prologue

Sluys Harbour, 24 June, 1340

The King must stand – the third attack

Under the swirling grey clouds, a strong south-westerly whipped sea-spray from the crests of the waves and into Edward's open wound every time the ship wallowed low into a trough. He clenched his teeth, not knowing which was worse; Morestede's needle or the sting of the salt water on his rent flesh.

"If Your Majesty would only be seated!" The surgeon exclaimed, exasperated.

"No! All of my men on all of my boats must see me upright. They must know I'm here, standing, ready to battle." The cog *Thomas*' sail was furled, and the flagship lay in the open sea beyond the harbor heads, surrounded by the hundred-and-more surviving ships of the royal fleet. All were anchored in place while the King's injury was attended to.

Suddenly, the high aft-castle bucked as the prow was lifted by the swell, and King Edward III took an involuntary step backwards, tearing the needle and cat-gut thread from the flesh of his own shoulder. He repressed a cry.

"George," the surgeon barked, using wool cloth to stem the flow of blood from this new tear "stand with your back against the King's, I must have him steady." His young assistant hesitated, for he had never touched the King's person, and wasn't sure he had the right to. "Hurry boy!"

Edward nodded to Morestede's apprentice. "Do as he says." Though only sixteen, George had a torso as stout and sturdy as many a grown man's. When Edward felt those broad shoulders lean against his back he nodded to the surgeon.

Morestede warned his King in a matter-of-fact tone before pressing the needle home for the first stitch. "Brace." Edward gritted his teeth against the pain. Suture after suture, Morestede continued. "Brace... Brace..."

The King spoke to the members of his Council who were anxiously huddled around him. "My Lords, be seated..." *Brace...* "clear the space around me. Our brothers in the other ships must..." *Brace...* "must see me up on my own two feet."

The men of the Council left, tottering on the moving deck like unbalanced toddlers in their plate armor. Among those English earls and barons was a dark-faced foreigner, a merchant-prince of Genoa.

"I shall be seated at once, Your Majesty." The Genoese declared in an unnecessarily loud voice. He had spent much of his life aboard ship, and showed off his greater poise to those who despised him by reaching the bulwark with a few sure-footed strides. Following the habit of a lifetime, the Genoese knelt gracefully on his left knee, leaving his right leg raised and ready should he need to spring up into combat. The left side of his body, clad in leather and light chain, was thus flush against the wood; his right hand rested on the hilt of his dagger at his right hip. Ready, wary and practical: a true Genoese. The lords of the King's Council regarded him with loathing.

"The King!" Came a distant shout from across the waves "Look, all of you, the King stands!" Now the space around Edward had been cleared, his dearest friend and deadliest fighter, Henry de Grosmont, had caught sight of him from the foremost ship of the left wing of the fleet. Rapidly the cry was relayed from ship to ship, crow's nest to crow's nest, and soon all the heaving green sea was ringing with the voices of a thousand Englishmen crying "The King stands!"

"Brace." Morestede was still calmly repeating at regular intervals as he stitched. "Brace... Brace..."

Edward made light of the situation, distracting himself with irony.

"Isn't it a pity, Messer Fieschi, that one of your country-men decided to spit me with his crossbow bolt?" The Genoese met his gaze with calm, steely eyes, ignoring the scowls of the King's councillors. "We would have been well into the third advance by now."

"My countrymen stationed on the French ships are mercenaries, Your Majesty." Fieschi coolly replied. "They are simply earning their pay. They know nothing of an agreement with my family. Rest assured that Boccanegra and his sailors on their galleys are different. They know my family will double what the French have already paid them if they honour our pact when Your Majesty launches the third attack on the French lines."

"Pay?" Blond and blue-eyed, the barrel chested earl, William de Montague came forward. "Indeed, if you want a Genoese man's soul, all you need do is pay." The mutters of the other members of the Council echoed his sentiments. "If we start the third advance and Boccanegra doesn't hold up his side of the bargain you brokered for us, what pay will you expect?" Montague narrowed his eyes shrewdly, and the tone of his voice became suddenly chilling. "I wonder if you know how to swim?"

Never had the animosity between the two men been so open. Fieschi astutely replied as though he had taken the question at face value.

"Of course I cannot swim, my Lord. I'm a man of rank, not a fisher-boy."

The scoffing of the English aristocrats at the word 'rank' was audible. Niccolò Fieschi boasted no title that to their eyes could be called noble.

The King intervened in an amused voice, his words punctuated by pained pauses as Morestede, the surgeon, deftly knotted the stitches tight.

"In truth, there was once a nobleman of the highest possible rank who… swam very well." He saw Fieschi's eyes widen slightly for a moment, and continued. "Did you know that my father, the late King Edward, used to be fond of swimming?" He subtly emphasized the past tense. Fieschi's gaze became impenetrable, his eyes like two pebbles of volcanic glass. The councillors instantly fell silent. All but Montague were bewildered by the King's change of subject. "Yes," Edward went on, lightly "he used to… to muddy the Royal Person in estuaries and streams the length and breadth of England. He enjoyed it better than hunting… Odd, wasn't he…?" No one dared reply. Though long gone, a king was a king, and only a sovereign might dare to publicly speak ill of him. Montague alone showed his teeth to the Genoese in a menacing smile.

"Since you can't swim to match our late King, I hope for your sake that Boccanegra moves promptly when the attack is launched." He spoke in a low voice, his fellow Barons left speechless by this confusing exchange.

"That's the stitches finished." The surgeon announced after a long moment, breaking the silence. "Step away, George, I need to bandage him."

"Are you nearly done?" Edward enquired calmly. When the surgeon nodded, the King spoke to his admiral. "Let the mariners open the sails, and signal the other ships to follow suit. Let's waste no more time." He turned his head to survey the sky to the rear of the fleet. "A break in the clouds is approaching. Not for nothing did we maneuver to have the sun at our backs. I want to be grappling with the French once more by the time the sun shines through to dazzle their eyes."

The admiral took a scarlet flag on a long pole, and swung it in three broad arcs. The signalers on the other cogs responded with green flags, and the third attack commenced.

Amid a cacophony of shouts and orders, sailors hurried up the *Thomas'* rigging and mast to unfurl the sail. For a short time Edward followed them with his eyes. Their supple bodies swayed high above the deck on the yard arms while the mast amplified the motion of the waves and described wild ellipses against the grey sky. The gyrating of the men's silhouettes made Edward realize that the wound had weakened his stomach, for nausea threatened to make him retch in front of his subjects. He turned quickly away, and focused on Morestede's calm eyes as he concentrated on winding the bandage tight.

Soon the admiral called out "The sail's full, Your Majesty!"

Beneath his feet, Edward felt the ship leap forward with the driving wind. He cried out in the English tongue in a great voice "Be praised and thanked, Mariners, that was well and swiftly done!"

Among the councillors all eyes were now turned toward the right wing of the harbour, where the huge and swift Genoese galleys were patrolling the straits beside the French ships. While the French ships were chained together, deck to deck, in lines blocking most of the harbour mouth, the galleys commanded by Egidio Boccanegra and his captains remained free to maneuver by both sail and oar. Agility and speed was where their strength lay, despite their greater size.

At the start of the day there had been no less than three parallel lines of French ships. Early in the morning the first line had been raided, ravaged and reduced to mere wreckage bobbing in the waves. In the fighting the French admiral had been killed. The English fleet's second assault had been broken off when the King had been struck in the shoulder by a crossbowman. Now they were attacking for the third time, hoping to break the second French line.

On the flagship, the great lords of the kingdom maintained their tense silence, straining to make out the movements of the galleys. All hoped that Boccanegra would be true to the un-chivalrous pact he'd made with the English King through Fieschi's mediation. Fieschi unconsciously half rose to see the better over the bulwark. His eyes seemed to grow darker, ever darker; with his stare he was willing his countryman to act. Finally, the galleys started changing course. Time seemed almost to stand still. Were their prows swinging toward the open sea? Or were they turning toward the English to meet the fresh attack? Should those fearsome galleys clash against Edward's slow, wallowing cogs, the loss of English life would be horrendous, and a French victory a certainty.

All held their breath, except Morestede the surgeon and his apprentice, George, who were fitting the King's shoulder plate back on over the bandaging.

Time passed with aching slowness, and then another. The galleys swung about on their keels, then one by one settled on a new course. Yes, there could be no doubt, the prows of Boccanegra's galleys were now turned as one toward the North Sea! The oars were working quickly, and all the sails of the three masts had been deployed, billowing in the south-westerly. Their speed was startling compared to that of the English fleet. Their graceful hulls seemed to skim the surface of the wave as they passed away, far from the battle and their French 'allies'.

"Boccanegra is true to his word!" cried Niccolò Fieschi, turning and rising in triumph to face the King and his councillor, defying Montague with his burning eyes.

"Not as far as the French are concerned." Laughed Edward. "He gave his word to them, also."

Montague stepped forward "Our naïve cousins of France simply failed to secure it with enough gold."

Fieschi was becoming angry with the bearded Earl of Salisbury. What did the man want?

"You know nothing of us Genoese, Montague. You know nothing of Boccanegra's motivations. The King alone knows the whole truth. Leave these matters to your betters."

"Do you dare reprimand my friend and councillor?" Edward interrupted sharply, the laughter fleeing his face, his voice lowering to growl. "Do you presume to instruct an earl of England?"

Fieschi took a hesitant step backward, his secure poise failing. Montague realized his foe was baffled. The King had never spoken to him in that manner before now, nor had Montague ever been so forward and public in his loathing.

"The time for your lording arrogance has passed, Fieschi." Montague stepped closer to him. "I *do* know about you Genoese, I *do* understand Boccanegra's motivations. Just as I understand yours."

"What do you want? What is the meaning of this?" Fieschi stepped sideways, giving himself space and moving away from Montague.

"Now that Boccanegra's well on his way to the open sea" Edward began dryly "what was the fee again? 2,000 marks for Boccanegra's betrayal, and that's fair. But as for those 3,000 marks you demand for your family's services in procuring this desertion… I rather think that's too much."

"Your Majesty," Fieschi was shocked, his eyes bulged, his face darted from side to side, taking in the stunned faces of the men of the Council. "not in front of these men! These are our private matters."

"Why not in front of us all?" Montague replied, savouring his enemy's discomfort. "What would you like the King to hide?"

Edward was implacable. "I see no reason why I should pay you so much as a single silver piece for your services."

Fieschi's jaw dropped. "How… … How can you…? How dare you….?"

"How dare I? Because I know that which you do not, Master Fieschi." He paused in triumph. "William de Tels is alive!" He took another, inexorable step closer to Fieschi. "William de Tels is alive, and his task completed. For the better."

Chapter 1

Three years earlier. Norwich, September, 1337

A stranger comes by night – English food for English stomachs – a lesson in secrecy

"... and as little Rose walked, with the black pudding in her basket, the trees loomed closer about her. They were taller, and taller, the further into the forest she walked, and the light of the sun was dimmer, dimmer..."

My eldest brother's little son, Robert, pushed his head further back into the crook of my father's arm, and his large dark eyes examined the whiskers about his grandfather's mouth. His brow knitted as he imagined the wild forest, listening to father's expressive voice.

"... She came to a huge old oak tree, with many knotted, gnarled arms, and each arm had long, barbed wooden fingers that reach down to take hold of her clothes, her cap..." his fingers snatched lightly at Robert's clothes, like so many twigs crowding low over a forest path. "Rose pushed through, and at the oak's feet the shadows were deep, and dark. Little Rose heard the sound of breathing, like this..." And father let his breath out slowly, with a hint of a growl in the back of his throat. I saw my Master, John de Ulgham, smile above the rim of his ale-cup on the far side of the hearth. We were enjoying the story as much as the child.

"... and out of the shadow stepped an enormous, grey wolf, with long yellow fangs and burning red eyes..."

"Papa, Papa!" Little Robert interjected urgently, starting up in the old man's lap. "Where is the wolf now? Where does it live? Is it near here?" His eyes were bulging in terror. Madge, the nurse, cast a reprimanding look father's way, as though to say *I brought him down because he wouldn't sleep. Now he'll be having nightmares the whole night long.*

My father's face took on a guilty hue, and he hastily told the little boy "No, no, don't worry. It's not near here at all. It's..." he hesitated for an instant, and looked over the fire-place at my Master. "It lives up in the woods near Ulgham. You know, where Master John comes from, near Newcastle-upon-Tyne."

Robert had no idea where these places were, but he did know that Master John spoke with a different accent, and came from somewhere many days' ride away. He looked across at my Master "Does the wolf live near your house?"

"Yes, it does. Far, far away." His voice was warm and gentle. "When I was a little boy just like you, I saw it." Robert gasped "In the distance." added Master John, not wanting to excite the boy further.

"Oh." Said Robert, settling back. My little nephew must have noticed how the adults in his family often turned with respect to Master John for the answers to mysteries, and accepted his explanations with absolute faith.

Robert curled up into his grandfather's arms once more, now content to hear the rest of the story.

"...and old Mister Wolf said to little Rose 'Oh, pretty child,'" The wolf's voice was low and gravelly " 'where are you going all by yourself in the dark, dangerous woods?' Now, little Rose was a silly girl," father continued in an admonishing tone "and she told Mister Wolf the truth! Would *you* tell him where you were going, Robbie?"

Robert shook his head slowly and solemnly. He was a serious boy.

"Of course you wouldn't." Father agreed, gratified. "But foolish Little Rose said 'I'm going to visit my Granny in the forest. Look, Mummy gave me black-pudding for her.'..."

Now my nephew was reassured that the Wolf was nowhere near, drowsiness swiftly came over him. His head nodded forwards, his eyelids became leaden, and finally he fell asleep just as little Rose was arriving at her grandmother's house in the woods. "And Mister Wolf said 'Sit down, and eat this meat, it's very tasty.' Poor little Rose didn't know it was her grandmother..." he tailed off, for Robert was breathing slowly and regularly, asleep.

"Sit still, Sir Henry." Madge instructed father, her voice hushed. "I'll take him up to bed." She delicately gathered the now sleeping Robert into her arms, and with a careful tread climbed the steps to the bedchamber. My two little sisters were already dozing in the great room upstairs, and Madge would settle the boy between them on the mattress. No sooner had she disappeared upstairs than a soft knocking came on the great door.

Father, Master John and I bolted upright in our seats, startled and suddenly alert. Had we imagined the sound? The knocking came again, unmistakeably. In spite of the curfew, someone was abroad and wanted to come in. Father looked searchingly at Master John and myself, but we could only shrug: we were not expecting visitors. We had returned just the day before from a long task abroad, and had been expecting to rest for some days without being disturbed.

"Come." Father commanded, and swiftly crossed to the door, and we came to stand at his shoulders. "Who knocks?" He enquired without opening the door.

"The Watch. It's I, Harold. Forgive our intrusion at this late hour, Sir Henry."

"You are forgiven, Harold." Father was mystified, but soothed by the civil tone and familiar voice. Since handing the management of his lands over to my elder brother and settling into his city-house, he'd come to know all the men of Norwich.

Father set his left foot an inch or two back from the door, to block it should anyone try to push it wide open from the other side, and lifted the iron lock-bar. He pulled the door open a fraction. Three men stood in the darkness, looking in. Two were of the city watch, one of whom was holding a torch, whose light bronzed the steel of their helmets and mail. The third was a knight in a great lord's livery.

"What service can I render you?" Father added, eying the knight and not moving his foot from the base of the door.

"Sir Thomas de Aldcliffe wishes to speak with you." Harold indicated the liveried stranger. "He bears two letters addressed to Master John de Ulgham, sealed by both the Earl of Lancaster and by His Grace, Richard de Bury. Bury also gave him a warrant to break curfew to reach you."

Father sighed, and turned his head to us. He had been hoping that we might spend some quiet time with him after our being so long abroad. It now seemed likely that our stay was already coming to an end.

"Were you expecting this visitor, John?" He asked my Master.

"Not at all. But if the warrant is truly Richard de Bury's, then we are bound to receive him."

The watchman beckoned the knight forward. "Sir Thomas, if you will, show these gentlemen Bury's warrant."

When it was handed through the crack in the doorway, Master John passed me the parchment, letting me examine it with my younger and sharper eyes.

"It is Bury's seal." I murmured when satisfied.

At that, father brought his left foot back, and opened the door wide enough for a man to pass through. "Welcome to my house, Sir Knight."

Thomas de Aldcliffe stepped forward, then halted on the threshold. He unbuckled his sword and dagger, announcing loudly in an important tone "It aggrieves me to disturb you so late, but my mission is urgent, and I was bidden to ride until I reached Norwich, even though night should come. I bring two letters to John de Ulgham and his pupil, William de Tels." He handed his weapons to father. "May I enter your household?"

"Of course, Sir Thomas. You are my guest."

With the air of a herald, Sir Thomas turned briefly back to the watchmen. He seemed incapable of moderating his voice. "Good men," he boomed "thank you for bringing me so well to Sir Henry's home. Tell your Captain that three shall ride out from Yarmouth Gate just before dawn. Let my horse be watered, saddled and bridled."

"It shall be done, Sir Thomas." Harold pushed forward the other, younger watchman, who was carrying Sir Thomas' heavy saddle-bag. He laid it on the floor just inside the door, and the two men withdrew into the night. Master John and I exchanged a meaningful look. Our stay at father's house, though hardly begun, was soon to be over.

"Sir Henry, you cannot imagine what a long, thirsty day I've passed, between sea and saddle." Sir Thomas was relaxing with extravagant sighs into the comfortable guest chair on the left side of the hearth, where Master John had been seated not long before.

"Perhaps I *can* imagine." Father replied dryly. "I may have ridden long and hard once or twice myself, over the years. Conquering Scotland in Edward Longshanks' host does spring to mind. There were also a few savage Highlanders along the road, to help bring on a thirst."

The young knight was eagerly taking a goblet of father's best wine from Madge's hands, and didn't seem to hear. "The sweetest wine is that drunk after such a parching day." He gratefully brought it to his lips. I noticed father's eyebrows twitch with the beginnings of umbrage.

"I assure you, this wine is sweet not only because of the dry road you travelled today, but also due to its natural sweetness." Just a few years earlier father's bellicose mood swings would have made us all tense at the prospect of an argument and even a challenge to a duel. Now, however, old age and grandchildren had blunted his sword and sharpened his tongue instead.

"It is indeed sweet," Sir Thomas gushed on, innocently "without even a spice to mull it. Is it claret?"

"That it is." Father was beginning to realise that Sir Thomas was simple, and gave him an indulgent smile. "Perhaps it reaches us more quickly here via Yarmouth than it does Lancaster, so it's sweeter. Did you notice the merchants off-loading wine barrels in the bay of Yarmouth this afternoon? The younger the wine the better."

With a child's fleeting attention, Aldcliffe was already thinking of other things.

"Master John," he addressed my Master, who was standing by the hearth with the two letters Aldcliffe had brought open in his hands "is the matter clear?"

Master John was staring at the wall, his eyes set in a hypnotic, steady gaze. I knew from long familiarity with his ways that he was memorizing some part of the letters' contents, but to Sir Thomas his expression must have seemed lost. Finally my Master snapped back to the here and now.

"Yes, yes, thank you." He stepped closer to the fire, as though to warm his hands, with his back to us for a moment. When he turned about I saw that the two sheets of parchment were now among the coals. "I was just thinking that my grandfather had vineyards of his own, in the north of England, back when the world was warmer."

Sir Thomas noticed the letters catching light in the fire-place, and started forward in his seat, slopping some wine on the floor-rushes. "Master John, the letters!" He pointed urgently.

Unlike father, Master John had realised that Aldcliffe was simple from the start. "Damn, they must have slipped from my belt." He swore, feigning concern and grasping the black spit. He made as though to rescue the letters from the flames, but of course, his poking about only made sure that the parchment disintegrated all the faster. Sir Thomas looked distraught, and I wondered with amusement how he could fail to notice how tightly Master John kept his belt bound.

"My long journey…" Aldcliffe was crestfallen "all for nothing…"

"No, no, Sir Thomas" my Master reassured him, leaning the spit back against the pile of hot-stones "I'm sure I can remember the important points."

"But the Earl instructed me to bring the letters to John de Ulgham and William de Tels." He glanced in my direction. "Your pupil didn't get the chance to read them."

I reassured him with a gesture. "It's of no matter. What is important is that Master John read them."

Sir Thomas slumped back into the guest chair with his usual dramatic air. "If you say so…" His brow furrowed as he thought for a moment. "I'll tell my Lord nothing of this. It might anger him. If you are sure no harm is done…"

"I'm sure." Master John told him firmly.

"So, we're to ride out before dawn?" I interrupted in a disapproving voice.

"Yes," announced Sir Thomas "a Lancastrian sea-captain who is loyal to my Lord, the Earl, is waiting for us at Yarmouth. I arrived on his ship early this afternoon. I told him we would sail with the out-going tide shortly after noon. As I know well after this evening's ride, we must allow plenty of time to reach Yarmouth."

"Will the ship-captain wait for us until evening if we don't arrive by the noon-tide?" My tone must have been a little more forthright than he was used to from people of my age, for he was startled.

"Why shouldn't we arrive in time?"

"My pupil" broke in Master John, who had understood what I was getting at "means to say that people will talk more about our leaving if we ride out at such an unusual time. In our line of work it's normally best to leave at the usual hour, and blend in with the bulk of travellers on the roads."

Sir Thomas dismissed such subtle reasoning with a theatrical wave.

"Don't worry, my friends, I told the Captain of the Watch to swear his men to secrecy. They'll have my horse ready shortly before dawn. If we don't ride out at that hour it will seem even stranger."

I opened my mouth to protest once more against this foolishness, but Master John almost imperceptibly shook his head. He was right.

There was no point arguing at this hour, now the damage had been done. I limited myself to saying "Then we should be getting to sleep."

Father's eyes took on a wistful and pained expression as he gazed at my face. He had suddenly realised that precious little time in our company remained to him. Madge intervened, tears already welling in her eyes and her voice a little choked.

"Get yourselves to bed, Master John, Master William. I'll wake before you in the morning and prepare your bags and saddle your horses. Need someone ride with you to bring the horses back? You can't take them over the sea with you this time, the King's banned deporting them for the war that's coming."

"I'm not boarding the ship, good woman." Sir Thomas told her. "I'll lead their horses back here tomorrow evening, and the day after ride for Lancaster, if you'll be so kind as to host me a second night, Sir Henry?"

"Of course, of course." Father mumbled, his eyes never wandering from my face.

As he wordlessly accompanied Master John and myself up to our bed, I could imagine father's thoughts. Each time we departed it was on the King's secret business, and Master John could never reveal to the old man how long we might be away, nor how likely it was that we might leave our bones in some foreign clime that father had never even heard of. The trust great Lords placed in us was a source of pride to father, just as every leave-taking was a source of feared grief. Until now that grief had only been imagined against some future date. Who could say when it might become reality?

I lay awake in bed for some time, listening to the mellow voices drifting up the stairs, picturing father chatting with his gallant, earnest guest, their faces yellow and red in the comfortable firelight as they smiled and shared stories. I imagined Madge in the cooking end of the hall downstairs, pushing a steel rod into a notched candle before settling down onto her mattress. How many hours would she sleep? Six? I pictured her sticking the rod horizontally into the wax at the sixth notch, then placing the lit candle carefully on a broad bronze plate. As I imagined the wax slowly dripping down, I fell into a light, restless sleep.

Somewhere in the shadowy space between midnight and dawn, the gradually descending candle flame melted the wax around the steel rod, which dropped with a clatter onto the bronze plate. I started from my dreams at the sound, and noticed that Master John beside me had also been woken. He got up, probably to help Madge get things ready, but in my youthful sleepiness I drifted rapidly back into slumber.

Soon after I felt myself shaken by strong hands, and I woke up feeling utterly disoriented, with no memory of why I should be waking so early.

"It's me, Will." I recognised Master John's voice, thinly whispering, and the previous evening's events came back to me in a rush, driving out my grogginess. I stared at the black silhouette of the man in the darkness for a brief moment, then slipped nimbly out of the bed. In those days every departure still made my blood sing with excitement, even if it meant being roused from sleep before the monks themselves were up and praying.

We padded our way to the top of the stairs. I hesitated for a long moment on the landing, my eyes searching through the gloom to where I knew my sisters were sleeping with little Robert in their alcove. They'd only hugged me a strong welcome back two days before. Now they'd wake up and find that, yet again, they'd missed the chance to hug me goodbye.

In the hall father was standing, looking grave, wrapped in a shawl, warming his back by the fire. Sir Thomas, beside him, was tying his belt in place. Madge was busy bundling up scalding hot bread and some seasoned stilton in kitchen cloth. There'd be no stopping for our main meal at mid-morning, as Yarmouth was half a day's ride from Norwich, and ships' captains liked their passengers to be aboard long before the tide started pulling. Master John and I took turns to embrace father.

"It takes me back to my young days." Father always said the same things at parting-time. "We rode out earlier than this with Longshanks, you know…" We waited while he mumbled some old fashioned but sound advice, then he gruffly cuffed me about the ear. "May the road rise with you."

Madge came outside with us to the horses while my father took to his great seat and stared into the hearth, his eyes alive with images of his own journeys past, and our journeys as he imagined them.

"I've already put a skin of ale in each of your saddlebags" Madge was explaining "and there's something to eat for this evening too, as I don't trust sailors to keep fresh food. That's the best I can do for you,

I can't give you food for a month, or however long you'll be away, so be careful what you eat overseas, and stick your fingers down your throats to bring it back up the moment you think it's playing tricks with your stomachs…"

"Madge, shhh!" I interrupted her, or she'd never be done admonishing. "We've done this before, you know, we'll be fine."

Master John smiled at her, and embraced her. "You sound like my old nurse, Madge, who never trusted grain nor cabbage unless it grew north of the Tyne, east of Corsenside and south of Scotland. Don't worry, in all the world people eat the food of the earth without falling sick."

"English bellies want English food." Madge stubbornly replied, taking another piece of cheese from her copious apron pocket and tucking it into my saddle-bag. "Every time you come back you're thinner than when you left, Master Will, and a boy of your age can't afford to thin out like…" Master John and I shared a smile, already nostalgic for when Madge would be far behind us. We let her carry on while we carefully slid our knives into their places and – no less importantly – our quills and ampoules of ink. We had rolls of parchment, and wax, and a variety of seals hidden in our bags, for as we needed a letter of commission on our travels we composed it ourselves. Our greatest seal was that of Melton, the Archbishop of York, who knew full well we had it and used it, but gave us his blessing and trust for the sake of his old friend, Richard de Bury, to whom our loyalty was sworn and proven.

While Madge kept protesting and finding new niches to stuff food into our saddles, Master John turned to Sir Thomas. "The Watch knows we're out by royal command, doesn't it?"

The Lancastrian knight only nodded, rubbing the sleep from his eyes. Like many men who are loquacious late into the night, he was far less talkative early in the morning. It was then that he gave Master John a small purse "From my Lord, the Earl of Lancaster." My Master slipped it into a hidden pocket. That would cover our expenses for the journey.

We led our two horses out onto the street while Madge's comments and reprimands faded behind us. Finally, in the silence of the pre-dawn city we heard her pull the great door of the house shut. In the still darkness, our horses' shoes struck echoes from the cobblestones. Twice we were stopped by men of the Norwich Watch.

Those grim, mailed and helmed men-at-arms had evidently received the order not to disturb the night's silence. Both times they waved us on, wordlessly, as soon as they recognised us. It was an eerie sensation to arrive at Yarmouth Gate and find the Knight's horse ready saddled and bridled, tended by a guard, and the small service door being unlocked and swung open for us, all in utter silence. The Captain of the Watch himself was there wish us well as we led our horses through and mounted. Once the city walls had disappeared behind us in the gloom, Master John voiced both our thoughts.

"Sir Thomas, was it really necessary to leave with such blatant secrecy?"

Sir Thomas replied with a blank look, and my smirk was hidden by the darkness. Master John had overestimated Aldcliffe's early morning wits. He sighed.

"The only secret actions that are *really* secret, my friend, are ones that look like normality. If we had left after the mid-morning meal, with all the other people bound for Yarmouth today, no-one would have noticed us, nor wondered why we were travelling. For all they would know we were off to bargain for smoked herring. Now all the men of the Watch know that we left on secret business. That's ten or fifteen men who know that a secret exists, when there might have been none."

"But I'm sure they're men of their word!" Aldcliffe protested. "They'll say nothing of our leaving to anyone."

"Not even when they get drunk? Not even in their sleep? Or when running a high fever and rambling nonsense?" Master John's voice remained calm, like a monk instructing novices in a ministerium. "Will they still deem it a secret in ten years' time, and keep it to themselves?"

"In ten years' time your task will long be over. What will it matter if they say what they know?"

"Sir Thomas, in the kind of work we deal in, a secret may matter more after ten years than it did at the start." He'd obviously decided to press the point. "Would those men keep their tongues still under torture?"

Sir Thomas gasped, and his eyes bulged. "Torture? Is the business so grave?"

Master John spread his hands before him in growing pre-dawn glow. "I cannot say. It's a secret."

For some time we continued along the deserted road in silence. Finally, Aldcliffe cleared his throat.

"Master John de Ulgham, Master William de Tels" he said slowly, almost ceremoniously, his tone acutely serious "I beg you to forgive my tactless behaviour. Even before you set forth on your journey your very lives were put in jeopardy by my thoughtless…"

"Enough, enough." I saw Master John's face break into the first smile of that day, of that journey. "This is all speculation, it may yet be that nothing at all will come of it. I ask you, however, to be more discreet in future. In particular, from now on William and I are Eilulf and Gerold of Ghent. I, Gerold, am a teacher of the *quadrivium*, and one-time student of Duns Scotus himself in Paris. Which, incidentally, is true." As ever, his voice warmed at the memory of his wandering student days. "Eilulf is my pupil and servant. We're men of the Word and learning." He stopped speaking in the court-French of England, and continued his speech in the French of Paris, thick with the characteristic Flemish accent. "We speak the Flemish of Ghent and Sluys, the French of Paris, the Occitan, and of course we argue our philosophy in the Latin. When you lead us to the ship you can whisper to the captain that we stink of kraut. That'll keep him happy." He flashed another wry smile.

"Kraut?" Thomas was bewildered "Ah… Of course, Master… Master Gerold." He paused. "But you needn't worry about the Captain. He's a man of Lancaster, and his greatest pleasure is to do the Earl's work. He's a man I trust."

"Nevertheless, Sir Thomas, believe me that it's better to let him think we're Flemish. Thus, from the port of Yarmouth onwards, our business shall start as it should continue: in secret."

Chapter 2

The Valley of the River Staffora, the Apennines south of Pavia, Lombardy, September 1337

*The Welshman in the pecking order –
Eavesdropping and gossip – A mystery blossoms*

The tall, greying newcomer who called himself 'the Welshman' stood among the chestnut trees, high on the mountain side, with a sack in hand. He had been sent there by Brother Demetrio, the healer at the Abbey of Sant'Alberto, to search for fallen chestnut burrs among fallen forest litter, and bring them back to the Abbey. But now that the sack was nearly full, he had become distracted by his surroundings and the haunting beauty of the woods and mountain flanks. When a slight wind lifted to softly stir the branches, he closed his eyes and threw back his hood.

The wind in my hair! How much time have I endured closed up, hidden away, wondering if I would ever see the sun again? The exalting words of his mind's voice were echoed by faint movements of his lips. *Now I just want to feel the wind in my hair.*

He was determined to seize the subtle pleasures of every moment in that tranquil place, lush with green beauty.

The browning leaf of a chestnut tree was loosened from its twig by the breeze, and brushed softly against his cheek as it fell. He opened his eyes and lowered them just in time to accompany its delicate descent with his gaze, down to its resting place on the forest floor. There he noticed another chestnut burr, half hidden by the undergrowth. This was a fine one.

Did you know bandages can be made of combed-straw, dearest? And did you know you can comb straw with green chestnut burrs? Brother Demetrio told me 'We need them still green, with each of the two halves intact and the spines still strong, for combing the straw to make bandages.'

The Welshman had been dumbstruck by the healer's strange request, and had inquired why straw couldn't be combed with boar-bristle, like hair. The old monk had shaken his head with a smile, and told him "the chestnut burrs are more delicate, able to comb the straw without shredding it."

Then the Welshman had rejoiced, understanding how marvellous was the meaning of this. "Brother Demetrio, it's no accident that the burrs start falling at the end of summer, just when the straw is ready, is it? God's will is evident even in these little things, is it not?"

Brother Demetrio had nodded at him with a quizzical smile.

The burr by the Welshman's right foot perfectly matched the old healer's request, the two halves like little cup-shaped combs, ready for use. He bent down to gather them up, and underneath he found a white mushroom. It had been a wet summer, and already mushrooms were pushing their way skywards through the forest litter high up here where the air was cool and moist. This particular one was speckled with flecks of yellow, and was wispy and fibrous.

The people hereabouts collect so many types of mushroom. The Welshman mused to his silent, unseen companion. *This may be a delicacy, or it may have some medicinal use. At worst, Brother Demetrio can throw it away as useless.*

He stroked the mushroom from the ground and tucked it into the sack, and hurried up towards the Abbey.

As he approached he could hear the voices of other lay-brothers, singing a working song as they tilled a field. Then, between the tree trunks, the magnificent Abbey came into view, sprawled across one shoulder of the mountain with the fields, animal pens and gardens below it, where monks and lay-brothers went about their business with an industrious air. Higher still was the more ancient, original little church built by the Saint himself, Alberto of Butrio.

Don't you think the church looks like a wise old owl, perched up above an enormous nest of stone buildings, watching over its little nestlings, the monks and lay-brothers, as they bustle about?

As he strode up on his long legs, the Welshman gave a friendly wave to some lay-brothers who were swinging their hoes in time to a working song. It was in the local tongue, and to his ears it seemed a strange blend of the Latin, the Occitan and some forgotten Germanic language of the far north. The men didn't return the Welshman's wave, they just followed him with a close, suspicious look. He didn't notice.

Brother Demetrio was working silently in the herb garden with his novice, Gilio. He looked up as his new labourer, the Welshman, came into sight, and considered him as he walked up the hill toward the apothecarium. He was decidedly odd. Often the old healer caught him silently mouthing words in some foreign tongue, as though speaking to thin air. Then the Welshman would cock his head, as though listening to a reply. In another man, Demetrio might have suspected either saintly inspiration or demonic intervention. But the Welshman seemed neither to be at the beginning of an upward climb, nor on the brink of a fall. Rather, he possessed a strange, neutral, almost child-like quality; like some world-weary innocent, though Brother Demetrio knew this was a contradiction in terms. The Welshman seemed aware of the simplicity of his soul, and had been resigned to his own naivety in this world of wolves for many, many years. Most people lost their innocence in the same, precise moment in which they became aware of it. The Welshman hadn't.

The new lay-brother arrived with his sack, and immediately, Gilio the novice looked irritated by the tall foreigner's presence.

"Salve!" The Welshman still spoke with them in his limited Latin.

"O, Gallese," Demetrio nodded to him in greeting. They had all called him that since he told them he was born in Wales: Gallese, meaning Welshman. The old man took the sack and inspected it.

"Good, good." He muttered in his own Greek-accented Latin. "And this?" he pulled out the strange white mushroom with an approving expression. "Excellent! Well done." A swift look of pleasure painted itself across the Welshman's face, and Brother Demetrio went on. "How did you know to gather it?"

Many people in his place would have feigned knowledge of mushrooms, to take advantage of the situation and avoid seeming ignorant. Such guile was foreign to the Welshman. "I didn't know to gather it." He was honest. "I've seen people picking many different kinds of mushroom in the woods, so I thought it was a good idea to bring this one back, too. Why, is it good to eat?"

Gilio snorted at that, and the tall, handsome foreigner reddened just a little.

"It's not edible, but it's considered very valuable." Demetrio told him. "When this type of mushroom has been dried out by the fireside it makes the finest tinder in creation. The slightest spark from a flint will light it, and as long as it's kept in a pouch it doesn't swell with damp and become immune to flame, even in the wettest weather. Travellers carry it, and in emergencies use a pinch of it to get fires going. Yes, it's a very valuable fungus." He glanced at the sack a little critically. "Next time you find one, bring it back in your hands. That way the spores scatter in the woods, and it spreads. Would you be able to take me back to the precise spot where you found it?"

The Welshman shook his head ruefully. "I didn't think to fix a landmark in my mind. It never occurred to me it might be valuable."

The novice, Gilio, smirked openly at such ignorance, but Demetrio was more understanding. He clapped the Welshman on the shoulder. "Never mind, you couldn't know. Over time you'll come to be so familiar with the woods, you'll have a map of the mushroom spots in your mind, like us old folk." Gilio raised his eyebrows, clearly unconvinced that the new lay-brother would ever reach that point.

Another monk, one of the scribes, approached Demetrio.

"I'm leaving for the village now. Did you want to send someone with me for your new pestles?"

"Ah, yes." The old man agreed. "Gilberto will have finished carving them by now. Very well." He turned his back on them for a moment, to survey the medicinal garden. "But there's also manure to be prepared. You go down to the village, while we get to the manure."

Brother Demetrio had not specified who 'you' and 'we' referred to: he took the question of who should do what for granted. Unfortunately, so did the Welshman.

"Wonderful," the foreigner said brightly "I still haven't had the chance to visit the village." He stepped toward the scribe with a smile.

"And today you won't have it either, lay-brother." Gilio swiftly retorted. He was nearly thirty years the Welshman's junior, but he was a novice and would one day be a monk. Lay-brothers were little more than labor for the Abbey's fields.

"Ah…" The Welshman stopped mid-stride, realising that he'd been presumptuous, giving Gilio another excuse to be irritated with him.

"Who do you think you are?" Gilio pressed on, angrily "And what would you know about pestles? Can you tell if they're weighted properly? You know nothing of our work."

"I'm sorry" the Welshman quickly apologised. "I had no wish to… I just…"

"What's the matter? Is your precious northern nose too delicate for manure?"

For an irrational moment, the Welshman wanted to imperiously command 'Silence!' But the word came to him in his own language, and he caught himself in time. He'd been strictly forbidden to speak in his native tongue. Sighing, he tried to explain.

"I've got nothing against manure. On the contrary…"

"I wonder if you can tell chicken shit from pig shit, Welshman?" Gilio was becoming aggressive.

"Let it be, both of you" Old Demetrio growled. "it's just a misunderstanding. Go to the village, Gilio, and see if the pestles are well-enough made. Welshman, you come with me."

Old Brother Demetrio was a practical man who liked to personally take care of every detail of his craft. To make medicine one harvested medicinal plants. To grow medicinal plants, one needed manure. Just as he personally supervised the harvesting of the plants and the making of the medicine, he also personally supervised the preparation of manure.

Together Demetrio and the Welshman strolled among the animal runs, the healer talking idly and the lay-brother carrying a pole on his shoulders behind his neck. Four small wicker buckets dangled from the pole, two on each end.

"Gilio is young and proud, but has learnt much." Old Demetrio was saying. "He was right about the manure. You can't give every plant the same type, nor the same mix. Some plants need raw chicken shit. Others need it mixed with sand, straw and dried cabbage leaves." They stopped in front of the chicken coop. Demetrio swung open the wooden door.

"There, scoop up half a bucket's worth of that while I keep the cock inside."

As he laid the pole down and set to work with his hands, the Welshman noticed some battered green stalks bound in a bundle against the door-frame.

"What's that?"

"They're cabbage stalks. After taking the heads of the cabbages to the kitchens, they tie together the stalks with the leaves still on them, and leave them on the door. The hens have pecked away the leaves, but they can't get their beaks around the stalks. I'll take them and we'll feed them to the pigs when we get there. Then the cabbages will have fed people first, chickens second, and pigs third. And the chickens and pigs will feed us again, with flesh, eggs and manure for the plants we eat. We never throw anything away here, ever."

The Welshman noticed how, unlike Gilio, the healer always spoke as though he was sure the new lay-brother could learn everything with time. It was encouraging.

"Brother Demetrio" he asked as he scooped up the chicken manure "don't you think I'm too old to learn healing?"

"Of course not." was the amused reply. "How old are you, anyway?"

"Fifty-three." He answered immediately. Demetrio raised an eyebrow, surprised by such precision.

"Well, I'm somewhere between sixty-three and sixty-five. That makes me at least ten years older than you. Do you think I've learned nothing in the last ten years?"

The Welshman had finished scooping up the dung, and rose to his feet. "I'm sure you have. You've got a curious soul." he said, trying to resist the urge to wipe his hands on his smock to clean them. He was proud that he hadn't pulled any faces because of the smell. He picked the pole and buckets up again. They started off towards the pig-pens.

"That's right. I've learnt a lot since the age of fifty-three, so you can too. When you stop learning, you're dead." He said this last phrase very simply, as though he was observing the colour of the sky. "What young Gilio doesn't realise, though, is that teaching is just as important. Knowing without passing on what you know is like a pear without seeds inside. You know, every now and then you find a pear with no seeds?"

The lay-brother nodded.

"The pear may be good to eat, but you'll never get another pear tree from it. That's what knowing without teaching is. Impressive, but useless."

They arrived at the dug-out pens where the Abbey's swine were grunting about in their muck. The healer tossed them the hen-pecked cabbage stalks, and the beasts crowded around them in excitement, their trotters squelching in the black mix of manure and mud.

"A full bucket, please." He ordered.

The Welshman could not avoid an expression of disgust this time.

"There's a shovel around the side there." Demetrio pointed, smiling. "You don't have to use your hands this time."

The Welshman was immensely relieved.

In the nearby village of Pizzocorno on the Abbey estates, the stranger's reputation as a living mystery was sown that very day. Gilio and the scribe were heard speaking of the newcomer to the monastery while they waited for Gilberto the carver in front of his workshop. Young Floria was gathering up the rushes in her father-in-law's tavern, a few metres down the same alley. When the monks started talking, she paused by the window, her ears twitching like a sheep dog's when it hears a lost lamb's bleating. She heard the words "lo gallese" and "the new lay-brother" repeated many times, interspersed in their conversation. She was curious about this new lay-brother at the Abbey, and assumed that Lo Gallese must be his name.

The growing mystery shot out a lively green shoot the next morning, when the baker fell behind with his baking. Fiorenza, Floria's brother's wife's sister, naturally already informed by Floria that a new lay-brother with a strange name had arrived at Sant'Alberto, bustled into the bakery not long before noon with her rolls of risen dough, sweet-smelling and ready for the oven. The previous customers, Donna Giovanna and Donna Saldina, were still there, waiting for their bread to come out. The three got chatting, and of course the name of the newcomer came up.

"Donna Giovanna," asked Fiorenza "have you seen a new lay-brother about the monastery?"

"I was up that way for green chestnuts just yesterday, but I didn't see anyone new. And you, Saldina?"

"As far as I know, no one in the village has seen him yet."

"So we can't tell yet" Fiorenza concluded "if he is handsome and kind, or ugly and rotten-mouthed. I wonder where he's from? Lo Gallese… Such a strange name!"

The baker's uncle, old Natalino, overheard the women's chatter while slowly hauling in some blocks of chopped beech-wood for the oven. He was aged and stiff, but he always liked to lend his nephew a hand.

"Lo Gallese, did you say Fiorenza?" He interrupted.

"That's right. I think that was his name. Floria says the Brothers from the Abbey kept repeating Lo Gallese. Why?"

"Oh, nothing. Probably just a coincidence." Stooping old Natalino had no love for gossip, and didn't want to waste his breath and half the morning with women's chatter.

"Now Natalino" Donna Giovanna, the eldest of the three, tried to sound stern "what do you know about this man?"

"Nothing, nothing." Natalino had finished stacking the wood, and went to the doorway with feigned indifference.

"Signor Natalino, who is Lo Gallese?" Donna Saldina called after him, but he only muttered as he disappeared down the road "No idea, sorry."

As a boy, Natalino had walked the salt-roads down to Genoa, and the sea. He'd sailed away a few years of his youth in hard work, salt wind and far-reaching adventure in the service of the Doria family, powerful merchants and money lenders. Natalino was no tongue-wagger, but he loved telling his family's youngsters of his sea-days in the evenings, when the hearth's warming light loosened out his memories.

"Grandfather" Tino begged Natalino after supper "tell us about the lands over the sea again."

Tino was six years old, and his real name was Natalino just like his grandfather, though everyone called him Tino. He was joy itself in the eyes of the old man, who couldn't say no to any of his requests.

"Of course. Let me see…" His eyes took on a far-away look, and the older boys and girls drew their benches and chests a little closer. They'd heard it all before, but they never tired of the stories.

"Did I ever tell you about the Gallea?" His memory was confused, and he pronounced the name of the land as though it were the Genoese word for 'galley'.

"Of course, the Santa Caterina." That had been the name of the galley Natalino had once served on.

"No, no, I don't mean the ship." He corrected himself. "I mean the land. The land of the gallesi."

Now Natalino had the full attention of the adults, too. This was a land he'd never mentioned before, but above all, its people bore the same name as the mysterious newcomer to the Abbey.

"I never visited it, for it's far to the north and I always sailed east toward Constantinople. But there were some sailors who talked about it. You know, many years have passed, but I think I recall them saying that the gallesi live on the island of Britain."

"Where the English live, grandfather?" One of the older boys interrupted.

"That's right, they share the island with the English. Of course, they hate the English and constantly fight them." Word of Wales's conquest by the Edward Longhsanks, grandfather of the present King of England, had not yet filtered through to the little village in the mountains of Lombardy, though more than thirty years had passed.

"They are Catholic Christians, like us." Truthfully, he remembered no other details of what his fellow sailors had told him, but he surveyed the expectant faces around the hearth and, like every storyteller, realised that something a little sensational was needed.

"But they're very tall, fair and good looking. They're said to be fierce when roused to battle, and there are some warriors among them whose heads take the shape of wolves' heads, and eagles' heads, when the fighting fury takes them!"

The children opened their mouths in awe, and the adults nodded with satisfaction. After old Natalino finished, others would vie with him in storytelling, and there would be good fireside fare for the imagination that night.

The news that a land populated by people called 'gallesi' existed far to the north spread to every last member of the village before the midmorning bells rang for main meal the next day.

Over the bread and stewed green cabbage cooked with spiced bacon, a heated debate arose. Did the stranger really hail from the island of Britain, on the far edge of the world, or were the 'gallesi' just another of the old man's tall-stories about his days on the great ships?

Natalino's son-in-law's aunt, Giuditta, was always ready to share every thought she had with the others. In fact, the villagers considered her to be something of a gossip. Unkind individuals had been heard to say that her tongue moved faster than her thoughts.

When she observed "he may well be from the northern lands, he's fair-skinned enough…" everyone's jaw stopped working on the cabbage and they all turned to gawp at her, and a dozen questions rained down on her in a thrice.

"Where did you…?" "Have you seen…?" "When did you see…?" "How did you meet…?"

Giuditta relished the attention, and determined to reveal the little she knew as slowly as possible.

"I can only guess it was him. How many new lay-brothers have come to Sant'Alberto this season?"

"One, just one." Everyone agreed, impatient.

"Then it was him, for sure. It was a face I'd never seen before."

"And what sort of face was it, Giuditta?"

She pretended to concentrate, summoning up the face in her mind and sizing up its features.

"Handsome. Handsome; I must say. Blue eyes and dark hair, a strong nose. Handsome."

The young men scowled a little, and one of them asked "is he young or old?"

"Well... old I would say. In his late forties, at the very least."

The youths relaxed a little, and the girls started losing interest. Giuditta sensed her audience slipping away, and volunteered a little more information.

"And he's very tall. They say the Northmen are tall, don't they? Perhaps he is one of Natalino's Gallese people, from Britain." Her listeners were as unaware as she was that the Welsh had no reputation for great height among Britons.

"And what was he doing when you saw him?"

"Brother Demetrio was showing him some herbs, and they were talking in... the tongue, you know, like writing."

For a long moment they chewed their cabbage boiled with smoked bacon in thoughtful silence. This was surely the strangest news yet of the newcomer. Lay-brothers came to the monasteries as adults, to do the dirty jobs in exchange for a sheltered existence after getting too much of life's rougher side. They were more likely to be un-lettered, like many of the people in the village, than speakers of the Latin, the language of writing. Only fully-fledged church men and nobles were likely to converse that way. A tall, handsome, aging Latin-speaker who was new to monastic life?

After a short while the leaders of the various families had them all swinging their legs out from under the benches and trotting back to the woods and fields. They worked in relative quiet for a long while, exchanging hushed gossip. Once they'd finally exhausted every variation possible on the theme 'what a mystery this man is', the villagers got their work-rhythm back, and the customary song and laughter of the working day began to ring out again.

Chapter 3

Yarmouth Bay and the North Sea, September 1337

Hordes of herring-workers – a storm, a blessing and a pirate-tale – the King's will is flaunted

In the port of Yarmouth we found ourselves weaving our way among long benches where herring were being gutted and packed by red haired and freckled girls from the Hebrides. Undeterred by the drizzle that fell from the grey skies, they worked in threes, their gestures perfectly timed like an elaborate dance. Two gutted with swift blows of the right hand, the fingers of their left hands wrapped in cloth to protect against knife-cuts while they held the fish steady. With one deft motion the silver-scaled bellies were opened and the entrails scooped out, then each herring-girl swayed her upper torso backwards and with a flick of the wrist tossed the fish to the third girl who packed it away into a barrel. Young boys, fishermen's sons, brought the still writhing herring from their fathers' boats in wicker baskets and dumped them on the benches to constantly renew the supply. As they worked, the girls chatted or sang in their native Gaelic. They came every autumn, following the migrating shoals from fisher-town to fisher-town. They started in the early summer in their native islands, and worked their way right around to Norfolk in late August as the herring swam. They spoke little English and no French at all, but that was no problem. They knew their work, and the people of Great Yarmouth, particularly the young men, were happy to welcome them every year.

Sir Thomas de Aldcliffe, Master John and I strode out onto one of the wharfs while the little boys darted to and fro about us with their brim-full baskets. Their mothers were busy on the waterfront repairing torn nets, while a royal inspector strolled among them, ensuring the width of the mesh conformed to the dictates of law. Out on the wharf's end a few grown men were enjoying a break from the tossing waves with flutes, tambourines and ale cups.

It was now past noon, and the tide was rising to its highest mark. A small rowing boat was waiting for us, to take us out to a ship, the cog *Richard*, lying a short distance away in the waters of the bay. From the wharf I could make out scurrying sailors readying her for sail. In the rowing-boat the sea-captain was waiting, along with a sailor whose densely scarred face startled me.

"The Lord's best to you, James." Sir Thomas greeted the captain in his fine court-French. "I present your passengers, Master Gerold of Ghent and his pupil Eilulf, whom you are to put ashore at Sluys. Master Gerold," he turned to us "James Ogden is a man I've trusted with my life upon the sea on many occasions."

"The Lord by your side, Captain. We're happy to be in good hands." Master John glibly greeted him, making his Flemish accent audible.

Ogden was a man of few words, and by way of greeting he held out his arms to help Master John clamber down onto the heaving boat. The scarred man held out his arms to me. I remember clearly how his hands reached up past mine and quickly wrapped about my forearms like iron manacles. "Hold my forearms the same way, boy, it's the safest grip." He grunted. He knew a little Flemish, as many English shipmen do, for it is the lingua franca of the North Seas. I clasped his wrists as ordered, then I half jumped, and half was borne by the man's strong arms, into the little boat.

Sir Thomas passed our bags down to us. "May the road open out before you both." He wished us well in a low voice, and a serious tone.

"Many thanks, Sir Thomas, you've truly been kind to us." Master John replied.

Aldcliffe opened his mouth, as though to say more, than hurriedly closed it again. I realised he was doing his utmost to be discreet, after the mess he'd made of our departure from Norwich. I waved him goodbye with a smile.

As Captain Ogden and the scarred sailor rowed us out to the ship, a familiar feeling came over me. We'd set out again, like two arrows shot into the wide blue. Where would our flight take us? What would we pierce in our passing?

On the evening of the next day rough weather blew up, so the entire crew of the ship was up on deck, tugging on ropes to tame the wild sails. That left us cooped up in the dark hold below to enjoy the unusual privacy as best we could. Master John started playing word games with me. It was a way to pass the time, but also to teach me how men in our profession should speak and think.

We were sitting on damp barrels of smoked herring, our feet propped up on beams to avoid soaking our boots in the several inches of sea-water that had collected on the bottom of the hold. Nothing could be done, though, about the miserable drips of icy brine that fell through gaps between the planks of decking above as sea-spray washed over the ship.

"…so let us imagine," Master John was musing softly in the Flemish tongue. If a sailor approached unnoticed in the dark and some words were overheard, they should be the Flemish we were expected to speak, not our English court-French. "that a gentleman who sometimes conveys me messages stopped me in the street in London two days ago. He said 'Master John, I'm a worried man. My eldest child's a very sick boy.' Now, what's strange is that I know for a fact his oldest child's a girl."

"He had a message for you, it's certain." I concluded with a grin. I loved these games.

"Of course - unless he'd got confused about how many children he had, as some men do!" We both laughed, for once my elder brother had let himself get very drunk, and when a townsman had asked after his family he'd forgotten one of his daughters.

"But this man hadn't been drinking. In fact, he then told me how a doctor had prescribed for his son a rare medicine from the orient, a most peculiar medicine that not many apothecaries keep in stock. What do you think I did then?"

"You paid a visit to that little shop tucked away in Alms Alley, back from the corner with Soapers' Lane." I replied promptly, pleased with myself. "The one with the green mortar-and-pestle hanging above the door, is that right? I know the apothecary keeps exotic powders… And I remember you went there once after asking me to feign sickness in front of that Spanish wool merchant."

"That's right, well remembered. You know, that apothecary is a special kind of man. If you see him once you would never remember his face thereafter. He has the singular good fortune of forgettable features. And he also forgets faces easily...." Master John chuckled. "When I arrived at his stall on Alms Alley I asked him for that same rare medicine, and he gave me a little leather pouch. I examined the contents carefully, without exposing them, for one never knows when a stranger might pass by a shop in a hurry. There was plain sand inside."

I was memorizing every action Master John described, for I knew he was revealing a partner in our work to me, and what signs to look for and give when contacting him. The sand where medicine should be was a typical ruse.

"That confirms that the apothecary was expecting you."

"Exactly. I told him that the medicine was just what I wanted, and when I'd paid he told me where to go to relieve myself, even though I hadn't asked him. I followed his directions, through a little arch and away from the street, and found a small courtyard. A servant was waiting for me there, and led me inside the building and left me in a room with another man. This last person was one of the most recognizable figures in the kingdom when seen from any distance, and one of the most difficult men to identify from up close. Who do you think that was, Eilulf?"

I thought a little while before answering, a smile of pleasure curling my lip. ...'a most recognizable figure from any distance'... 'a difficult man to identify from up close'... I had a sudden insight.

"The Bishop of Winchester?" I replied.

Master John laughed. "You're quick" he congratulated me "and I like your reasoning. You recognize the figure of a great bishop by his robes and regalia and colours, even at a distance. No common man remembers his features, for there's no need to: his clothes tell you who he is. It is the trappings of his office that you see. A man, on the other hand, is recognized by his face, as you know well. So, strip a great bishop of his regalia and at close quarters he might as well be anyone. He can safely slip into any commoner's household in the land, like an apothecary's, for example.

"And I think you know, for I've told you to keep abreast of these things, that Winchester was in London in the last few days...."

Master John was interrupted by an angry yell from above us, and soon after the sound of a man being struck hard. We grinned to each other. A slack sailor was probably receiving sound instruction.

"So well done, Eilulf, you reasoned well. Now..."

He cut himself off as the Captain's men came sliding down the wet ladder through the hatch from above, one by one. The captain arrived last, and spoke to us in the Flemish.

"The wind's brought up a friendly little storm for you." The ship bucked suddenly, as though to emphasize his words. "We've lashed the sails down in good time, so we'll wait it out. I don't think it'll be too bad. Just try not to vomit, boy." He winked at me. "That would really foul the air down here."

He turned to the men, to give them orders in their familiar English. As the captain spoke I let my expression go blank, then looked away as though losing interest, for such is the natural reaction of a person who cannot understand the conversation he is hearing, and Master John did likewise.

"Right, let's bail the water out of here." Ogden began. "Robert, Roger, Nick, Tom and Anthony, form a chain and get to work." One of the men he mentioned flushed violently red when he was named.

"Now, Tom," the captain spoke in a matter-of-fact way "you don't want to work with Nick after the blow he gave you. I say he did well, for the knot you tied was loose and dangerous. You're one of the freshest men here, so you'll work to clear the hold. Don't get any wild ideas about accidentally tripping over and falling on Nick with your dagger in hand. I'm a man for the old laws, and I'll have you trussed up to his corpse and thrown into the swell before the evening's out." Out of the corner of my eye I saw Tom pale rapidly back to a normal colour. I liked Ogden and his disciplined ways, I decided.

"Master Gerold" the captain turned to my Master, speaking again in the Flemish. "Will you say a prayer for the ship and her company? Ask St James' blessing, if you will." He was keen that his namesake's goodwill in heaven be invoked.

This was not the first time that Master John had been taken for an ordained man in our travels, for un-lettered folk tend to think all clerics are priests, and Master John could play the part beautifully. In the meager light that filtered down to us from the black-clouded dusk above, he took out the small silver cross he wore about his neck, and said prayers in expressive Latin, now bowing to the floor, now raising his head towards the invisible heavens. He called upon Saint James, the Virgin Mary and Saint Martin. "*Jesus cum Maria sit nobis in mare. Amen!*" He intoned in conclusion.

"Amen!" The sailors repeated gratefully.

And so we passed the evening tossing about in the pitch dark, shivering under constant drips of cold water, while the sailors told each other stories to stay awake, in case they were needed on deck. Each spoke roughly in his own dialect, for they hailed from all parts of England. Master John and I pretended to try and sleep, since we couldn't let it show that we understood the sailors' tales.

Steven, the sailor who had come to ferry us onto the *Richard* in the rowing boat the day before, told of the time he'd exchanged blows with the famous Flemish pirate, John Crabbe. Steven's face, though mangled with scars, was expressive, and he gestured like a true storyteller, though his left ring finger was a severed stump.

"It was the eighth year of ol' King Edward-the-Second's reign. God forgive me speakin' ill o' the new King's father an' all, but the land was truly in a sorry state back then. Scotland was fresh lost at Bannockburn Woods, an' the King was playin' the bloody fool at court wi' them boy-favourites as was always pressin' about him lookin' to get lands and castles as never was thems by rights. An' to make matters worse, the coasts of all the land was plagued by pirate reavers. Only brave ol' Sir John Buteturte had the gumption to raise a fleet an' go after 'em. I was a-servin' on Admiral Buteturt's flagship. There are times I touch the scar I got that day, but never I rue how they put me to serve the Admiral. I was little more'n a boy, an it was the greates' honour in the wide worl'! We was sailin' down the east coast of England - seven ships in all, we was, on the King's orders. It was early Fall and the seas was often rough.

"We went a-scourin' the sea-ways off Great Yarmouth coast – lookin' for pirate ships.

"Finally we came upon Crabbe an' his ships just north o' the town. I was on the aft-castle wi' the other baggage-boys. God's truth what fear! What fear, but we was reckless bloody bold!

"Far off I saw him, John Crabbe himself. He was pointin' to our ship and tellin' his pilot to bear down on us, hopin' to take ol' Buteturte on, hand to hand.

"Now, as every man knows, the sea-beasts is like carrion birds – they can smell battle miles away, and come crowdin' up under the waves waitin' for them morsels as might be had. That mornin' they scented a great battle in the water, and the sea twixt the ships fairly heaved wi' them, great scaly heads like slimy green lions, and others like snakes wi' green fire in their bellies, and all about were long, boneless arms lined wi' suckers, ready to grab knights and sailor and pirates alike.

"Now, Buteturte was a man o' both the Royal blood and the Fey blood, and stood he up on the prow wi' his blade drawn, and like swee' thunder and summer lightnin' came his voice a singin', a song o' might. So strong he was that the sea-beasts quailed, and hid them heads a-neath the wave-tops. What a sight, what a sound! And the ships came on…

"Our boys wi' their bows let fly from a good way off, killin' a fair few o' the pirates before they got under cover. But they couldn' hit the crossbowmen in the pirate ships, as they was crouchin' behind their shields, loadin' up their bolts. The wind was drivin' our ship hard, and our boys had scarcely the time to loose three rounds when the pirate archers fired. All I heard was a whistlin' sound, for I was young and didn' know to get behind cover. One o' them bolts punched a ruddy great hole through me left under-arm before I coul' so much as blink, but I was out o' me mind with fear, and didn' even notice it.

"Tomorrow, when there's light to see by, I shall roll up me sleeves and show yous all the scar, should there be any as don' believe what I'm a tellin'.

"So then the two ships pulled alongside. Our knights and men-at-arms leapt onto the Flemish vessel, but one young knight jumped awry as the ships rocked. He let his sword drop, and grabbed for the bulwark wi' both hands, but found no grip! He fell into the sea… But he was a strong feller, and fought the water long enough to get his head out for scream. Lord it made my blood curdle! Then under the water came the heads o' the Great Snake – it's eyes was like burnin' coals and on each head there was lots o' little snakelin's in the place o' hair. One o' the heads took the knight by the waist, and the other by the legs, and it ripped him fairly in two, it did! Then took him down below for feedin' its younglin's…"

The younger men in the hold gasped, and crossed themselves fearfully.

"I was still on the aft-castle o' the Admiral's cog wi' two other boys. A goodly number o' the pirates were swift o' foot, and skipped past our English knights and boarded us. Right'way they bore down on the aft-castle, to take the rudder. Before Buteturte had the time to double back, I was caugh' twixt the railing and Crabbe, who was roaring like a lion! Before I could blink, I'd parried two blows. The third blow struck me short-sword from my grip and sent it flyin', and I swear before God I saw Death herself bearin' down on me!"

By now old Steven had all the sailors twitching on their cold damp barrel-seats.

"Jus' then, brave ol' Sir John Buteturte shouted out to the John Crabbe in his voice like summer thunder: 'Turn and fight a grown man, you stinking cur!' Crabbe turned away to meet Buteturte's sword, and I got me-self up righ' quick. Them blades was a-clashin' and a-clangin', and two finer swordsmen did I never see. But more o' Crabbe's men crossed over behind him, and came to corner the Admiral on the aft castle. 'To the Admiral! The Admiral's in danger' I screams at the top o' me lungs to the Knights as was fightin' on Crabbe's ship. 'Back, back, to the Admiral, or all's lost!' Two fine young fighters heard me, an' slashed an' stabbed their way loose o' the pirates to come a-leapin' back to the flagship. I threw me-self at the bloody pirates, who wante' to trap a gallant such as Buteturte like he was a rat in a barrel, and the two knights came at their backs, and afore them swords was raised they was chopped down and their blood was a-washin' the salt from the deck.

" 'By God and Mary, Buteturte, damn you to Hell!' ol' Crabbe bellowed, seein' 'twas now him was cornered, an' wi' three mighty strokes he cleared his way to the bulwark and jumped clear o' the snappin' jaws o' the Serpent, an' back to the pirate ship an' his mates.

"So Crabbe got away, that day," The sailor told his spellbound listeners "and many an adventure more did he have. Now he's stewar' of Berwick, an' servan' to our King. He's old, is Crabbe, but damn tough to slay."

At some point in the various tales they told that night, in spite of the wet and the rocking of the ship, I fell asleep.

Sluys bay had become busier and busier with the passing years, its enormous expanse of greenish-blue waters cluttered with ships from around the northern seas. And not only from the northern seas, for that afternoon Captain Ogden's good cog was dwarfed as it pulled into the harbour by a Genoese galley as it rowed out to the open sea.

"Master, it's huge... how can such a great bulk possibly stay afloat? Is it some magic?"

"Eilulf, I'm dismayed. I have taught you of the revelations of Archimedes. How can you forget that the more voluminous a vessel is, the more water it displaces and the more, proportionally, it is buoyant."

I shook my head in a display of feigned ruefulness for the benefit of Captain Ogden who was beside us, admiring the galley.

"I know, Master, I am a poor student of numbers." In reality, of course, though Master John was indeed well acquainted with the Quadrivium of arithmetic, geometry, music and astronomy, it had never really been the subject of my instruction. He had always had more pressing things to teach me for our work than the liberal arts. "But look how it seems to glide over the water. How can it move so swiftly?"

"That, I suspect, is not a question of arcane arts. There's nothing magical about the way they ply their slaves with whips." Master John's voice was dry.

Captain Ogden nodded in agreement as he waved a seaman's greetings to the Genoese captain in passing.

"Many's the time I would have liked a team of oarsmen to take my ship into the wind as I pleased." He told us. "It's a shame we hang our thieves and murderers, instead of putting them to good use as the Genoese do."

I couldn't but agree with the Captain.

Once ashore, we said our farewells to Ogden and his crew, who were busying themselves off-loading their cargo before night fell. All of the men spoke enough Flemish to wish us well on our way, and accept our thanks and blessings. Ogden himself refused payment, explaining that Sir Thomas de Aldcliffe would settle the account when the Captain returned to Lancaster.

"Sir Thomas always clears his debts, I've no worries of that. Be on your way, and God's speed to you."

And so we were back in familiar old Sluys, among the busy throngs of merchantmen, tradesmen and financiers. Flanders had become our second home, as much of our service to Richard de Bury and the King had been carried out there, guarding the interests of the King's English Wool Company. We mingled easily into the jostling crowds, and disappeared into the narrow streets of the city itself.

Though it was still sunny and pleasant, darkness would soon gather in.

"Before curfew we must order our horses for tomorrow morning. We're leaving straight away." Master John informed me.

Until that moment I had not known that we were to travel beyond the port town of Sluys. I was used to being kept in the dark about our aims. Master John would say that a secret existed between two men. When a third man was told, it was no longer a secret but a rumor in the making.

We started toward the artisan's quarter, near the south-gates, from which the roads for the rest of the continent stretched away. Clustered around the streets leading to the gates were the saddlers and lorimers, ready to sell their wares to travellers setting off for the south. On the way, as we normally did when in Sluys, we made a detour through the Genoese enclave. My Master explained that he simply wanted to 'breathe in the air of the money-market', to keep abreast of the situation there. It was a professional habit.

"The Earl of Lancaster's man gave us a number of promissory notes, small and large." Master John confided to me as we crossed the city. "I'll change one of the smaller ones into coin as an excuse to be in the money-market. Listen carefully to whatever you hear in the northern tongues, while I concentrate on the Genoese, Occitan and the Florentine, the tongues you understand less well. In particular, listen for mention of wool."

The interests of England had been inextricably tied to the wool trade in those years. The King had tried, in vain, to finance his fleet and army with revenue from the English Wool Company. His design had been scuppered both by the untrustworthiness of the English merchants, who often falsely declared low profits in order to pocket the difference, and by the fact that Flanders, where the wool was transformed into cloth, was deeply influenced by Paris. Now the King had decided to block English wool from arriving in Sluys, hoping that the shortage would bring the marketplaces of France to a crisis. We were curious to see what effect the blockade might be having on Sluys.

The Genoese enclave huddled around the church of St Augustine, where the monks rented space to keep documents and coinage. All about the church the money-market had grown up, where equivalent value was calculated, assurance against the risk of sea voyages was bought and sold, and where ledgers and promissory notes, with more 'zeros' than real numbers, were filled out.

We ambled slowly past the stalls and notaries' benches, taking our time in order to overhear as much as possible. The words 'wool' and 'shipment' stood out of the background babble in many different tongues. It soon became apparent that a famous merchant of our land, whom everybody was careful not to name, had brought a consignment of English wool to the town that very morning, flaunting the King's blockade. Now the various Genoese, Florentines and Milanese were calculating how much the price of wool could fall in the markets of nearby Bruges as a result of the shipment, and speculating on the price of finished cloth in Paris. How could King Edward ever hope to bring war to France if his efforts were continually undermined by his own countrymen?

We sat down in the street before a Genoese change-bench, and produced our promissory note. Master John, who spoke some Florentine volgare with a creditable Flemish accent, dealt with the matter. In the meantime I looked discreetly about at the faces. Finally I saw what I'd been hoping to see: a familiar English face. Rather, I should say, a familiar English nose-bridge and pair of eyes. The rest of the man's face had radically changed in the year since I'd last caught sight of him. Master John had taught me to memorize the set of the central part of a face, for it is the part that changes the least over time. Beards can come and go, hair can shorten or lengthen, teeth be knocked out, ears and tips of noses cut off in battle, but the set of the central features of a face remains more or less the same.

As we wandered out of the money-market, I murmured "I saw Henry Tideswell talking to some Danes."

Master John swore softly. "Did he see us?"

"No, I'm sure of it."

"Good. So…" He paused. "Henry Tideswell and his ilk… I wish the King had never put his faith in such men." He sighed. "Money lovers, and money grubbers. Our poor England is short of silver coins, so their loyalty is drawn elsewhere."

"That's the truth of it." I agreed.

For a moment Master John was silent, and I knew he was thinking about how to confront the situation. Finally his face split into a broad grin.

"Tell me, Eilulf, did you ever get your amorous way with Anna, the wife of Jooris the lorimer?"

I grinned. "No, I didn't, though not for want of trying, nor for want of willingness on her part. I was determined enough, and she was more than open to the idea, but her husband kept arriving at the wrong moment."

"Good." He said brightly. "Then we'll go straight to Jooris now and ask him to arrange our horses for us. I'm counting on his good wife to use the late hour as an excuse to invite us to stay with them tonight. After all, we're trusted loyal clients. She'll be hoping to get Jooris and myself well into our cups and snoring the night away, so you can do with her as your heart desires. What do you say?"

The prospect was pleasant. Anna was a fine, busty young wife, with plenty of fat on her hips.

"I say it's a fine way to get us board without paying, and it would be my solemn duty to please the craftsman's wife in exchange. But what's it got to do with Henry Tideswell's wool?"

"Ah!" Master John indulged in a cunning expression. "We'll leave their house after midnight when both Anna and Jooris are sleeping. If we stayed in a tavern, we'd never be able to slip out into the night unobserved."

I nodded. In a tavern, our fellow lodgers would surely include sailors, bent upon drinking, singing and dancing until dawn.

"What are we going to do, Master?"

"You'll see. Henry Tideswell and all those speculators at the money-market will wish they had never crossed the King's divine will!"

Chapter 4

London, September 1337

Reaction to a brutal murder – an agent has left the country – the mysterious behaviour of Henry de Grosmont

The door closed behind the two men. For a long moment there was no sound but the distant dripping of water. It was always raining in this dank, moldy city.

"A number of members of the Council have expressed their abhorrence of the murder of the Spinola boy two weeks ago."

The Englishman was taking the trouble to speak in his best Occitan for the foreigner's benefit. He was met with a raised eyebrow in the olive-skinned face, nothing more. Those dark eyes let no meaning or emotion show. He continued.

"Our ways are not your ways, Messer Fieschi. We are not accustomed to this... style of politics. Should your family have chosen to exercise its power in its own territory, neither I nor His Majesty would feel any need to intervene. But here, in London..." He vainly searched the listener's features for some hint of his thoughts.

"While the King's father, Edward of Caernarfon, did nothing to repress such violent games at court, His Majesty King Edward the Third has no intention of playing host to foreign blood baths and feuds. I understand that this agent of yours... Francesco Forzetti... is valuable to you, and we are prepared to forego the pursuit of justice for this heinous act. But you will find something useful for him to do overseas. Immediately." Still no reaction. The dark eyes moved about naturally from the speaker's face to small objects around the room, as though the listener were wholly at ease.

"Such a transfer might ease the anger of the lords of the Council to some extent."

There was another long moment of silence. When finally the other man spoke, it was in the Latin, disdaining the English earl's Occitan as inadequate for holding a real conversation. The arrogant tone of the reply was calculated to make sure it was understood that in no way was a concession being made to his English hosts.

"Our agent, Forzetti, left two days ago by ship. Discreetly. Pressing business of ours had already called him away to the continent."

The Englishman's jaw dropped a little in surprise, before his expression quickly froze with irritation. He, too, took up the Latin.

"Do not vex the men of the council, Messer Fieschi. There are other forms of power than money."

By way of answer the listener only inclined his head, as though to sardonically acknowledge that this might, possibly, be true. It was clear, however, in which form of power he put his trust.

As soon as Messer Fieschi had left, Richard de Bury came forward from the drapery-hidden recess where he had been listening to the conversation in absolute silence.

"Now, William, I think you understand why I am so concerned." The old man said, taking the seat just left vacant by Fieschi. "You've witnessed how detestable he is first hand. And just think: the King admitted this man to the Council within a month of his arrival in England."

William de Montague's face was grave, and he brought a stout index finger to his blond-bearded chin, as he always did when choosing his words carefully.

"I agree, the man is detestable, and yes, I am concerned. This interview with Fieschi has left me…" his mouth twisted, as though full of some bitter liquid "with a sour taste in my mouth. On the other hand, might we not be underestimating the King? He's truly come of age in the last few years, largely thanks to you, Richard. He might be keeping us out of his own thoughts for some good reason of his own."

"Edward's coming of age is as much your doing as it is mine." Bury commented. "I have been his mentor in matters of the head, but you have been his model with the sword and the heart." Both men paused, remembering the night, seven years before, when Montague and a small band of brothers-in-arms had led the young King Edward, a boy on the cusp of conquering manhood, along a pitch black tunnel, up through the bedrock beneath Nottingham Castle and out through a secret door to arrest the traitor-tyrant, Roger Mortimer, and reclaim his kingdom.

Bury leaned forward, his hands clasped together on the marble table, just as Fieschi had done shortly before.

"Now our pupil has outstripped us. He has won the people's sincere love, his feats of arms are already legendary, and his head for diplomacy is as subtle as the Pope's. He may well have a secret agenda in his dealings with Fieschi that we cannot guess at. But I am the overseer of the King's secret business, and I know nothing of it as yet. What could be so secret that Edward keeps it from his own secret-keeper?"

Montague shook his head. "I agree, that is strange."

"And there is something even stranger, William." Richard de Bury took a deep, troubled breath before continuing. "Some months ago, Henry de Grosmont came to me asking a favour. He told me that he was profoundly troubled by a matter of state, but could not be more specific. Henry seemed transformed from his usual self. You know Henry. He lives every moment, be it a private conversation, a public feast, or a stately dance with a courtesan, as though he were boisterously battling in a tournament. His every move, his every word emanates that beaming joy with which he wins his every fight. But that day he was reserved, close, and troubled. I was startled, and yet hopeful. I remembered when he was a boy, and came to me for lessons with his cousin Edward. Henry would ask Edward to do his Latin exercises for him, because he loathed writing and wanted to go out and play-joust. If Henry were to mature into his role as his cousin has done, it would be the best of outcomes for us all. With his father ailing worse every day, he will soon inherit the broadest and richest power base in the land. Henry is a man of great talent and intelligence, though he pretends to be brawny but brainless in public."

"I agree with you," Montague nodded "there is far more to Henry than he reveals to the world. But what was the favour he asked of you?"

"He requested that I loan him some of the King's agents to investigate a certain matter. He told me he would reveal the matter to me when he was sure his fears were not mistaken and he was not wasting my time."

"And did you loan him these agents of yours?"

"I did. I wanted to encourage this new seriousness of his. After all, his loyalty is absolute. I wrote a number of warrants instructing agents to serve Henry de Grosmont as loyally as they would serve me, and I left it at that, choosing to trust in him and let him follow his own initiative. There is no other way for a young man to come of age. Then, two days ago, I discovered that Henry had used one of the warrants to take John de Ulgham and his pupil into his service. Ulgham is my senior agent, the finest in all the land. I have pressing need of his services in Flanders now, where the wool shortage is starting to pinch and we need to turn the loyalty of cities like Sluys and Ghent from France to England. And here I find him, gone from under my nose, whisked away by Henry de Grosmont. Concerned, I called in some of the other agents that had served Grosmont, to ask what they had been doing for him. They had been gathering information on the dealings of one Niccolò Fieschi."

William de Montague nodded. He had seen it coming.

"And what had they discovered?"

"Many things, but I have no way of knowing their significance."

Montague raised his eyebrows in surprise.

"But they are your agents."

The old man spread his hands, helplessly.

"That is the nature of the secret business. You gather crumbs of information from the most disparate sources, and only when you piece them all together do you start to understand what they mean. No individual agent ever understands enough of what they are doing to give a really useful appraisal. Unfortunately, most spies are utterly prosaic men and women, whose degraded moral state leaves them incapable of appreciating the finer points of anything but money. After all," Bury sighed "that's why they're spies."

"And so you're saying that you cannot know what Henry has discovered by questioning your agents?"

"For some months now, Henry has been piecing together information from far and wide. He even sent one of the warrants to William Bateman in Avignon, my key agent in the papal city. It would take weeks to get word back from Avignon about exactly what Bateman discovered for him, and even then it may be just a small part of the puzzle. And that is where you come in, William. That is why I requested that you be the one to meet Fieschi today, to help you understand why I am so concerned."

"What can I do?"

"Henry de Grosmont is a young and bold creature of chivalrous deeds. I am merely a crafty old Bishop, but you are a man of the sword and of honour, a model for him. You have often been a mentor to Henry just as you were to the King. He still calls you 'big brother', William. Use this bond with him. Talk to Henry, and try to discover what he has learnt. How has Fieschi become so close to the King in such a short time? What is the source of his influence over the King? Why has Henry de Grosmont suddenly become so interested in the affairs of the Genoese?"

Montague nodded. "In other words, you want me to dig discreetly."

Richard de Bury smiled. "Quite."

Chapter 5

Sluys, September 1337

The pleasure of a craftsman's wife – Ave Maria – Lady Fortune's choice?

Our old friend Jooris was at his workbench in the street. He was bent over, finishing off a set of bridles in the last light of day.

"Master Gerold, Eilulf," he caught sight of us "bless your heads, hearts and hands! Back in Sluys for some time, I hope?" He was always keen to take advantage of potential drinking companions.

"Not at all, Jooris, I'm sorry. We're here for the night. Will you have time tomorrow morning to help us with fresh mounts and gear?"

"Of course. I always have time for my best customers. Come inside for a ladle-full of beer. You look tired." He gathered up his tools and the bridles, then led us into his shop.

"We caught a storm last night crossing over from England, and hardly slept." Master John explained. I was looking forward to that beer, and my stomach grumbled. I had finished off the last of Madge's cheese and bread at lunchtime.

"Then it's little wonder. Tonight you'll be at the Scheldtswass Tavern?" He set his gear down on a bench and took a candle to the fireplace to light it. "Anna," he called out through a doorway at the back of the shop-front "Master Gerold and Eilulf from Ghent are here."

"Of course, we'll stay at the Scheldtswass." Master John confirmed. "In the morning we have to be on the road."

"So soon? That's a shame…" he fell silent

We were now speaking by the most haunting illumination: the flickering brazen light of the fire, the steadier, paler gleam of the candle, and the last hues of the sun from the open window. Old

Jooris' seemed concentrated, as though calculating something, and I knew he was counting up the number of beers that might be drunk between now and curfew. He sighed wistfully.

"Just one night in Sluys, and it's nearly curfew… You'll at least take a traveller's breakfast tomorrow with us…" At that moment Anna, his wife, interrupted her husband as she came into the room, and I caught her eye with ease.

"You'll take both your breakfast tomorrow and your dinner tonight with us, and be our guests, too." She came forward and kissed us both on the cheeks. Anna was rosy, and smelled pleasantly of cooking. "We can shift Jan to our side of the room to sleep, it's only one night." Though it hadn't been his idea, Jooris seemed pleased. It was the best way to make the most of our company.

Master John surreptitiously winked at me. Everything was working to plan. We were regular customers of theirs for our horse-wear, but Jooris and Anna's affection for us dated to the time Master John had successfully treated their son, Jan, when he'd been taken by a bout of vomiting. Once the fear for her little one's well-being had passed, I had taken a better look at Anna in particular, and decided that I liked what I saw. From then on, every time we'd visited I'd pushed myself into some tight corner with her. She was a pretty young woman, married to a much older man, and was not at all displeased at the situation. Neither was I. Whilst an English peasant's daughters are bony and hard from their work, a Flemish craftsman's wife is soft and chubby, and childbearing makes her buxom. It is an altogether finer pleasure, though unfortunately much harder to get. Her husband had the knack of innocently bumbling into view when he was not expected. Now that we would stay the night with them, the prospect was better.

Master John was the perfect actor that evening as we sat down together to Anna's specialty, leeks and bacon baked in savoury custard, with slices of roasted sour-apple strewn over the top. Whenever Jooris passed us the jug of strong black beer, my Master and I only half drained the ladle, while Jooris gulped all of it down, every time.

After a few hours' talking about saddles, stirrups, studs and spurs, Master John and Jooris both climbed upstairs to sleep, my Master making a show of staggering as badly as the lorimer. Anna went up to tuck her husband into bed, while I stayed by the fire warming my toes. Soon enough the raucous snoring of two grown men echoed through the shop. I was sure that Master John was not really sleeping, for he had serious business on his mind for that evening. Then Anna slipped back down to the hall, a coy smile toying with the corners of her mouth.

"I forgot to stoke the fire and take tomorrow's porridge off the heat." She explained, and bustled over to the hearth.

"Let me help Anna. You must be very tired, Anna, after a long day." I rose from my bench and went to her side, as though to warm my fingers. She bent over the coals industriously.

"Not at all. It wasn't a busy day, and Jan was with the other boys learning his letters all morning." Her hips swung as she worked, and her breasts fell full against her thin linen tunic.

"Then you must be glad I've not fallen asleep like Jooris and Master Gerold. It must be boring in the evenings when…" I broke off deliberately, enticing her to finish for me.

"…when Jooris rolls into bed drunk." She obliged. "Here, take the other side of the pot."

I obediently wrapped my sleeve-end around my fingers, bent over and grasped the handle on my side. We were now face to face above the sweet, simmering oats.

"You poor thing, Anna." I sympathized as we straightened up, the pot between us. "How can a dutiful husband fall asleep imagining that his pretty wife's thirst is slaked, just because *he* has drunk his fill?"

"After too much beer, judgment is not the only thing that fails a man." She sighed as we stepped toward a large cooling brick. We bent over once more carefully set the pot down on the brick, taking an unnecessarily long time over it. I was well placed to admire her, and she was enjoying my admiration.

"Dearest Anna," I leaned forward before she could rise again and placed my hands lightly, caressingly on her shoulders. "not all men seek beauty in the bottom of a beer-jug." I stepped forward, around the pot, as we straightened up, so that she stood within my arms, the rich brown hair of her fringe almost brushing against my lips as I spoke. "I, for one, seek and find elsewhere. Of course, as an honourable guest I yearn to do my hostess…" I trailed off as she closed her eyes, tilted her head back, and her warm, richly scented lips pressed urgently upward toward mine, while her full breasts strained forward against my chest.

How could I have neglected my duty to befriend such a kind, generous woman? In our professional interests, I had to bear in mind that we might return to Sluys many times in future on business, and many times be in need of the goodwill of the locals. It was my job to forge ties with them, was it not?

I was patiently sitting by the ember-light downstairs in the shop, singing troubadours' poetry in my mind to avoid giving in to slumber, when I sensed rather than heard Master John stealing down the steps. The barely restrained excitement and determination in his eyes brought me wide awake in an instant. He put a finger to his lips, then crossed to the fire place. He took out a small leather pouch, and some rags. He dipped the rags into the clay hot-water pot that always lay on the hearth-stone, wetting them with simmering water. Then he wrapped them around his hand and fished a good sized coal from the edge of the fire. He swiftly trussed the coal up in the damp rags, then dropped it into the pouch, which he loosely tied shut. He passed the pouch to me with a level look. There was no need to say more. I tucked it into my clothes against my chest.

The evenings were not yet cold, and Anna had not yet stretched panes of thin hide across the street-windows to keep in the warmth. We listened carefully for sounds of the city watch, and when we were sure the street was empty we slipped out of the window into the night.

In a low voice, Master John explained.

"We're going down to the wool-houses by the wharves. You're lighter on your feet. I'll give you the distraction you need, and you'll go in and out in the time I give you. When the time's up, I'll make a second distraction, and then we'll both get away and back to Jooris' shop separately."

We padded through the familiar lanes and alleys, our ears sensitive to the slightest suggestion of noise. Rats scurried in the drains in the centres of the streets, and once we surprised a cat crouching low on the cobbles as it stalked its midnight meal. As we approached, a dark smudge stretched its wings and fluttered off, and the cat turned two glowing eyes on us in a reprimanding glare, then vanished.

The pouch containing the coal wrapped in wet rags had become warm against my skin.

Twice we passed in front of well-lit taverns, the sound of laughter, harp, flute and song, making me yearn to be in the hall with the other guests. Only once did we have to duck into an alley to avoid being seen by the steely eyes of the watchmen on their rounds. Finally, we were under the city walls in the vicinity of the docks. We crept within sight of the wool-houses, on the far side of the narrow street. There were night guards, two mercenaries who mumbled to each other in a Swiss dialect as they leaned self-confidently against their pikes in front of the main entrance. We crouched down in the shadows to wait. After some time, the watch passed by, exchanging wary greetings with the two mercenaries. There was no love lost between the Watchmen, born and bred of Sluys, and these foreigners who fought for the highest bidder.

Then we waited. I knew that Master John was singing the *Ave Maria* to himself in his mind, to a slow beat. Time passed. How many times had he sung the prayer? Thirty? Thirty-five? Finally, the Watch patrol came back into view, exchanging nods with the mercenaries again. About forty *Ave Maria* rounds had passed.

I tensed as the patrol walked away. Soon our moment would come. Master John reached across to me, and closed his fingers about my wrist. He squeezed twenty times. That was the number of rounds of the prayer he would give me to get in and out: half the time it would take the Watch to come back on its round. That would leave us time enough to deal with an emergency should something go wrong.

After a long pause, Master John squeezed my wrist three times with a slow rhythm. I picked up the beat in my mind, and after the third squeeze started to intone in my mind the *Ave Maria*. I knew Master John was also intoning the same prayer to the same melody and to the same tempo that he had just given me with his fingers. In an instant he was gone from my side. Though we were now out of each other's sight, we were linked by an invisible thread of song, as the *Ave Maria* echoed simultaneously in both our minds.

An eerie calm came over me, as the rhythm of the prayer soothed the pounding in my veins. *…benedicta tu in mulieribus…* On cue, at the start of the second *Ave*, I heard a pebble drop somewhere far to my left. The night guardians heard it too, and as one they fell silent to turn and look. I did not take my eyes from them, but somewhere to my left Master John started to conjure up a low growl in the back of his throat. The sound was ambiguous, and the night could play tricks on the keenest ears. Was it a human, or was it a quarrelsome he-cat? The guards took two steps in that direction, and I silently crossed to their side of the street, in time to the prayer in my head. The growling continued, and I was safely into the shadows of low-hanging gables.

I watched as one of the mercenaries ordered the other to stay put, and with his hand on his dagger, he went to investigate. Master John was nowhere to be seen.

...nunc, et in hora mortis nostrae. Amen... At the start of the third *Ave* Master John darted out from the shadows into the moonlight that filtered through the thin clouds, running away from the wool-house to towards the narrow streets of the city.

"Stop!" The investigating mercenary called, and followed, his feet pounding. His companion's attention was focused on him, and I stole unseen into the alley that ran along one side of the broad, low warehouse. My nose wrinkled involuntarily. It was a pissing alley. There was no help for it, I had to enter through one of the windows that gave onto it, above my head. I still had seventeen repetitions of the *Ave Maria* during which to get in, do my work, and get out.

The pouch against my chest was now scalding hot.

With my hands raised as high as I could reach, I ran my fingers along the brickwork, searching for a window. I kept the rhythm of the prayer in my mind. Master John and I had practiced keeping our rhythm when separated many times. It had almost become second nature.

Finally, I felt the brickwork change. Here was an airing window, but it was as high as the tips of my outstretched fingers. I would have to be grimly careful. The guards would be by the doorway now, especially watchful, and the slightest sound from the alley would draw them toward me with daggers unsheathed.

I slipped off my shoes directly beneath the window, then began to search for gaps in the mortar of the wall with my toes. Fortunately the brickwork was old and had fallen out in places. I found a toe-hold and hoisted myself up, then got my fore-arms over the window-sill. As silently as possible, I pulled myself up and onto the sill, then dropped quickly down inside.

It was pitch dark in the wool-house. I dared not wander about, or I might never find the way out again. I stood with my back to the wall directly under the window, and took carefully measured steps forward, one for each beat of the prayer. After seven steps, I encountered the outer sacking of a bale of wool.

I was relieved. We were half-way through the eighth *Ave Maria*, and I could finally take the burning-hot pouch out from under my tunic.

I knelt down, and carefully took the coal from the wet rags with my fingers. In spite of the great heat it still emanated, the surface of the coal was as black as the darkness around me, dampened as it was by the rags. With infinite care, by touch alone, I placed it under the wool bale sacking. All the while I gritted my teeth against the blistering heat on my fingertips, but I did not lose contact with it, for I would never find it again in the gloom. I had to bring my chin down to rest on the back of my hand and blow directly along my fingers onto the invisible charcoal.

...*Sancta Maria, Mater Dei, ora pro nobis peccatoribus*...

I blew on the coal, and it flared against my fingers. I snatched them away, for I could now see the faint glimmer of the coal to blow on, and did not need to keep touch with it. ...*nunc, et in hora mortis*... I blew again and again. The coal was now the colour of anger, but still I blew. ...*Ave Maria, gratia plena,*... A tiny flame licked against the wool bale, and still I blew. Soon it was no longer a tiny flame, but a flickering golden crescent in the dark, which arced along the curved side of the sack like some infernal scythe-blade. I closed my eyes, so as not to be blinded, straightened up and turned my back to the bale. As the tenth *Ave Maria* ran through my mind, I opened my eyes again. The window was now visible in the growing red light of the fire. I reached it as my back started to feel the heat. Silence was still paramount as I climbed up onto sill. With the toes of my right foot I felt about for a foot-hold on the outer side of the wall. I dared not drop into the alley, even though it was a tiny drop. Who might know what I would land on? I found my footing, and carefully stepped down onto the muck and rubble of the street.

When I knelt down to recover my shoes, I brushed against the rotting corpse of a rat, and the sharp tips of its rib bones pricked my palm. I hurried to slip on my shoes. It was the start of the thirteenth *Ave Maria*. The sacks of many of the heaped wool bales would now be ablaze. Though the wool itself would probably only smolder, it would be blackened, stinking and un-sellable. But how soon would the crackling of the fire be audible?

I edged toward the mouth of the alley, but did not look out onto the street. It was not yet time.

...Dominus tecum. Benedicta tu in mulieribus, et benedictus fructus ventris tui, Jesus...

I tried to breathe shallowly, silently, in time with the prayer. At the start of the twentieth *Ave* I edged one eye past the wall of the wool-house, to see what was happening. The two mercenaries had regained their usual relaxed posture. They probably thought they'd seen a frightened beggar earlier.

I waited.

...et in hora mortis nostrae. Amen. Twenty. In case things didn't go according to plan I raised my fist with my knife's hilt in it. I almost hoped things didn't go according to Master John's plan. What better way to polish off the perfect night? After good food and beer, love-making and arson, a lusty little fight.

An instant later, Master John sent a rock flying from the shadows like Thor's hammer, striking the further guard's helm before he could so much as open his mouth. Then my Master darted out into the moonlight and started running. The mercenary who'd taken the rock was half dazed, cradling his head in his hands and groaning, his eyes shut. The other guardian instantly leapt after Master John. I casually stepped out of the shadows and brought the heel of my knife down on the base of the groaning guardian's neck. He fell to the road, stunned. I shook my head. There was no satisfaction in felling a man so easily. The other guardian's footsteps and shouts were fading in the distance as I made off in the opposite direction. The fire in the wool-house would soon rouse the whole city to the docks quarter, and ensure that Master John and I could get back in safety to the far side of Sluys. My heart slowly calmed to a normal pace. Now the task was done I smiled, suddenly exquisitely exhausted.

Jooris came to the breakfast table with a cheerful air, accustomed as he was to recovering from hard drinking. He took Master John's and my haggard faces to be the result of the previous nights' beer-bout, and clearly suspected nothing of our night time adventure. I was worried Anna might notice that my feet were unpleasantly fragrant this morning after scrambling about in that pissing-alley, but she didn't seem to have noticed anything. As she nimbly moved about the kitchen, fetching us salted herring and twice-cooked rye bread bathed in hot salty water, she cast many a sly look in my direction, but I was too tired even to let my eyes play with hers.

"Don't worry, Gerold" Jooris assured Master John "you'll be on the road before long, then you'll be able to sleep it off as your mule waddles along."

"Horses, not mules" he lifted his heavy-lidded gaze to our Flemish friend "We need two decent road-horses. We have urgent business in the south, I'm afraid."

"Even better!" Which was true for Jooris, who would take a larger commission buying horses on our behalf than mules, and could sell more expensive examples of his wares to us.

It was not until we were outside the house that we saw the smoke that darkened the morning sky in the direction of the port.

"What happened?" Jooris asked his neighbouring shop-owner, who was busy setting up his work-bench in the street.

"The wool-house down at the docks went up in flames during the night. Full of wool. It took them hours to douse it down, I heard."

"The wool-house?" Jooris scratched his stubbly chin. "I thought it was empty, now the English King refuses to ship to us."

"Seems someone ran the embargo just yesterday with a hefty shipment."

"Bad luck it went up in flames the very same night."

"Luck?" The shopkeeper shook his head. "I doubt it was luck, so much as arson." My heart started to race, but he went on. "I'd lay a bet on one of those damned Genoese or Florentines, someone who was counting on a high price in Paris. When he saw the shipment come in, and prices falling, he must have set the fire to raise the market again."

Jooris nodded. That seemed plausible.

It took Jooris over an hour's haggling in the shops and stables around the south-gates to purchase our horses, then he supplied us with his best bridles, saddles and stirrups. When we'd settled our bags onto our new horses' backs, we said farewell to our friends. Jooris shook our hands, and bade us good fortune on the road. "Please return soon." Anna said fondly, and her kiss on my cheek was slightly more lingering than courtesy required. Old Jooris either didn't notice, or didn't care.

The walls of Sluys were still tall behind us when Master John beckoned to me to veer toward the side of the road. We extricated ourselves from the flow of hundreds of in-comers and out-goers, and reached the margins, where the well-trodden earth gave way to scraggly grasses and thorn-bushes, and the well-dressed citizens on mule or horse-back gave way to rag-clad outcasts, hovering about the fringes on bare feet, hunger in their eyes.

"Wait here for me with the horses." Master John instructed in a low tone, dismounting. "I want to slip back into the city among the crowds. It's vital to know the effect of our deeds last night on the money market. I want confirmation that we forced the price of wool up. Only if the spinners and weavers of Flanders are desperate will they turn their backs on the French in the war that is soon to be declared."

Long after Master John had disappeared among the comings and goings close to the city gates, I had dismounted for my horse's comfort. A grubby looking boy with a pox-marked face caught my attention. He stood in the roadside scrub on scrawny, muddy legs, his knees showing beneath the rough sacking he wore, and he clasped a crooked stick in one hand. He eyed me thoughtfully, slowly taking in my clothes, face, and the two horses. I felt that, had I been dressed as anything other than a cleric's pupil, he might have come begging to me. Instead, discouraged by the miserly reputation of clerics, he turned away. He soon caught sight of a well-to-do lady leaving the city on a pony, accompanied by a maid on mule-back and a manservant on foot. I was impressed, though disapprovingly so, of the way the urchin now drew his left leg up carefully until it had completely disappeared beneath his sacking, and leant upon his stick like a cripple. Next, he carefully concealed something slight and small between the fingers of his right hand. His back now twisted until he was frightfully hunched over, and he somehow managed to hobble over to block the path of the pony whilst never losing his new posture.

"My lady, spares-you a crumb for me, my lady, and God blessing your..."

The beggar was interrupted by a slap in the face from the manservant, and a brusque "Out of our way!"

The boy clutched at his face in exaggerated pain. I was sure the manservant had dealt him nothing but a light blow, and yet as he drew his hand away I saw blood running from his cheek.

"Guy, leave the poor thing be," the lady called back her manservant "he's done nothing to you, and meant you no harm. Did you, child?"

"God bless you, lady, I surely meant no harm ever in my life, I didn't," the boy bleated "but since my mam were taken by fever and my pa were killed in the wars, all as I've gotten is blows and ill words…" he continued to describe his dire plight to the lady with many sad details, such as how he lost his left leg after a crazed horse trampled him. I was sorely tempted to cross back into the road and inform the wide-eyed lady that the urchin was an outrageous liar. However, I was alone with our two horses, and I could not lead them back into the road without causing much rage to other travelers whose path I would block. I was considering crying out to her in a loud voice, but by the time I made up my mind the whole scene was played out. Hushing the manservant's protestations, the lady had taken a coin from her purse and thrown it to the beggar, who was now scampering away as fast as his crippled play-acting would allow.

By the time the boy was safely on the fringes again, the lady and her retinue were lost in the multitudes on the road, and he miraculously rediscovered both his lost leg and his straight back. He grinned, pleased with himself, and as he slipped his ill-gotten coin into a fold of his tunic, he tossed that strange, slight object he'd concealed between his fingers up into the air. As it tumbled and turned in the air, I realised that it was broken-off knife blade. Perhaps he'd scrounged it from the gutter by a tinker's stall somewhere, and now kept it for the purpose to which he'd so ably put it. That little blade turned the blows he regularly received in the course of his 'work' into bleeding skin and sympathy from gullible ladies on the road. As the trickle of blood dried on his grimy cheek he slipped the blade into a fold of his sleeve, then he scanned the passers-by for someone else to fool. Suddenly I understood that the scars all over his face, which I had at first taken for pox-marks, were in fact self-inflicted. I felt repulsed by the boy. In that moment he seemed beneath even an animal, for animals at least live according to the laws of their kind, not against them.

"Good news, Eilulf," Master John exclaimed as he slipped out of the traffic behind me with a broad smile "prices have soared like a hawk on the wing. Now all that remains to be done…" He paused, catching sight of the urchin standing a little further on, still on the look-out for fresh quarry.

"Perfect." Master John murmured, nodding, and to my surprise called out to him. "Boy, come here if you want to earn yourself a coin."

Naturally, the boy scurried over, though a little fearfully at first. Two grown men would always be more likely to beat him than to help him, he must have thought. Before I could protest, Master John took a coin from his purse and held it out to the boy together with a tiny leaf of old parchment. The pauper took the first with glee, and the second with bewilderment.

"You are to deliver this parchment to the guards by the city-gates. Do you understand?" The boy nodded, clearly intrigued. "I will watch you from horse-back here. Be kind enough not to slip into the crowds, but let me see you all the way to the gates, so I know when your errand is done."

As Master John finished, the boy's face slowly broke out into a coy grin, looking my Master challengingly in the eye. He had clearly taken us for two slow-moving laggards, for he chuckled in his barely intelligible street-dialect "I thinks I knows the game. You's done something as oughtn't you did, this here as being your confession, but you wants to be off yonder afore it were read. And with a second coin in me hands, I mayn't be telling what's your faces like, and what's the road you were taking…"

This was more than I could bear. I acted without thinking, as though my own limbs were not mine to control, but slaves to my anger, still smoldering after the previous night's excitement had ended without a fight. With one hand I lunged for the little blade where I knew it to be hidden in his sleeve, and caught it between thumb and forefinger. My other hand shot out and around to take hold of the hair at the scruff of his neck before the shocked pauper could so much as blink. I pulled his head up close to my face.

"If he didn't do as he was told, a beggar-boy like you could die in the night, and no-one would ever notice." I grated, startled to hear that my voice had, almost of its own accord, become as cold and menacing as I had ever heard it. I pressed the blade to the side of his neck below his left ear, and "Be thankful I haven't slit your throat for insulting my Master."

"Eilulf" Master John interjected "that's enough!"

As though starting from a day-dream, I jerked guiltily, but the boy chose that moment to try to struggle free, and I resisted. I could never have guessed he kept that broken-off bit of knife so sharp until I saw the blood well from his ear and realise that the lobe had somehow been snicked off by our confused movements.

I released my grip and the boy staggered away, pressing his hand to the wound.

"That's something to remember your duty by," I told him, as though I had injured him on purpose "Now go to the guards at the gate, and forget our faces." The wretch scampered off toward the city, whimpering and terrified, clutching at his bleeding ear as he went.

Master John was appalled. "What has got into you?"

"He's a pauper and a liar." I began to justify myself. "He had no right to speak to you like that."

"But what need was there for such an act? Now he'll bear that scar for the rest of his life. The poor and innocent deserve charity, not violence."

"Innocent? That boy's a trickster. I saw him, while you were in the city. He pretended to be crippled, with a missing leg and a hunched back, and provoked a lady's servant on the road, the way he provoked you. When the servant struck him, he cut his face with this" I gestured to the blade, smeared with blackening blood "and pretended he was cut by the servant's hand, so the lady was moved to give him coin. All those scars on his face aren't from the pox, he did them all to himself."

Master John stared hard at me in silence for a long moment.

"And now you compound his misery with violence that is far beneath you, you who have mastered violence in the service of king and God?"

"I didn't mean to cut his... But he's a beggar, a commoner...Why does it matter so much?"

"A commoner like me?" Master John could not trace noble Norman lineage in his ancestry, as I could, and occasionally reminded me of it.

"No, that's not what I meant-"

Master John interrupted me, his voice rising.

"That boy is the son of a woman. *You* are the son of a woman, God bless your poor mother's soul in Heaven. Our Lord Jesus was born of woman. We are all the son of a woman, regardless of her rank." As Master John remounted, his face was red with anger. I was speechless at such a tirade for a country orphan.

"Think, Eilulf," he continued, his voice more controlled now and his eyes piercing "that boy could have found any number of tricks with which to beg a living from the road. What hatred drives him to mar his face again and again, chuckling afterwards and playing with his knife as though delighting in the pain? Can you even begin to imagine the life that poor soul has led?"

"But you gave him a coin..."

"And so? Can coin make up for misery and fear?"

"But we endure fear in our work, and we're paid in coin."

"Fear like you felt last night?" His eyes held mine, and I nodded, swallowing. "I think that was more excitement than fear, last night. And even if sometimes we are afraid, this was the life we chose for ourselves. That little wretch never chose to be powerless against bullying strangers. Blind fortune chose for him. We are all on Lady Fortune's wheel, and none of us can ever know if it is lifting us up or hauling us down. Might we not one day be brought as low as that beggar boy, and be in need of kindness in the place of injury?"

"But we often do far worse injury than that in our work..."

"In the King's name, knowing that God is on our King's side. But we do what needs doing, and there was no need for what you just did. Do you have the healing hands of a king?"

I opened my hands with a helpless shrug.

"No."

"Then do not injure the innocent on a whim, since you cannot heal them after."

I decided to change the topic.

"What was written on the parchment, Master?"

"That Henry Tideswell's wool was burnt, just as Henry Tideswell will one day be burnt for flaunting the King of England's law."

I nodded, understanding. "He'll be fleeing Sluys in a hurry, if that message gets about. The owners of the wool-house will want to kill him for being the cause of the fire!"

Master John smiled tightly. "Pray they don't beat that boy for bearing bad tidings. He's on your conscience."

I said nothing. I would have preferred a dozen beatings than to have those words, and that beggar's face remained burned on the inside of my eyes.

"Mount, Eilulf." Master John ordered, and while I obeyed he explained "It's time I told you where we are going. We're not taking our usual roads, this time. We're going to Avignon."

Avignon, the city of the Popes! At once my imagination took flight, preferring to dwell on the prospect of visiting one of the great cities of our time than on the shame of what had just happened. What curious people would I meet in Avignon? What unfamiliar food would I eat? But the finest thing would be to perfect my command of the Occitan language first hand.

Master John continued. "We're going to take the road to Strasbourg at the first opportunity, then ask for directions for the Rhône. Then we'll follow the river south towards the Occitan, and Avignon. We have to hurry, from now on, and won't be stopping more than a night in any place. If you're quick with your wooing, you can warm some lass's bed, otherwise you'll have to be content with my snoring."

With that Master John, his manner still slightly colder than usual, spurred his horse forward, and our journey resumed.

Chapter 6

Valley of the River Staffora, October 1337

The trials of a roasted chestnut – a boy is sick – the beginnings of a friendship

It was one of the season's first ripe chestnuts, and it was large and round, which augured well for the harvest. Inside the cramped stone drying-hut it lay with hundreds of its fellows, all strewn out over a thin lattice-work of overlapping branches and twigs, that stretched horizontally from wall to wall at a height of about four feet. They had been slow-roasting for days above the glowing coals carefully laid out on the earth floor of the hut. They were dried through, and rock-hard inside their brittle shells.

"Grab handfuls, stop passing them out one by one, or we'll never finish." Matteo, the tall boy at the entrance to the hut, shouted impatiently at his little cousins inside.

"They burn my fingers!" A tiny boy complained, scampering barefoot over the lattice-work to reach the back of the hut. "And my feet."

"Get used to it, and stop whining. I did it for years, till I got too big." Matteo was unsympathetic.

The chestnut, along with two others, was clasped by grubby, awkward little fingers. The child could only get a hold of three chestnuts in one five-year-old hand, which he passed on to another small child, who in turn passed them to the impatient cousin standing outside the drying-hut.

"Finally." As another boy took his place by the door to receive more chestnuts, Matteo raced to where his older brother, a bearded and muscular young man, stood waiting beside a large, solid wood bucket. His brother held a curious club vertically with both hands. It was a long and heavy pole, broad at the base with a number of sharp spikes, like an upside-down wooden porcupine.

"Here you are." Matteo panted, and dropped the chestnut, with the others, into the bucket. His brother brought the club down with a grunt of effort, once, twice, three times. The chestnut, hard as a pebble and as wrinkled as a centenarian's brow, was unscathed, but its shell had been splintered into dozens of fragments.

Matteo scooped up the mix of nuts and shell fragments with his bowl. While another of his cousins brought up more intact chestnuts to have their shells broken in the wooden buckets, Matteo scurried off, glad to get away from his big brother's club. It was not unknown for the porcupine club to be applied to boys' backsides if they were too slow in their work.

Matteo reached the women, holding their big wooden tossing trays.

"Here." he dumped the contents of his bowl into one of the trays, then darted back to the drying-hut to start his round again.

The chestnut, along with the bits of broken shell and the other nuts, was now in a broad wooden tray with a deep V-shaped depression in the middle. The young woman, Matteo's cousin Fiorenza, gripped the tray with both arms around the rim, then swished her shoulders in a swift figure-of-eight that tossed the mix into the air. The chestnut flew straight up into the autumn breeze. The shell fragments were caught by the wind, and blown off to fall to the ground a short distance away. The chestnut, though, was heavy, and fell back with a wooden 'thunk' into the sorting-tray. Once, twice, three times it flew up with the other chestnuts, till Fiorenza was happy the nuts were cleaned of their shells. With another strong swish of her shoulders she tossed the now-naked nuts over her shoulder onto a broad canvas spread out on the ground.

There, the smallest children in the family were picking up the chestnuts as fast as they fell, and passing them up to their grandparents. Natalino and Maria stood by with large sieves to separate off the last little pieces of shell with vigorous shaking, and discard any nuts that were either rotten, too roasted or too raw.

The chestnut was dropped into old Natalino's sieve. It was rolled around for a moment, then his crabbed old hands tossed it into one of the big sacks.

"What are you doing, you daft old sod?" Old Maria's voice was so cutting that they said she could be heard scolding all the way up at the Abbey when she got angry – which was often.

"That one's too roasted, fool. Don't put it in the good sack, or you'll make the flour gritty. Throw it into the pigs' sack."

"You're as blind as you are stupid, woman." Natalino had long since given up being diplomatic with the mother of his eldest son's late wife. "There's nothing wrong with it. If it was up to you, we'd all starve."

They had been bickering all morning, but they never tired of it.

"And if it was up to you" the old woman retorted "we'd have pig swill for breakfast every day."

"In the meantime I've filled nearly two sacks, and you've not finished your first. Do you want to be here till sunset?"

Maria growled in the back of her throat, and quickly reached across to try and fish the chestnut back out of the bag. Her fingers, blackened by time and labour, just managed to brush it, before Natalino roughly battered her hand away with his sieve.

"Leave it, you're wasting time."

"You'll have us breaking our teeth!"

"What teeth? You've none left!"

"Papà, Donna Maria." Natalino's son, Don Rogerio, had arrived. His father and his mother-in-law grudgingly quit their bickering. Rogerio was the head of the family now Natalino was elderly. He was both loved and respected, for he was fair, hardworking, and had two fists like a blacksmith's hammers. Now the entire family was cautious in his presence, for the sudden illness of his youngest son had made him tense.

Don Rogerio looked around at the work-chain, counting the members of his house-hold who were working on the chestnut flour. He turned to Maria.

"Where's Anna? Don't tell me she's ill, too?" He meant one of the girls, who he had thought was up at the drying-huts, working.

"She's weeding," Maria replied matter-of-factly "her first period has come. It started last night." During menstruation, no woman could touch any food product that was meant to be preserved, for it would surely spoil.

Rogerio nodded with mixed feelings. He was pleased that Anna had become a woman, and could now be entrusted with more responsible work, but at the same time knew what a handful girls could be during this time. But there were more pressing matters at hand. He looked over at Natalino. "Papà, how long will the good weather hold?"

Natalino paused in his sieving, glanced up at the sky, sniffed the air, licked a fingertip and held it up to the wind, then slipped one crabbed hand under his tunic, to feel an ancient scar on his back.

"Another two, maybe three days. There'll be clouds about tonight, but when the weather changes by night it never holds up. When it does change, we'll get the first bit of snow. It should fall for a night and a day, I'd say."

Rogerio nodded again, for such was typical weather for that time of year.

"When it snows I'd like to slaughter a couple of pigs. Mother-in-law, how many will we have to work the meat?"

Now it was the old woman's turn to pause in thought. She turned to the south east, where the moon would rise within hours, and in her mind's eye imagined the shape it would have.

"Today's the nineteenth day of the moon, isn't it?" She fell to counting in her mind. Finally she told him "There'll be six women, if you need them all. I'd leave Jacoba out of it this time, to be safe, and Marta won't be able to work. Let's hope none of the other children come down with Tino's ague."

Rogerio nodded gravely, but said nothing. He wasn't one to waste breath on things that were beyond his control, no matter how deeply they touched his feelings.

A polite voice at their backs caught their attention. "Don Rogerio, we're here." It was Brother Demetrio and his new assistant. Although the old healer came from far afield, from Squillace in the Kingdom of Naples, where the common folk still spoke the Greek of their forebears, he had long since learned the local dialect.

"Ah, Brother Demetrio, God and Mary be with you. How is it with you and the Brothers?" Rogerio was speaking with Demetrio, but he was struggling not to stare at the Welshman, the talk of the moment in the village. All the family members on the work chain discreetly cast curious glances at *lo Gallese* as they worked.

"Today we're all well. Let's hope this new sickness won't change that."

"Let's all hope for the best." Rogerio agreed, ruefully. "Would you bless these sacks of chestnuts, Brother Demetrio?" As ever, he was thinking of the future good of his family. A third of the harvest was the Abbey's by right, and a further part went to the Lord of Auramala, but the rest would keep them through the winter.

"Of course, of course." The monk touched Maria's sack first, and uttered a blessing. When he approached Natalino's two sacks, Maria became agitated.

"Bless those ones twice each, Brother Healer, twice, if you will! So many rotten chestnuts made their way…"

"I'll gag up your foul old gob with rotten chestnuts in a moment, old blitherer." Natalino retorted.

"Knowing your eyesight, you'll mistake the best ones for the rotten ones, and it'll be my Christmas dinner."

"I've got more eyesight that you've got sense, you old baggage…"

Brother Demetrio pretended not to hear, and blessed each sack. Once.

"Shall we go, Don Rogerio?" Demetrio asked "I can see everyone here has a lot of work to do, and can't waste their breath chatting." The old monk added pointedly, not quite looking at Maria and Natalino.

"This way." Rogerio led the healer and his assistant down towards the village, commending those who remained to work hard. Rogerio was as intrigued as anyone in the village about the stranger, but he couldn't stare over his shoulder at the Welshman while they walked. It would have been bad manners. When he did glance back, fleetingly, he saw that the mysterious newcomer was in turn staring curiously back over his shoulder at the work-chain beside the drying-huts. This made Rogerio think he really was from far away, for if he had never seen the work of the chestnuts he couldn't be from anywhere nearby.

"This is the south-gate of the village." Demetrio explained to the Welshman in the Latin as they approached the low fortified wall, Don Rogerio leading the way. "It opens onto the road to Auramala, the fortress of the Malaspina family. Therefore it is the most protected part of Pizzocorno. Whenever the village comes under attack – and it has happened in living memory - troops riding out of Auramala to aid the villagers come first to this, the south-gate. That's why the neighbourhood of this gate is a sought after place to live. Don Rogerio is the head of one of the most favoured families in the community."

"Isn't there a castle in the village itself? Isn't that a tower, over there?" The Welshman enquired.

"True, the cousin of the Lord Malaspina has his own little castle within the walls by the Abbot's concession, but it is little more than a tower, and is never garrisoned with more than about a dozen armed men. Here are two, now, they always guard the gates. Salve, Bernaldo, salve, Martino."

The healer hailed the two soldiers, who were at ease chatting with village girls. The Welshman could understand little, but it was clear from the tone of their return greetings that Demetrio was well loved here.

"Here," the old man continued "you see, just inside the gate is Don Rogerio's house."

The home of nearly twenty people, it was not grand, but it was practical. The thick, rough-hewn stone walls rose up to where great wooden beams were inset, supporting the mixed thatched-and-slated roof. The hall, which gave on to the street, had fresh rushes on the floor, an open hearth in the centre and wooden chests to store possessions in and to use as seats in the evenings. There were a couple of small windows, which were closed with wooden shutters against the ever colder autumn breeze. Rogerio made as if to open them, to let in extra light, but Demetrio stopped him.

"It's best not to set up a draught. Your boy has to keep as warm as possible. Just take me to him."

Rogerio took a candle and lit it with a smouldering coal from the fire, and led them up the stairs.

On the first floor there were three small bedrooms in the same space that on the ground floor was taken up by the hall. Only Rogerio's, the closest to the stairs, had a door to close the entrance. Furthest from the stairs was the room where the little boy was lying on his side on a narrow mattress, his back to the door. When he heard them arrive he turned weakly to face them, the beech-and-chestnut-leaf stuffing of the mattress rustling like forest litter under foot.

Brother Demetrio knelt on the floor by his side, pulling back the furs that all but hid young Tino from view. "God be ever by your side, little one." he murmured softly, pressing his palm against the boy's forehead. "Have you vomited at all?" The child shook his head. "And have you coughed?" By way of answer the patient broke out into ugly phlegmy splutters. "And can you drink, boy?" Tino nodded.

Brother Demetrio rose and moved to converse quietly with Rogerio.

"He's not as bad as I feared. If he can eat, he must eat, that is important. Small portions, but frequently. He must also drink a decoction of plums with elderberry. Here are some elderberries for this evening" He passed the worried father a pouch-full of the latter "but you can gather many down the hillside tomorrow. This year there's a good harvest of them. Give him the decoction twice a day. And your daughters are to add two pinches of this to each cup." He passed the head of the family another leather pouch "It is a strong medicine that should help him. They're not to let the decoction boil too long, mind, and let it stand a while till it's tepid. Very hot liquid will make him sweat."

"So you're not very worried, Brother Demetrio?" Rogerio's was anxious for reassurance.

"Not yet, no. It may pass sooner than you think. Saturn is soon to cross Cancer, and over the next few days will bring protection to his chest and throat."

"Saturn? Cancer?"

"The stars, Don Rogerio, the stars."

The big man looked unconvinced.

"A barn owl alighted on the roof above this room this very morning, and hooted three times, Brother Demetrio. Mightn't that be significant?"

The healer sighed. "Animals are lesser beings than we are. If we cannot divine the influences that govern us, how can they? The heavens are the highest plane under God. The harmony of the stars and the planets is the only guide we should look to for the things of this world. For the world beyond, the Word of God is enough for any man."

Don Rogerio, lost, waited a moment and then, as though Brother Demetrio might have changed his mind in the meantime, said "If I catch that owl, you could read its innards…"

"Never mind, Don Rogerio. Just do as I say and cease worrying. Give him the decoction, and keep the other children away from him, so he can sleep peacefully when possible. In particular, keep your elder daughter Clementia away from the boy; away from the house altogether, till there's no more ague here. If the Lord Malaspina's baby should come down with the illness, give no-one cause to say Clementia's milk carried the evil spirit to him.

"These ai89ilments are inevitable, Don Rogerio. If God wills, and the child is strong, he will soon be up and about, and stronger than before." The old healer thought for a moment. "And make sure your daughters-in-law change the floor-rushes daily. And they are to wash him well in the mornings with an infusion of oat-bran in hot water, just like you do a new born baby. Cleanliness is to be observed."

"You're not going to let any of his blood?" Rogerio seemed as dubious about any treatment that didn't include blood-letting as he was about divination by the stars instead of animal guts.

"No, no," Demetrio shook his head "if he is coughing up phlegm it shows there is no need as yet. If the cough passes and the fever stays, I'll consider bringing down my leeches to balance the humours."

In that moment they were distracted when little Tino was seized by a coughing fit that was so strong he half fell from the mattress to rushes on the floor. Demetrio's newest assistant was closest to the child. The tall foreigner was down at the child's side with a swift, smooth motion. He reached out with both arms, then hesitated, as though he had never put a child to bed in his life and wasn't sure how it was done. Awkwardly, he gathered up Tino and put him back in the bed. Then he picked up the blankets and laid them across the child. This was clearly an act he had never performed in his life, for he didn't notice that he had left the little boy's toes uncovered.

"Thank you." Murmured Tino in the Occitan, for he was a bright boy and realised the stranger couldn't speak their language.

"You're welcome." The Welshman answered in the same tongue, smiling, and gently smoothed back a lock of the boy's hair that had fallen over one eye. Now the Welshman paused, looking at his own hand with a sensation of wonder, distantly remembering another hand performing that same caring gesture. It had been the nurse, Margaret, as she put his own little son to bed on one of the very few occasions the Welshman had been present to witness the act.

That night I wanted to come forward and help Margaret settle him beneath the blankets. That could have been my hand, brushing his hair back from his eyes, not hers. And do you know why I didn't do it? Earlier that day old Aymer had spoken to me at length about my habit of behaving in ways more suited to commoners than to men of my rank. He used to do that regularly, in the hopes I might heed his words for more than a few hours at a time. How sad that to think that, of all the foolish customs I had back then, the only 'common' act I forewent before forgetting his advice once more was letting my son glimpse for an instant that I loved him.

Tino wondered why the kind old foreigner had frozen still, mouthing silent words to himself. Rogerio noticed, too, and approached a little consternated.

"Gratias ago tibi." He thanked the lay-brother with one of the simple formulas in the Latin that he knew. The Welshman rose, smiling, and backed away, murmuring a longer phrase that Rogerio couldn't quite grasp. He sensed, however, that the Welshman was congratulating him on having a fine son.

The boy's father tugged the clumsily arranged blankets down over his son's toes as discreetly as he could, renewing his thanks. The two men looked at one another for a long moment, then Brother Demetrio called to them.

"Let's give the boy some peace, and your daughters can get to making the decoction. If the boy has been well-mannered of late" he said, casting a feigned stern glance little Tino's way "they can add a drop of honey to it. Let's get back to the hall."

All four men passed out of the room, leaving Tino alone. He realized that he had been the first person in all of the village to speak with the newcomer. His first impression had been the great height of *lo Gallese*, who was much taller than most men in the village. Then he had noticed his white, thinning hair, and had thought he was very old, perhaps as old as Brother Demetrio. Then *lo Gallese* had knelt down to help him back into bed with graceful movements, and Tino felt he might be younger than he seemed. When he had looked closely at his face, he had been struck by the handsome, regular features, well matched with the kindness of his gesture. Tino sighed. He couldn't wait to be better so he could tell the other boys all about his encounter with Brother Demetrio's mysterious assistant.

Chapter 7

The banks of the river Rhône and Avignon, October 1337

A new identity is acquired – Wiligelmo stumbles into our journey – the House of Fieschi

South of Lyon we reached the Rhône and started following it toward the Mediterranean. A jumble of ancient flagstones from an old Roman road tracked through mud and fields east of the river banks. It was the high road for the many hundreds who wished to go either north or south.

While we were travelling through the Occitan region, it was my duty to perfect my command of the Occitan tongue, the *Lengadòc* as it is known in that language. I was to listen to one individual speaker and imitate his every inflection. Having learnt to emulate his speech exactly, I could plausibly claim to be from his region, should I ever need to disguise myself as an Occitan. And so it was that, when we met a friendly merchant with his pack horses and servants journeying south towards their home in the city of Orange, we matched our pace to theirs and rode with them. Jehan de Blanhaco was his name. He was perfect to practice upon, as Orange lay along the road to Avignon, and he would leave our company before we arrived at our destination. Any lies we told him on the road would not encumber our movements in the papal city.

For more than a week we strolled by the fickle Rhône, Master John pretending to be the silent type, letting me chatter away. Our new merchant friend never noticed how my accent gradually became more and more like his own as each day passed.

Jehan de Blanhaco's mode of speech was typical of the town of Orange. "Friend Eilulf, what fine bridles!" He loved complimenting me. "You must have bought them in your land of Flanders, *lalà.*" He would close any exclamation of surprise or appreciation with that tell-tale 'lalà', and soon I learnt to mimic him.

"The best lorimers live in Ghent and Sluys." I replied. "If anyone from another town starts to excel in the craft, we import him right away, and force him to set up shop in our city, lalà!" I replied playfully.

"But my bridles are very nearly as fine, oc est?" That was another of Jehan's mannerisms, asking for an opinion with an 'oc est' in a rising cadence.

"They are indeed. Your supplier will just have to come to Ghent with us on our way back, lalà!"

Master John and I spent the evenings reviewing my progress in hushed tones in the dormitories of taverns. We retired early, while most of the others were still drinking away in the common rooms, and he had time and privacy to point out my mistakes and any hints of the English accent that remained.

"You still have your guttural Norfolk 'D'." Was his comment one evening. "Can't you hear how Jehan says his 'D's with his tongue forward, against his teeth? Try."

As ever when speaking the Occitan, I felt an urge to sing, for it was the language of the troubadours. I eagerly launched into a melodious verse by one of my favourite troubadours.

"C'aitals amors es perduda…"

"Stop, stop. Get it right speaking first, and then you can sing." Master John interrupted, shaking his head as ever at my love of song.

"Very well, Master." I submitted. "I'll try:

C'aitals amors es perduda

qu'es d'una part mantenguda…That's a little better now, oc est?"

"Yes," he chuckled "the 'D's are perfect now."

I sang the song through, pronouncing the 'Ds the way he wanted, and Master John patiently but unenthusiastically listened. As soon as the last note of the ballad had died away, he asked me an important question.

"Have you thought about the name you'll travel under as an Occitan? The identity must be complete."

"Can I keep my own name in the Provencal, since I'll pretend to be from Orange? I've dreamt so many times of being Willame d'Orange…"

"Who's that?" Master John asked in all innocence, and I had

to mask my surprise. How could he not have heard of Willame d'Orange, the hero of so many songs?

I sang the beginning of one of the songs about the legendary knight, hoping to jog Master John's memory.

Plaist vus oir de granz batailles e de forz esturs,
De Deramel, uns reis Sarazinur,
Cum il prist guere uers nostre empereur ?
Mais dan Willame la prist uers lui forçur
Tant qu'il l'ocist el l'Archamp par grant onur.

His only reply was a bored expression. I sighed discreetly.

"Willame was a knight in the service of Charlemagne, who fought the Saracens… It's a famous… Well, it's a beautiful story."

My Master never could bring himself to approve of my love for knightly antics and honour, which he thought foolish, at times barbarous. I'm sure he worried that my judgement in a moment of great tension might one day be clouded by my yearning for chivalry.

"It's best to avoid the equivalent of your real name," he said "it makes it safer for everyone. What about Guiraut? Don't you like it?"

I sighed and, as I often did, changed the subject of conversation.

During the journey southwards Jehan de Blanhaco chatted to me at length about his town, his friends and his family. Still to this day, if ever I must play the part of an Occitan, I introduce myself as Guiraut de Faya, a merchant's son from Orange. I freely give details about the city, though I've never actually seen it, then go on to recall my 'old friend' Jehan de Blanhaco. I speak easily of his wife, his children, his sister and brothers as though I had passed many long hours in their company. I sometimes wonder what they looked like.

We said farewell to Jehan and his company when they turned off the main road to go towards Orange late on a beautiful, sunny afternoon. By noon the next day the towers of Avignon were visible in the distance, as was the magnificent Bridge of Saint Bénezet leading over the river to the city, its light grey stone luminous. I had never seen such a bridge in all my life. I counted twenty-two arches and as many buttressed piers. An elegant Romanesque chapel rose on the second pier out from the city-end. The bridge disgorged teeming crowds of travellers into the city through high arched gates on the Avignon side. It truly was the marvel of all my travels up to that time.

"There you are, Will," Master John smiled knowingly at my awe "that's the true wealth of Avignon. From Lyon to the sea, there's no other place to cross the river in real safety. They say Saint Benezet was a shepherd boy who heard the holy voice of an angel telling him to build the bridge. Well, now the Popes have heard some unholy voice, surely not an angel's, telling them to put a steep toll on it.

"Look behind the bridge, up on that hill of rock. Do you see all that scaffolding? Look at those piles of fresh masonry. It's immense! The new Pope is extending his residence into a mighty palace, lest anyone doubt that Avignon is the new Rome. The locals call it the Palais dei Papas, and every traveller in the land is paying for it with his toll."

A queue had formed in front of the gate onto the bridge as merchants, pilgrims, adventurers and clerics alike were held up while the laws of the city were read to each newcomer, and the bridge-toll was exacted. Finally we managed to pass the gate-keepers, one of Master John's purses considerably lightened. As we set foot on the stone-flagged back of the bridge I was startled by its breadth. Such was the throng trying to cross into the city that we were forced to dismount and lead our horses.

We had nearly reached the Avignon end when we met Wiligelmo for the first time. We were passing the beautiful bridge-chapel, and had just made the sign of the cross upon seeing the shrine of Saint Nicholas through the entrance, when a fair-featured man a little younger than I came hurrying through the crowd. His gait was so chaotic and uncoordinated that I at once thought of a seven-legged crab scrabbling over slippery ice. He dodged one of our fellow travellers, only to collide heavily with Master John. He tripped, and would have hit the cobbles headlong, giving his chin a bad crack, had I not lunged forward and softened the worst of his downward momentum with my arms.

He quickly got up, but was so strongly lacking in grace that even when he was rising to his feet his movements seemed those of a man in mid-stumble.

"I'm sorry, I'm sorry!" He breathlessly apologised to Master John, then turned to me. "I'm so grateful, yes, so grateful. And sorry!" He looked back to Master John. "And grateful to you sir, if you forgive me, sir. And sorry," he turned back to me "You must forgive me." Then back to Master John. "Forgi..."

"Hush, boy," my Master interrupted, smiling "no harm was done, and none was risked either, except to yourself."

"I know, I'm sorry, I was in a hurry..."

"Boys of your age always are. Is it a young lady?"

Our new acquaintance blushed furiously, but did not deny it. "I'm late, I'm very late! I was to meet her half-way to vespers. Do you think she'll have waited for me?" I had to keep myself from laughing. He tripped over his own words like he tripped over his own feet, while he ingenuously asked complete strangers what his lady friend, was likely to do.

"Well, it normally does no harm to keep a girl waiting..." Master John was pragmatically answering when the bells of the bridge-chapel started ringing the vespers. "But on second thoughts, you may be running a little *too* late." Master John slapped him on the back in a companion-like way. "It's all very well to keep a girl waiting, but you're very late indeed. I suspect she long since gave up."

The young man's face froze into a stricken expression. I spoke up for the first time, and like Master John I let a Flemish accent taint my Occitan.

"That said, it may be a blessing in disguise. When a girl thinks you're losing interest in her, it may heighten her interest in you. Female pride is behind it."

New hope dawned almost comically in his eyes, and he looked to Master John for corroboration. My Master nodded.

"My pupil, Eilulf, is not a bad strategist..." He was admitting, when a gravelly voice behind me loudly interrupted.

"Clerics! You bed more girls than you bless." It was a burly carpenter, his tools at his belt, whose pack-mule was held up by our conversation. "If you've finished corrupting the lad, some of us would like to get across before nightfall."

Behind him I could see a long line of angry merchants and craftsmen peering around his bulk. We'd brought a large part of the traffic on the bridge to a halt. Master John hastened to apologize.

"We're most sorry, Mary be our witness. May Angels kiss your children's heads."

He put an arm around our new acquaintance's shoulders, and started leading him on toward the city, his horse's reins in his other hand.

"My new friend, why don't you forget about your young lady, and be our guide? We're looking for an inn for the night. I remember there used to be a place - I can't recall the name - frequented by our countrymen of Flanders. It was down by the milk markets. That was fifteen years ago now, though. Is it still there, do you know?"

"You mean the *Brugesfort*?"

"Ah yes, that's the one! Why don't you take us there, and it shall be our pleasure to drink with you before we part company. I am Master Gerold of Ghent, and this is my pupil, Eilulf of the same city."

The young man, who we took to be Occitan, lit up with enthusiasm. The object of his romantic desire seemed to have been wiped clean from his mind.

"Of course, it would be my delight to show you the way." He gave a bow that was reminiscent of a duck's bob. "My name is Wiligelmo."

"Wiligelmo?" I asked, astonished. That was when I realised he couldn't be a native of Provence, though his Occitan was perfect. "You're not from Avignon?"

"No, I'm from Campione, in the Alps of northern Lombardy. Have you heard of my town, you who live away north in Flanders?"

"Of course." I assured him. "At least, I've heard of the Masters of Campione. You must be a craftsman – a marble sculptor?"

"That's right. Or rather, my father, Pietro, is. He's a *magistrinus*, a 'little master'. That's what they call my family, because we're all short." I was surprised at the thought that such a clumsy young man could be a marble carver, and wondered if his father, the 'little master', was just as clumsy. Wiligelmo continued. "I'm learning the *mano de Roma* from him every day as we work."

"The *mano de Roma*... the 'hand of Rome'?"

"'Hand' meaning 'art'. That's what we call the marble-craft. Rome is where it came from. Ancient Rome. My *barba*, that means 'grandfather', but it really means 'beard'... my old *barba*, who was Wiligelmo like me, would always say 'we of Campione are the only ones who learn the hand of Ancient Rome.' I think he was right, because nobody else works stone in quite the same way we do."

"Well, they call on your services from all over Europe. Even in Ghent we know the Masters of Campione are the finest." I agreed, warming to our new companion. He was as refreshing and genuine as he was clumsy and naïve.

"And where are you and your father engaged right now?" I was curious.

"On the *Palais*." he said, as though it should have been obvious. After a moment's thought I realised that it *was* obvious. From miles away the hive of activity around the Pope's new palace was clearly visible. Surely there must be hundreds of craft-masters working there. I was instantly curious to see what such a large worksite might look like, to see the scurrying, digging, hewing, cutting and measuring.

"Of course." I nodded. We were finally passing through the great-gates into the city, closely scrutinized by liveried guards. "But the palace must be vast."

Master John came to a halt, and turned back to Wiligelmo.

"Left or right, my friend? Or straight ahead?" A narrow ring-road skirted the inside of the city walls, winding away to our left and to our right, while a broad, paved avenue stretched away before us.

"This way." Wiligelmo cantered off to the right. "Yes, the Palace is vast. We're under the charge of Master Pierre Poisson de Mirepoix, working on the new tower, the *Tour des Anges*, making carven window arches. Father likes them, he says it remind him of the time when he was working in a church crypt in Genoa. That was when he met our great patron and friend, Cardinal Fieschi, who brought us to Avignon."

Later, after discovering how deeply our task was entwined with the House of Fieschi, I realised just how much finesse Master John displayed in that moment. Wiligelmo had revealed a tie between himself and our enemies, and yet my Master gave no outward sign of surprise nor interest.

For my part, I was still unaware of the true motivations behind our journey, and continued to chat lightly with Wiligelmo as we wound through the streets.

"Then I'm sorry for your loss. I know Cardinal Luca Fieschi passed away two winters ago. He's a sorely missed man."

"Yes. Life just isn't the same. His successor is from a different family, and lacks an eye for true workmanship. The new overseer he's appointed is constantly approving our sketches, then telling us to start again from scratch when he sees the shapes beginning to emerge from the stone. Father tells him to wait to see the final effect, to trust us, but he never does. Old Cardinal Luca *always* trusted us, and would often come to admire our work in person, rather than delegating to an overseer."

"I'm sure your father's frustrated with the new situation."

"Of course. He's always grumbling about our conditions. To make matters worse, the stone-cutter's cough has come on much worse the last few winters, and what with the new overseer…" He shook his head. "Well, he's talking seriously about leaving Avignon for warmer climes. Relatives of the Old Cardinal down on the Genoese Riviera, all the way past Camogli to the east, need Campionese Masters for new churches. The weather down there is warmer, the lands are rich in the best foodstuffs and grapes, and we'd be far away from all the squabbling and rivalry of life in Avignon."

In contrast with the idyllic description he gave of the Genoese Riviera, his tone was down-turned and sullen.

"Aren't you happy at the prospect?" I enquired.

"And Maddelene?" He cried, aghast "I would never see her again!" I gathered she was the young lady he'd been hurrying to meet when he'd stumbled into us. "And then, my friends…" He looked utterly bereft at the prospect of leaving. "The sons of the other masters? The world is so vast… When will I ever come to Avignon again? And my friends the scribes, too… It would be farewell to all."

"The scribes? What do stone-masters have to do with scribes?"

"Avignon is full of scribes, didn't you know? It's hard to *not* to be friends with at least a few. Rotbert, Girart and Miquel are copyists. Rotbert and Girart share a room in the same building in Charrieira Sant Stefan, where father and I were granted lodgings by Luca Fieschi. Together with Miquel, they used to work for the Cardinal's family before he died."

I wanted to ask more, but we had arrived at the *Brugesfort* and he proudly gestured to the wide open door.

"Here we are, your tavern!"

Master John thanked him warmly.

"Will you stay to drink something with us?"

Wiligelmo was not much younger than I in years, but far younger in experience. He doubtfully eyed the common room through the open door, and the bearded northerners swilling beer from their great tankards along the wooden benches.

"Father doesn't want me to frequent the taverns. He's very concerned about our good name, and says that beer makes your hands tremble and your chisel slip. He only drinks wine and cider."

"Your father is a wise man. Before we leave Avignon, however, we will come to your workshop to say goodbye, and congratulate your father on his worthy son."

The compliment brought red to Wiligelmo's face, and after shaking Master John's hand he kissed me on both cheeks like a brother. He then strode happily away, his legs threatening to catapult him into passers-by at any moment. Wiligelmo's friendliness and openness were so contagious that neither Master John nor myself could help but feel affectionate toward him, though we'd only just met.

Master John paid handsomely for the privilege of a room to ourselves, and when the landlord had led us up the rickety wooden stairs and left us torches for the night, Master John set us straight to work.

"We must write a message and send it with a runner-boy to my contact here. It's past mid-afternoon now, and I want the reply by tonight, so we have to be fast in encrypting it."

"Shall we use a key-phrase, master?"

"That's right. The message is for William Bateman, have you ever heard of him?"

I drew in a sharp, surprised breath.

"The famous auditor? He's a Norwich man like myself."

Master John smiled.

"Of course, I was forgetting. Well, years ago I was able to convince him to help Richard de Bury organise our work, and I taught him the secret writing. I think that's been one of my most important accomplishments, for he is one of the best informed men in Avignon. He has numerous contacts in all the church factions here, and very little escapes his notice."

"What message must we encrypt?" Since the encryption process was slow, and prone to error, we normally encrypted half of any message each, then swapped results and cross checked our work.

"It's six words long. You take the first three, and I the rest. The message must read 'Welsh Pilgrim, Year III, Pope, Fieschi'."

"Fieschi. The House of Fieschi." I gasped. "Then Wiligelmo and his father…" I paused, unsure of what to think. "Are the Fieschis our enemies?"

Master John's penetrating eyes held mine for a long, thoughtful moment, before he slowly nodded.

"I believe they are."

"You don't know?"

"The message Thomas de Aldcliffe brought us from Henry de Grosmont was… enigmatic. It only named the House of Fieschi, but said nothing more about it. I hope Bateman will be able to make things clearer for us."

"Then at least for the time being we should avoid contact with the House of Fieschi, including the late Cardinal Luca's following?"

"Don't worry about our encounter with Wiligelmo. Craftsmen in the service of a Cardinal can hardly be a party to the secret business of their patron, whatever it may be. And in any case, as he said, since the Cardinal's death they've fallen on hard times, so I imagine the House of Fieschi no longer employs them directly. Rather, I think that if we had the time and skill to read the stars tonight we might discover that our meeting with Wiligelmo was meant to serve some cause that we cannot yet guess at. What do you know about the House of Fieschi, Eilulf?"

"Little more than any freeman in London might. They're from south of the Alps, so not to be trusted." My Master nodded his approval. "They're Genoese, so fabulously wealthy." Again, he nodded. "They have cousins and nephews ensconced in half of the dioceses in Europe, who each have a finger in every pie on the table at the local court. The Genoese ships we saw in Yarmouth bay and at Sluys could easily have been running their errands. But more to the point, they've been linked with the papacy for a century or more. The patriarchs of the House of Fieschi must be among the most powerful men alive. Two popes and a host of cardinals and bishops have come from their family. Their heraldic animal is the seated cat, and their motto 'I act sitting down', which perfectly describes the way they insert themselves into key positions in the church and then hold their seats for generations. It must be the least chivalrous motto of any great family of Europe!"

"A different sort of power to that of a king," Master John commented "but a great power nevertheless. Now that you're starting to understand to what level of politics our task is taking us, let's get to work on the message. We must be quick if we want a runner to take it to Bateman and return with the reply before curfew."

Chapter 8

A game park near London, October 1337

A secret meeting – the King's new favourite – honour without armour

The two earls passed their falcons delicately from their own gloved hands to those of their squires, who then discreetly let their horses drift a little forwards into the sunshine. Their lords remained in the shade of the two oak trees. When it was clear that the squires were too far away to hear them, the two English earls began to converse in their native court-French.

"You wanted a secret meeting with me, William?" Henry de Grosmont's long, dark locks tumbled merrily about his handsome face. "How exciting. Perhaps this means I'm becoming important in the scheme of things. Shall we agree on a code to identify one another in future? We might need to meet in disguise next time, big brother." An expression of cultivated vacuity lay broadly on his face.

William de Montague kept his voice dry. He wanted to bring out the serious side of his young friend as quickly as possible.

"That won't be necessary, Henry. I would know you anywhere."

"Really? I'll have to test that someday." Was the playful reply.

"Henry, set aside your boy-face and let me speak to the man. This is a matter of the greatest importance to England, and we need you."

"We?" Grosmont's eyes had narrowed a little, and his child-like demeanour was wavering.

"Richard de Bury and I. We have recently become concerned about the influence of Messer Niccolò Fieschi at court."

"Fieschi? Is that the tall, blonde, friendly man from Florence?"

"I know you know who I'm talking about, Henry." William snorted. "Be serious. Bury told me he lent you some of his agents, and you have used them to investigate the dealings of the House of Fieschi.

What have you discovered?" Grosmont finally began to assume the expression of an astute adult, but he did not speak. Montague continued. "A young scion of the House of Spinola, rivals of the Fieschi in Genoa, was recently found mutilated to death beneath Westminster on the banks of the Thames. The Spinola have held trading interests in London for years, honestly paying fees and taxes to the Crown. They're threatening to empty their warehouses and move on because of the incident. I believe the crime was perpetrated by a Fieschi agent. When I spoke to Messer Niccolò, he refused to cooperate with the most arrogant bearing imaginable. Why do you think Fieschi allows himself such airs with an earl of England?"

For a long time Henry de Grosmont made no reply. At last he murmured "It is true, I have been gathering information. I went to Richard de Bury asking for the loan of some agents. I thought he would dismiss the idea out of hand, remembering how I used to make him angry by never doing my writing when he used to tutor Edward and me, but he agreed, and gave me warrants."

"And what have you found?"

"It seems that," he spoke slowly "recently, large sums of royal money can only move about if a member of the House of Fieschi is involved."

Montague looked at him levelly for a long moment. "Tell me more."

Grosmont went on, gradually speaking more easily now he had begun to open up to his old friend.

"The King started contracting enormous debts with the bankers of Florence three years ago; debts worth more than all the English coinage that's been minted in the last twenty years. Before that time the Florentines wouldn't so much as fund one of our hunting parties, for fear that Edward wouldn't be able to pay the loan back. What changed their minds about the King's solvency, to the point that they would lend him so much? That was the question I sought to answer."

Montague nodded, taking Grosmont's transformation in his stride.

"I noticed the change, too," he commented "but I don't know why they suddenly became so trusting."

Grosmont continued. "Those damned promissory notes, those pieces of paper with numbers scribbled all over them that the Genoese and Florentines and Lombards love so much… What you probably don't know is that those 'banking notes' are being brought back and forth between the King and his Florentine bankers by trusted cousins and nephews of the late Cardinal Luca Fieschi. Does that seem normal to you?"

Montague replied thoughtfully, his voice lowering. "Florentines loathe the Genoese... They wouldn't entrust them with important work without good reason... Go on."

"The old Cardinal died two winters ago, and this awful Niccolò got the upper hand in the family politics. He arrived in England last April, and on the very same day the King gave a Fieschi agent, a certain Montefiore, 3,000 marks and sent him off to France. He spent a part of that sum paying the royal pensions of a number of Cardinals, then sent the rest off to another Fieschi man in Genoa to contract two galleys for England."

"What's so strange about that, Henry? We both know war's brewing, and Edward wants to arm himself for it. There's no finer warship in the world than the Genoese galley."

"Two ships alone? What use are two ships in a war? And the amount of money he sent was far greater than the price of two ships, even considering the value of Genoese galleys."

"Perhaps the contract was officially for two ships, but there was a secret agreement to send more. I believe that any Genoese family must first ask the permission of the government of their republic before selling more than two galleys, for it becomes a matter of security for their city. Perhaps this was a grand scheme to smuggle out more ships. Have you found out how many actually arrived in England?"

"None. The money was impounded en-route, and never made it to Genoa. And that's a part of this story that may interest you. The money was impounded by one of King Robert of Naples' marshals, a certain Gherardo Spinola of Genoa..."

Montague's calm blue eyes suddenly darkened. "The Spinola boy who was murdered a week ago was his nephew. It must have been a vendetta for his uncle's actions."

"Indeed." Grosmont confirmed, grimly. "I'm sure it was a warning from the House of Fieschi to the House of Spinola."

At that moment their conversation was interrupted by the calls of their squires, alerting them to the presence of approaching horsemen. "Here comes Messer Niccolò Fieschi, my lords."

"Speak of the Devil, and the Devil comes." muttered Grosmont with an ironic smile. Montague tensed.

The dark skinned and dark eyed Genoese was dressed in his customary family colours of blue and white. On his raised left arm a particularly fine falcon perched on the great glove, its hooded head darting from side to side as if locating prey by hearing alone. Montague fancied that the bird and the owner were strangely akin. Fieschi had a Sardinian man on horseback to serve him, who promptly joined the two English squires away out of earshot.

"Good morning, my Lords." Fieschi hailed them both in the Occitan.

"A good morning also to you." replied Montague in the same tongue, though his sentiments far from echoed his words.

As though he were some poorly learnt, unworldly baron of the provinces, Grosmont replied in the court-French of England with his native Lancastrian accent "And Mary and her Son by your side." His expression had now returned to his familiar easy, handsome vacuity.

"Have you had no luck, either, this morning?" Fieschi continued in the Occitan.

"None at all," Grosmont cheerfully admitted "though I fancy I came close to a speckled pheasant a short while back. Nothing more spectacular than that, I'm afraid."

"The deer are sensibly keeping their profiles low." Montague commented.

"Indeed, I just glimpsed a fawn soon after we rode out, but I clean missed it." Fieschi lamented.

"Oh dear." Grosmont gave a pleasant laugh. "Then you comfort me, my Lord Fieschi." If it hadn't been for his ingenuous tone one might have thought that he was being ironic, for Fieschi had no aristocratic title to speak of. "If even a Genoese can shoot wide of his target with a crossbow, my poor archery may be excused!"

Fieschi allowed a tiny smile to steal across his lips. "I am far from worthy of my countrymen's fearsome reputation with the weapon." He did not bother to correct Grosmont's mistaken use of title.

"But I hear you make up for that with the sword." Grosmont replied. "It pains me that you have never accepted my many invitations to take part in tournaments with me, for the honour of England and of Genoa."

"It has pained me, too." Fieschi spoke as an adult humouring a child. In truth, he had no right to participate in tournaments due to his lack of heraldic title, nor was he even remotely interested in the sport.

"It's of no matter, Messer Niccolò." Montague addressed Fieschi by his correct, humble title. "Jousting is a foolish pastime for hotheads like my friend Henry, here. More sensible men like us must take care of our nations' interests." He habitually teased Grosmont about his sporting obsession.

"Ah, but it is for this reason that I have come to speak with you. I understand that the rules of the sport allow one who is unable to joust to choose a champion, is that right?"

"Yes, of course." Montague was mystified.

"Then let me finally accept your invitation, my Lord Earl." Fieschi turned his dark eyes to Grosmont, who reacted to his title, granted just a few months before, by artfully beaming like a child who has received a treat.

"You have a champion to fight with me? Genoese, I hope."

"Not Genoese, I'm afraid, but Savoyard. He is the grandson of my aunt Beatrice Fieschi. She married Count Gotofredo de Challant, and their grandson, Ubaldo de Fénis, is an athletic youth, who jousts with passion. Will my Lord Earl choose a champion to meet him, when it is convenient?"

"A champion to fight for me?" Grosmont laughed out loud. "Where would be the pleasure in that? I'll meet him in person."

"Very well, it shall be a memorable occasion."

Grosmont hadn't finished being the over-grown boy. "Ask him if he will truly put his life and honour into the Good Lord's palm, and let us fight without armour."

Fieschi's face froze at the mere thought of it. "I have no doubt that he will decline such a great… pleasure… my Lord Earl. You will forgive me" he shook his head, as though clearing it of the image of men fighting a tournament without protection "but I have great need of Ubaldo, and don't wish to see him needlessly die."

"What a shame!" Grosmont's beatific smile hid pure mischief. "Nothing matches the thrill of combat without armour."

"I'm… sure that's true." Fieschi murmured. "Now, if your Lordships will excuse me, I'll continue with the hunt and leave you to your counsel. Good morning."

When the Genoese merchant prince and his hired man were lost amid the trees, Montague expressed his admiration.

"What a knack you have of seeming the simpleton, Henry. Even your eyes seem to go blank, and brainless. How do you do it?"

"It just comes naturally." the keen intelligence returned to Grosmont's gaze. "Now I will fight Fieschi's man, and vanquish him, and it is almost a pity. The satisfaction of seeing his champion fall will ease some of the ill feeling that is building toward Messer Niccolò among the Lords of the Council. I would prefer it if that ill feeling were to boil over, and force Fieschi out of the King's affairs."

"You could let his champion win." Montague suggested.

"What?" Grosmont nearly scoffed "Who would ever believe that *I* had been honestly beaten in arms? Absurd."

"Ah yes… of course." Montague hid a smile. Whether feigning simplicity or discussing the finer points of politics, Grosmont was incapable of modesty. "In any case, let us come back to our previous discussion. After years of refusing the English Crown credit, the bankers of Florence now seem confident that the King will pay back their loans to him, and you feel that Niccolò Fieschi is somehow involved in this miraculous shift in their attitude."

"Exactly. He and his family are acting as mediators. But why? Why does Edward trust them so, and what warranty have they given the Florentines as bond for the loans?"

"Is that what you sent John de Ulgham to find out?"

At the mention of Bury's most trusted agent, Grosmont's complexion darkened. Montague was astounded to realise that his toweringly confident young friend was blushing slightly.

"Did Richard tell you that?" Grosmont asked

"Yes. He was concerned. The situation in Flanders is particularly delicate now, with the wool embargo, and he wanted his best men to be in the thick of it in Ghent and Sluys. When he realised that you had called Ulgham and his pupil away, he came to speak with me about the affair."

Grosmont nodded, recovered. "Yes, yes of course. I sent Ulgham out to discover exactly what it is that the House of Fieschi is using as leverage with both Edward and with the Florentines. I'm concerned that it may be a case of blackmail."

"Really? Tell me more."

"I can't." Grosmont hastily dissembled. "It's just a feeling. That it may be a case of blackmail, I mean. Just intuition, that's all. I really can't tell you any more than that. We will all have to wait for Ulgham to return."

Montague scrutinized the younger man, but could find no outward sign of deceit. Nevertheless, there was a hard kernel of doubt within that would not go away.

"In that case," he urged his steed into motion, storing away his uneasiness "let's see if we can find some deer to shoot."

Chapter 9

Avignon, October 1337

Secret writing – Bateman the auditor – the Palais des Papes

In the privacy of our room in the tavern, Master John and I set to work on the message for Bateman.

"I write to Bateman with a particular type of secret writing that you have never seen before." Master John told me. "This is the most challenging encryption, but safer than all the others." He paused for a moment, a look of thoughtful surprise in his blue eyes. "You know, Will, after today you will have learnt every last one. This is the last." His lips curved into a nostalgic smile, and he gruffly put an arm round my shoulders. "I fear Richard Bury will soon separate us, and send you into the world on your own."

My excitement at the prospect must have shown in my face.

"I know that seems grand to you, lad" he sighed "but it will make me feel lonely, and when a man's lonely he counts his years and scars and mopes…"

He suddenly drew himself up, and shook his head. Just as water flies from a dog's fur when he shakes himself, so Master John seemed to fling his melancholy off. "Let's get to work." He sat down and readied a quill.

"For the method to be successful, you must agree before-hand on a key-phrase with your contact. It must be a secret phrase that has the same number of letters as the alphabet. The English is a good tongue to use, so few Europeans can speak it. So the phrase must be 28 letters long, like the English alphabet. It need not be in English; it can be in any language you choose, what is important is the number of letters."

As he spoke I committed every word to memory.

"Now, let us imagine our key-phrase begins: In nomine Domini amen. You line it up with the true alphabet. I'll show you."

He took his sand-pouch and spread the fine grains over the parchment, then wrote in the sand with the dry nib.

I	N	N	O	M	I	N	E
A	B	C	D	E	F	G	H

"To encrypt our message, we will substitute the letters of each word with the corresponding letters in the key-phrase. So, the letter 'A' in the message becomes the letter 'I' in the encrypted version. The letter 'B' becomes 'N', 'C' also becomes 'N', and so forth. Now, encrypt for me the English word 'beef'."

He passed me the nib. I hardly needed to concentrate at all to complete the exercise. So far this technique did not seem so complex. I wordlessly inscribed the letters 'N-M-M-I in the sand.

"Good, good. But I had no doubt you would take to it immediately." Master John then assumed a shrewd expression I knew well, and I realised that the hard part was still to come.

"In fact, Will, this is far from perfect. Can you see what the great problem with it is? It is the same problem most encryption techniques create."

I frowned, and thought it over without success.

"I can see no problem, Master, unless the contact forgets the key-phrase."

He shook his head, and the shrewdness in his eyes deepened.

"Are you sure? Try to imagine a parchment with such a message written on it being intercepted by an enemy."

I pictured such a manuscript in my mind, and pictured it falling into the hands of an intelligent foe. I saw the seemingly random text on the page, and the insight leapt into my mind from the string of jumbled letters.

"Master, I understand. Once intercepted, it is obvious that it is secret writing, and the enemy will start trying to decipher it."

"Precisely." Master John was satisfied. "Now, would *you* be able to decipher it?"

"To be honest" I shook my head "I doubt it."

"Perhaps. Or perhaps you underestimate yourself. In any case, Will, you and I, though learned and intelligent, do not devote our entire lives to intellectual beauty. We must constantly hone our skills with the sword, lance, bow and knife, not to mention our bare hands. We must often practice praying to a steady, constant beat, to work together in harmony when we are separate. But think of Richard de Bury. He is beyond such games, and his mind is active every instant of every day. Would *he* be able to decipher the code?"

I nodded without hesitation, knowing my Master's master well.

"Indeed, Will, he would. And men like Richard de Bury also exist in Europe, and many of them are belligerent to us. As a consequence, I have invented a way to make this secret writing truly secret. The letters of the encrypted message become the second letter of every second word of an apparently normal prose text; a letter, or a memorandum." He looked at me penetratingly, to see whether or not I had understood.

"Master, perhaps... Would you give me an example?"

He nodded.

"So, the word 'beef' becomes N-M-M-I..." His face assumed the serene, meditative expression I had come to know meant his mind was immersed in the mechanics of secret business. A short time later, he began to write in the sand.

Are any good, ample barrels among the wine stocks?

"To anybody but the contact, this might seem to be a letter from a shipping merchant to a cart hauler. But the contact would know to take out only the second letter of every second word, so obtaining: N-M-M-I, and could then decipher it using the key to obtain the word 'B-E-E-F.' This way, with a little imagination, you can write a seemingly normal text in prose that, in reality, contains an encrypted message."

My face broke into an admiring grin, as the brilliance of the method dawned upon me.

"Master, did you really invent this yourself?"

Suddenly modest, he shrugged and gave the barest of nods.

"It's marvellous!"

Though Master John was not of our nobility, his forefathers being minor Saxon thanes, he was perhaps the most formidable man I ever met, short of the King himself. Nevertheless, he was only human, and blushed slightly at my compliment.

He cleared his throat uncomfortably. "Let's get to work. While we were chatting the shadows turned from west to east, so time is short." He carefully smoothed the sand on the parchment, ready for the drafting of the letter.

"We shall compose a request to Bateman asking to meet with him tomorrow to discuss a matter of ecclesiastical law, his speciality. The words of the secret message are: Welsh Pilgrim, Year III, Pope, Fieschi. How would you begin?"

Later that afternoon we sealed the finished parchment with red wax, went down to the street and waited just outside the door of the inn for a runner-boy to pass. With all the Cardinals' palaces and ecclesiastic offices, Avignon in those days was alive with runners, like so many bees in a busy hive. They were mostly around the age of twelve, and wore a bright green ribbon around their left wrist to be recognisable. They were famous for their discretion, and any boy who was found to have delivered a message to the wrong person, or – far worse – broken its seal, would be beaten by his fellows and have his ribbon taken away. Soon enough we saw one at the nearby crossroads. We hailed him, and he came hurrying up, a bright look on his face now he was sure of an extra coin before nightfall.

"This is for Master William Bateman, the Auditor Lawyer." Master John passed him a coin and patted his shoulder in a friendly manner. "Lift your feet like Mercury, lad, we need the reply this evening."

The runner's eyes widened when he felt the unexpected weight of the coin in his hand, and sprinted off with a grateful grin. Master John and I exchanged a glance, and I knew we were both thinking of the beggar I had threatened into delivering a message just outside Sluys. I could still see his haggard face before my eyes.

We sat down to wait for the runner in the common room, as far from the open door as possible, for even in the Langedoc the afternoon breeze could be chilly in October. When the runner finally returned with a written and sealed reply, Master John sat him down at our bench.

"Will you bring a cup with some clean water for the boy's wine?" He asked a serving girl, as he broke the seal on the parchment. She arrived with a cup half full of fresh water, and I filled it the rest of the way with wine from our jug. The runner gratefully sipped it while we waited for Master John to finish reading the reply.

"Come back tomorrow morning before sext, for we're to meet Bateman on the bell, and I want you to guide us. Now go off to your family." The runner scuttled home a happy boy, already certain of receiving at least one coin on the morrow.

The next day, we started off as soon as the runner-boy came to collect us. The papal quarter was a maze of grey stone streets with high buildings blocking out the sunlight. Everywhere you looked, tonsured scribes and officials darted in and out of doorways, urgently speaking to their companions. The impression I had was of an immense bureau, spread out over many streets with all their buildings and palaces. The runner led us to the street where the Englishmen lodged, and one of the finest buildings, which housed Bateman's apartments.

An orderly greeted us, and after Master John tipped the runner and thanked him, we were led in and across the courtyard to the hall that lay at the back of the house. At one end, on a slightly raised dais, the master of the house sat among myriad books and sheets of parchment, spread out around him over no less than three tables. He rose as we entered, in a long action that seemed never to end. How tall he was! Tall and slim. The thinness of his body seemed to exaggerate his height further, and long wiry fingers completed the effect.

"Master Gerold." He greeted Master John, for we had signed the letter the previous afternoon with our Flemish identities.

Master John smiled broadly. I could tell his affection for the lawyer was genuine as they embraced, though I had no idea when and where they had first met or had made friends.

"I'm pleased that you're finally meeting Eilulf. He's my brother's second son, and I've promised to educate him myself and show him the world."

Bateman clapped me on the shoulder, warmly.

"God keep you, lad, you're welcome in my home. How is it with you?"

"A little weary for the road, but happy to be in Avignon at last." Master John and I kept to the French of Paris with Flemish overtones, while in Bateman's French the Norwich accent ran strong, making me yearn for a ship back to Yarmouth, and home.

Bateman looked me over well, and seemed satisfied. He turned to my Master.

"Gerold, you've finally found an assistant. You've done the right thing. Neither of us is counting less wrinkles day by day… Fresh blood is what's needed. I have my own protégé now, Simon, but he's away on errands so you shan't meet him. Take a seat, friends, take a seat."

They started by chatting idly about Flanders, London, and old friends for a short while. Then Master John made good the pretence we'd used in the letter by asking Bateman about an obscure question of clergy-law. It is always best to keep your outwardly visible actions coherent, he used to say. Bateman had probably destroyed our letter as soon as he'd decrypted it, but we couldn't be totally certain it hadn't fallen into other hands by chance. In our profession, you must always play it safe.

After a short while, Bateman subtly worked the conversation around to matters of money, and with seeming innocence asked us "By the way, what toll did you pay on the bridge, as foreigners travelling without goods?"

When we told him the sum he laughed lightly. "So much? I'm sorry. But then, it is a most precious bridge, in every sense. Saint Benezét was just a shepherd-boy, out watching his flock when he heard the voice of an angel telling him to come to Avignon and….

"We're all grateful he did so. Ferries and fords are not a sound option in these parts. The waters of the Rhône are unpredictable, and often violent, as are all the waters of creation, in my opinion. Even smaller rivers can surprise us with their capricious fits."

I realised that he was making this speech for the benefit of some secret communication. What did we care about the violence of waters? How was it connected to church-law? No, this was another secret message. When you realize that a contact's words are important, you must clear your mind of all else and memorise every word, to ruminate on them later at leisure.

"Yes," Bateman continued "one might find ruin even in the waters of smaller rivers, washing down from smaller mountains. It seems their currents and eddies just cannot wait to reach the great plain rivers, like the Danube, the Rhine, the Po or our own Rhône." His eyes burned with hidden meaning, though the rest of his face bore the expression of a man rambling idly. I felt sure we were hearing the crux of what Bateman needed to tell us.

"And when the stars and planets clash in the heavens, as my learned friend Opicino de Canistris, who works in the household of Cardinal Gauscelin de Jean, the Penitentiary Major, often says: 'storms and lightning then rage over the hills and mountains, and the waters come rushing down with anger'."

A delicate pause, and then he repeated the word unnecessarily. "Anger."

He brought the conversation abruptly back to the matter of church-law, and we realised that the secret communication had come to an end. Finally the old lawyer came to the subject of friends and family. Once again he meandered into mysterious discourse.

"I heard, Gerold, that your good sister Marianne lost her husband last winter to a fever, may his soul rest in peace." Of course, 'neither Master Gerold' nor his sister Marianne really existed. Why should Bateman be inventing this story about the death of a fictitious brother-in-law? I resumed memorizing every word.

"Be sure to look after her, and her children. The loss of a father is a terrible thing for a son, as you know. The effects are felt long after the event. Yes… It is an ill wind that brings such a fever. An ill wind indeed."

"Don't worry," Master John reassured him "I keep a close eye on all my family. I'll let no earthly harm come to them, God be willing. And your own sister, in Norwich?"

The conversation concluded soon afterwards, with no further odd moments. We both embraced Bateman, and took our leave of him, making him promise to visit us in Ghent the next time he passed through the city.

Out on the street, Master John put an arm around my shoulder, and whispered to me "Hear how he weaves kernels of information into his speech. He is smart, but not only. That is truly a gallant man. Can you imagine how many have tried to seduce Bateman with gold into taking other loyalties? And yet, I'd swear by the Virgin Mary that he's never sold himself to anyone, but is the King's true man, and from the King he'll take no gold; only thanks.

"Now, let's get to a market place. We need the privacy to talk over what Bateman told us."

Speaking softly amidst the hustling of merchants as they haggle with housekeepers over prices in a market-place is the safest way to discuss secret business in a city. A market had grown up at a broad crossroads near the Papal quarter to cater for the requirements of the clergy and their servants. We strolled from stall to stall, discussing in hushed tones in the English of London, as it was mostly unknown in Provence.

"Where do you think we must go next, Will?" Master John wanted to test me.

"Lombardy, Master." I replied, happy to show that I was reckoning well. "The lawyer mentioned four plain rivers, only one of which lies near the family we named." By 'the family' I meant, of course, the House of Fieschi. "The Po is in Lombardy. It flows from the sunset to the sunrise, doesn't it?"

"Yes, it does, and leads to the Adriatic, south of Venice."

"And south of the Po at some point there is Genoa, but I don't know how far."

"Nor do I, Eilulf, I admit. But there are low mountains between Genoa and the plain where the Po flows."

"That's right. Genoa stands on the sea, and the mountains at its back are the low mountains they call the Apennines." Master John had described the lay of the land in many parts of Europe to me over the years. Now my thoughts were racing as I remembered his teachings. "The lawyer mentioned small rivers whose waters come down from hills and lesser mountains towards rivers like the Po. I'll wager there are many small rivers that flow down from the mountains of Genoa towards the Po, where the family we named have lands or influence."

Master John smiled approvingly. "It's true. The family's lands are vast, and spread far and wide in that part of the world. However, perhaps our loyal friend of England has told us which part of their holdings to search in."

"You mean somewhere along one of the rivers that flow down to the Po from the Apennines of Genoa?" My tone was dubious. "There may be dozens of rivers that match such a description. Neither of us knows those lands. Where must we go in particular?"

Master John was silent for a long moment, letting his gaze linger on a bunch of fennel on a grocer's bench. Then he turned to me with lively eyes, and I knew he had a solution.

"Bateman told us more things of use than I thought. He mentioned a certain Opicino de Canistris, and told us he works for the Penitentiary Major here in Avignon. Have you ever heard of Opicino?"

"Never."

"From what I've heard, he's a visionary priest. Brilliant, but in a dark way, and as steady as the hare who fell in the ale barrel." Master John paused to frown "He's also a gifted astrologer, illustrator and map-maker. They say he's quite an impressive preacher, that his voice holds the congregation in absolute thrall. His sermons are said to be entrancing. I know for a fact that old Pope John was fond of him and had him brought here, where he's useful. It's also safer not to have him out and about preaching to the common folk.

"The key point is that he is originally from Pavia, near the Po, north of Genoa, and can surely tell us more about the region. He's known as a map-maker, after all. If we ask him about the rivers flowing into the Po, we could find a clue to confirm our conjecture about what Bateman said."

I thought over his words for a moment as we strolled past varieties of broccoli that I had never seen before. "What business shall we tell him we have in Lombardy? We shall need to question him closely without arousing suspicion."

"That is simple enough. We can tell him we wish to worship on the bones of Saint Augustine in Pavia, and converse with the Augustinian Brothers."

Abruptly, Master John halted. We'd drifted close to a particularly well-looked-after section of the marketplace, where a notary was conducting business from behind an oak table on the stone pavement. Such an educated man might recognise the English language, and perhaps even understand it a little. We stopped talking while we passed him by.

Two men stood in front of the notary's bench, one looking angry and the other smug. The notary was reading aloud claims pertaining to a contract to supply urine. Periodically he seasoned his speech with glib Latin phrases, just to remind his listeners that they were in the presence of an educated man.

"… and furthermore, you are held to deliver the barrels of fresh urine no later than the third hour. The gentleman tanner informs me that on many occasions stale urine has been delivered as late as sext. And, *dulcis in fundo*, unstrained urine at that!"

 I mentally grimaced, imagining what gunk the tanner had found in the bottom of the tanks.

When we were safely past the notary's bench, Master John resumed his reasoning.

"We can tell him we're headed for Pavia. At this time of year it would be folly to try and get there by land, crossing the Alps. It would be faster and safer to sail from here to Genoa, and cross the smaller Apennines as the snow melts in early spring. The best way over any mountain range is to cross a mountain pass, then follow a stream down toward the plains. We'll ask him about the rivers running down to the Po, and hope we hear something that Bateman hinted at."

"Master, what did you make of Bateman's enquiries after your family in Ghent? It must be significant, for him to invent for himself a part of your identity in that way."

"I don't know, to be sure," Master John mused "but I'm certain it's going to become clear sooner or later. As God's my witness, Bateman never wastes a word nor wanders from his purpose. Soon, we'll understand.

"And now, let's go to the new tower of the Pope's palace, where Master Pierre Poisson de Mirepoix is in charge. Do you remember that Wiligelmo da Campione told us some of his friends are scribes? One of them can surely guide us to Opicino de Canistris, and we'll both be happy to renew our acquaintance with our new young friend."

The buildings in the heart of Avignon stand along close, curving, cobbled streets, and lean crookedly towards one another at their tops like merry drinking companions looking to each other for support. The sky is visible only in patches, and even the mighty *Palais dei Papas*, which at a distance is visible from all sides, rising as it does from its high rocky hill, is blocked from view. Nevertheless, that afternoon the creaking and groaning of the tread-wheel cranes, the work-songs of the labourers, and the signal-whistles of the work gang supervisors were audible long before we saw the Palace itself.

The first thing we glimpsed through an opening in the maze of streets was one of the faces of the enormous new square tower that Master Poisson was building. It was already well over three storeys high, and above the rising line of masonry a gangly tread-wheel crane, perched inside the tower on the roof of the third floor, stretched up and out, slowly winching a broad wooden basket laden with hewn stone blocks upwards. Impoverished men, desperate for scraps from the work-site kitchens to take back to their homeless families, drive the tread-wheels with bare feet on building sites everywhere. At the *Palais dei Papas* there must have been more than a hundred such wretches, their sweat and suffering lifting the walls of the Pope's fortress-residence toward the sky.

As we came closer, we saw that a ramp, fixed with wooden beams and iron bolts to the outside of the masonry, spiralled upwards around the tower from the rock at the base to the top of the unfinished construction. Men carrying great buckets of wet mortar on their shoulders toiled up the ramp to where their superiors, journeymen of the craft, waited with their levels and plumb lines to fix each stone in place. Down on the ground, stone-cutters were working the rough blocks into the exact shape required with sharp clangs of hammer and chisel. Around them other workers gathered the resulting rubble up with broad wooden pans, shovelling it into buckets that were sent up the ramps to fill up the interior gap in the walls.

We identified a work-gang leader by the sharp whistles he used to catch workers' attention, and the big framing square he held up to the stone blocks to check their shape before they were hauled up by the crane.

"Good man, we're looking for Master Pietro da Campione and his son Wiligelmo." Master John addressed him.

The big fellow was obviously more used to whistling than to words, for he merely gestured roughly at another half-built section of the Palace, and said nothing. We picked our way among workmen and piles of stone in that direction, and soon found ourselves on the site of what we realised were the foundations of a vast chapel. We stopped another gang leader, who directed us to the cover of a large wooden shed, where stone craftsmen were working side by side on long benches.

Standing in the doorway, it took us a long moment to recognise Wiligelmo among them, for his identifying characteristic at our first meeting had been his outward clumsiness. Now, standing still and utterly engrossed in the stone before him, he was another person altogether. He moved with a dignity he could never reproduce in any other situation, lightly tapping away with a small wooden hammer in his right hand as his left seemed to use his chisel as a natural extension of his fingers, delicately caressing a curving form that was not yet entirely free from the original block. We waited until he had removed the chisel from the sculpture for a short pause before hailing him, not wishing to startle him into a costly mistake on the marble.

"*Salve* Wiligelmo!"

He looked up, blinking wildly, his concentration broken. When he realised who we were he smiled warmly and set his tools down.

"Master Gerold, Eilulf, a blessing on you! Wait there, I'll come forward, there's no space back here."

He squirmed and wriggled his way past the rapidly moving elbows of his fellow craftsmen until he was at my side, and embraced me as though we were old friends.

"I'm so glad you came to see me here." He enthused. "Father's with the supervisor, otherwise I'd introduce you right away. Come, come out where there's space so we can talk."

He led us out of the shed through the door on the far side, and in the afternoon sunlight I could see the whole city below us, the rooftops, the courtyards, the curtain wall studded with towers and the bridge of St Bénezet that stretched over the waters of the Rhône with its impossible number of arches. The market squares teemed with people and animals, smoke rose merrily from the many palace chimneys and humble roof-holes, and all about us the faint strains of work-songs and prayers overlapped into a murmuring musical cacophony.

"We came to see the *Palais,* but also to ask you for some help." Master John told the young sculptor.

"It's my honour to be able to help you."

"Thank you. But first – have you seen your fair Maddelene since yesterday? Has she forgiven you for not meeting her?"

"Yes, yes, I saw her this morning." Wiligelmo's eyes first lit up with delight, and then became lost in the general bewilderment of his features as he remembered the encounter. "But… I don't know if she's forgiven me. At first she was very angry, and I had no chance to speak for all her yelling and raging. When she finally stopped, I didn't know what to say, so I just turned my back, so she wouldn't see my face. I thought it was all over, and I was very upset. I thought she'd never speak to me again, so I just started to walk away. At first she did nothing, and my stomach felt as if I'd swallowed roofing-lead. And then…" He blushed.

"And then?"

"She ran after me, grabbed my arm, and spun me around, and kissed me! It was... wonderful." He blissfully breathed in conclusion.

I embraced him, delighted. Master John, however, after an amused chuckle, wanted to come to the business at hand.

"Wiligelmo, we must speak with a certain priest here in Avignon. Unfortunately, the city is vast and there are many hundreds of priests and residences and bureaus, and we don't know where to find him. Do you think one of your friends, the scribes you mentioned, might be able to help us?"

"Of course." He was eager to help. "If they don't know him personally, they must know someone who does. I can introduce you to them this afternoon, after vespers, then tomorrow one of them can take you to your appointment."

"Unfortunately it's a pressing matter. I had hoped to speak with the priest in question this very afternoon."

"I'm sorry, Master Gerold, but I have no leave to go away from the worksite." Wiligelmo thought for a moment, then sudden delight in his face showed that he'd found a solution. He slipped something small and round with a pointed end from his pocket. It was a wooden spinning top.

"Take this as a token. It belongs to Miquel's little sister, Elionor. My own little sister, Alehandra, who is a terrible pest, borrowed it and never gave it back, so I took it from her and brought it with me today to return to Miquel. You can go to find him, he's not far from here. Explain to him that I sent you with Elionor's spinning top, and I'm sure he will help you."

This seemed promising to us, and Master John made Wiligelmo explain carefully where we could find Miquel in the city below. This wasn't easy, for his mind was as scatty about destinations as his legs were in getting him to them. He knew, however, which landmarks were close to the building where his friend worked, and the rocky plateau jutting over the city, the building site of the *Palais dei Papas*, was the perfect viewpoint from which to make them out. When we were sure of our destination, we thanked him profusely, and before we parted company Master John recommended warmly "You can expect to meet us again before long. We still haven't had the pleasure of congratulating your father on his fine son."

Chapter 10

Valley of the River Staffora, October 1337

Encounter in the woods – an invitation, a language lesson and a story - a day of fasting for the pigs

"Welshman, I have a pleasant job for you now." Brother Demetrio called to his lay-brother as he came walking through the workshop door. "Do you remember the sick boy down at the village? He will have finished the medicine I left for him."

The Welshman looked up eagerly from the parchment he'd been scraping clean. "Yes." This might mean another trip to the village.

"I have another pouch of medicine." The healer continued. "You can take it down to Pizzocorno. Just ask for Don Rogerio, the boy's father."

"Isn't it Gilio's place to go?" He had become cautious about the novice, liable as he was to take offence wherever possible.

"Gilio's taken up with his studies. He and the other novices are with Brother Fiorello, taking a lesson on Boethius."

"Boethius?" Startled by the name of the Roman philosopher, the Welshman found himself a young man again, more or less the same age as Gilio, marching toward his first taste of warfare. He had tarried for twelve days in a Dominican abbey with his companion, preparing himself for battle. They had lived and dined with the monks, insisting upon being served the same modest portions at mealtimes as they, and had participated in all their prayers and lessons.

The day the Prior told us that King Alfred the Great translated Boethius into the old Saxon tongue for the betterment of his people, you turned to me and teasingly asked me if I would do the same one day. I was so eager to please and impress you that I swore I would, pretending to myself that my command of the Latin was sufficient.

My pride often tricked my mind into believing such falsehoods about myself, back before this new life began.

"Gallese?" Brother Demetrio was struck by the ease with which the Welshman could wander from the world, and begin mouthing those mysterious words. So intense was the lay-brother's expression that the healer could almost feel a third person in the room with them, listening and answering.

"Gallese!" Brother Demetrio raised his voice, and the Welshman's eyes focused on him once more. "I've got work here to do that doesn't require your presence, and that boy needs his medicine. You got on well with him last time we were there."

"Did I? I helped him when he fell."

"There you are. I think he likes you."

The old healer picked his way carefully through his cluttered workshop, careful not to knock into anything in the vast array of curious objects that lay haphazardly on shelves and benches. There were mortars and pestles, knives with strangely curving steel blades, and others made of warmer metals such as bronze and pewter, for not all plants could bear the harsh touch of cold steel. Bulbous glass vessels adorned shelves, and beneath them were chopping boards both of wood and marble. On the top shelves, little clay vases contained a variety of multi-coloured powders and syrups. Brother Demetrio carefully took down from a shelf a vase containing a fine green-and-red specked powder, and delicately poured a dose of the precious substance into a waxed silk pouch.

"This is the medicine. They'll take this pouch and give you back the empty one I gave them the first medicine in. Be sure to bring it back to me."

The Welshman gladly received the pouch, his passport to the village. He nodded solemnly as Demetrio continued giving him instructions.

"You're to ask Donna Maria, the grandmother, about all the symptoms of his sickness. Can you manage a little Occitan, to speak with them? Good man. Can you find the village again, by yourself? Good, good. If you see that the boy is visibly worse than before, tell them I'll come to read his stars. Actually no," he changed his mind, half closing his eyes as he thought "I can play a little trick. Tell them to find a frog, to tie up its legs and put it into bed with the boy for the night, and I'll come down tomorrow to read its entrails and discover what ails him still. That will keep them happy while I consult the stars for the truth of the matter."

"Brother, it is a sin!" The Welshman was too shocked to phrase his protest more respectfully.

"Reading the frog guts? Maybe, but what is best before the eyes of God: while using real magic to help the boy I read some entrails to keep them happy; or letting them abandon my Christian aid because they do not understand it? They would just end up going to Silva for some good old fashioned soothsaying."

"I did not mean reading the frog guts, I meant the deception. To lie is a sin." The Welshman proclaimed, as though Brother Demetrio might not know it. The monk realised that his lay-brother had entered into another of his child-like moments. He definitely needed more contact with the village folk, the old man thought, to counter all this conversing with the unseen and reasoning like a seven-year-old. The simple, but practical and keen nature of the peasants should help bring him out of it.

"Listen," Brother Demetrio commanded "Never mind about the frog, just take him his medicine and see how he feels. Anyway, if you did mention the frog they would ask me to make the trip down tomorrow anyway, whether Tino is feeling better or not. Save me the bother!"

The Welshman thought nothing more of the incident, and immediately forgot the fact that the healer had said the villagers could *'go to Silva'*. In the Latin 'Silva' simply meant 'the woods', and he assumed the old man meant the villagers might go to the woods searching for animals to sacrifice for their fortune-revealing entrails. It never occurred to him it might be the name of a woman.

Impatient to reach the village, the Welshman took the shorter path through the thickest part of the woods down the mountainside toward Pizzocorno. Though there were still enough leaves on the trees to block out the sky, the path was becoming thickly covered with fallen foliage. It hadn't been thoroughly cleared for more than a year, and in some places new growth had narrowed it to little more than a wild boar track. The Welshman arrived in one such place, where he knew the true path swerved, but was no longer sure whether to the right or to the left. It looked cleaner and straighter to the right, so that was the way he took.

After treading the blanket of fallen leaves for a short time it became clear he'd chosen wrongly, for the path dissolved into shrubs and tree roots, shrouded by litter. He looked backwards, but the point where he'd left the way was no longer in sight. He turned about face, and started walking hurriedly, sure he would find the path. Soon, however, he found himself treading downwards into a shallow gully that he couldn't recall crossing on his way out. With a sigh, he realised he was lost, and cursed ever choosing the shortcut.

What do you think the best way out is, dearest? Across, till I reach the stream, or up till I reach the main road? Let's try across. The village is downhill, heading uphill will only mean walking for longer. Sooner or later I'll find the stream.

He carefully turned perpendicular to the upward slant of the land, and started treading carefully among tree roots, chestnut burrs, shrubs and the autumn's last mushrooms. He had not gone far when he stopped again, concerned, for another silent consultation.

Do you think my back is toward the monastery, or toward the village? Where is the sun? There are no clean-cut shadows down here beneath the crowns of the trees. How can I tell this is the right way?

"That way leads back to the monastery."

The Welshman halted at the quiet voice, somewhere to his right, which seemed to have answered his inner question. Stock still, for a long moment he searched for the owner of the voice. With a start, he finally made out the shape of a woman, hunched down low to the ground, perfectly blended with the woodland. Her famine-thin arms like fallen branches sprouted hands and fingers like dried out old twigs. Her clothes were made of overlapping patches of earthy reds and yellows, echoing the forest litter. Her wild hair was a criss-cross mass of white filaments like the dense webs that spiders weave in dark places, and her eyes gleamed like two pinpoints of distant blue sky that, against all expectation, penetrate into the deepest forest.

"How did you know… Who are you?" He asked without thinking.

"When a stranger walks uninvited into a Lady's home, it is she who asks the question, 'who are you?'." She replied with a calm smile, rising to her full height, which very nearly matched his.

"A Lady's home?" He looked about him at the tree trunks and underbrush confusion. "Who I am?"

The strange woman hushed him. "Don't speak. I already know as much of the answer as I wish." She fell silent, and stepped toward him, studying him from his clogs to the tip of his hood. "You're an exile who has spent too long alone. As am I."

He stared at her lined features as she came face to face with him. She was about his own age, he thought, and must once have been a most beautiful young woman. Beneath her queer woodland vestments, the line of her cheeks and her delicate mouth betrayed her as a woman of that region, of the same race as the folk of Pizzocorno.

"I'm just a lay-brother." He dissembled.

She took his hands in hers, and lifted them up, palms to the forest canopy.

"Are these the hands of a lay-brother?" Whenever she spoke, her voice was soft, constant and caressing, like a seamstress slowly smoothing the folds on a bolt of silken cloth.

He looked down at his pink puffy palms and fingers, and realised they could never be taken for a labourer's hands, but he had no desire to bare all so easily.

"I am a lay-brother, and they are my hands." He said, simply.

The peal of laughter came like a songbird's mirth in the pre-dawn dusk.

"Of course. What an honest man you are. They *are* a lay-brother's hands, but they are also the hands of one who was once a nobleman, who was caught up in terrible intrigue, and now after many years of hiding in solitude has come to hide in company."

He blanched, not at the word 'nobleman', nor 'intrigue', but at the one word she had said that still mattered to him.

"Solitude? What could you know of my solitude?"

"Your silent speech with your companion when you are alone…" The Welshman flinched with an almost physical stab of pain.

"I've felt what you feel, lay-brother. I know. But now, in a way, you have come back to the world. This I can never do."

"How do you know? Who *are* you?"

For a long time she said nothing, her hands cool to the touch as they gently held his. He wanted to pull them away, but something prevented him.

At long length she replied "A friend".

He suddenly felt something cold and odd-shaped in his left hand. He looked down, and nearly dropped it. It was a tightly curled snake, frozen in cold, dark grey stone, whose tail-tip and head were tucked somewhere out of sight among its motionless granitic coils.

"What is it? Is it dangerous?"

Again the bird-like laughter flowed away through the woods, taking his apprehension with it.

"No, it's not dangerous. Now: tell me about it." She commanded.

"It is a snake."

"Ah, again your peculiar form of honesty." She smiled patiently. "You are a lay-brother, therefore your hands are a lay-brother's hands. It is worm-shaped, coiled and scaly, it is a snake. Think, man! Not what it is, but why. Not that it is a snake, but which snake, and how it has come to be stone. All things have a story."

As a child and young man the Welshman had often eluded his tutor to slip into pantries and cellars with pages and other boys of no rank for riddling games, in which, to his tutor's infinite dismay, not only did he always seem to lose something valuable to his crafty playmates, but he showed far greater enthusiasm for word-sports than he ever did for the arts of war or hunting. He wondered if the lady of the woods was playing such a game with him.

"Is this a game of riddles?"

"Perhaps." she replied slyly. "As with riddles, there is a prize at stake. You don't know where you are, nor the way to the village. I can show you, but first I want to hear the story of this snake."

He was about to claim that he would find his own way out of his predicament, but stopped himself. There was something compelling about this queer woman in her rags and skins. She was asking for the stone snake's story. Perhaps he would be wise to oblige her. But what could he say? He attempted the riddling style of his childhood.

"It's the snake that swallowed its own tail, then, while it was hiding its head in shame, a salamander came along bit it on the rump, and it turned to stone."

She arched one eyebrow. "That is more of a child's joke than a story. Can you not do better?"

Feeling almost chastened, the Welshman now fell back on the long hours he had spent as a young man in the company of abbots and bishops to avoid his blustering, sword-and-lance smitten peers. "Perhaps it is the snake that bit Saint Paul on the shores of Malta. Its eyes fell out and it was turned to stone as a consequence of its violence against an Apostle of our Lord. That's why we can't find the head. We are looking for the eyes which are now pebbles on a Maltese beach."

"Saints and apostles?" The lady of the woods seemed repelled by these images. "You may as well say it is one of the snakes St Patrick banished from your land long ago, Gallese. With the magic in his ash-wood staff, he flung them to all corners of the earth."

"So you are not all-knowing after all, strange Lady." The Welshman felt just a little triumphant at finding a gap in her knowledge. "They call me the Gallic man, but I was not born in Eire, and do not speak the Gaelic." He said no more of his origins.

The lady of the woods turned her head in curiosity at this. "Ah? You teach me not to take anything for granted. Indeed." Strangely, she did not ask further. "So… let us come back to the story of the snake."

The Welshman paused to think, knowing something more was required. He recalled the marvellous stories sung by the great minstrel, Robert Craddock, while he bowed his crwth among dozens of dignitaries and high tables laden with the fattest meats and finest delicacies of the land. The Welshman had listened, spellbound, to stories such as Y Ddraig Goch, while beside him his father had continued to discuss wars and similar affairs with grim-faced counsellors. His father had been irked because his son paid more attention to fairy tales than to matters of state, and had loudly muttered to his interlocutors "It's a pity that boy is not listening to us. He might learn something." It was neither the first nor the last time that the old warrior had seemed to barely recognise 'that boy' as his son. The Welshman had long since learnt to push his father out of his memories. Now he deliberately recalled only Craddock's gripping narratives, and wondered if even a miniscule part of the minstrel's craft might be hiding within him.

"It is a snake fallen from the head of a gorgon." He began. "It grew too long for its own good and bit his mistress on the nose, so she flung it in a heap on the ground and glared at it. It tried to hide its eyes in its coils, but it was already too late. It was turned to stone." Even as he concluded, he felt unsatisfied, and the lady of the woods smiled just a little.

"I see the beginnings of ability in you. With time you will learn to tame and twist stories you have already heard. But storytelling is much more even than this. Return the charm to me. It can only awaken abilities that lie dormant in each of us, and mine are modest. But perhaps I can show you enough to let you understand." She took the cold stone from his hands, and her eyes slowly focused on a scene he could not see, but which soon appeared vividly in her tale. Her words were deceptively few, but colours and sensations came to life in her tone and gestures.

"This snake... is that ancient serpent which emerged from the woods into a fragrant spring meadow long ago, and found two lovers there. One was a lissom young lady, lying in the grass," and her voice melted like the sigh of a young man as he sees a beautiful lass and wonders what it would be like to embrace her and kiss her "with a garland of freshly picked flowers in her hair." Somehow the scent of those flowers sprang into the Welshman's nostrils, sharp against the autumn odour of dry litter. "The lady's suitor sat on a rock and sang to his lute songs of intense beauty that made the birds stop their warbling to listen." Now her voice became musical, melodious, and one could hear the wonder of the songbirds as they met their match. "And so the serpent came closer to hear the music, too, but as he passed her, the lady moved her leg, and blocked the sunlight from the serpent's eyes. It thought she was going to stamp on him" the snake's terror was a gasp in the story-teller's voice "and bit her ankle in fright. And when the lass succumbed to the deadly venom and breathed her last breath the minstrel's grief was so heavy that his song became like the granite of tombs, and the serpent himself turned to stone as he listened." The Welshman felt the cold, hard, mourning quality of a boulder that blocks a path and brings a journey to its end.

"Strange Lady," he breathed, a little awed "after hearing this tale I believe it is indeed the snake which bit Eurydice, for that is the name the Greeks gave to the lady you described. But the story as they told it does not end there."

"Then take the charm, and learn to use it, and one day you will tell me the rest of the story. This snake" she continued, placing the coiling stone in his hand "is all of the snakes we mentioned, if you know how tell their stories. And you, Gallese, and I, are just like the snake. Can you see why? No one knows where we begin, nor where we end, and no one really knows our story. But each person tries to imagine it, by inventing it. You will see. So we are many people, one for every story they tell."

The Welshman felt uneasy. "But *I* know my story; the real one."

"Do you? Perhaps... Or perhaps your silent companion is the only one who truly remembers it."

"But my silent companion…" he paused, then admitted with difficulty "is not here. Not anymore."

"Not here?" She inclined her head in negation. "You are wrong, Gallese. He is present."

The Welshman was puzzled and in pain. His next question required a courage that once, before he began his new life as a laybrother, would have been unthinkable for him.

"Then why does no one hear him but I?"

"Because you are the only one who needs to hear him."

The Welshman shivered, and looked away, down at the stone snake.

"Lady, do not take offense, but I want to go… what did you say, earlier? Back to the world. Show me the way to the village, back to the world, I beg of you."

She nodded. "I will show you the way."

"Here, please take the snake back. I don't want this gift."

"It is not a gift. It is only in your keeping. It is a story charm, and you in turn will pass it on one day. I cannot take it back, now that it has found a new keeper."

"Pass it on? To whom?"

"I don't know. But you will."

His glance shifted uneasily from the snake, to the woman, to the forest floor, and to the snake again. He had heard that such objects existed, and often harboured magical qualities. Should he take it? He was attracted by it, by the thought of telling stories as powerfully as the lady of the woods. In the midst of his indecision, she took a step backward, raising her left hand to point over his shoulder.

"Look. There is an ancient holm oak, with two gaping hollows and low, thick branches."

He turned to look, and there on the far edge of a small rise on the mountain slope stood a black-trunked and gnarled old holm oak.

"Stand tall on the first branch and look sun-wards," her voice became fainter "and there you'll see the tower of Pizzocorno."

"So close?" The Welshman looked back, and the lady of the woods was already walking lightly away from him through the underbrush.

"Wait, where are you going?" He took two hurried steps after her, then stopped, realising that if he lost sight of the holm oak he would be as lost as when he'd met her. He stared helplessly at the fast vanishing back of the lady, the snake heavy in his palm.

"Who are you?" He called after her. "Are you a hermit? A saint? A…" He interrupted the very thought, and looked back over his shoulder at the great old oak. Gratefully, he saw that it was still there, still twisted and gnarled and solid reality, not illusion. He looked again after the white haired lady of the wood, but she had already vanished among the trunks. He shivered again, and fixed his eyes on the tree she had pointed at.

When he arrived at Don Rogerio's house, the Welshman was attracted by the noise of many people chattering and shouting to one side of the building. Finding the front of the house apparently lifeless, he followed the sound of the voices. As he rounded the corner of the building he saw what all the mirth was about. The children and the women of the family were working together under the supervision of an old woman, whom he guessed was Tino's grandmother, Maria.

"Bring another log, Matteo, and stoke the fire." She ordered in a whip-like voice, standing by the side of an enormous, water-filled bronze cauldron above a crackling open fire. The boy, whom the Welshman had already seen in the work-chain by the chestnut drying-huts, fetched the wood in a trice.

"Stop spilling the water on the coals!" the old lady punctuated her words to one of the younger women by firmly prodding the unfortunate girl with her foot. Like all the women present, she was carrying a clay jug, with which to take hot water from the cauldron, and a wooden cup for scooping up ashes from around the fire at the base of the cauldron. Some of the women were taking their jugs and ashes over to a broad, slate-paved porch. They were sprinkling the ashes over the slates, pouring on a little hot water, then scrubbing the slates with boar-bristle brushes, down on their hands and knees.

When Matteo had stoked the fire, the old lady barked "Take the little ones to the stream to rinse the cutlery."

Matteo gathered the smaller children together with kicks and pinches and took them to where some other women were standing to one side of a sandy patch, using the ash and hot water to clean frightening-looking knives, wide wooden buckets and thick chopping boards. The women gave each of the children one of the foaming, scrubbed objects, and Matteo herded them away down an alley to where a little stream gurgled away out of the village under the defensive wall. It was the stream that crossed the entire village from top to bottom, the Welshman realised. Naturally, the utensils were rinsed where the stream exited the village, so other householders wouldn't find ash, or worse, in their water supply. Once they'd rinsed the foaming ash away, the little ones brought the bright, clean objects back for old Maria's inspection.

"Fiorenza, do you call this clean? Scrub it again, it's still dirty." One of the scrubbing women was thus reprimanded and the chopping board was given back to her to be cleaned again. Fiorenza scowled and glared at the child who had rinsed it, as though it was the child's fault that it hadn't come through spotless.

The Welshman sensibly waited for a moment when the old lady seemed satisfied with the cleaning, and hailed her in his faltering Occitan.

"Excuse me, good woman, I've brought medicine for Natalino."

Maria hadn't realised the foreigner was there. She cast him a suspicious look. The village folk were relatively used to people from outside, what with the salt roads passing so close by, and with the Abbey of Sant'Alberto itself attracting all kinds of learned travellers. Still, a foreigner is a foreigner, and you could never be too careful. She stepped through the group of working women to warily greet him. "God and Mary by your side, stranger." She prided herself on being able to get by in the Occitan. "We're glad for the medicine." She added, almost grudgingly.

"How is the little boy?" asked the Welshman. Maria frowned, and didn't open her mouth. "Brother Demetrio asked me to enquire." He added.

"He's a tough one, our little Tino." Maria couldn't refuse to reply, if it was Demetrio asking. Now she was closer, Maria caught a better glimpse of the Welshman's eyes. She was taken aback, but politely said nothing. Her tone softened a little. "I think he's getting better every day."

"Will you take me to him? Brother Demetrio instructed me to look at him, and ask him what he feels personally."

"Of course. Come this way." She turned and spoke sharply to the women, warning them not to be slack in her absence, and led the Welshman away.

Little Natalino was sitting up in his bed, visibly pinker and healthier.

He smiled as the Welshman entered, and greeted him. "God by your side!"

"And by yours, little one." He replied, and knelt down by the mattress. "How do you feel today? You look better." He hoped the boy understood the Provencal.

"Yes, I'm feeling better." He understood, but replied in his dialect. It was still strange to his ears, but the Welshman could make sense of it. "My throat is still sore, but my cough has gone away." The boy delightedly thumped his chest with one hand. Then he ingenuously reached forwards and touched the Welshman's face with his right hand. *"Biànc"* he breathed, wonderingly. How could anyone be so white?

"Tino! Don't be rude!" Maria reprimanded.

The Welshman understood the little boy's wonder.

"I'm from the far north. All the people there are as fair as I am."

"Are you really from the land of the Gallesi?"

"Yes, yes. I was born there."

"And does your head really turn into a wolf's head when you get angry?"

The Welshman gave Maria a startled look, who disapprovingly said "His grandfather likes telling stories."

"Ah. No, don't worry." After meeting the woods-woman, and making his first foray into the difficult art of invention, he was sensitive to the boy's grandfather and his tall-tales. "It *might* turn into a dog's head one day, that happens among the Welsh, but so far *mine* never has."

"Good!" The little boy replied emphatically. "So... you're not white in the face because you're sick, like I am... was?"

"No, don't worry, I'm fine." He laughed. "It's you we must worry about."

"I'm *much* better, really I am. I'm going to the *frittura* tomorrow."

"The *frittura*?"

"The pigs..." the boy didn't know how to explain. For him it was obvious what a *frittura* was.

Maria stepped in. "Tomorrow we're slaughtering the first three pigs. That's why we're cleaning everything this afternoon. Every time we slaughter, we have the *frittura* at lunchtime. We cook the hearts, livers, lungs and kidneys all together, chopped up in little pieces with onion and seasoning." She paused for a moment, warring with her own good manners. It was deeply rude in that country to mention a feast to a person and then not invite him or her. She finally, unwillingly added "Will you come to eat with us?"

Tino, who was far too young to share his grandmother's most sensible distrust of strangers and foreigners, became doubly animated.

"Yes, yes, please do…" He paused, concentrating, wanting to show the Welshman that he was the son of one of the village dons. Latin was the language of importance, and he had occasionally heard his father use a few phrases in the Church-tongue to speak with foreigners, just like the day the Gallese had first come to their house. Now Tino repeated a phrase he heard often during masses in church: *"Veni mecum…"* he hesitated, unsure of the next part *"convivio…"* He concluded. 'Come with me… by the feast'.

The Welshman smiled, and without thinking corrected him. *"Veni mecum ad convivium."* 'Come with me *to* the feast."

The little boy looked puzzled, but curious. The Welshman remembered Demetrio's words about seedless pears, and for the first time in his life he felt the urge to teach.

With the two longest fingers of his right hand he showed a figure walking, and with his left hand he pointed in the direction of travel. *"Ego venio af conviviUM,"*… 'I come TO the feast'… *"non conviviO"*… "not BY the feast". The boy nodded, but it was clear he was struggling. There was a wooden cup on the floor-rushes by his bed. The Welshman pointed to it. *"Domus est."*… "This is a house" …. *"Ego venio domUM"* his right hand walked up to the cup, his left hand pointing to emphasise the direction, 'I come TO the house'… *"Non domO"*… 'not BY the house'.

Suddenly the boy's eyes lit up. He waved his hands excitedly, thinking, then pointed to the wooden cup himself. *"Castrum"*… 'Castle'… With the two fingers of his own right hand, he imitated walking up to the castle *"Ego venio ad castrUM"*.

The Welshman laughed out-loud, delighted, and ruffled Tino's hair with his fingers. *"Sic est, optime!"*… 'that's right, good!'.

He made as if to stand up, but little Tino tugged at his sleeve.

"Please, won't you tell me a story from your land, Gallese?"

"Tino" Maria said sternly "I'm sure the man doesn't have time for telling stories."

"It's true, Tino, I must go back to Brother Demetrio at the Abbey." Seeing the boy's disappointment, he added "But I promise you that another time I'll tell you the story of the Red Dragon, whom they call Y Ddraig Goch." He fervently hoped in the power of the charm given to him by the lady of the woods. Tino's eyes widened with anticipation.

"Tomorrow, when you come for the *frittura*?"

"I can't come tomorrow, Brother Demetrio has work for me all day. Perhaps another time."

He smiled fondly at the boy, then stood up and went back to Maria, who was watching the scene closely from the doorway.

"He's a strong fellow. I'll tell Brother Demetrio he's getting better. In the meantime, here is his medicine." He handed her the pouch.

"Come with me," her tone was more respectful, he noticed "and I'll give you the empty pouch Brother Demetrio gave us a few days ago."

The Welshman waved goodbye to Tino, and followed the old lady down to the hall.

In the main room of the house, Maria went to a wooden chest covered with cloth. Removing the cloth, she took the lid off the chest and started rummaging around.

"So..." The Welshman thought of what Tino had said "they say my head turns to that of a dog when I'm angry. Are there any other stories like that circulating?"

Maria rose from the chest with the empty pouch in her hand and a smile playing over her lips.

"Quite a few, actually. Some even said the rest of you changes, too, and you were a werewolf. But then when you came to the village everybody dismissed that one. No offence, but you're so soft-looking."

He blushed, glancing down at his soft hands.

"And... who is the lady in the woods? With white hair?"

"So you've met Silva? She is..." Maria paused, searching for words to describe her. Finding none, she replied "For the moment there are many more stories about her than there are about you. But I tell none of them, for I think none of them are true. She is... a friend. More than that I cannot say. Now come, I have to get back, they'll be making a mess of everything without me."

On the way to the door, the Welshman noticed an alcove with piles of dry acorns inside it.

"Are those for the pigs?" He asked, pointing.

Maria nodded. "Yes, but not for the ones we're to slaughter tomorrow."

"No? Can't a pig enjoy a good meal, his last day on this earth?"

She looked at him oddly, half smiling. "The pigs could, but those of us who make salami prefer them to fast for a day before dying. That way their guts empty out a little. Otherwise, when you come to clean them they're full of shit." He looked a little taken aback by that, and she chuckled. "That's life for us who work the land."

Chapter 11

Avignon, October 1337

Interview with a visionary priest – the sack of Pavia – the key to Bateman's speech

Wiligelmo's friend, Miquel, was a sunny-faced youth. He quickly seized on helping us find a famous priest as an excellent excuse to escape from his scriptorium for a short time.

"Of course I know where Opicino de Canistris is!" He exclaimed, taking his sister's spinning top from Master John "He's Rotbert's master. Rotbert is both a friend of mine and of Wiligelmo's. You should have mentioned the name of the priest to him, it would have saved you some time. They're in an old building just inside the Portail des infirmières."

As he led us through the streets, chatting about life in Avignon, we noticed we were drifting away from the fashionable centres of power within the city. The roads narrowed, and were no longer cobbled, and the mud of autumn rains, mixed occasionally with the muck of animals, squelched underfoot. We started to see grubby children, who ran away giggling when they caught a glimpse of us, then crouched at a safe distance in grimy side alleys to watch while we passed. At one point we were pinned to the walls while a dense flock of goats was driven past by its herder.

Our destination was a nondescript wing of a building that looked out over the Portail des infirmières, or the "hospitalers' gate", where the Carmelite monks have their charter-house. Miquel cheerily took us to the first floor of the decrepit building. There we found a room where a young man was squinting by the light that filtered through the thin-scraped hide which covered the window and blocked out a little of the afternoon draught. It was now late October, and the afternoons in the narrow city streets were neither well lit nor warm.

He was far too young to be Canistris. Master John and I let Miquel go in, and stayed at the door to observe.

"Rotbert, how goes it?" Miquel greeted his friend.

The boy stood up immediately, but strangely did not come forward. He stood with his back against his writing desk and his legs close together, like a child when he's trying to hide something behind him. From the doorway I smelt smoke in the air, though I could see there was no fireplace.

"Miquel, welcome." Rotbert seemed like a serious boy, with gloomy eyes, unlike his friend. Around the folds of his tunic and tucked away under the writing bench I was just able to see glowing coals.

"Is your master here? These scholars are planning to travel to Pavia, and want to ask his advice."

While Rotbert answered his friend in low tones, I murmured to Master John.

"He's brought in some clay bricks and made a tiny fireplace under his desk." I murmured. "There were live coals there. He must be freezing."

Master John nodded. "He probably goes to fetch some more from time to time from the main fireplace below, when no-one is looking. This building is so old and draughty…"

"How was a famous priest like Opicino relegated here?"

"He must have fallen out of favour when his patron, the old Pope, died."

Miquel came forward with Rotbert, who looked miserable.

"Friends," said Miquel "I must be back to my work. Rotbert will take you upstairs to speak with Opicino. Good luck!"

We took our leave and climbed the stairs behind the silent Rotbert. On the second floor we discovered a long room with three writing benches and a bookshelf. At the far end a window with no hide covering let the autumn chill through. This room was colder still than the one where the young scribe worked. On the nearest bench hunched an old cleric, busily writing on one piece of parchment amidst a jumble of many other documents, some of which had the appearance of epistles, while others were clearly astrological charts and maps. He worked away, apparently oblivious to the chill. It was strange to find a master had less care for comfort than his pupil. Even if there was only one pane of hide left for all the windows on the building, surely the master had a right to it?

Rotbert wordlessly gestured us forward into the room, and as soon as he saw Opicino turn around on his stool he scurried away, wide-eyed. Thus we met the great visionary priest unannounced.

Opicino had a posture like that of the drunken hare Master John had mentioned, and hair like a wet horse's tail draggling down from around his shaved tonsure-patch. His chin was almost bare, but for a few straggly whiskers, many of which grew out of warts. His clothes were un-sellable antiques and his clogs were worn almost as thin as linen cloth. But his dark eyes were disturbingly penetrating. As they met mine I felt a presence, intangible but as cold and sharp as a steel blade, probing through the layers of my being. Master John, however, seemed unaffected at first.

"Father Opicino?" he began in flattering tones. The old man nodded slowly, his unblinking black gaze settling on my Master's face. "I am Master Gerold of Ghent, a teacher of the *quadrivium* and once a student of Duns Scotus. I have heard tell of you all over Europe, and know you once lived in Pavia. My pupil, Eilulf, and I intend to kneel before the bones of Saint Augustine there, but we must know the road to travel."

Opicino rose with surprising grace from his chair. "The Lord himself has sent you to me." His voice! It was… melodious. Fascinating. It seemed to come from on high, like an angel's announcement. I remembered what Master John had said about the Church's fear of the trouble that might arise should he preach to the common folk, and I believed it.

"The Lord in his wisdom has chosen my words to guide you. Those who seek to kneel before the shrine of our most Holy Saint must trace on the cold Earth with their footsteps the paths set out in the heavens by the stars in their courses." As he spoke, I was sure he was listening to some voice from far - a voice that only he could hear, and which spoke in a fey language that he alone could comprehend. Even Master John began to be swayed by the man's presence.

"Like Capricorn himself in the vault of night, the pilgrim must bend his knee, and sink down, down toward Pavia." I shivered involuntarily. He was, I thought, interpreting what he heard in the language of the Angels into the Latin, that we might understand.

"Pavia…" He lowered his eyes and breathed a long sigh. After a long pause, his whole body became suddenly animated, his gaze lit up like fire and he swept dramatically in one graceful, mystical movement to a codex-laden shelf. He carefully took a manuscript down, and brought it to the writing bench, his eyes alight and intense.

"This is my *Book of Praise for the City of Pavia*." He laid it reverentially on the wood, as though it were the work of an ancient philosopher and not a book of his own writing. I had the impression that he himself stood in awe of some higher quality that the book possessed. He opened the manuscript at a fold-out page, where there was a beautiful illustration.

"Here you see the mighty twin-cathedrals. The greater of the two is the summer cathedral, St Stephen's, with its carved arches, and the smaller is St Mary's, for the winter services, but inside the two buildings are joined, and the worshipper finds himself in a veritable sea of columns." His eyes became unfocused, and it was clear he was reliving hours spent there in prayer as a young man. He turned to another page.

"This is the tower where the philosopher, Boethius, was imprisoned by Theodoric the barbarian King. In his cell in this tower he composed the *Consolation of Philosophy*, that work of wisdom we all study, before they took him down and tightened rope about his forehead until his eyes were forced from their sockets, and then they beat him to death!" I was impressed. This man had walked the streets where the great Boethius himself had lived, worked, and finally been executed. Master John, too, was now utterly fascinated.

"Here, instead" another intricate drawing unfolded "are the three rings of the city walls, for as each line of bastions was created to house the city-folk as their numbers grew, the old defences were preserved. This is how Pavia has resisted so long to so many mighty sieges."

This map was potentially of great use to us, and we both came as close to Opicino as we dared. We struggled in those few instants to memorise the image as best we could. Now Master John spoke.

"Father, are you able to instruct us on how the land lies between Genoa and Pavia? We wish to travel first by sea to Genoa, and then cross the Apennines towards Pavia."

The priest's eyes focused for an instant on Master John's face, and then something seemed to burst into hissing sparks behind his eyes.

"How the land lies? How the land lies… It lies most vilely!" His voice was rising to fever-pitch "Vile, lascivious, the land lies about the testicles of the Great Goat, fornicating with Africa. Look!" He jabbed a finger down on the parchment he'd been working on when we arrived.

We saw that it was an enormous, bizarre image of a goat whose grotesque lips touched those of a woman beneath him, and whose giant phallus extended toward her bloated vulva.

"What is it?" Master John breathed, awed by the detail and craft of the drawing.

"A map! A map of Europe and Africa… A map of their disgusting fornication that embraces us all!"

We backed away, struck dumb.

"Here, look, the islands of Spain, the beard of the goat's sweaty chin, and Gibraltar his vulgar lips which brush… brush *sensuously* against Africa's."

I had never before seen a map like it, where the shapes of the continents were clearly outlined, the coastlines in their vast physical forms. It was not unlike the best of the Spanish and Catalan maps we see today, but at the time it was something unheard of. Indeed, neither of us really understood at first what we were seeing.

"Greece and Macedonia, here and here" Opicino jabbed at the Europe-goat's legs "are his hind-legs, pushing, thrusting his hips onwards in his lust… and the Italian peninsula his engorged sex, eager for the gulf of Tunis, Africa's sinful vulva!

"The land lies in unholy, immoral embrace with Africa, and my poor Pavia lies here, at the base of the Great Goat's phallus…"

We took another cautious step backwards, away from the desk and Canistris. I cannot remember all the words he said, for he raved for a long while, his finger stabbing the map viciously again and again. The spirit that was in him, and which revealed these miraculous secrets of the world to him, frightened us not a little. I began to wonder if the voice from afar he seemed to hear spoke to him in the tongue of Angels, or in that of Demons.

When, after a long while, he had finally finished his feverish speech, Master John delicately changed the subject.

"Will you not show us more of your magnificent *Book of Praise for the City of Pavia?*"

Unnervingly, in less than an instant Opicino' reverted to the calm, reverent, mystical mood he had displayed at the beginning of the encounter.

"Of course…" he spoke musically once more "Let us begin at the beginning…" He opened the first book once more, and there, on the second page of the manuscript, was the map we'd been hoping for.

"May I see this page better, Father? May we not light the candle? The afternoon light is fading."

"Of course, of course… *Boy! A light!*" he cried out in a high nasal voice, and we heard the young scribe from the floor below come scurrying up the stairs with a glowing coal in a steel pincer. He held it to the wick of a fresh candle in the centre of the bench, and blew on it. When the flame had sprung up, he hurried back down the stairs. He hadn't said a single word, but his eyes were wide and darted about like a mouse in a corner with a hungry cat. I pitied him, for it must have been a mental torture to work with Opicino. The spirit that was a gift for the Master was surely a heavy burden for the Pupil.

With the candle lit we could admire the map. It took the form of a great wheel, a circle of which Pavia was the centre, and red lines indicated the flow of the rivers. Pavia was shown, standing on the banks of the Ticino, which flowed into the Po as it ran west to east. A couple of smaller rivers ran approximately south-to-north into the Po.

"Might we follow one of these rivers from Genoa to the plain, Father?" Master John indicated the most likely-looking one.

Opicino thought for a moment. "There are no rivers that run from Genoa to the Po, for the land runs uphill from the city. I know well, because I once spent time in exile there."

"Father, you were sent from Pavia in exile?" Master John made it seem an innocent exclamation, but I knew he was hoping for more details about our destination.

"Yes…" Opicino shook his head sadly "I had been teacher and guardian for some time of the children of Lord Filippone Langosco, Palatine Count of Lomello and rightful Lord of Pavia. There came a time, however, when Filippone Langosco was opposed by another nobleman of Pavia, the Ghibelline traitor, Musso Beccaria."

I could tell that Opicino had launched himself into a tale he'd told many times before. Master John and myself lost a little of our tension, relaxing into the account and letting the mellifluous voice wash over us with its highs and lows, quickenings and pauses.

"Musso Beccaria had made a pact with the Visconti family of Milan. Lord Langosco had a powerful ally, Lord Monferrato of Acqui, but the Milanese were too clever. Galeazzo Visconti, a fearful strategist, at first hid the greater part of his troops from the Lord of Pavia when they met. With a small party of knights that seemed vulnerable, he taunted the men of Pavia and Monferrato from the far side of a stream. Filippone Langosco was fierce, and eager to meet Visconti and Beccaria in person. He would have killed them, hand to hand!" He brought a fist down hard on the bench in emphasis, his expression fiery. "So my Lord Langosco rode out into the stream with his men first. Before the men of Monferrato could begin to cross, though, Visconti brought up his hidden reserves. Monferrato had started crossing the ford, but some cowardly worms in his ranks turned to flee in mid-stream, blocking the rest of their troops from reaching the far side. The militia of Milan and of the Beccarias swept aside Langosco's guard, and he was captured. They formed their ranks again on the bank of the stream, their archers forcing Monferrato and his men to retreat.

"They threw my Lord Langosco into the lightless dungeons of Milan, where he rotted until he died." A gleam appeared in his eyes. Were there tears forming in them?

"The Viscontis completed their victory over my beautiful Pavia just a few years later. An honour-less man in his pay, one Marchetto Salerno, the wretch! opened two of the outer gates. St John's gate could not withstand their advance, and they erupted into the city as curfew was being announced. Filippone's eldest son, Ricciardino, gathered his men around the gate in staunch defence, but to no avail. He had had no time even to put on his armour, like the many in his guard, and the Milanese archers had an easy time picking them off, one by one. Every time the city's defenders sought to rally behind the wing of a palace the Milanese threw burning brands into the building, forcing them out into the open.

"I heard the sounds of battle, and took my charges, the daughters of Filippone, and hid them in the cloister of the church where I sang the mass in those years. Then I took a mace, and would have joined the battle, but as I approached the scene of destruction I overheard two of the bastard children of the Beccaria brood, boasting of the battle.

"*'We're to hand the eldest daughter, Elena, over to Musso'* they were saying, *'but we can do what we like with the little ones. I've wanted that blond girl since the day she refused my kiss under Porta Calcinara. If I find her...!'* They were men of Pavia, fighting for the Milanese! May they writhe fearfully in the fires of Hell, just as the poor people of Pavia writhed in the flames of battle that night! The fog glowed red with fire above the rooftops, and I realised that I must take the girls and flee.

"I ran back to the church and took the children out of hiding and through the back streets where cowardly citizens were watching, trembling from upper windows. I shouted to them *'Arm yourselves! To St John's gate! Pavia is burning.'* But the wretched fools pretended not to hear, hoping the battle would leave them unscathed if only they stayed hidden in their homes.

"At the bridge I was forced to use my mace on the guard there, for he blocked my way, and I took the girls over the river and south, as my Lord's son was dying, stabbed by a dozen Milanese swords.

"Ricciardino!" The priest had real tears in his eyes. "Ricciardino! So fair, so brave, so honourable…"

He paused, slumping over his manuscript, his dilated pupils black and desolate now the last of the daylight had vanished and the candle-glow was our only illumination.

"The next day, while Musso Beccaria was declaring himself lord of the city, Ricciardino's noble mother uncovered her son's broken body among the bricks of a fallen palace, and fell dead on the spot, her heart rent by the sight…" He wept silently. "Twenty-two years have passed… He would have been forty by now, the master of his family and of his city…"

Master John let the crazed priest weep a while, then gently spoke to him.

"You said you spent time in exile in Genoa…?"

Opicino gradually recovered his equilibrium. "Yes, yes… I was able to lead the children of Langosco south in secret to the town of Calvignano, where the Bottigella family, allies of the Langoscos, helped me. They gave me an escort to take me south to Varzi, along the River Ira…" My Master and I both started at the river's name "and from there we followed the salt roads over the Apennines to Genoa. When we arrived there, the Langosco girls were exhausted, but we found shelter in the bosom of the Spinola family, friends and allies of the Langoscos and of the Bottigellas."

Master John and I exchanged a surreptitious glance. … *the River Ira… the Spinola family…* Suddenly many disparate words in William Bateman's speech were starting to make sense.

"Father Opicino" my Master began, weighing every word before uttering it "it is the first time I have heard of these places, of the River Ira, for example…" He tailed off, waiting for Opicino to tell us more.

"The Ira? Have you never heard of it? It is famous, but perhaps you know it as *Iria*, as later historians call it. Now in Lombardy we say *Staffora,* but as the *Ira* it is famed because on its banks Majorian, the Roman emperor, was killed, betrayed by his general, Ricimer."

I'm sure my expression was blank in that moment. Opicino was vastly overestimating my knowledge of the lives of Roman emperors. Even Master John looked a little bewildered, for he had always cared more about the liberal arts than history.

"By chance is the Ira a tributary of the Po?" Master John inquired.

"Of course, all the rivers which run down from the Apennines flow into the Po, or one of its greater tributaries."

That was the confirmation we'd been waiting for. It was a river flowing down from lesser mountains to the Po, just as Bateman had rambled about, and its name was *Ira*, which in the Latin meant 'anger', the word Bateman had curiously, unnecessarily repeated.

"And you mentioned a town called Varzi, and roads across the Apennines toward Genova?" Master John persisted.

"Yes, the salt roads. Varzi is a beautiful town in the valley of the Ira, watched over by Auramala Castle, the great court of the Malaspina family, lords of much of the Apennines from Genoa right down to Tuscany." Once again, Master John and I exchanged a meaningful glance. *Auramala* meant *ill wind* in the Latin, another phrase Bateman had repeated unnecessarily during our conversation. It was the second confirmation that these were the places we needed to reach. "Salt merchants, and many other kinds of merchants," continued Opicino "carry their goods over the mountains to Varzi, where buyers and sellers from the plains gather. The salt-road, they call it."

"And are there any particular places of worship and of learning where we might stop along this route?"

"Of course, there is a monastery. Sant'Alberto's Monastery, at Butrio, is a short walk from Auramala Castle. There you will find hospitality in abundance, and you will be able to discuss theology with learned doctors of the Benedictine order, and worship before the bones of Sant'Alberto himself."

Opicino rambled on for a long time, describing the mountains, the plain, the city of Pavia and the salt roads. He spoke of churches, castles, fields and forests, his eyes never focusing on any point in the room, lost as they were far beyond Provence, in the lands beyond the Alps to the east. Finally, my Master decided that he had enough information.

"I cannot thank you enough, Father Opicino" he said "for all the knowledge you have shared with us."

Opicino seized my Master's arm before he could make a step. In an urgent, hoarse whisper, he said "My words shall be as a light for you on the dark paths of the mountain valleys!"

Master John freed his arm as delicately as he could, and we realised that Opicino's mood was transforming yet again.

"Your footsteps must trace the paths set out in the heavens by the stars in their courses." He continued in his low whisper. "Your footsteps must trace the paths set out in the heavens by the stars in their courses..." He repeated the phrase, again and again.

"We beg your leave!" Master John told him "Soon curfew will fall!"

"*... the stars in their courses!*"

We hurried down the stairs, unable to endure more of that powerful, bewildering, enthralling presence. We strode past the scribe's room, where young Rotbert looked up at us with a forlorn expression that seemed to say *'Take me away with you! You've only had the smallest inkling of what it means to be here with Opicino, day after day after day'*. I pitied him.

Once out on the darkening street, Master John took my hand discreetly and guided my fingers beneath his cloak, until I felt the familiar crackle of parchment.

"It's one of the astrological charts Opicino had composed, and left lying on his desk." He whispered. "I slipped it from under his very eyes. We have to find a quiet, private corner of our tavern. I want us to have a letter from Opicino commending us to his friends in Lombardy. By God's good will, he seems to have been friends with the Spinola family and their allies, the opposite faction to the Fieschis. We can avoid the Fieschi family all the better if we make use of the hospitality of their rivals.

"On this chart there are plenty of phrases in Opicino' handwriting. There must be the complete alphabet. So, Will, it's time you showed off your forging skills!"

Chapter 12

A field near London, October 1337

The scene is set for the tournament – a private conversation in a public place – a gallant rescue

The preparations for the tournament had been truly impressive, William de Montague thought as he surveyed the field from the height of the Royal stand. It was to be a lavish showcase for the young King Edward III before a host of foreign dignitaries, among whom five honoured guests had brought their champions to represent their various kingdoms and dukedoms in the mock-battle.

A shallow green vale had been left un-ploughed after the harvests, the dividing lines between the various peasants' strips removed, and the whole area fenced in with a line of stakes. Each wooden stake bore a red and white tassel, the colours of the cross of St George. One end of the vale was lightly wooded, and the boundary stakes embraced the trees three or four deep; enough to provide obstacles to make the fighting more exciting, but not so far into the wood that the spectators might lose sight of the combatants.

A natural depression in the centre of the vale had been paved over with stone, and a nearby stream temporarily drained into it to form a little lake. On one side of the lake stood a small stone tower, complete with tiny crenellations and a turret. An open spiral staircase circled the outside of it, leading from the ground up to the top. It was not the only such miniature tower to have been erected especially for the event. Five in all dotted the vale, one for each of the guests of honour, and banners bearing their coats of arms hung from each turret. Montague easily made out the three golden lions on a red background which marked out his friend Henry de Grosmont's tower. The blue and white Fieschi colours had been placed on the tower by the lakeside. 'Of course' thought

Montague 'Genoa is a port-city'. The champions, their squires and their men-at-arms would fight to protect their own towers, and to conquer those of the others. It was surely going to be a magnificent show.

Around the vale were a series of stands for viewing the spectacle. The King's was naturally the highest and finest, but the merchants and minor nobility were more than satisfied with the views from the other stands. Undeterred by the cloudy morning, people had travelled from far afield to witness the tournament.

Montague took advantage of the noisy chatter in varied tongues all around them to murmur quietly to Richard de Bury, seated beside him. "As you requested, Richard, I spoke to Henry. He has gathered a surprising amount of information through your agents. He really is a remarkable man, in many ways."

"Indeed," Bury nodded "remarkable both with the mind and with the sword. Everyone is expecting him to put on quite a show here today."

As if on cue, an excitable young Spanish lady to Bury's left broke out into a song about Henry Grosmont's bravery that was lately to be heard in every marketplace in the country. The lyrics spoke of a young minstrel's heartbreak, caused by falling in love with a succession of young ladies, each of whom refused him because they were already deeply in love with the dashing Earl of Lancaster.

"I can't be certain, Richard," Montague murmured "but I strongly suspect that Henry composed that damn song himself, to enhance his reputation. His opinion of himself never was understated. But one wonders how he got it about? You hear it everywhere. Perhaps he secretly paid a minstrel to spread it."

The Spanish lady was gesturing excitedly to her maid and pointing at Grosmont's coat of arms, fluttering in the breeze out in the vale.

"If he did write the song himself" Bury replied "it appears that much of woman-kind agrees with his assessment of himself."

Montague came back to the matter at hand "He told me a great deal of what he has discovered through your agents, but there is a part of me which remains certain he didn't tell me everything."

Richard de Bury slowly breathed in as his gaze swept over the elaborately prepared vale. He held his breath for a thoughtful while, before slowly expelling it in a long sigh. "So Henry was close even with you. I am more concerned than ever. What can this matter be?"

"He obviously thought it unwise to tell me everything." Montague spread his hands.

"To be truthful, that is not actually un-sound policy." commented Richard de Bury, the Bishop of Durham, Lord Chancellor and chief overseer of the King's secret business. "In our line of work, one should never discuss delicate matters with more people than is strictly necessary."

"And yet Henry did say…"

Montague's voice was at once overwhelmed by the blare of trumpets, the pounding of drums and the throaty song of shawms, signalling the arrival of the champions and their men. Heralds in each of the stands announced the groups as they marched into the field. Each knight was accompanied by nine squires and men-at-arms of his household. The first to enter was Niccolò Fieschi's champion "Ubaldo de Fénis, Knight of the Duchy of Aosta, son of Aimone de Fénis, son of Beatrice de Fieschi of the House of Fieschi of the Most Serene Republic of Genoa!" His glittering armour, broad shouldered steed and elaborate lance from which hung his patron's colours, all made a fine impression. He arranged his men around the 'Genoese' tower by the little lake, and planted his lance upright in his stirrup.

Henry de Grosmont and his men, the pride of England on their shoulders, were the last to set foot on the tournament field. This was ostensibly to honour the foreign guests by allowing them to enter first, but it also provided Grosmont with an excellent opportunity to put his fine sense of drama to good use. He held his men back, deliberately making the spectators wait to see him. Finally, when delaying any longer might have risked seeming rude or cowardly, he kicked his war-horse forward in a brisk, prancing gait, and as he came into view the spectators erupted. There was no doubting he was the man they had come to see fight, both Englishmen and foreigners among them. The heralds tried in vain to announce him, but their voices were lost in the tumult.

When the young English warrior-earl had placed his men around their tower, the King rose from his seat, and silence fell. The young Edward III was dressed in the bright arms of Lionel, Knight of the Round Table of King Arthur. Indeed, his subjects lovingly called him 'our little lion, the King'. In his right hand, he raised a wine-filled silver chalice.

"To the honour of England, in the name of King Arthur, Saint

Cuthbert and Saint George!" The King exclaimed, his voice relayed to the other stands around the vale by heralds. With a gesture toward the soon-to-be combatants, he drained the cup in a single draught and toasted their honour. It was the signal for the tournament to begin. Predictably, Henry de Grosmont was the first to urge his horse into motion for a charge.

The crowd assumed an air of expectation, and William de Montague took advantage of the hush.

"And yet Henry did tell me much that is of interest concerning our... Mediterranean acquaintance." He nodded toward the far side of the stand, where the dark features of Niccolò Fieschi, intent on what was taking place in the vale, were visible among the men and women of his household.

"Excellent," Bury leaned slightly toward Montague "tell me as much as you can." He gestured toward the action on the field as he spoke, so casual onlookers would believe they were commenting on the combat.

Before Montague could begin, a thundering crash from the vale brought the crowds to silence. Henry de Grosmont had crossed lances at a gallop with a young Spanish knight, halfway between the two champions' respective towers. After the impact the Spaniard cantered on, but it was clear he had lost his balance in the saddle. When Grosmont saw the man drop his lance to grasp his saddle with both hands in an attempt to stay on horseback, he doubled back. One of the Spaniard's men-at-arms was on foot nearby. Grosmont approached him, raising his lance-tip to the sky, assuring the foot-soldier he meant no harm. His voice rang out across the fields, deliberately raised so all could hear.

"Since your Lord has lost his lance, I entrust mine to you, soldier, that your Lord and I may fight on equal terms: with the sword!"

The onlookers applauded this chivalry, and the Spanish soldier bowed as he took the lance from the earl, for an instant feeling himself at the centre of the crowds' attention. In that moment, the many other men engaged in skirmishes all around the vale might as well have ceased fighting, for the eyes in the stands were now all fixed on Grosmont and his adversary.

"Did Henry also mention Ulgham to you?" Richard de Bury whispered tightly.

"He did."

"And?"

In the vale, Grosmont and the Spaniard met on horseback to the sound of sharp peals of steel on steel. The murmuring of the crowd rose apace, covering their conversation.

"Ulgham's involvement is precisely what I'm suspicious about. That was when I felt Henry was hiding something from me. But I should start from the beginning before getting to that."

Gasps escaped from watchers all around them as Grosmont roundly struck the Spaniard about the helm, dazing him a little, and immediately started pressing home his advantage.

"A hit." Bury acknowledged in a louder voice. He thought for a moment, then continued softly "Very well, start from the beginning. And what, incidentally, is the beginning?"

"Fieschi's arrival in England, and immediate admittance to the Council. Ah, look, that didn't take long!"

The Spaniard had lost his balance again, his sword had been dashed from his grip and sent flying, and the weight of his armour had pulled him from the saddle and down to the soft earth with a thud. He had obviously broken some ribs or an arm, for he was now rolling back and forth on the ground in agony while his squires came to his aid. Grosmont saluted him, and abruptly lost interest. He took his lance back from the Spanish foot-soldier, and rode off to look for a better test of his mettle.

In the stand the young Spanish lady was melodramatically whispering in her maid's ear, no doubt torn between her sense of loyalty to her chastened countryman and her attraction to the charismatic English hero. Montague observed her, yearning for his youth when he, too, had had the luxury to agonize over such petty problems.

"Henry has found Fieschi's mark on every financial transaction of substance the King has made since Fieschi arrived in the country." Bury was listening intently. "He noted that the Florentines have become so trusting of the Crown's solvency as to lend enormous sums of money to Edward. Then he mentioned a certain Montefiore, to whom the King gave 3,000 marks in order to contract the purchase of war galleys. That money was impounded on route to Genoa by a marshal of the King of Naples, who happens to be Gherardo Spinola, the uncle of the murdered boy and one of the Fieschis' main rivals. Of course, when Henry told me all this I realized it had been no coincidence when Fieschi's killer, Forzetti, brutally murdered the youth. It must have been in payback for the impounding of that money."

"And what are Henry's conclusions about the affair?" Bury's eyes darted about the vale, seeing not the combatants, but Fieschi, Forzetti, and Spinola, Montefiore and Florentine bankers.

"He feels that Fieschi is acting as a go-between for the King with the Florentines. And to ensure that the King gets his loans, he must have some kind of… warranty, some means of reassuring the Florentines that Edward will, indeed, pay the money back."

"And Ulgham?"

"I asked him if he had sent Ulgham to find out what it is that Fieschi is using as a warranty, and for a brief instant Henry looked slightly… sheepish."

"Sheepish?" Bury was discreetly shocked. "Henry?"

Out in the vale, Grosmont was suavely saluting a beautiful damsel in one of the stands after deftly downing his second knightly victim.

"Sheepish." Montague confirmed.

Bury swore under his breath. "Damn the boy, why didn't he tell me first?"

"Tell you what?"

"That he has sent Ulgham to take some form of… direct action. Ulgham is no information gatherer, he is a man who carries out the most important secret tasks for the Crown, I told Henry this. Henry is astute, and brave, but he has little experience of the intricacies of politics. What if, as we surmised the day you met Fieschi, King Edward has his own secret agenda in the affair? Ulgham's actions may upset the King's best laid plans. Henry should have sought my advice before assigning him a task."

On the tournament field, fate had seen to it that Henry de Grosmont levelled his lance in a climactic horse-back charge against Ubaldo de Fénis, Fieschi's champion. Even Montague and Bury ceased their whispering now to watch, for Ubaldo had already cut a fine figure that morning, laying another opponent low. This was to be the match of the day.

While the Genoese men-at-arms clashed hand to hand with the Lancashire men, their respective lords thundered towards each other, their heavy war-horses churning up the damp ground by the lakeside. Finally they met, the Fieschi champion planting his lance tip in the centre of Grosmont's shield. But the Earl of Lancaster had fared just as well, his own lance taking the tanned southerner on the left shoulder-plate. On impact, both lances shattered, and slivers of timber sprang high into the air. As one, the earl and the knight reeled backwards in the saddle, sliding out of place. With practiced movements, they both kicked their feet free of the stirrups as they realized it was too late to get their balance back, and controlled their falls as best they could. Nevertheless, there was a long moment of terrific clatter as they came to the ground, bending their knees and rolling with the momentum. Their horses galloped on, foaming at the corners of their mouths with the battle-lust, Grosmont's only rearing to a halt when it came to the water's edge.

Neither Grosmont nor Ubaldo were hurt, and after a few moments of giddiness they rapidly gathered themselves on their feet, with the help of their respective men. Grosmont, as ever, was the first to make a move, drawing his broadsword. "*Pugnandum est!*" he cried, and struck with such force that the Knight of Savoy was pushed back as he parried. Grosmont's stamina seemed infinite as he lunged again and again toward his opponent, who slowly retreated. But Ubaldo was no newcomer to this game, and refused to be easily beaten. When Grosmont once swung a little too wide, Ubaldo feigned a defensive parry, but then stepped lightly shifted his sword aside, avoiding Grosmont's. The Englishman, who had been waiting for the parry to curb his inertia, stumbled forward, and Ubaldo had time to lunge at his side. Grosmont laughed with delight, and easily recovered with side-step and a deft parry. Now, however, he had his back close to the Fieschi tower, with its blue-and-white flag.

Rather than concern at his lack of manoeuvring space, Grosmont's eyes through his visor came alive with joy, much to Ubaldo's surprise. The earl made two rapid thrusts of frightening strength, forcing Fénis back a pace or two. Then with a yell of triumph he leapt onto the second step of the open spiral staircase that circled the outside of the tower.

Now Grosmont had just a small step for his footwork, but he had the great advantage of extra height. Ubaldo fearlessly closed in, aiming at the earl's legs, hoping to bring him crashing down in a fall. But Grosmont was faster, and transformed his first parry into a lunge that took Ubaldo on his shoulder plate, making him stumble, then he reversed the arc of his blade and brought it down on the Savoy Knight's helm. Dazed, Fénis took two full steps backwards.

With a cat's sure-footedness, Grosmont started running up the steps.

The Knight of Aosta's squires shouted to him with alarm in their musical Mediterranean tongue: "Lord, the flag! Guard our flag!"

Ubaldo regained his wits in time to follow Grosmont up in hot pursuit, lest the Englishman cut down the flag and shame the Fieschi champion.

"Turn and fight!" He snarled as he cleared the last step and landed on the tower-top. "The flag's not won while its champion is on his feet."

"My pleasure is in the fight." Grosmont joyfully replied. "Guard your banner if you can!"

Somewhere in the back of Montagu's mind, as he looked on in the grip of the spectacle, was the conviction that Grosmont, when climbing the tower, had been far more interested in heightening his visibility before the many ladies present, than in cutting down the Fieschi flag.

The two warriors exchanged blows in a frenzy of flurrying attacks and counter-attacks. It seemed the sun itself wanted to watch, for it pushed through a break in the clouds and bathed the vale in its golden light. The shields shone, and in the breeze the swords sang, and nothing in the world could have been a finer sight for the spectators.

Sooner or later, one of the two would have to make an error. As fate would have it, it was the young Ubaldo, who backed up against the miniature crenellations and stumbled. The entire crowd moaned as one when he toppled over the side of the tower-top, and fell flat into the water of the lake.

De Grosmont was as astonished as anyone, and more than a little disappointed with such an anti-climax. He then realized, however, that his best and worthiest opponent would soon drown in the water under the weight of his armour. The earl saw the squires scramble fearfully to the water's edge. The lake was shallow, but none of them could swim and all were armoured, and their eyes betrayed their terror.

"Hold where you are!" Grosmont bellowed to them, and with great flair threw his sword and his shield aside. He drew his dagger and cut the leather straps of his armour with swift strokes. He pulled off his helmet first, so the crowd could see his bold features. Then he half slashed, half tore off his shoulder plates and mail coat, cutting himself a number of times in the process. All the while, a gurgling sound came from below as Ubaldo on the lake bottom slowly let his breath out under the crushing weight of water and armour. Grosmont tore off his leg guards, then planted his left foot onto the top of a crenellation. Though Ubaldo's life was passing before his eyes beneath him, Grosmont paused for an instant in that pose, his knee up high and his thigh muscles rippling under his hose. He knew he had the finest thighs in the land, and didn't want them to be lost on the ladies. Then he leapt into the lake.

Grosmont splashed down right on top of Ubaldo, which was both unfortunate, for he pushed the last of the drowning man's air from his lungs as his legs came driving down, and fortunate, as he wasted no time in searching for his erstwhile opponent in the turbid lake. The water came halfway up his chest. He took a deep breath and knelt down. He got his arms under Ubaldo's prone form, one under his shoulders and the other under his buttocks, then heaved upward with every ounce of strength in his muscular body. His back strained, and his knees felt like they would burst, and after a split second he could no longer feel his arms. Somehow – and afterwards he could never recall those moments – he lifted the Knight, armour and all, clear of the water. With leaden steps he made his way to the lake-side, as water drained out of Ubaldo's helm and armour like a fountain. At the shore he let the Baron drop unceremoniously to the ground, for his arms and torso were on the brink of collapse. Then he sank into the mud, utterly exhausted.

For a long moment the spectators were silent as the squires hurried to remove their lord's helm and let him breathe. Then the whole vale erupted into deafening applause. Grosmont looked up into the sky, black dots swimming in front of his eyes. His entire body was alive with pain like white hot fire, and his lungs were raggedly heaving in desperate gulps of air after the superhuman strain they'd been subjected to. Suddenly, a convulsion seized him, and he turned over and started vomiting with exertion-sickness. As he brought up wave after wave of bile, he wondered whether, given the circumstances, even vomiting might be manly.

In the royal stand, the Spanish lady pretended to faint with relief, while Montague and Bury shook their heads disapprovingly at the whole performance, which neither of them deigned to discuss. As the crowd erupted with delight, Bury took the opportunity to murmur to Montague:

"I've been thinking, and I may know where Ulgham is going."

Montagu stared at him.

"Tell me."

"Of course, of course…" He laid a reassuring hand of Montague's arm. "It's just speculation, but… I know for sure from an agent in Great Yarmouth that he embarked for Sluys. From there he may have headed south."

"South? You mean toward Genoa?"

"It may be," Bury replied, guardedly "though the easiest way to reach Genoa is to pay one's way on a merchant's galley. Perhaps he is going to Avignon."

Montague spread his hands helplessly.

"I have no idea… And what is his task? Henry spoke of gathering information, but you have excluded that."

"Information is gathered by people who live in key places, like William Bateman in Avignon. John de Ulgham has no one abode, though in recent years I have sent him most often to Flanders, where he has perfected the identity of a Ghentman. He even owns a home in that city."

"Then… what is the typical task men like Ulgham perform?"

De Bury was silent for a long moment. The applause was dying away, to be replaced by a hubbub of excited chattering and exclaiming.

"Most often they are sent to 'remove a weed'." He finally admitted.

Montague's eyes widened briefly. "Let's hope" he muttered grimly "that whoever the 'weed' is that he has been sent to remove is not essential to the King's designs."

"We will only discover that when the task is done. Not even Henry can call his man back now." Bury said gravely. "He would need the wings of an eagle. All we can do is try to convince Henry to tell us what his orders were – or trick him into revealing it. And hope we can counter whatever damage may be caused, if his orders to Ulgham were rash."

Chapter 13

Valley of the River Staffora, October 1337

*Salami and black-pudding in the making –
the story of the Red Dragon – the dragons' shrieks*

"The real reason why you are being allowed to come for the meal this time" Gilio taunted "is not to deliver the Abbot's salt and pepper to Don Rogerio. It's that you are so useless in your work, you may as well not be there."

"You are right, Gilio." The Welshman's expression was humble, but he was hardly even listening.

"You'd barely even picked up that hoe when your hands began to blister."

"Yes, yes, it's true." He replied automatically. One of the mailed and helmed guards at the south-gate of Pizzocorno hailed them as they emerged from the woods before the village walls.

"Good day, brothers. You may pass."

As they passed beneath the stone arch, the Welshman concluded that Gilio was envious. He would at last enjoy the invitation he had received from Tino and Signora Maria, whilst Gilio was to pass the morning visiting ailing villagers from other families.

"Well, here is Don Rogerio's house." Said Gilio. He made a last attempt at nastiness. "If you steal any of the Abbot's salt or pepper once my back is turned, you'll be flayed."

"A good morning to you, Gilio." The Welshman smiled into the novice's sour face, then turned his back and started down the path. He could still feel the red heat on his hands where the hoe-handle had pinched his skin.

I never had this problem when I used to dig trenches for sport, to spend a little time with the common folk, and get to know them, and let them know me. He mouthed, and then listened for a moment.

Of course, you're right. The spades I had back then were made of sharpened steel, not blunt iron, and peasants used to discreetly loosen the soil with harrows before I arrived. Even I noticed that at the time, but pretended to myself it wasn't true. And then, I was wearing silk gloves, and could give up the game as soon as I wearied of it, and a servant would bring me a cup of ale so I could play the merry farmer while I rested. Tilling the herb garden this morning was a far more painful, affair. He concluded, ruefully.

At the corner of Don Rogerio's broad, squat farm house he paused, fascinated by a sound like a hundred storks all rapidly snapping their beaks together again and again. When the scene came into view he understood.

Many benches had been set up in the open space with its stone paving that Signora Maria with the women and children had been cleaning the day he'd been invited. The dismembered limbs, heads and rib cages of at least two pigs were strewn about on them. Five women, with a hatchet in each hand, were mincing bits of meat on wooden boards in a flurry of sharp chops. This was the sound the Welshman had heard. He looked around and slowly started making sense of the rest of the activities.

"Tino, another piece." Little Tino's youngest aunt paused, scooped the meat she'd just minced up in one hand and threw it onto a broad sheet of cloth where an enormous pile was being amassed. Tino, who'd been up and healthy for more than a week now, promptly slapped a new piece of meat to be minced down in front of her.

On other benches, the men were breaking up spines and leg bones with small axes and hammers.

"Hold it firm." Don Rogerio ordered to two of the younger men. One seized the thigh, the other took a firm grip on the trotter, and the bearded head of the family positioned his blade above the knee-joint. With three powerful blows of his big wooden mallet on the axe head, the hock and trotter fell away from the ham.

Squatting on the pavement around wooden boards, the older children were paring fat away from the cuts of meat and skin. They threw each off-cut onto one of three piles on a broad sheet of cloth, depending on the type of fat it was: jelly-like fat from the under-neck, firm lard from the flanks, soap-like suet-fat from under the skin of the back. Matteo, as the tallest boy, felt he ought to be in charge.

"Maria, sharpen this for me." He thrust his fat-blunted knife at Don Rogerio's second daughter, one year his junior.

"It's your wits that need sharpening, if you think I'll be doing your work for you." She shook her long plait indignantly, not even deigning to look at the proffered knife.

In a corner old Natalino was slowly stirring a large bucket full of the pigs' blood to prevent its clotting. A nephew by his side was gradually trickling honey into it. The sweet black pudding it would become was a delicacy, and they would take it down to the traders' village of Varzi for sale at the markets.

"Slow means sweet, old man." Donna Maria harangued from behind Natalino's back. "Stir it more slowly. Slow means sweet."

"Then yours is the quickest tongue a woman ever had." The old man retorted.

Donna Maria herself had the worst job of all, the Welshman noticed. She was slowly untangling a mass of pig guts and cutting away the surrounding fat, which was glossy and stringy and clung together like a thousand greasy spider-webs. She was assisted by Don Rogerio's younger sister, Alberta, one of the few people with whom Maria moderated her tone of voice out of respect.

"Alberta, please hold the knife point away from the guts, or we'll prick them."

As they freed each portion of slimy gut, the two women slowly emptied the membranous tubes of the yellow, squelching mush inside them, half way between digested food and faeces. As it was dropped into a big wooden bucket, it released a stomach-wrenching stench. The Welshman was suddenly very glad they had not had their acorns in the last days of their life. In another bucket nearby, coils of cleaned and rinsed guts from the first pig butchered that morning lay soaking in vinegar, to rid them of the last remnants of their horrid contents.

"Patience, Alberta, patience. One pig is done, this second one is half finished, and after lunch the third's to be stuck. By this time tomorrow these guts will all be salami skins."

The intense activity all around him made the Welshman think of the work-chain he'd witnessed at the chestnut drying-huts, but it was far denser and more chaotic to the eye. Everybody was excitedly chatting, and the more responsible members of the family were forced to shout out their instructions over the hubbub.

"Welshman!" He heard a child's excited voice, and turned to see that Tino, slab of meat in hand, had finally noticed he was there. "Welshman, you came!"

He dropped the meat he was holding down in front of his aunt, and rushed over to where Donna Maria had finally reached the pig's bloated stomach.

"*Nonna, nonna, lo Gallese.*" 'Granny, Granny, the Welshman.'

"Ah! This time they let him come." She looked up and across at the grey-haired stranger, her expression far less enthusiastic than Tino's. "Everybody," her voice rang out around the work-site "our company is complete. We'll start frying now. Matteo, Maria, bring up the frying-fat for Alberta, she's doing the cooking."

The two cousins glowered at each other as they obeyed.

"Stay with me, I'll look after you." Tino told the Welshman proudly, coming and taking his hand. Evidently, he'd been told he was responsible for his own guest that day.

"Welcome." "Welcome." All the members of the family he passed greeted him courteously, their expressions a uniform mix of curiosity and distrust. They cleaned some of the work-benches and pushed them together to form a long table. Don Rogerio, wiping his hands on his cloth apron, came to greet the Welshman.

"*Salve, bene vales?*" 'Welcome, are you well?'

"*Gratias, sic est.*" 'Thanks, yes.'

"I'm glad you were freed from your duties to come, this time." Don Rogerio continued slowly in the Occitan. "After today, I'll have no more pigs to slaughter, and you would have had to wait until next year."

"You're very kind, Don Rogerio."

"But so are you. Signora Maria told me how you taught the boy to speak a little of the Latin." The Welshman was embarrassed, knowing how poor his own Latin was by comparison with a true scholar's.

"It was nothing. He is a bright boy, and should I teach him he would soon outreach my own learning."

Don Rogerio nodded, thoughtfully. The Welshman wondered if the boy's father were considering a life of prayer for the little one. Perhaps he had older sons to take his own place, and a piece of land that would make a suitable gift for the Abbey in exchange for taking the little one in. There were far worse destinies for Tino.

"Don Rogerio," the Welshman remembered the reason he'd been

sent "I've brought the Abbot's salt and pepper. I was told to say the Abbey wants its share of the hams and salamis spiced, not smoked."

"Very well." Don Rogerio took the heavy sack from him, regarding it with slight disapproval. He preferred his salamis sweet-smoked with beech wood, after the ancient manner of the mountain folk.

Soon everyone was seated around long tables under the portico, all rugged up in warm woollens and with braziers placed at intervals beneath the tables to warm them from below. Amid the chatter and breaking of bread, they chewed on raw, crisp chestnuts and roasted apples, and their cups were filled with the previous year's vintage. The Welshman had not drunk wine since he had come to the valley, except during communion, and was surprised to see that the rich ruby liquid was not still like claret, but frothed slightly, almost like freshly pumped ale. The effect, however, was both refreshing and pleasant.

The Welshman had one of just four pewter cups in the family's possession. Don Rogerio, his father Natalino and his cousin, the village baker, had the other three. All four had clearly been handed down from generation to generation as treasured marks of rank at the dining table, and over the years had received a number of batterings, though they had been repaired to the best of the peasants' abilities.

A far cry from our feasts of long ago, don't you find? The Welshman paused over his wine cup to comment to his unseen companion. *Back then we were not even satisfied with silver chalices to show our rank, but wanted gold filigree and gemstones. And yet, amongst these cups of clay and pewter, there is greater warmth than at many of those banquets.*

And then, as ever when he thought of such occasions, the memory of one particular night came unbidden to mind. He wished he could have forgotten it, but no number of years passed nor leagues of road walked seemed capable of banishing it from his mind.

He was transported back to that cursed evening, and once more the sick, grieving, intoxicating joy for the death of his father, which had at long last given him control over his own destiny, coursed once more through his veins. He had been so wildly and recklessly elated to be able to make his own choices that he had agreed when his dearest companion wanted to tell the world for once and for all who his true soul's mate was.

And so there we sat, you and I, in that hall bedecked with our two coats of arms as though we were consorts, laughing and chatting over our bejewelled cups at a table apart from everyone else. We were uncaring of the food that arrived late and badly prepared, for even the cooks were offended by your place at my side. And we utterly ignored my cousins, my other friends, and above all my new wife... that poor girl, just twelve, she who so adored both you and me in those early days. And then my first cousin, almost speechless with anger, came to me and whispered in my ear that he swore he would kill you for the insult you had flung in everybody's teeth that evening... My cousin, who so loved me, and desperately hoped that I would one day return his love just as fervently.

With painful effort, the Welshman tore away from those melancholy memories, and focus on the present. He looked at Tino sitting bright and happy beside his grandfather. With a determined smile, he turned his back on the memories and set his wine-filled cup in front of the boy.

"Tino, tell me: what does our Lord say in his prayer in the garden of Gethsemane?" The Welshman knew the boy must have heard the passage many times at mass, and had chosen the question on purpose. Tino's brow wrinkled as he struggled to remember. The Welshman jogged his memory. "*Pater, si vis transfer...*" Around the two a little circle of curious faces looked on, waiting to see if Tino was able to reply.

"*transfer calicem a me...*" Tino finished from memory. It was not quite right, but the important words were there.

"Yes, good." The Welshman congratulated him.

That sparked appreciation and encouragement for Tino from most present, and black looks of jealousy from some, like the older boy, Matteo. Donna Maria had settled into the seat opposite the Welshman to keep a watchful eye on the foreigner, stopped glowering long enough to pragmatically sum-up the peasant's prospects.

"Learning could earn you a place in the world beyond the village, Tino. Your sister Clementia also has a place in the world now, up at Auramala," she made a vague gesture in the direction of the great tower "nursing the Lord's little son at her breast. But once he's weaned that place won't be certain. She may stay on as a maid, or they might send her back to us. But if you learn letters and the Word, we may be lucky if *you* come back to visit *us* from time to time. The rest of us will work away here till we die, and most of our sweat will always be the property of the Abbey and the Lord of Auramala."

"Go away? Come back to visit?" Tino was crestfallen. He loved his family and their working feasts, and couldn't imagine another existence.

"When you're older" the Welshman assured him "the prospect won't seem so awful." He cut himself another piece of bread then set the broad, flat loaf back down on the table on its rounded top. Three hands belonging to three separate people quickly reached across to turn it over, so it rested on the flat bottom, and Donna Maria muttered darkly.

"I'm sorry, have I done something wrong?"

"Doesn't it bring bad luck in your land to put bread down the wrong way up?" Maria was almost gleeful to have a fresh reason to be suspicious of him.

"No, no it doesn't. Forgive me."

"Don't worry, you couldn't know." She admitted grudgingly.

In that moment the first plates full of diced pieces of heart, lung, liver and kidney, all spiced and deep fried in fat, were laid down along the long table, alongside smaller bowls of apple and honey sauce. Everybody became suddenly too busy with their mouths to converse.

It was not until the curb had been taken off his hard-earned hunger that Tino piped up again.

"Welshman, you promised me a story about your land. Don't you remember? The red dragon?"

The mere suggestion of a story was enough to bring silence along most of the table. This was what the Welshman had been half dreading, half looking forward to. His hand went automatically to the stone snake under his tunic, feeling the smooth ridges of its scaled body.

"Yes of course." The Welshman smiled weakly at the expectant faces. "Y Ddraig Goch."

As the Welshman began his tale old Natalino, who was used to being his grandson's storyteller of choice, watched the foreigner darkly. Who was this foreigner, perhaps the same age as Natalino, but so handsome and young seeming, to take his place? However, he reminded himself that, according to Maria, the last time he had come to their home the Welshman had graciously refrained from ridiculing the idea that his head at times transformed into a wolf's. And besides, Natalino's storyteller's curiosity soon got the better of his jealousy.

"The land of Britain had been at peace for one hundred years after the revelation of our Lord Jesus was brought by the Saints, and the Red Dragon of the Britons slept happily in the knowledge that his people prospered. Then one day, in the time of the good Prince Llud, a terrible White Dragon came from the East while the people were feasting, and singing to their harps. It was a long, cruel fire serpent, and its spit was venom. It began to lay waste to the green hills and mountains, and the desperate cries of the people awakened the Red Dragon, who rose up from its cave dwelling to fight the invader and protect his people.

"The White Dragon was nearly as strong as the Red Dragon, and the two inflicted terrible wounds upon one another. They leapt and slithered to and fro over the rocks, which were now blackened and roasting-hot from their fire-breaths. Every time a cruel, curving claw dug into a neck, or a rump, or a leg, thick dark poisoned blood gushed out, and where it fell the grass withered and died, and never grew back again, and the beasts shrieked, and shrieked… A terrible sound!" Instinctively, the Welshman winced as though he was hearing that awful sound and it was physically painful. His audience winced with him, hearing and feeling everything through him. "Their shrieking was so awful, and blood-curdling, and carried so far, that women with child in the villages across the land went into labour, and their poor sons and daughters were born stiff and cold, struck dead by the dragon-shrieks."

A number of people shivered or shuddered, and the smaller children looked aghast. No one present was more surprised by those words, and their effect, than the Welshman himself. He had not known he was capable of such drama, though he was nearly sweating in the cold air with the effort.

Tino, who was more than a little frightened by the description of the fighting dragons, leaned surreptitiously across to his grandfather.

"*Nonno*, are there really dragons like that?"

Natalino paused, melting at the touch of his grandson's little hand on his forearm, and met the Welshman's gaze before he replied.

"Don't worry, Tino, the land of the *Gallesi* is very, very far away. I've never seen dragons *here*abouts."

This was the first time the Welshman had ever encountered the universal code of mutual support among storytellers, whereby the impossible was not vanquished from young children's minds too soon. He smiled warmly at the old man, and continued his tale.

"And so Llud went to his wise brother, Llefelys, and begged him 'brother mine, how can I protect my land from the devastation wrought by these duelling dragons?' and Llefelys told him what to do. Llud dug a wide, deep hole in the ground at the foot of the sacred hollow hill of Maes-y-Gaer near the sea of the Irish, and had his people fill it with the sweetest mead, for as all the world knows, when a dragon takes a deep draught of mead he cannot keep his eyes open, and falls into a long, slumbering sleep. Then he took his long horn from his belt, and blew three mighty blasts. The dragons both turned at the sound, and spread their bat-like wings and took their battling toward the sacred hill. At once they smelt the sweet mead, and fell to the banks of the mead-lake to drink. Soon they were deeply asleep, and Llud bound them up in cloth and buried them, still dozing, beneath Dinas Emrys." Now, without knowing why or how he was doing it, the Welshman allowed drowsiness to creep into his voice, which lowered and grew sluggish like the sleeping dragons.

"Then peace reigned once more in the land for many long years, until the Saxons came into Britain, and there was much slaughter of the good Britons. Finally the two sides laid down their arms for a time of truce, but they never loved one another nor trusted one another. Then a Saxon king came to power whose name was Vortigern, and he decided to build a castle at Dinas Emrys. As his masons worked to lay the foundations, they must have woken the dragons, and that very night when the workmen lay down to sleep there came from the site of the castle hideous sounds of stones cracking, grinding and crumbling…" The Welshman was startled to hear the way his own voice evoked the rending of the rocks. "The next day, the builders saw that what little they had built of the new walls had been razed to the ground. Busily they started work again, but once more that night their work was undone to the sound of cracking and grinding. Day after day the same thing happened, and King Vortigern was becoming furious. He called his astrologers to meet him, and asked them what he should do.

"They replied: 'Your Majesty, the stars reveal that among the Britons there is a boy who has no natural father.'" The Welshman now held his head high and proud, like a wise astrologer announcing his prophecies to a court " 'You must find him, and let his blood spill upon the bed-rock below the castle until his heart stops, and he is no more' the astrologer told him, and the good King quailed at such an awful remedy. But his knights and men-at-arms searched throughout the lands of the Britons for the boy, and finally they found him, and took him to Dinas Emrys.

" 'Child' King Vortigem told him 'I must sacrifice you to appease the spirits below this hill who destroy my masons work every night.' " Now the Welshman's voice carried the sadness of the King as he pronounced that sentence, and his eyes became compassionate. "But the child replied 'Spirits? There are no spirits beneath Dinas Emrys. Do not be foolish, my Lord King, for my blood on this rock would solve nothing. Here lie the ancient dragons who fought and were put to sleep in the time of Prince Llud, who was Lord of the Britons long ago, before your people came and brought slaughter to our land. The dragons must be freed from the hill, to finish their fight, or your castle will never be built!' " Somehow, as he spoke, the Welshman attained the youth and agility in his voice of that lively astute child.

"So great was the power of the boy's words that King Vortigem ordered his men to dig deep into the hillside, and soon the dragons were freed, and sprang up into the air to resume the terrible struggle they had begun so many years before. And again the roaring of their combat filled the air, and dragon-blood sprayed all about. But soon the Red Dragon showed his greater might, and struck a deadly blow to the White Dragon with his talons, and the invader fell to the ground, dead, and where he fell the grass never grew again." The Welshman's expression was now solemn and wise.

"Then the boy with no natural father turned to King Vortigem, and told him 'Behold, my Lord King, the Red Dragon is victorious. He is the protector of my people, the Britons, and the White Dragon is the spirit of the Saxon invaders. Remember this always, that we may appear to be beaten, and our swords may sleep for many years, but in the end we will always rise again victorious in our own lands!' And King Vortigem heeded the boy's words, and so it was that his people left the Britons in peace for a long time thereafter, and they were the Welsh, while Vortigem's own people carved out the Kindoms of the Saxons to the east. And the boy with no natural father was that same Merlin, the Wizard who came to the aid of King Arthur long ages afterwards."

As the story came to a close there was profound silence at the table, and it took a while for his listeners to shake themselves from the world of the tale. The Welshman's true gratification, however, was in Tino's wide, story-struck eyes. In them, dragons and knights and wizards could clearly be seen fighting, making chivalrous vows and uttering powerful spells. He immediately started repeating random moments of the story at a gabbling pace to his grandfather in their native tongue, as though the old veteran of the sea hadn't understood the tale in the Welshman's Occitan.

Soon, however, the sound of a panicked animal's hoarse cries interrupted his chatter, and the Welshman craned around to see what was happening. Lunch was clearly over and the family was getting back to work. Two men of the family were dragging another pig out of its pen, a thick hemp rope slipped over its snout and clamped between its jaws. Two other men got behind it, and pushed against its backside with their feet, forcing it in the direction of the granite slaughtering slab in the centre of the yard, where Don Rogerio was waiting with his knife in hand. As the pig reluctantly moved forward, spluttering and snorting in its struggles, it left a trail of faeces behind it in its fear. Once it was on the grey stone, more ropes were fixed about its hind legs, and six men held it firm. Don Rogerio stepped up without hesitating, and stuck the pig through the base of its fat neck.

Everything happened so quickly that the Welshman had barely realised he was witnessing the slaughtering. Then the pig began to shriek and writhe in agony, a shocking sound that pierced the blue sky and the dark woods. Old Natalino darted in, wooden bucket and stirring stick in hand, and as the crimson blood violently spurted out to the rhythm of the animal's wildly beating heart, he collected it and slowly stirred the thick, blackening liquid.

The awful, unearthly shrieking continued, while the pig broke into convulsive shudders that wracked its entire body, its trotters clattering futilely against the stone. The Welshman felt its pain and turned away, and saw Tino looking at him. Every year of his young life he'd witnessed the macabre spectacle many times over, and was not at all disturbed by it.

As soon as the pig had collapsed, buckets of steaming hot water were brought up and thrown over its flanks to loosen its black bristles so that the men could get to work scraping away with their knives, leaving the bare white skin visible. Some of the women collected the fallen bristles and started to wash them, ready to sell to the brush-maker.

"I imagine the cries of the two dragons fighting sounded something like that poor animal's shrieks." Said the Welshman, summoning a smile.

Tino's gaze was quizzical. "That was much worse than this." He assured the old man.

The Welshman was about to comment upon this scene to his companion, but stopped before formulating the first word. He looked at Tino, and thought of the boy's eyes while he had been listening to the story, and then thought of the grandchildren he might well have, but would never meet. Strangely, in that moment it didn't seem necessary to say anything to his companion.

Chapter 14

Avignon, October, 1337

Who is trying to kill whom? – Francesco Forzetti – flight through the river-gates

We became momentarily lost while returning to our inn from the meeting with Opicino. As we searched for a familiar landmark, we wandered the labyrinthine heart of the city, which was curiously melancholy now that the various craftsmen were packing away their stalls for the evening. Finally we passed the opening of an alleyway, and saw a familiar church tower at the far end. We both thought it was the church nearest our tavern, and decided to follow the alleyway toward it. As twilight with its queer shadows settled upon the city, we were dismayed to discover ourselves in a street rife with decay. The walls of the houses were cobbled together with crumbling mortar, and rusted rein-loops jutted out at random heights and angles, cluttering the line of sight all along the alley. The sewer down the centre of the street was foully clotted with dung, both human and animal, and half way along a poor family's hovel had half collapsed, the stolen timbers buckled by wind, rain and time.

We had just passed that wreck of human dignity when we noticed a young man ambling toward us in the opposite direction, his hood half drawn, his unfocused grey eyes lost in thought, a slight smile playing across his lips, and we realized that we knew him. We could not know, however, that we were being observed from behind our backs, and that the anxious hurry in our gait was being interpreted as murderous intent. Nor could we know that yet another person had entered that alley, his attention most definitely murderous, and focused on the youth walking toward us.

At our backs a now-familiar voice, cracking with desperation and fear, burst out "Miquel, run! They're killers!"

Behind our shoulders Wiligelmo was standing in the mouth of the alley. Ahead stood Miquel, his hood falling backwards from his face, his legs frozen in place by shock.

I don't remember which way my head was turning when I felt Master John throw himself forward from my side, and out of the corner of my eye I saw, in a patch of particularly impenetrable murk, a dark arm whip around like a sling-shot. There was someone else in the alley. A rapid flash of metal cut through the air toward Miquel.

Master John had no hope of reaching the young scribe and shoving him out of the path of the flung knife before it struck. Instead, his leap was intended to frighten. He raised his arms high, he contorted his face into a grimacing mask and growled like a trapped tiger. Miquel shrank back instinctively in fear, like a child before his mother's upraised, punishing hand. His startled movement took him a step back, out of the path of the flying weapon. It whistled passed his eyes, and the hilt thudded into decaying masonry on the far side of the alley.

Master John was now falling to the ground off balance, and the unknown knife thrower was running through the gloom, the alley suddenly too crowded for his liking. He took the path of least resistance, in the direction of the youngest, most innocuous seeming person there, Wiligelmo.

I only realized I was running when my foot squelched into the sewer in my second stride, but I didn't lose my balance. I had a formidable turn of speed, and the unknown assassin could not have suspected that I would pursue him, rather than dissolve into shock or run in the opposite direction. As I ran, I dimly heard bells start pealing in the distance.

"Wiligelmo, get aside!" I screamed, even as I closed on the back of the fleeing, would-be murderer who, now warned of my proximity, skipped left for two steps instead of running forward. I was forced to swerve in mid-stride, scrabbling over the street-grit, and nearly lost my balance.

"Wiligelmo, move!" I shouted again, but the killer had drawn another short knife, ready to slash the still motionless young sculptor from his path.

"Will, down!" I heard Master John's voice, and knew he'd regained his stance and was ready, in turn, to throw. I bent double still running, and heard my Master's knife slice through the air above my head. As I straightened I saw it embed itself in the right shoulder of that mysterious man who, in a short, compulsive twitch of breathless time, had both entered our lives and become our mortal enemy.

The man uttered no sound, but for an instant he twisted his head, his hood fell back and his bearded, dark, pain-wracked face was toward us, Master John's knife deep in his shoulder. He slowed for a fraction of a pounding heart's beat, but it was enough time for me to close the gap between us. But that terrible man was no novice to the game, and stretched one leg out behind him in a swift kick that struck me on the shin and checked me for an instant. With cat-like agility he swiped across at Wiligelmo, who was now finally starting to move out of the way, and I lunged toward the assassin's arm with both hands outstretched. I caught his sleeve with three fingers of my left hand, and dragged his knife arm down and away from my friend, but my grip wasn't good enough to hold on, and he wrenched himself free and away, out of the alley, and down the main street to the left, Master John's knife still in his shoulder.

I stood panting at the mouth of the alley, the air vibrating around me with the metallic cacophony of bells. Master John came up beside me, another knife in his palm that he hadn't been able to throw for fear of striking me. Behind him, Miquel was running up, confused but wary. In one hand he held the knife that had been thrown at him. Wiligelmo shrank backwards against the corner of a building, gibbering.

"Murderers... killers... knives"

"Wiligelmo..." I tried to reassure him, but he drew back.

"Killers!"

"No, Wiligelmo" Miquel interjected, speaking for the first time "they were protecting us. Didn't you see how the young man here stopped that other man from slicing at you with his knife?"

Wiligelmo closed his mouth abruptly, surprised, and stared at me. He was probably seeing every action that had been played out in the alley again in his mind from a different point of view.

"Protecting us?" His eyes nervously went from Master John's face to mine and back again "But Miquel, they killed Girard and Rotbert."

"What?" both Miquel and I exploded together. The scribe's fingers whitened as they clenched around the handle of the knife he was carrying.

"Girard and Rotbert… are dead?" Miquel continued.

"Girard… died…" Wiligelmo stuttered "he was found with a slit… a slit throat the afternoon these clerics arrived." He stopped, incredulously. "You are not clerics." He pointed at us with dreadful certainty.

"And Rotbert? I saw him this very afternoon!" Miquel couldn't bring himself to believe it.

"I know, you led these two… killers… to his scriptorium. And I gave them your sister's top to make you trust them." Wiligelmo's voice became wracked with guilt. "After they released me from work I went to see Rotbert. There were Papal guards everywhere… He was dead… a knife…" He was trembling, white faced, remembering the sight. "Now they must want to kill you!"

In the heat of the moment Miquel didn't see the absurdity of the situation as Wiligelmo described it, and raised the assassin's throwing-knife as though to protect himself, its tip skyward. It was clear he came from a well-to-do, pampered family, and had never so much as seen a street fight. The most useless place for a knife tip in a moment of danger is raised and pointing to the sky. I almost negligently reached across, twisted it from his grip, and stuck it in my belt. He snatched at his stinging hand.

Master John nodded, and spoke for the first time, putting his own knife away out of sight. The sound of bells was beginning to die away.

"You have both seen what we are capable of. I threw that knife into the other man's shoulder at twenty paces as he was running. My pupil just now disarmed you as though he was taking a toy from a new-born baby. If we wanted to kill you, we would have by now.

"I threw a knife at a man who threw a knife at you, Miquel, and Eilulf here stopped that same man from slitting your throat, Wiligelmo. Isn't that enough to show you that we're friends?"

Both Miquel and Wiligelmo began to register the truth in what my Master was saying.

"Now, you must believe me when I say that we never met your friend Girard, much less killed him, and when we left the scriptorium of Opicino de Canistris, Rotbert was alive and well."

"Then who killed them?" Miquel breathed.

At first, Master John did not reply, but gave the scribe a shrewd look. Then he began to speak slowly.

"Wiligelmo told us that he knows you because you three, Girard,

Rotbert and yourself, were once members of the household of Cardinal Luca Fieschi. I think I can be more precise than that. You were responsible for copying the papers of members of the Fieschi family in the clergy. Including – or am I wrong? – Manuele Fieschi."

Miquel stared hard.

"How do you know that, if you arrived in Avignon only yesterday?"

"I know more. You copied letters in triplicate, you three. And once you copied a letter with no addressee, but which spoke in the second person, and told the tale of a pilgrim's escape from prison in England and voyage through Ireland and Europe toward Lombardy. Is that true?"

By the vanishing light, it was clear that Miquel was honestly, transparently confused. He struggled with his own memory.

"I… I don't know. Maybe. Can you imagine how many thousands of papers we copied in triplicate? How could I remember one individual letter? That's impossible!"

"I know, I know. But there was always the risk you might remember it. That's why that man had to kill you. All three of you."

Both Miquel and Wiligelmo were looking at Master John in awe. I was as surprised by this revelation as they, but knew how to hide it. Master John began to speak sternly.

"A moment ago the curfew bells rang. If we're caught out and about we'll be put into the provost's prison. That may be the safest place for you, though, because not only did you copy that letter, but now you have seen the assassin's face. So have you, Wiligelmo. That man is a fearsome professional. Before a day has passed you will both be dead. Unless you accept our help, and give us yours."

"What help, Master Gerold?" Miquel, for want of a better title, still addressed us as clerics.

"We can help you through the city streets unobserved, to Wiligelmo's home. We will take your father and sister and go down to the river port, and go downstream to Arles where we will board galleys for Genoa. Wiligelmo, you said your father wanted to leave the city for the Riviera di Levante? Now is the right time. Put your faith in us, and you will live.

"Miquel, you have father, mother and siblings here?"

"Seven brothers and sisters in all."

"Then you must leave them here. I'm sorry, you have no choice. But perhaps, in time you will be able to return safely.

"Now, Wiligelmo, take us to your home."

After a long, helpless moment of indecision, Wiligelmo was swayed by the authority in Master John's expression, and led us away.

Wiligelmo, his father and his little sister lived together in a single room where the only luxury was a fireplace. The great bronze cooking pot, full of black cabbage, was simmering over low flames and exuding something one would have to be gracious to call a smell, not a stench. On the edge of the hearth a closed clay pot was warming. A little girl was fast asleep in her corner of the room, oblivious to the conversations around her that were transforming her life forever in hushed tones. Wiligelmo and Miquel were speaking quickly to the grizzled old master sculptor, Pietro, whose green eyes frequently flicked across at us and looked us up and down suspiciously. His long white beard was tucked into his belt, and his head was nearly bald, but his arms had the same look of silent strength as the roots of great oak trees, which can shape or split the bed rock with their patient work.

Master John and I, on the other side of the hearth, waited patiently for the man's decision, murmuring to one another in the Flemish.

"Master, who was that man in the alley?"

"I don't know for sure, but my instinct tells me it was Francesco Forzetti."

"He killed that Genoese boy in London just before we left, didn't he? The Spinola boy." I asked. Forzetti, a Lombard, was famous in our profession. Though he lacked some of our finesse, he compensated with utter ruthlessness and cunning.

"I know the boy you mean. Yes, I believe so. He must have left the country immediately. That would have given him time to be in Avignon before us, or around the same time."

"And the letter you described to Miquel? How did you know about it?"

"It was one of the documents Aldcliffe brought with him to Norwich that evening. There were two sheets of parchment, do you remember? One had Bury's warrant in Bury's hand, committing us to the Earl of Lancaster's service, and underneath, in Lancaster's hand, were the Earl's orders to us. The other sheet contained a copy of the letter. I burnt both sheets."

I recalled the event with a smile.

"It is only an educated guess of mine," he continued "but the letter is the best explanation for why the scribes had to be killed. They were never meant to copy it. Manuele Fieschi must have made two copies, one to be delivered to England and the other for his own keeping. He must have been careless with his copy, and it was caught up by mistake with other, official papers. Then the bureaucratic machine got to work, and it was automatically copied in the scriptorium in triplicate and filed away. The scribes are innocent victims of being conscientious workers."

"You said the letter described the journey of a pilgrim. The Welsh pilgrim we mentioned in code to Bateman?"

Master John hesitated before answering. "Lancaster's orders were… very concise. I was told to consult with Bateman about a Welsh pilgrim, and I was given Manuele Fieschi's letter to read, which speaks of a pilgrim."

Just then, Wiligelmo's father broke into a painfully hoarse cough. Thumping his chest, he rose to his feet. Stiff and slow but erect, he took a ladle and went to the pot that was perched on the hot stone a few palms from the fire. His work-hardened old hands clearly didn't feel the heat of the clay as he lifted the lid, and the sweet scent of the season's first cider filled the room. The old man inhaled the rising vapours to calm his breathing for a short while, then offered a ladle-full of the golden liquid to Miquel.

"Have some, boy, my bread is your bread, my drink is your drink."

Miquel thankfully emptied the ladle. Next, Pietro offered the cider to Master John.

"Master Gerold of Ghent, or whoever you are, my bread is your bread, my drink your drink."

My Master willingly took a long draught.

"Many thanks."

While he served me in turn, Wiligelmo's grizzled old sire spoke roughly.

"I understand that I must thank you for saving my son's life this evening. Though I'm sure you endangered it for him first." His proud eyes were challenging. "If everything I'm told is true, Wiligelmo's life is forfeit unless he escapes, and young Miquel's, too. I'm told you will pay our way on a galley to Genoa, is that true?"

"I want to set sail from Arles with a mid-morning ship tomorrow." Master John confirmed. I let the warm sweetness of the cider trickle slowly over my tongue as I watched old Pietro's reactions. "The man who attacked Miquel and Wiligelmo this evening now knows there are two others, equal to him in skill, somehow involved in the same business as he. This will worry him, and he will no doubt come back with more men, to eliminate both us and the boys he failed to kill.

"Arles is a day's hard walk away." Pietro's face was expressionless, and his tone was of comment more than objection.

"For us, it is a hard night's walk away. As soon as you have agreed to come with us, we'll leave." Master John was calm.

"Under curfew?"

"We'll leave in the time honoured way: bribing a fisherman to take us out in hiding, and giving him coin with which to bribe the city watch."

Pietro nodded with such understanding that I felt sure he had already left a city that way, perhaps even more than once.

"Master Gerold, when men like you enter one's life, one either does as they say, or one dies. You will kill us if we don't come, won't you?"

"It won't be necessary to make that decision." Master John replied levelly. I could tell from the set of his shoulders that he liked this straight-speaking artisan.

"No. It won't." Was there the hint of a smile beneath those whiskers? Perhaps the liking was mutual. "What can we bring with us?" And we knew he had capitulated.

"Nothing, just the clothes you're wearing and one or two of your finest tools. I can replace the ones you leave behind when we reach Genoa. We *must* be on a ship leaving Arles by mid-morning tomorrow, and it has already been dark for some time."

"Very well." said Pietro matter-of-factly. Once again I had the distinct impression that it was not the first time he had left everything behind and moved on in the greatest haste. He was a Lombard, after all, and his land was ever the hunting ground for looting armies from north of the Alps in search of fat spoils.

"I'll waken my daughter." The old sculptor grunted.

The canals of Avignon leading down to the river-gates in the city walls were lined with stone, unlike many places where such canal banks are nothing more than mud. The stones in turn were lined with filth, for the good citizens often disobeyed the laws and tipped both their human and their animal muck into the canals when no-one was looking. As I looked out through a gap between the tarpaulin and the rim of the fisher-boat I saw the gunk floating on the surface of the water. There must have been an awful stench out there, but it didn't reach my nostrils. It was masked by the even more pungent smell of eels in the little boat.

We were all lying down in the damp hull of an eel-fisher's long boat, hidden by a greased tarpaulin, Master John, Miquel, Wiligelmo and his family and I. Actually, there were no eels in the boat yet. The fisherman perched on the stern, punting us along, was on his way out for a fresh catch, but the slime and odour of his past victims constituted an overpowering presence.

Periodically, Pietro was forced to hush his little daughter, who wrinkled her nose and would have complained bitterly about the situation. Her father in turn had to smother his own frequent bouts of coughing.

An approaching gleam caught my eye.

"Torch light." I said in a low voice.

"We're nearly at the canal-gate." Master John replied. "Alehandra!" he took Wiligelmo's little sister by the hand. She regarded him with wide eyes. "If you are a brave girl, and stay silent now till your father tells you to speak again, I shall kneel and kiss your hand again, and Eilulf here will sing you a song of chivalry."

The girl was half excited, half terrified. She pressed her mouth to her father's ear and said something in a tiny voice. The old man related with a tender smile.

"Alehandra wants to be sure you won't forget the word given. You'll truly give her a song and a kneeling kiss?"

We both solemnly swore. She smiled with delight, and said in a more audible voice.

"I'll be silent. Look!" and the little girl pressed her lips together tightly, her eyes wide with earnestness.

A few moments later there came a hollow thud as the fisherman lifted the tip of his punt from the water and set it against the wooden boardwalk to halt our progress and announce himself to the watchman.

"Gilbé," we heard a new voice hail Gilbert, our trafficker "how is the little girl?"

"Still a-bed" the fisherman's accent was so thick as to be almost unintelligible "and the fever's not abated."

"I'm sorry. Have you coin for medicine, or at least broth?"

"I do, Roger, thanks to this night's work."

There was a pause. No fisherman could ever know if the night's catch was good before he caught it. He must be sure of his coin for some other reason. The watchman said in a coy, understanding voice "Then you and I are both content, Gilbè, and I've already inspected your boat and found nothing amiss."

There was the unmistakable clink of coins being dropped into an open palm. Some of the very same coins we'd received for our promissory notes in the money market of Sluys.

"No, no, keep this last one, there." Came the watchman's voice. "Tell your old woman 'twas I got a second cut of pork for the lass. She's a good girl, is your daughter."

As we felt the boat push away from and resume its progress we heard Gilbert call out "God bless those bulky britches o' yours, and strike the fleas dead from about your balls, Roger!"

Soon we felt the tug of a real current on the boat, and it swung about into the open river. Shortly afterwards the fisherman threw back the tarpaulin, and we all sucked in heady breaths of fresh, untainted air. The quarter moon, low over the tops of the trees on the river banks, was nothing but an outline of silver behind a cold grey curtain of cloud. Gilbert signalled to us to be silent. Here and there over the water the lanterns of other boats were visible intermittently, as other fishermen sought to draw a catch into their nets. After a while he turned the boat into the mouth of a narrow tributary, and heaved us upstream against the current.

When Gilbert the eel-catcher set us ashore far up the rivulet, near a ford where the footing was firm, we each thanked him effusively. His replies were curt but courteous, and his expression was inscrutable. As we started away on our forced march through the woods and fields toward Arles, I felt he must be asking his heart whether coin and pork-broth would really suffice to make his daughter well again.

As soon as the poor fisherman had pushed his boat out into the current again, Master John knelt theatrically in front of Alehandra, whose eyes shone in the darkness with pleasure as he decorously kissed her outstretched hand. Then we set off at a brisk pace, and I commenced to sing the deeds of Willame d'Orange. Alehandra fell into step beside me, her head eagerly cocked to listen. It was going to be a long, unpleasant march, but song could make it a little more bearable for all of us.

Chapter 15

London, November, 1337

Two birds with one stone – at the Sign of The Laughing Earl – Ubaldo de Fénis' first secret

If he hadn't been so distracted riding through the crowded London street, William de Montague might have recognized the minstrel immediately. But he was exceedingly distracted, and passed by the upturned, grinning face without a second thought. He caught just a hint of irony in that smile as their eyes met, but let it pass. He was not the man to publicly challenge commoners for insolence and have them arbitrarily whipped. Such excesses were, by his own recommendation to the King, a thing of the past: a thing of the King's father's reign, and that of the traitor Mortimer.

The smile and the dark eyes slowly filtered through his worried thoughts as he rode forward, until he abruptly reigned in his horse and swivelled in the saddle to look backwards. The minstrel had disappeared. Not even the tall neck of his sheathed citole was visible anymore among the crowds of bobbing hats and ambling pack mules.

Montague laughed silently to himself. It had been Henry de Grosmont. Had he not said he would test Montague's ability to recognise him anywhere? The Earl of Salisbury had nearly failed the test.

Even a great lord, particularly a great lord, could become invisible simply by assuming the clothes of a common man. All he need do was keep away from the eyes of his powerful peers, who saw him regularly in the flesh, and he would be unrecognizable to the masses. Often this little game was played for the most mundane motives. Some wished to play dice without their vice becoming known to political enemies, whilst others were on the prowl for prostitutes. It was much rarer, but did occur, that a great lord wished to confess his sins to an honest village priest in complete anonymity.

On either side of him, Montagu's squires looked puzzled.

"My Lord?"

"Nothing. Forward, I'm late."

The crowd parted respectfully before him, his livery known in all the land, and he had nearly arrived at his destination when he was struck by a thought. Grosmont's little game might have provided him with the solution to not one, but two problems.

It was perhaps the same hour the next day when William de Montague started putting on the unfamiliar clothes of a moderately wealthy townsman, fumbling without the aid of a squire. There, in the private antechamber of his London residence, he felt like a novice, great lord though he was.

Henry de Grosmont was by his side. The younger earl was clearly far more accustomed to dressing by himself. He was already cocking his bright green minstrel's cap, with its garish peacock feather.

"How many times have you already done this?" Montague enquired.

"Dozens. I love the life of a minstrel so much, that perhaps I should have been born one."

"And was it you" Montague decided to test his theory "who composed that song about the broken hearted minstrel, rejected by a string of young ladies who are all in love with the Earl of Lancaster?"

Grosmont grinned.

"I may have done. And I may have accidentally sung it within earshot of some genuine minstrels, too, so it just happened to get around."

"Don't be offended, but I'm sick of hearing it."

De Grosmont laughed lightly. "Then I'll compose another one, so they change their tune."

"If you're ready, can you help me with these sleeves?" Montague, whose sleeve laces had just slipped from his fingers a third time, decided to swallow his pride and ask for assistance. "How the Devil do you tie them on single handed?"

"Big brother, big brother," Grosmont chuckled as he deftly knotted first one sleeve to a shoulder, and then the second "you're a babe in arms without your squires." He swiftly drew the offending laces tight and made a deft knot. "There, done. If you get into the habit of masquerading as a commoner, you'll soon learn the trick." He looked Montague up and taking, taking in the effect of the earl in his merchant's costume. "I was right to insist that you dress like a man of moderate wealth, and I as your minstrel. You'd never manage to cut the figure of a lowly servant."

"Henry, I'm only doing this because it might prove to be for Edward's good. I have no intention of making a habit of such games." Montague replied drily. "Now let's go before I change my mind."

With the help of Montague's steward, sworn to secrecy, the two slipped out through a servants' door into a side alley. Grosmont was immediately off at a bound over the packed earth.

"There's a high street down there. Come, we look ridiculous in these alleys."

On the main streets they mingled so well that the crowds pressed in around them, and Montague felt almost overwhelmed. He was not used to being on foot in the teeming city streets. He had always passed through on a powerful, armoured war-horse, with mounted and armed squires on either side. He'd never needed to worry about his personal space. Now, other men, and even *women*, brushed right against him as they jostled past, and barely even looked at him. Grosmont seemed to actually enjoy being at such close quarters with the multitudes.

"Those are two fine chooks, lass!" he glibly exclaimed in very convincing English to a young woman. She'd bumped into them while hurrying along with a basket of vegetables on one hip and two beheaded fowl hanging from the other. "If you need help eating them, I'll be along in a trice."

"If your woman's not feeding you enough, man" she snapped back at him lustily, striding away "it means she's found someone else to feed, cuckold!"

Grosmont broke into a delighted grin. Montagu shook his head.

"Henry, only you could actually *like* being told certain things."

"Like it? I love it. It's exhilarating. Liberating." Abruptly he paused, and pointed at a roll of gloriously violet silk at a clothier's stall. "Look at that cloth, William, isn't it lovely?" He called out to the owner. "How much to the yard, sir?"

"Four shillings and tuppence to the yard. But it's not the best by far. If you come here I'll show you and your master the finest cloth I have." He gave Montague a moderately respectful nod.

"I'm afraid we haven't the time, sir." Grosmont replied, never slowing his pace. "We're awaited."

The clothier wasn't one to give up easily.

"Then let your master's butler come to find me when there is time."

"God willing, he shall." Henry was calling back when his brisk eyes seized upon another bright stall, a few yards further along the street.

"Oh, oh, just look at that hair!" He said in a crowing whisper. "Hah! Won't they pay for it if the inspectors come. You see, the cornettes they're selling over there have braids of real hair, I swear it."

"Is that a problem?" asked Montague, eying the suspect hairpieces as they passed the stall.

"The Archbishop has decreed that all women's hairpieces be made with flax braids, to make it obvious they're false. Otherwise it would be immoral deception."

"The message hasn't yet spread at court." Montague shook his head. "The older ladies are all sporting cornettes made with the tresses of golden-haired lasses these days."

Grosmont snorted. "Not even the Archbishop would ever dream that the ladies at court might stifle their fashion to obey his decrees." His eyes now widened at the sight of yet another stall. "William, have you ever seen such fine ribbon work?"

"Never. Nor will I see it now." Montague decided enough was enough. He gripped his young friend by the arm, and quickened his pace. "We have a meeting at the Sign of the Laughing Earl, and I won't be late for the sake of baubles and ribbons. Concentrate on the business at hand, Henry."

Niccolò Fieschi kept his dark, impervious eyes fixed on his companion's face as they spoke intensely at a bench in a corner of the inn. Though the unknown man he was conversing with often gesticulated and clearly raised his voice from time to time, the cool-headed Genoese merchant-prince gave no sign of excitement. From time to time he acknowledged the other man's words with the slightest of nods.

Montague and Grosmont were seated among the crowded benches on the far side of the bar, unnoticed across the thronging tavern, observing their opponent and his mysterious interlocutor. In spite of himself, William de Montague was struggling to keep his gaze focused on Fieschi. Whilst he had seen the streets of London many times before, albeit from the great height of his warhorse, this was his first visit to a common man's drinking den, and many things distracted him.

As the maid brought two cups of ale to a nearby bench, Montague's eyes couldn't help wandering briefly to her exposed cleavage. As she strode away, the tight sash about her waist made the outline of her swinging hips temptingly visible.

"Clearly a prostitute, that wench." Montague whispered to his friend disapprovingly.

"Of course not. She's just a maid. Her cleavage is part of the warm welcome you get here. If she were a prostitute she wouldn't be…"

"Look," Montague interrupted him, nodding toward the far corner of the tavern, "Fieschi's about to speak."

Fieschi had raised one hand for silence, and the other man had abruptly closed his mouth. Fieschi took a leisurely sip of wine from his pewter cup – had he brought it with him, or had the tavern-keeper known to treat him singularly? – and patted his lips with his napkin before speaking. His words then came slowly and calmly. His expression, though, remained as inscrutable as a bust sculpted by an artist whose touch and technique were perfect, but who knew nothing of conveying emotion in marble.

"I wish your would-be protégé would arrive." Montague murmured to Grosmont. "He could listen to their conversation, and then report it to us if we're clever enough to win him to our cause. I have no idea who the other man is, but whatever they're saying might be of interest."

At that moment, a boisterous group of men in muddied clothes came in from the street and burst into a rough group-song in the English. The tallest among them was holding aloft an inflated and cured pig bladder in one hand, and a coloured banner in the other. Everyone else present immediately erupted into cheers, and there was much back slapping and clinking of ale-cups. Montague barely understood a word in the tumult, though he prided himself on understanding the English of London fairly well. Suddenly, the tall man with the bloated pig's bladder leapt up onto a bench, and started tying it to one of the rafters. His mates then passed up some of the coloured banners, which were then draped over the skin.

"What *is* that thing?" He nudged Grosmont amid the hubbub.

"William, how can you not know? It's a football."

"Ah, I see." Even among the high nobility it was known that the sport wrought havoc in the back streets, and whole districts were sometimes wrecked by the violent mobs of players from opposing city blocks as they kicked, punched, bit and sometimes slashed their way to victory.

"Of course," Grosmont added "it's been banned."

"Like using real hair to make cornettes." Montague observed.

"Indeed. The common man can no more bear city-life without football than a duchess can bear court-life without a pair of flowing golden tresses. And then, given that many of the keenest players are watchmen, how can it ever be banned?"

"Watchmen, eh? That's good to know." He frowned. "And so, after the match the ball becomes a trophy for the victors."

"And hung up in their local alehouse until it's won by another block." Grosmont confirmed.

As the mob of excited footballers settled into their pints, the back corner of the inn became visible once more, and both earls were startled. A third man had joined the conversation. Montague sighed with relief.

"He's finally come. And in time to meet that other fellow, so now we'll discover who he is."

"Yes, that's my man." Grosmont agreed. "Ubaldo de Fénis."

Ubaldo greeted both Fieschi and the stranger, and the conversation resumed. After a short time, the unknown man rose and took his leave of Fieschi and Ubaldo, who continued to speak for a short while. At length, Fieschi also took his leave of Ubaldo, and strode from the inn, being careful not to brush his finery against any of the Englishmen, all merry on a potent concoction of sporting victory and mellow ale.

Ubaldo remained at his bench with his unfinished wine and a troubled expression. Soon, a prosperous-looking merchant with his minstrel, who wore a bright feathered cap, approached him.

"Ubaldo de Fénis? St Elaeth's blessing on you, sir." In the Occitan, Montague invoked the English saint whose mass was being sung that day.

"I am, gentlemen." Ubaldo replied in the same language. "But I do not have the pleasure of knowing you. Will you join me?" He was happy just to have some company that spoke the same language as he.

"With pleasure." They sat. "It is true, you have never met me. But my young friend here is a different matter. Look at him closely."

Ubaldo, surprised and mystified, looked long and hard at the minstrel without understanding. When the jaunty musician removed his cap, however, the young knight gasped, and half rose from the table, spilling his wine.

"No, no, sit down, and be calm." Montague told him quickly. "We have come to speak with you... without our meeting becoming common knowledge at court. Act as though we were what our dress implies."

"My Lo... Good sirs, you cannot know how joy suffuses me in renewing our bond." Like many noblemen whose court-tongue was the Occitan, he tended to speak in poetry. "My defeat at your hands" he looked at Grosmont "was a higher honour than a thousand victories against lesser opponents."

While Grosmont basked in the worshipful tone Montague started on the business at hand. "Sir Knight, we came as soon as we could when we discovered you were lodging here."

At once Ubaldo glanced around him at the inn and its customers, then embarrassed by his London residence.

"Though my rank is far beneath yours, I assure you I am of the noble blood, and far from accustomed to living in... such places."

Montague's expression was now suave, by contrast to the dark intensity that had dominated his face while Fieschi had been at the inn. "I am perplexed" his soothing words were calculated to rile "that a man of such wealth as Niccolò Fieschi cannot situate his champion, who is truly one of the great combatants of our time, in more salubrious apartments."

"Situate? Niccolò Fieschi?" came the bitter reply "That shipbanker has not 'situated' his champion at all. London is an expensive town, and he prefers to hoard coin, not spend it. I have been forced to situate myself, and as my county can spare little for a younger son... here I am."

"But why did you come so far from home for that man? I presume Fénis is a county of Provence?"

"No, I am a vassal of the Savoy. Fénis is near Aosta, high in the Alps. I came because I had been told that my grandmother's kin were generous, and that Niccolò required a champion whose noble birth enabled him to fight in a royal tournament here. My grandmother

Beatrice was the daughter of the House of Fieschi, and a grand lady. It was in her honour that I came to fight in the tournament."

Grosmont nodded. "In that case, your grandmother was one of the purest ladies in all Christendom, for her honour in your heart lent your lance and sword fearsome weight in the tournament. I confess, my own heart quailed at every blow, though I sought not to let it show. And yet, honour is an intangible weight, and as I lifted you from the lake in my arms you were as light as goose-down."

Montague groaned inwardly, and leaned forward impatiently, knowing that Grosmont was soon liable to start composing an epic if this lyrical mood continued.

"It seems to me, Ubaldo" he said levelly "that you owe your honour to your father, your life to Henry, and nothing at all to Niccolò Fieschi."

Ubaldo, who had been ready to launch into a flowery reply, hesitated. The hard-talking Englishman had brought him roughly back to Earth from the clouds of chivalry.

"Fieschi is my grandmother's kin." He replied, but the tone was uncertain. He was clearly attracted to Grosmont's glamour, charisma, and above all the sense of high honour that he exuded. Montague sensed this, and continued.

"A knight like you has more kinship with a man of honour than with a money-lender. Just think: the Genoese measure the Good Lord's time, and sell it, calling it 'interest'. They weigh up Fortune's caprices, and trade in them, calling it 'insurance'. One day they will try to measure honour, sell that too, and who knows what vile name they'll call it by. But you and I know that honour cannot be sold. It is an inseparable part of a man, and all men of honour are a brotherhood. We, Ubaldo, are brothers therefore!" He reached forward to firmly clasp the knight's forearm. "Niccolò Fieschi, who slices up God's time for sale like a butcher at a marketplace, has nothing in common with you. Besides" he lowered his voice "the man's awful character denotes him as a bastard. You may well have no tie of blood at all."

Ubaldo's eyes widened, and something deep within him relaxed. This last comment had given him the excuse he needed to finally deny any duty to Niccolò Fieschi.

"By the blood of the Martyrs, you're right!"

"My brother!" Grosmont, too, rejoiced in Montague's eloquent argument. "Let's drink to our kinship." He flagged down the maid.

At first she addressed them with a tired voice. "Yes?" Then she noticed that one of the newcomers, the tall minstrel, was a very handsome man indeed. She straightened her shoulders. "How can I serve, good sirs?" Her eyes dwelled slightly upon the ripples beneath Grosmont's tight hose.

"Lass," the minstrel told her in the English "this gentleman is from a foreign land, and all his life has drunk nothing but wine. Bring us all a cup of your best ale. Let our guest taste England's finest."

When the maid had gone to fetch their drinks, casting appreciative glances back over her shoulder at Grosmont, Montague decided to press home their advantage.

"Sir Ubaldo, you would surely be dead now had Henry not rescued you from the lake. That makes you brothers twice over, once in honour, and once in battle. Now, we find ourselves in difficulty. We are seeking to defend the honour of our King and our country, and perhaps you can help us."

"I know, I know." Fénis nodded immediately. Had Montague been less astute, he would have let his mouth hang open with surprise. *How* could he already know? The young champion continued.

"I'm sure that the Englishman who was speaking with Fieschi just now is the cause of your problems. He is nothing but a miserable scoundrel, a cheat, and a traitor to his nation."

"Indeed, it was about him that I wished to speak." Montague swiftly recovered. "What do you know of that vile creature?" He was hoping that the stranger's name would arise before his own ignorance was unmasked.

"What do I know about Henry Tideswell?" Montague was inwardly relieved. "Not a lot, but I assure you I have no qualms in telling you, for the man is a traitor to his own King and it's no business of mine to protect him. He is a wool merchant who smuggled wool against the blockade a month or so ago, but the wool soon burnt to ashes in an accident at Sluys."

"Exactly." Montague's tone implied he had known that from the start. "Now, what we need to know is why Fieschi has taken an interest in the man. Was it Fieschi who urged him to smuggle the wool in the first place?"

"No, I think that was his own idea, originally. If I understood well, the rivals of the Fieschis in Genoa, the House of Doria, lost a lot of money because of Tideswell, because of prices rising and falling, I believe. It was a very complicated explanation. In any case, Niccolò was pleased. Now it seems the Doria family and their allies in Genoa have issued a warrant for Tideswell's arrest. Niccolò Fieschi was offering him protection in exchange for favours."

The two earls exchanged a long, meaningful look as the maid, carrying their ale cups, interrupted the conversation. They had come for information about Fieschi's relationship with the King, not Genoese power games with corrupt English merchants. And yet, the desired effect had been achieved. Fénis had passed on his first secret, justifying it to himself by the fact that he was exposing a common scoundrel. Now he'd had his first taste of it, passing them secrets could become a habit.

The seductively playful maid returned with their ale-cups. "The inn's best ale, Sirs." She lingeringly placed the fullest cup in front of Grosmont. "We bitter it with yarrow, juniper and ground ivy, sir." She hovered over him, waiting for him to taste it.

Grosmont took a savouring draught.

"Ah, that's the best I've drunk in a long time." He complemented her, his brown eyes rising to hers. They exchanged a lingering glance.

Ubaldo de Fénis hesitantly brought the cup beneath his nose. As he delicately inhaled the bouquet his eyes widened slightly in alarm, but he put a fine face on it.

"Hmmm…" he forced himself to sound appreciative, not wanting to offend. "What a… complex… bouquet." Once more he inhaled. "Are there, perhaps, faint over-hues of… perhaps… of quinces?" The maid, who spoke no Occitan, blankly observed this strange behaviour, far more interested in casually laying a hand on the back of Grosmont's chair. Ubaldo took a small sip of the brown liquid, dutifully swirling it over his tongue. Despite his best efforts, his mouth twisted into a grimace of disgust, and he was so shocked that he lost his chivalrous veneer for a moment.

"Is it not horse-piss?" The maid fortunately did not understand.

"Ale is not wine, to be sipped slowly." Grosmont told him. "You must drink it in long gulps if you want to appreciate it." He demonstrated by draining half his cup in one draught.

The young knight was very dubious.

"Sir Ubaldo" Grosmont insisted "we two are brothers. Trust me." He caught the maid's hand and squeezed it. "Another round, if you will." He ordered in the English, then turned back to Ubaldo.

"Believe me, by the time you've had a few pints you will love it."

Ubaldo brought his cup to his lips a little stiffly, but obediently took a long drink. He didn't seem much more enthusiastic then he had after his first sip.

Montague pressed on, impatiently.

"Sir Ubaldo, you told us that Henry Tideswell has placed himself under Fieschi's protection. That means the two will do business in future, and given Tideswell's talent for smuggling, I've no doubt his future actions will be harmful to the King and to England. A thought has occurred to me." He thoughtfully swirled the ale in his cup. He had barely drunk from it at all. "It occurs to me that we might be able to help one another, and kill three pigeons with one stone. If you were to discover when, and where, Tideswell is to set sail with illicit cargo, we could arrange to have him caught red-handed. It would then be a simple matter to grind a confession from him, and have him admit to working on Fieschi's behalf."

Grosmont was nodding approvingly, but Ubaldo had suddenly become pale at the prospect.

"Then what would befall *me*?" He nervously drained his cup with two draughts worthy of an Englishman.

"We would discreetly inform the King where his gratitude should lie." Montague reassured him. "And with Fieschi publicly decried for treachery, you would be free to renounce your ancestral bonds with him while maintaining your own honour. Actually" Montague almost smiled at his own cleverness "you would be obliged by honour to sever your bonds with him. You would be free of the man."

As the maid placed three more over-flowing cups on the table, allowing herself to brush lightly against Grosmont's shoulder, Ubaldo de Fénis started to look decidedly agitated.

"But Niccolò Fieschi will know that it was I who led you to Tideswell…" He trailed off, and grimly seized his second cup. "The Fieschi's have men in their employ… fearful men… They settle their debts with blood." He took great gulps of ale like a drowning man taking gulps of air.

"Fieschi will never know. We will make it seem like a routine inspection that just happened to find its mark."

"And what do you stand to gain, my lords?" Ubaldo asked, with an uncharacteristically penetrating look, his ale-cup frozen just in front of his lips.

"Tideswell and Fieschi's guilt bared before the King." Montague answered truthfully. "The first is a traitor, and the second is too deeply in his Majesty's trust without merit. If we can open our King's eyes to this betrayal, it will be a gift to him and to our land. And to ourselves."

Ubaldo de Fénis nodded. "Very well. I will find a way to obtain the information you require. But you must be patient, he is unlikely to sail again before the spring sun calms the waves."

"In the meantime" Montague encouraged him "you will watch, and listen."

After a long pause, Ubaldo seemed to come to a decision.

"Very well. I will do it." He drank deeply again, and looked at his cup in surprise. "You were right, brother." He turned back to Grosmont with a smile. "I'm starting to like this… ale."

Many cups later, they were forced to haul the merry knight up to his lodgings with the help of the maid. There were only two rooms: a modest parlour, with barely any furnishing, and bed chamber with a straw mattress stretched over two broad, low trunks. Soon Ubaldo was snoring his way through a misty ale-sleep, and Grosmont, Montague and the maid quietly slipped the curtain over the doorway.

"But where is the Knight's armour, and where are his harnesses?" Montague asked, mystified by the lack of possessions.

"I've heard the tavern keeper say that he often complains." the maid told him "He says his patron keeps everything locked away in his own lodgings. He doesn't really get on with that man." She was clearly referring to Fieschi.

Grosmont slipped her some coin. "Lass, this is for your kind service."

"Many thanks. I'll spend this in Soaper's Lane, on a jar of walnut dye. Tomorrow at vespers." She looked into Grosmont's eyes as she spoke, her pupils wide and alluring. Montague briefly and wistfully wondered why attractive young women never spontaneously said where they were going to be at vespers looking into *his* eyes that way.

When the maid was gone, Grosmont exalted with Montague.

"Big brother, this is better than I dared hope for! We came seeking information, and we now have the makings of a trap. If we can catch Tideswell red-handed, and extract a confession from him that he is working for Fieschi now, we can completely discredit Fieschi with the rest of the Council, and have him expelled."

"True, true." Montague decided the time had finally come to dig into his young friend's secret plans, now his tongue was loosened by ale and excitement. "So you're not concerned that the assassination Ulgham is to perform will jeopardize the trap?"

"That's still months away." As Montague had hoped, the young Earl of Lancaster let his caution slide for a moment. "Oh… Damn!" He looked at the older man with dismay.

"Who, little brother," Montague spoke slowly, deliberately "is Ulgham going to kill?"

Grosmont opened his mouth to say one thing, but changed his mind. He took a deep breath, then broke into a roguish grin. "Richard de Bury put you up to this, didn't he?"

"Richard and I," Montague was aware that he sounded like a scolding father saying 'your mother and I' "both feel it's in England's best interests that we know exactly what you sent Ulgham to do. Whoever he has been sent to strike at, it may be that the King has laid plans that will be thwarted as a result. Bury informed me that Ulgham is no information gatherer, as you tried to make me believe the day of the hunt. I know he's a man of action, so you might as well tell me what action he has been sent to carry out."

Grosmont remained silent for long while before answering, his eyes closely examining a set of possibilities and choices that only he could see.

"I'm sorry, William," he said finally "I'm not going to tell you."

"It's pointless not telling us. We already suspect too much. Suspicions and half theories may be dangerous. It's better if you tell us everything now, so we can all three act together, and avoid clumsy mistakes. It's for the King's sake that I ask you, Henry."

"I'm sorry," Grosmont's ale-clouded eyes became almost entreating "but it *is* necessary, please believe me. One day, perhaps in a year's time, I'll be able to tell you. For now, please, trust and wait."

Reluctantly, Montague realized that he was not going to get any more information from his friend.

"Very well, I trust you. I hope you will eventually repay my trust."

Chapter 16

Genova, Palazzo Spinola, March 1338

Focaccia and passito aboard ship — the cell where a million lies were told – gaol-breaking after the manner of an English traitor

On our graceful Genoese galley, time seemed to glide slowly by. Before, during our flight to Arles, the moments had seemed to scurry along like our own feet, hurried forward by the fear of pursuit. Once aboard, however, the moments trickled gently by like the Genoese passito wine as it is poured into one's cup. Day after day we were offered a measure of that dark golden liquid with slices of twice-baked bread, while the marshes, cliffs, fishing villages and beaches of the Occitan disappeared one by one astern like the fading recollections of a pleasant dream when a busy morning drives it from mind.

I came to the end of the page and sighed. "Wiligelmo, here is yet another unsuspected talent of yours. Your prose is so sweet and lilting, it is almost poetry. That's what comes of growing up in the land of the Troubadours, where the air itself is lyrical. How I envy you that! And now… such a shame."

Wiligelmo stopped scraping the page he was working on and looked up. "Thank you, but I'm sure my prose is very poor. At least, father thinks so."

I smiled, and set my knife blade to the parchment. With just the right pressure to strip the ink from the page without damaging the hide, I started scraping the page clean.

"Even great poets scrape their parchment clean again and again for their drafts. Only abbeys can afford to keep permanent codices. If your father thought badly of your prose, he wouldn't have given you the parchment in the first place."

Wiligelmo looked unconvinced, so I cast about among the pages spread out on the bench in front of us until I found a particularly appealing passage.

"Here, listen to this. Isn't it nearly poetry? *'For ten days Marseilles was our home, as one storm followed another, driving the sea to a frenzy, and launching was impossible. Then finally came a night of serene luminosity, with a cold but light wind which swept the mist and clouds from the air until the stars shone through. The morning brought us a radiant sun, whose light rolled down the coast toward the sea whilst, from the East, the scent of oregano, fennel and myrtle wafted across the harbour on the breeze.'* There, a few retouches here and there and it could be song."

"Thanks, Eilulf, I'm glad you like it."

But Wiligelmo was scarcely comforted by my words, and heaved a sigh as he went back to erasing. At that moment we heard the sound of wood against tiles, and Miquel's sister's colourful little top span past the door of the room. It was Alehandra's top now. Miquel had left it to Wiligelmo's little sister when he had left us in the port of Toulon, where distant relatives of his had offered him hospitality.

"Aleh," Wiligelmo reprimanded as Alehandra darted down the corridor and scooped up her toy in a flurry of blonde hair. "you're not allowed to play in the corridors, I told you."

Always game for a squabble, his little sister ran into the room, her eyes defiant.

"Why should I care what you told me? If father tells me, that's different." She lifted her nose imperiously, having put her big brother in his place.

"Father doesn't have time to waste on instructing tiresome little girls." Wiligelmo retorted. "That's why I'm stuck with you." He concluded ruefully.

Alehandra noticed our busy scraping, and flounced up to her brother triumphantly.

"Hah! You're cleaning off that stupid diary you wrote on the ship, aren't you? Father shouldn't have let you write it on skin in the first place."

"You're just jealous because you can't read or write."

"Not because I couldn't if I wanted to! Nobody ever taught me. Mother could read and write, so I should learn too." She was indignant, but mentioning their deceased mother made poor Wiligelmo wince. I imagined he remembered her much better than his little sister did.

"Just shut up."

She skipped to the doorway with a mischievous smile and knelt down, her top poised against the red clay tiles, ready to spin out into the corridor again.

"Alehandra…" Wiligelmo started to rise "don't you realize we're guests in the palace of one of the great families of Genoa? You can't go around disturbing the Spinolas with toys. If nothing else, think how badly it would reflect on Master Gerold and his friend Opicino, thanks to whose letter of commendation we've been given hospitality."

"You'll never catch me, Wiggy, you'll fall over your own feet." She paused coyly, and looked at me. "But… I promise I'll behave if Eilulf sings me another song."

"Aleh, don't be silly-" Wiligelmo began angrily, but I raised a hand to acquiesce.

"Very well, Alehandra. I'll sing you a song."

"Yes, yes, yes!" She crowed joyfully, and ran over to sit down cross-legged in front of me.

"You have to close your eyes." I told her solemnly.

"Ooooh." She breathed in anticipation, and closed her eyes tightly. When I was sure she wasn't peeking, I looked over at the next page of Wiligelmo's diary. My eyes settled on his description of our passage of the point of St Martino last autumn, more than half way through the sea voyage to Genoa. I playfully started to sing Wiligelmo's words to an old Troubadour's air, the kind of tune most poems will fit. It was a simple thing to adapt a few words here and there to the metre.

"Long we dwelt about the deck with a flask of Vermentino,
Anchovies and tuna stewed with olives from the groves,
And a crust of focaccia, soaked in the juices of the pot.
The chill October breeze upon the famous Sea of Genoa
Grew warm and aromatic thanks to that flask of wine!

As he listened, Wiligelmo's expression went from puzzled, to startled, and then delighted, and he broke into a broad grin. As I started the melody again from the beginning, as though moving into the second verse, I began to add supple, fluttering trills and embellishments.

"Then Master Francis asked the Captain 'Is port still far?'

Captain Petracco was ready with words of comfort for all:

'We're rounding Cape San Martino, 'neath Roccabruna,
A garden of olives and castles atop steep Alpine slopes,
We'll sail the night long in Genoa's welcoming waters."

When I let my voice die away on the final note, Alehandra clapped with enthusiastically.

"Did you like my song?" I asked her, with just a hint of a wink at Wiligelmo.

"Yes, yes, you sing so well…"

"Was the poem beautiful?"

"Oh, it was absolutely lovely…"

"So you don't think Wiligelmo's diary is stupid after all?"

"What?"

I chuckled at her confusion.

"The song I just sang was from your brother's diary. It was the night we passed Cape San Martino. Don't you remember? I changed Master Gerold's name to Master Francis, and Captain Christoffaro's name to Petracco, and sang it to an old troubadour's tune, that's all."

Alehandra clasped one hand over her mouth in dismay, while Wiligelmo burst out laughing.

"It's true, I remember it now. That's how it happened." She said.

"Well, thank you for the compliment, little sister." Wiligelmo was ironic. "I'm glad you like my writing. And now that you've had your song as promised, you have to behave."

Alehandra turned a light shade of violet as she screwed up her face in anger at her brother.

"Uh uh, I was promised a song. That was a trick, not a song, and I won't do anything you tell me to do!"

"Aleh!" Wiligelmo was exploding and I was laughing when Master John appeared at the door wearing a scowl, and we all fell silent.

"Eilulf, Wiligelmo, can't you keep it down?"

"I'm sorry, Master. We were trying to keep little Alehandra entertained," I explained "but the winter has been long, and she's starting to get restless."

"So now it was *my* fault?" The glare Alehandra turned on me was edged with more than just anger, and I was flattered to realise she was a little in love with me. Even the furious adoration of a seven year old is pleasing to a young man.

"I understand completely, Mistress Alehandra." Master John nodded to her with grave seriousness, as though she were the lady of the house. "It has indeed been a long winter, and you have not even had the chance to visit the fairs of the city. But if you are patient a little while longer, the spring will come, the waves will settle, and the ships will set sail again. In the meantime, you must lend me your minstrel, Eilulf."

Alehandra, seeing an opportunity to regain a little face, drew herself up haughtily, and in the tone of a dame replied "Of course, Master Gerold, I understand. You may borrow Eilulf if you need him."

Concealing a grin, I stepped to the door.

"Thank you, Mistress Alehandra," Master John completed the little fancy with a half-bow "with your permission, we shall take our leave of you." And Alehandra answered him with a little curtsy.

As we strode along the corridor, Master John murmured.

"Have you been regressing to your childhood, Will? It's time to come back to the present, there's adult play afoot."

He led me through the palace of the House of Spinola that had been our home since our arrival in Genoa the previous autumn. To my surprise, he stopped in front of the archway leading to the chambers of Messer Gherardo Spinola himself.

"I have revealed our profession to the master of the house, Eilulf." Master John murmured to me in the Flemish. His choice of language and use of my Flemish name told me that he had revealed our profession, but not our identities. Soon there appeared a servant wearing the red and yellow livery of the family, who ushered us in through an antechamber and through an imposing carven bronze door, and promptly disappeared.

Sitting in front of rich draperies on an ornate chair that was little short of a throne, at the far end of a room that was little short of a hall, Gherardo Spinola looked up as we entered, his greying hair and short beard framing a swarthy Mediterranean face and keen hazel eyes. One of the most powerful magnates of the House of Spinola, Messer Gherardo had personally taken Opicino de Canistris and the fugitive daughters of Filippone Langosco of Pavia into his protection after the sack of Pavia. It was he who had inspected the letter of commendation from Opicino that I had forged, and given us hospitality out of love and respect for his old friend. Furthermore, Gherardo's nephew Corradino had been horribly murdered by Forzetti in London shortly before our departure from England.

"Ah, so this is the second player in the ruin of the House of Spinola." Gherardo rose as the door was shut behind us, a slight ironic smile underplaying his dramatic words. "My compliments, Master Eilulf."

I looked enquiringly at Master John, who clapped me on the shoulder reassuringly.

"It's a long story, Eilulf. Soon you'll understand."

"Shall we be seated?" Our host beckoned us to a cushioned horse-shoe-shaped bench. As we took our places he handed us pewter cups brimming with saffron-laced white wine from a fine earthenware jar. "You must allow me the honour of serving you personally, though I'm no dab hand at it. If what you told me about yourselves is true, Master Gerold, the sensitive nature of this conversation will no doubt mean no servants may attend us. Now," he settled onto a cushion opposite us "tell me more of your destructive exploits in Sluys."

"It was Eilulf here who actually set the wool-sacks alight." Master John began. "I was merely keeping watch outside, and distracting the guards."

"Is that so?" Gherardo turned to look me in the eyes. "With that flame you sealed a loss of face worth a thousand marks for my family. But of course, you could not have known."

I was mystified that Master John had chosen to reveal so much to our host, but I had long since learned to trust my Master completely.

"I sincerely apologise for the harm we caused the House of Spinola, for you have been the most generous hosts I have ever known. It certainly wasn't intentional. I confess that I cannot see how our actions can be connected with you…"

"It's quite simple, really. I can explain." Gherardo began, taking first a thoughtful sip of wine and then a deep breath. "My brother-in-law, who resides in London, had come to know of Henry Tideswell's planned illegal wool consignment through paid informants. As a favour to our Doria allies, he informed the Doria agents based in the money market of Sluys that the price of wool cloth was soon to drop in Paris due to an unexpected increase in the amount of raw material available to the manufacturers in Ghent – Tideswell's smuggled shipment, naturally. The Dorias, who had been stocking a considerable amount of un-dyed wool cloth ever since the King of England had announced his blockade, promptly went to our ancient enemies here in Genoa, the House of Fieschi, and took out an insurance policy against falls in the price of wool cloth. The Fieschis, unaware of the upcoming illegal shipment, charged the Dorias an unexpectedly low premium. Sure enough, the price of wool dropped when news got around that Tideswell's shipment had arrived in Sluys. However, before the Dorias could cash their insurance pay-out from the Fieschi bankers, the whole shipment was rendered useless by your good selves, causing the price of finished cloth in Paris to return to its previous levels and annulling the insurance pay out, because the Fieschis had cleverly inserted a clause into the contract specifying that variations in market prices must last for a minimum of two calendar days, the time it takes for a certified message to reach Sluys from the Paris wool market, before they can constitute a valid cause of payment. The Dorias thereby lost the money they had been charged for the premium and, of course, the face the House of Spinola lost with its greatest allies was proportional not to the money they effectively lost, but to the earnings the Dorias might have made had the deal gone according to plan. I am sure you can see the problem."

As Messer Gherardo came to his conclusion I realised that my mouth was hanging open in dismayed bewilderment.

"I'm sorry, Messer Gherardo, but didn't you say the affair was quite simple? I can make neither head nor tail of it."

Master John chuckled beside me.

"Don't worry, Eilulf, it took me quite a while to get my head around it too. What's important is not how it happened, but the fact that we really did inadvertently cause a serious diplomatic incident for the family that has given us so much here in Genoa. By sheer luck, I overheard one of Messer Gherardo's stewards discussing this misfortune while I was playing chess with Captain Cristoffaro, and I realised not only that the damage was our own fault, but that we could help repair it."

Messer Gherardo inclined his head in a sign of both respect and curiosity.

"When you asked to speak with me in private, Master Gerold, I admit that I was fascinated. What exactly do you propose to do, to make up for what has happened? You could easily have said nothing at all, and I would never have known you were responsible. I presume you have an excellent idea already in mind."

Master John nodded, suddenly wearing that expression that I had come to know and love as a harbinger of adventure: at once shrewd, astute and amused, like a university student about to play a clever prank. I leaned forward, eager to hear his plan.

"I will give you the opportunity to arrest Henry Tideswell, and hand him over in secret to the House of Doria, giving them the opportunity to put him on trial and convict him of betraying England as a gift to the English Crown. This will ingratiate you with the House of Doria, with the King of England, and even with the Emperor himself, who is intimately engaged in negotiations with King Edward as we speak. If you manage the situation with skill, your London agents will probably be able to extract an audience with Edward himself, perhaps even setting a wedge between him and the House of Fieschi."

Messer Gherardo was almost unmoved, just the hint of a smile curling one edge of his mouth.

"This is a pleasant fantasy, and no doubt I could gain much from the arrest of this clumsy smuggler. But he is tossing about somewhere on the north seas, and we are here in Genoa. How do you imagine to organise his arrest?"

"You will arrest me, and I shall pretend to be Tideswell."

Messer Gherardo laughed aloud.

"And do you really think you can convince the Dorias that you are an English smuggler? What will you do, speak in the Frisian and hope nobody notices it's not an English dialect? I'm sure they'll find someone who can at least recognise the language."

"I speak fluent English," Master John did not add that it was his mother tongue "and you will be surprised by my skill in convincing the Dorias. I am much better acquainted with the north seas and the ways of English sailors than you might think, and can skilfully play the part. And there is no risk that the real Henry Tideswell will show himself. If he ever finds out about it he will be delighted that some impostor is taking the blame on his behalf,."

Messer Gherardo shook his head in near disbelief.

"You are a truly surprising man, Master Gerold, and I imagine your pupil is equally so. But, once arrested and imprisoned, what will you do? Rot in gaol?"

"That is where my pupil, Eilulf, comes into it. Since this affair touches the English, the feat of a famous English baron came to mind. It was during the fifteenth year of the reign of the old King Edward II of England. Baron Roger de Mortimer of Wigmore, on his way to seducing Queen Isabella and leading a rebellion against the old King, escaped from his cell in the Tower of London in a rather spectacular fashion. I would like to try my chances using the same technique here in Genoa. Eilulf is more than capable of carrying out his side of things. It will, however, require the help of a prison guard in your pay."

"Indeed, the Mortimer incident is notorious even here in Genoa." Messer Gherardo made a steeple of his hands, and thoughtfully leant his chin upon it.

"But I have a request to make, if we are to go through with this." Master John smiled, his eyes shining. "I understand that Marco Polo was captured and detained by the great Lamba Doria, and dictated the story of his travels while in a prison cell in the *Palazzo del Mare* of Genoa. It stands to reason that his cell was in the part of the city prisons given over to the use of the House of Doria. My one request is that you organise for me to be kept in that very same cell, where Marco Polo dictated the record of his journeys. That would be… an emotion to remember forever."

Messer Gherardo laughed aloud, throwing back his head in mirth.

"Is that what this was all about? All this intrigue and secrecy to organise a scholar's pilgrimage to a literary anti-shrine?" Master John simply shrugged, his smile broadening. "Master Gerold, you are an extraordinary man indeed. I wonder… I wonder who you *really* work for?"

Master John disappeared from the Spinola palace a few days later, without saying a word to anyone. Master Pietro da Campione seemed entirely unsurprised.

"Young Master Eilulf, you've been a good friend to me and above all to my son. Wiligelmo will be sad when you vanish into thin air too, like Master Gerold, but I will distract him with some good news. We have been commissioned to work on the frame of a rose-window for a new church in a town called Corniglia, far to the West in lands connected to my old patron, Cardinal Luca. After Avignon it's hardly a move up in the world, but it should be the right climate for my sick old chest. I'll let Wiligelmo do the bulk of the work. He can sculpt in peace there, with no one to rush him, and put his own name to a set-piece for the first time. Perhaps it will lead on to work in Modena, or Parma."

Of course, I knew that Master Pietro was right, and that I would soon be disappearing without a trace from their lives.

"You will be safe there." I told him. "The man who murdered the scribes in Avignon, who we fled from… He will be coming after us, and not you. I'm glad you'll be able to live in relative peace from now on. May Lady Fortune smile on you."

It took a little over a week for the House of Doria to subject Master John to a trial as Henry Tideswell and sentence him to imprisonment until such time as the King of England sent word concerning his desired punishment for the miscreant. Then Messer Gherardo invited me to his chambers again. A guard of the prisons beneath the *Palazzo del Mare*, the 'Sea Palace' of Genoa, who was somehow indebted to the House of Spinola, was waiting there to provide a thorough description of the entrances to the prison, the cells and the guards' routines.

On my last day in the Spinola palace, I spent some time with Wiligelmo, singing songs and talking of faraway places over a cup of passito, trying not to reveal the melancholy I felt at leaving him. In part to say farewell and in part to raise my spirits, I spent the first hours of the night with the young scullery maid who had often warmed cold nights for me over that long winter. Then, toward midnight, I prepared for the prison break.

As Master John had planned, we were going to use the same technique as the infamous Roger Mortimer, with some colourful touches of our own devising. I took a long rope ladder that Messer Gherardo had procured for me, and carefully wound it first around my hips and then my chest until I was satisfied that I had obtained the figure of a buxom young lady. After a close shave, I massaged some cheap rouge onto my face, and flushed my lips with red clay-water, then donned the distinctive green striped hooded gown and flat red clogs of a Genoese prostitute.

It was well after curfew when our corrupted prison guard came to fetch me from a rear door, and guided me through the streets of Genoa. I had seen little of the city since our arrival, for we had kept a low profile, knowing that Francesco Forzetti was likely to be tracking us. This was a peculiar problem in our profession. We saw many of the world's most marvellous cities and monuments, but often only by night. And so it was with Genoa: I saw one of the wealthiest cities in the world by the light of a torch, peering through gathered edges of a prostitute's hood. 'A fine story this will make one day for a grandchild!' I remonstrated with myself.

Nevertheless, the city's haunting ambience did not escape me. We were walking down vertiginous, man-made canyons, whose floors of great flagstones sloped steeply down from the higher regions of the city toward the seafront. The buildings rose to seemingly impossibly heights, their summits so far above and so close together that only a sliver of starry sky was left to see. And yet, at ground level, there was no sense of being hemmed in, for the base of every building opened into a sequence of broad, elegant portico arches in alternating layers of white marble and black slate. By day I knew they were teeming with shopkeepers' and merchants' wares and customers, but in the silent stillness of night, at such depths beneath the buildings, they seemed to me like shadowy galleries in some mystical subterranean city. My imagination had unwittingly conjured up a sight Marco Polo himself might have described in one of his million lies, the lies that fascinated Master John so.

At one point we passed the watch on its patrol, and the squad captain hailed my guide in a coarse voice.

"O, Lucchino, that's a pleasant night's work you've got ahead of you."

"Not for me, I'm afraid Raimondo." The guard replied bawdily. "This bird's to spend the night hopping up and down on a rich prisoner's perch!"

And that was the same story he told the gatekeeper at the postern gate of the *Palazzo del Mare*. I ducked under the low frame of the door, thinking it was a shame that I should see nothing more than the back door of the famous palace that enshrined the might and wealth of this great city. As the door closed, the sudden silence made me realise that up until that moment the lapping of the waves against the seawall of the great port had been audible.

I was led through the passages to the anteroom where the guards relaxed in between their rounds. Of course, numerous cups of wine that looked like they had already been emptied and refilled a number of times, lay on chests and benches around the room. It was just as I hoped: the guards were not ones to spend their free time in prayer.

"Good evening, lads." How carefully I had rehearsed that phrase! Not only the right intonation for those few phrases I would have to say in Genoese, but also the feminine tone. The key to seeming a woman when you are a man is not to resort to falsetto or other such tricks. A high and light, delicate tone with a man's voice will seem the low, alluring tone women of the night tend to cultivate.

I pushed back the hood, confident of my disguise in the dim, flickering light. "I can't spend any time with you, I'm afraid, for it's to be a busy night, but the Guild sends this with its regards." I held out a loosely tied pouch. "Opium and spice for your wine."

The five men in the room gave a cheer, and the sergeant-at-arms took the pouch with a grin. I nodded to my guide, and he quickly led me to the cells. Behind me, just as the guards of the White Tower had done years before on the night Roger Mortimer had escaped, the men gullibly drank their laced wine and quickly started falling into a deep sleep. The drug Master John and I had concocted for the purpose was sure and strong.

While the corrupted guard went back for the keys, I soon located Master John behind a tiny wooden door. I simply sang one of my favourite songs, like Blondel the Minstrel and Richard the Lionheart, and he soon answered my voice.

"Eilulf… tonight I'm actually glad to hear one of those ridiculous songs of chivalry."

"And I'm glad to hear your complaining about it for once, Master." I affectionately replied.

When I sorted the right key from the ring, the door swung open with difficulty, and a candle soon lit the tiny space to reveal Master John, smiling even as he stooped under the low ceiling.

"Look!" He pointed at the wall with boyish pleasure he rarely allowed to show through. The wall was littered with rough letters cut into the rock, perhaps with the sharp corners of manacles, spelling the names of countless prisoners past. Where Master John was pointing, I could make out MARCVS PAULUS VENETUS. To the right, my Master had managed to inscribe JOHANNES VLPHAMENSIS.

"You see, Eilulf, I'm in notorious company. This dungeon stone might preserve our names side by side for centuries. Now, shall we be going?"

The guard took us to the dead-end of a corridor. "Here, this is the place." He grunted. "Below there are the rocks at the base of the seawall."

By the candlelight we saw that he was pointing at brickwork beneath a ribbed stone arch. Probably it had once been an open portico giving onto the sea, perhaps where passengers used to disembark. Since the stone arch above was carrying the weight of the building in that point, the wall itself was likely to be just a couple of bricks thick.

"Let's get to work, Eilulf." Master John commanded, taking two metal bars from the guard, and handing one to me. He turned to our accomplice.

"While we work, man-at-arms, you had best take a distance from us and draw your dagger. Our friends back there are dreaming happy dreams, but their captain may arrive at any time, or one of the doorkeepers looking for a cup of wine. If someone arrives, try to look like you've just arrived and are trying to apprehend us. Otherwise," Master John shrugged "it's your skin."

The guard saw the sense of his words, and backed off a little, drawing his weapon. We got to work on the mortar, which was probably weakened by years of exposure to sea spray. Soon it was crumbling and the first red bricks came away to let in a damp, cold draught directly from the waves. Soon the gap was large enough for a man to squeeze through.

"I've got the ladder." I told Master John, and started stripping my clothes off. Master John looked with admiration at the way the rope-ladder beneath was wound about my body to give me womanly proportions.

"Well done, Eilulf. Two birds with one stone."

As I unwound the ladder from hips and bust, he started lowering it through the gap.

"You know, Eilulf, this is a trick we learnt from the Scottish. They took many a castle and made many a prison-break using these ladders in silence by night. Mortimer used one as well, on his way out of the White Tower."

The ladder was almost fully unwound, and I was therefore almost naked, when Master John's fears proved correct. At the far end of the corridor a new light appeared. It was one of the doorkeepers. As he turned the corner at a run, his dagger already drawn after he had passed his drugged and sleeping comrades, he took in the scene before him. Another guard, dagger in hand, perhaps come to stop our escape, a fleeing prisoner and a young man, all but naked, his face alluringly decorated with rouge and his lips reddened with clay-water like a prostitute's.

Our accomplice played his part as Master John had suggested.

"Stop, stop! They're escaping, we have to stop them!" He shouted, starting to run toward us. The newcomer was faster though, and overtook him in the narrow passage, dropping his candle.

"Finish the rope." Master John muttered, stooping to retrieve the iron bars, then he ran forward at a low crouch.

"Hold!" The guard cried, his dagger in a backhanded grip for close combat. With one bar Master John stunned his dagger-hand while landing a strong jab on his left kneecap with the other. The guard curled in agony, and his dagger was soon dashed away. A blow to his head promptly knocked him senseless.

Master John turned to our accomplice, who swallowed nervously, only now fully realising that he was in the company of extremely dangerous men.

"I think it's best, now, if I knock you out, too. Otherwise, you'll come under suspicion."

The guard nodded slowly, swallowing.

"Are you ready?"

"Just do it."

With a metallic thud, the man was down. Master John turned to me.

"This is going to make a fine story. It will no doubt greatly enhance Henry Tideswell's reputation, when it gets about. Now, is the rope ready and tied fast?"

"It is. Just one thing, Master." I looked down at myself pointedly. "I might see if one of the guards has a similar build to me, and take his clothes."

"Of course," Master John chuckled "and we should take a dagger each, too. You never know."

A short while later we climbed carefully down from the breach to the wet, slippery rocks below. It was so dark that surely only the cats of Genoa could have seen us. Now, the problem was to get up the seawall and into the city before the hue and cry went up from the garrison at the *Palazzo del Mare*. At noon of the following day a servant of the House of Spinola would be waiting for us at a town called Busalla, more than half a day's walk from the city. He would have our possessions and a mule ready for our journey across the Apennines toward the River Ira.

Leaving the rope ladder hanging where it was, we both dropped to all fours, the better to negotiate the slippery rocks. The smooth outer surfaces of seawalls are always punctuated by narrow stairs to let people onto smaller boats at the base, or carry out work on the walls themselves. After much scrabbling and oath muttering, we came to the base of just such a flight of steps. Master John now allowed me to take the lead, with my younger eyes. At the top of the stairs, however, a low growl followed by wild baying told us that we had disturbed one of the port guard dogs, set to watch over the top of each flight of steps. It was making enough noise to bring every man in the port, awake or not, to the scene, and to make matters worse, we couldn't even see him. This problem, at least, was soon solved by the Genoese themselves. To the cry of "Genoa and Saint George! Who goes there?" a fire-arrow rose high in the air, flaming drops of oil dripping from its flaring tip, shot from the nearest galley lying at anchor in the harbour. By its light I saw a great hound, on a long chain tied to a crenellation, come charging toward me with a black snarl that made every hair on my body stand on end.

"My ankles!" I cried to Master John below, and prepared to face the dog in the only way I could. As the fire arrow reached its zenith and the hound was almost on me, I lunged toward and under those blood-thirsty jowls, seized the first few links of its chain, then launched myself bodily from the narrow steps. Man and dog, we catapulted out and down from a great height, just as Master John's steely fingers caught my ankles. I let go of the hound's chain, and slapped hard against the rock below Master John, but that was nothing compared to what awaited the dog. It snapped about in mid-air as the chain pulled taught, and whipped through a savage arc into the stones some yards below, ribs, neck and back all broken in one long, sickening impact. I pitied the beast as I seldom pitied the men who got in our way, for God's lesser creatures are as innocents.

Master John swung me onto the steps below him. The fire arrow had not quite finished its blazing course, and still illuminated our corner of the vast port. The men on the galley had certainly seen everything. We scurried to the top of the wall as the hue and cry sprang up from all sides of the port, and ducked into the nearest of the cavernous, shadowy city streets.

"Master, we have to reach the city walls in the south east of the city, near the castle. Spinola told me there is a section of wall to the left of the castle where the poor folk have built dwellings up against the inside of the ramparts. There the walls may be climbed."

"Be my guide, Will. I'm glad you thought of everything. They're sure to have men-at-arms inspecting everyone leaving the city gates by morning."

By keeping the sea glow to my right at every corner, I navigated the vast labyrinth of streets that was Genoa toward the south eastern quarter, and the castle. Fortunately any pursuers could have no idea of what direction we had taken, and the sheer complexity of their city would work against them. We were like two straws of barley in a stack of rye-stalks.

Soon I was reassured to find that we were moving steeply uphill, for I knew that the castle occupied a height over the city. Finally, when we were nearly winded with the effort of running up those sloping streets, one corner of the castle and the beginning of the city wall loomed up ahead. I turned left, skirting the city wall until we came to the area Messer Gherardo had told me of. A ramshackle jumble of badly-built, windowless houses clustered up the inside of the city wall like a series of wasp-nests, one built on top of the other. I was surprised that here, so close to the castle, the city of Genoa had allowed such a risk to its security to grow up. Perhaps this was a part of the town rarely visited by the authorities, and the soldiers of the garrison that patrolled the walls did not report the houses of such miserable folk out of a sense of pity.

The walls of the poor-houses were built with un-hewn stones. Even though the only light was cast by a slim sickle-blade of crescent moon, it would be possible to climb them. As we sought out footholds and handholds with aching slowness, taking the utmost care not to make a sound nor commit an error, the eerie sound of prayers drifted to us along the silent, empty streets. *Ut sine timore, de manu inimicorum liberati, serviamus illi...* The monks in some nearby monastery were towards the middle of Lauds. We would have to hurry once out of the city, but we should make our appointment.

The roof of the tallest of the makeshift houses was lower than the walkway of the city walls by a little more than the height of an outstretched man. Master John, being taller than I, crouched and jumped up with all his strength. The roofing slates were irregular and were not fixed to the timber frame, and moved noisily beneath his feet, but his fingers just managed to grip the edge of the walkway.

Controlling his breathing, and without so much as a grunt of effort, he slowly pulled himself up. I reached up to take his hands, and we were soon both on the ramparts. We had no way of knowing how soon a member of the garrison might come on his rounds, so we immediately began lowering ourselves down the outside of the city walls. Seldom in one night have I faced so much climbing! And the city walls were a very different affair to the roughly made walls of the houses of the poor down below. The stones were finely hewn and fitted, so it was far more difficult to find holds. At one point we froze to absolute stillness as we heard footsteps on the ramparts above us. Two men were passing on patrol, muttering to each other in their Genoese dialect. The only word we understood clearly was 'fugitives', and we realised that the alert had reached the castle garrison. Fortunately, however, they did not think to look down at the outside of the walls, and passed us by.

After a great deal of time and exertion, we came within a safe fall of the ground at the base of the walls, and we gladly relaxed our grips and dropped down.

"Now, Master," I murmured in a low voice "we are awaited in a village called Busalla, a fiefdom of the House of Spinola, where they will meet us at the stables with our possessions. It's a little more than half a day's walk away. I listened carefully to a description of the road, I'm confident we can do it."

"I'm in your hands, Will." Master John told me "and there are no better hands to be in. Let's go."

I spent much of the gruelling march that ensued wringing my fingers, which were stiff, sore and stinging from clinging to hard rock and being dug into tiny gaps in mortar. A brisk pace kept us warm against the chill until the sun had risen, and we saw the magnificent city of Genoa laid out below us, her towers, steeples and rooves, her mighty cathedral and her sprawling port with its myriad bobbing masts. No doubt traffic away from the city would be held up all day, as the city watch inspected everyone leaving to be sure that Henry Tideswell and his 'accomplice' were not escaping the city undetected. As we climbed the stone steps of the steep mule trails up, away from the city and toward the Apennines, the fortified town of Busalla gradually became visible, nestled into the green slopes above us. Well before noon we were standing at the gates.

As soon as we identified ourselves as Master Gerold of Ghent and his pupil, we were ushered through the gates toward a princely house in the centre of the town. The servant who welcomed us at the door wore such a grave expression that we became nervous, a sensation that heightened as he bade us enter the house. I was expecting to be taken to the stables, not into a house.

"Come with me." He ordered, swinging the small service door open.

"Our agreement with Messer Gherardo was that we would be taken immediately to the stables, where a pack mule would be waiting with our possessions."

The servant's expression did not change, and he gestured through the door. "Come with me."

Eying one another, our hands lowering to our dagger hilts beneath our clothes, we ducked through the door and followed him through the house to a chamber with a heavy wooden door. He knocked respectfully, and a faintly familiar voice answered "Enter."

As the door swung open, we were astonished to find Messer Gherardo himself waiting for us. We were at once pleased and cautious. It was an honour to be taken once more into the presence of such a magnate, but at the same time we wondered why he had not given the task of helping us on our way to a trusted servant.

"Welcome, you are most welcome Master..." He paused, a clever little smile playing on his lips. He glanced at the servant, who immediately left, closing the door.

"Master... who? Gerold of Ghent? Or John de Ulgham?"

Our hands dropped to our dagger hilts.

"Come, be calm." His voice was soave as he raised his hands in a placatory gesture. "There's no need to slaughter me."

"Messer Gherardo," Master John was the first to recover from his surprise "you once described me as a truly surprising man. I think the same can be said of you." Though his voice was calm, he did not take his hand from his knife hilt.

"The merit of discovering who you really are is not mine." His broadening smile seemed not to hide malice. "The House of Fieschi has that brute, Forzetti, who destroys everything he touches, but the House of Spinola has far more subtle agents in its employ. I have known who you were since Captain Cristoffaro sent a description of you to a loyal informant of ours in Arles. My compliments, in any case, for your forgery of Opicino de Canistris' script. It was utterly convincing."

Master John accepted the compliment on my behalf with a wary nod.

"And so," Messer Gherardo continued "the King of England's finest agents, and so far from home. When you first arrived I assumed you were here to negotiate the return of the English royal money I impounded. And yet you have never sought to approach me concerning it."

"You impounded English royal money? We had no idea of this." Master John's surprise was genuine.

"Oh yes," Messer Gherardo laughed lightly "no less than two thousand marks. It was being carried by a Fieschi man named Montefiore. Officially, he claimed it was for the purchase of two galleys, but such a sum is worth far more than two. Genoese law dictates that no more than two galleys may be sold to any foreign power, to preserve the security of the city. I am a Marshal of the King of Naples, who is nominally Lord of Genoa while it is convenient for the houses of Spinola, Fieschi, Doria and Grimaldi to let him play the part. As Marshal, it was my duty to impound the money to prevent the illicit sale of three or more ships. As a Spinola, it was a pleasure to impound a vast sum intended for our dearest enemies, the Fieschis. Even though" Messer Gherardo's voice modulated with suppressed pain "it cost me dear, when Forzetti murdered my nephew to settle the account, right under the King of England's nose." A hint of the fury that seethed within him showed in his eyes. "When you first arrived, I assumed you had come to negotiate the return of that sum. Now that I know your mission has nothing to do with this, I am most intrigued. Why exactly have you come, agents of England?"

Master John spread his hands in conciliatory gesture.

"I cannot tell you, Messer Gherardo, Marshal of the King of Naples. It is the secret business of none but our King." He carefully did not correct Messer Gherardo's assumption that we were working on direct instruction from the King himself. "However, for the sake of our friendship, which I hope you will extend in our honour to our King and country as well, I will stretch my mandate a little to tell you some good news. Of course, I must swear you to secrecy."

Messer Gherardo at once agreed "As secret as the tomb."

"Our task has brought us into conflict with the House of Fieschi, and we are being pursued by Francesco Forzetti himself, who is already leaving a wake of blood behind him." Master John placed a firm hand on Messer Gherardo's forearm, and spoke earnestly. "Sooner or later he will find us again. I promise you that, one day, your nephew's murder will be avenged either by my hand, or by that of my pupil, William de Tels."

At these words my heart surged in my chest. Seldom did Master John enshrine our actions with an oath worthy of a Knight.

Messer Gherardo nodded gravely. "I am glad. This is the best news I've had since…" his face suddenly glowed "since I heard that Henry Tideswell had been arrested!"

Then, this most honourable of merchant princes handed Master John a folded sheet of parchment bearing the seal of the House of Spinola.

"As you travel in Lombardy this may be of help to you. And it will save you having to forge one…" He smiled a little mischievously. Clearly, it was a letter of commendation on our behalf to all those who called themselves friends of the House of Spinola. "The first part of your journey will take you toward the lands of the Malaspinas, and there you may prefer to hide this parchment, as there is no love lost between them and the House of Spinola, whilst their ties with the Fieschis are very strong. But as you near Pavia you will cross lands belonging to Messer Matteo Bottigella, a noble and wealthy woad merchant whose mother was a Spinola, and whose wife, Filippina Langosco, was once the pupil of our friend Opicino de Canistris, one of the daughters of Count Filippone Langosco that he brought to my care in Genoa after fleeing the sack of Pavia. And now, I have kept you from your journey long enough. It's time you turned your backs on my enchanting, perilous city of Genoa, take your pack mule, which is already laden with your belongings, and may Mary and Jesus walk by your side as you cross the Apennines."

Chapter 17

Valley of the River Staffora, March 1338

The powder woodworms make – the Welsh Pilgrim's tale

"Welshman, stop your work awhile, you have a duty to a child."

It was Brother Demetrio's voice. The Welshman straightened up from weeding the medicinal gardens and saw that the old monk was accompanied by Signora Maria and – he broke into a smile - her grandson, Tino. The old lady was burdened by a heavy-looking basket, while her grandson carried two small sacks over his shoulder. The Welshman hurried over to them, cleaning the mud off his hands with a moist rag.

"God and Mary be with you, Signora, it's good to see you. Tino," He knelt down to greet the boy "you must be starved of my stories. I haven't seen you since the Feast of Saint Anthony the Abbot, in January, when we ate the chestnuts cooked in milk. Before that we saw each other more regularly."

"He found out I was going to the Castle," Maria explained and begged me to bring him as far as the Abbey. But truly, Brother Demetrio" she turned respectfully to the healer "if the Welshman has work to do I'll take Tino to Auramala with me and leave you all to your tasks."

"It's really no trouble, Donna, even lay-brothers are allowed rest. He would have rested after the main meal and worked before. Now he will rest before the main meal and work after. The boy will eat with us this morning, and you can collect him on your way back from the Castle."

"Will the Brothers not mind?" Maria glanced up the hill in the direction she knew the Abbey stood, its towering stone walls hidden by trees.

"I won't tell them." Brother Demetrio replied simply. "We'll be here in the gardens all morning. And… thank you for the pudding." He half winked at the old lady, and patted a tunic pocket where something weighty bulged against his hip.

"It was the least I could do… to stop this one complaining from dawn till dusk!" She gave Tino an affectionate clip over one ear. Then she gave him a look of warning. "Natalino, if you don't keep the good manners of a Bishop this morning I'll never bring you again. Do you understand?"

"Yes, *nonna*, of course." Tino was almost hopping in his excitement while passed his grandmother the two sacks he had been carrying.

As Signora Maria slung the first sack back over her shoulder, a puff of the finest white powder escaped the tied neck. The second sack was lumpy, the neck glistened with drying blood, and a squelching sound came from within as it settled against the old woman's back. The Welshman looked so curious that Maria paused to explain.

"This bag has chicken-necks in it, for making broth. My granddaughter Clementia is up at the castle nursing two babies, her own and the son of the Lord of Auramala. If she eats chicken-neck broth it will help make the babies' necks strong, so they can hold their heads up the sooner."

"That makes sense." The Welshman nodded. He wondered whether peasant mothers back home did the same.

"May I ask what's in the other, the one that seemed to hold powder?"

"Of course you can ask. It's shit!" Maria exclaimed, for the pure enjoyment of seeing his surprise.

Brother Demetrio, observing the exchange, suspected that Maria's brash manner with the Welshman was a veil for growing affection toward him, in spite of the strong duty she felt to be mistrustful of strangers.

"Then it must be ant-shit, it's so fine." The Welshman rebutted almost playfully. This earned him an appreciative chuckle from the others. Brother Demetrio was pleased. As he had hoped, the time the Welshman had spent over these past months with the peasant family had brought him out of his inward looking isolation a little. He had even gradually stopped conversing in silence with that unnerving invisible companion of his.

"Ant shit?" Maria was smiling. "Very nearly, very nearly. It's woodworm shit. We lay cloths under the wood piles to catch the dust the woodworms make as they eat the wood. Their shit, that is. It's perfect for powdering babies' skin, to stop them getting rashes in their swaddling. I'm taking it up to Clementia for her baby and the Lord Malaspina's."

"You never waste anything here, do you?" The Welshman was appreciative.

Signora Maria wagged an emphatic finger at the Welshman. "Never ever. Now, I'll leave Tino with you."

"Very well." Brother Demetrio turned away. "I have some things to do, but you stay and chat a while with Tino, Gallese, until we stop for little food."

As the monk walked stiffly away to his garden beds, Signora Maria spoke in a low tone to the Welshman. "Please, as you eat together with Brother Demetrio later, speak a little in the church-tongue with Tino. Show Brother Demetrio that the boy is learning, and can speak it a little. The healer is the wisest of the Brothers. We all hope he might speak up for Tino with the Abbot."

The Welshman promised to do so, finally understanding why the old woman had gone to such lengths to bring the little boy with her, even sacrificing a precious black pudding. He was thankful that Gilio was not present that day to spoil the meal with his jealousy. As Maria walked away toward the path for Auramala, he settled down on a log bench.

"Well, Tino, what story shall I tell you today?" His fingers unconsciously brushed against the stone snake in the folds of his tunic. "Do you want to hear the tale of the Green Knight?"

"Hmmm." The boy replied noncommittally. "Maybe. But… You know, Nonno often tells me about the things he did when he was young and sailed on the ships of Genoa. Won't you tell me what you did when you were young?"

"What I did when I was young?" The Welshman was suddenly very uncomfortable. "What do you mean?"

"Well, maybe… Did you sail too, like Nonno?"

"I did." The Welshman did not wish to admit as much, but nor could he lie.

"Really?" Tino's eyes widened, and he half jumped up from his seat with glee, but he caught himself in time and kept his bottom on the wood. A polite young man, he knew, neither sat down nor stood up before his elders did so.

"Did you sail with the Doria family, like *nonno*, or with the Grimaldis? Or the Boccanegras?"

"With none of these." The Welshman replied, and when he saw the boy's confusion he explained without thinking. "The sea does not belong to Genoa, Tino. It is wide and vast, and bathes the shores of many nations."

"And what nation did you set sail with when you were young?" To the Welshman's dismay, Tino was fascinated.

"When I was young… I set sail on the ships of the English." He cut himself off abruptly, knowing he was saying too much, but Tino didn't notice, and filled the ensuing silence with his piping voice.

"And what else did you do when you were younger? Did you rescue any maidens? Did you fight in many battles?"

The Welshman could not lie. "Yes, yes I did."

"Many?"

"Yes, many. Well… I fought in some, and at others I was… present."

Again, Tino seemed not to notice the Welshman's hesitation in speaking about himself.

"And did you escape from any castles?"

"Well… yes. Actually, from two castles." The Welshman earnestly hoped that Tino would soon tire of these questions.

"Ooohhh!" Tino breathed in mix of awe and anticipation. "And… and did you ever rescue any maidens?"

In spite of his tension, the Welshman chuckled ruefully. "No, I'm sorry. Quite the opposite, many would say."

Tino went blithely on to make a catalogue of the stories he might hear.

"Sailing on the seas, escaping from castles, fighting in battles…" He mused. He'd heard of the sea many times from his grandfather, and there was an old man down in Bagnaria who often told of his younger days spent as a mercenary in the service of Milan. "Tell me… Tell me…" He finally made up his mind. "Won't you tell me about the escapes from the castles?"

The Welshman said nothing as, for a long moment, he warred against a profound need to tell his own story. He looked into Tino's pleading eyes, and thought *Surely it won't matter if I tell a peasant boy. I can leave out names, and ask him to keep it a secret. It can't do any harm.*

In truth, he had already told his story once, more than a year before, when he was still a guest of the hermitage of San Ponzo, near Cecima. A member of the House of Fieschi, Manuele, an ordained priest and papal notary, had visited him there. The Welshman owed the Fieschi family an enormous debt for the generosity the now-deceased Cardinal Luca Fieschi had shown him in the early years of his flight from the world. He had therefore agreed to confess to Manuele Fieschi on the eve of his becoming a *conversus*, a lay-brother beholden to the Benedictine Order.

"A long time ago, I was married to a good and brave woman, but I did not always treat her as a man should treat his wife. I loved her very much, but I... I loved others above her, and she became bitter. Finally, she betrayed me with an ambitious Baron, who desired nothing more than to take my place."

Tino was disconcerted by the start of the tale. Firstly, the Welshman seemed to have lost the zest and compelling manner with which he normally told stories. And then, he had never thought of the Welshman as once having had a wife, and perhaps children, and perhaps even grandchildren to compete with him for the old man's affection.

"By vile trickery, my wife and her lover captured me and locked me in a dark cell in a remote and virtually impregnable castle. But many people still loved me, and wanted to free me. On one occasion, a group of loyal warriors assaulted the castle by night. A storm was blowing up without, and as I lay in my cell I heard strange noises, clangs and hammerings, and thought it was the wind scattering objects around the courtyard. Instead, it was my rescuers fighting their way into the castle after they climbed over the walls on rope ladders. When they unlocked my cell I was so grateful that I wept in their arms. We rode hastily away into the night, but my wife and the baron had been informed of the plan to break me from prison, and were soon coming after us with their men-at-arms."

The Welshman was doing his best to warm into the story, but it was a very different experience to the storytelling he had done until that day. Not only did he have to remind himself constantly not to name people and places, but he found himself listening to his own words with just as much attention as Tino. It was almost as though he was discovering this narrative for the first time, and not at all liking what he was hearing.

"We rode hard through the night and morning, but when we came to a river we were forced to coast it for some miles before finding a ford, and there our pursuers caught up with us, and there was a bloody skirmish. All of my defenders were slain, and I was taken back to the castle in chains. However, my captors soon moved me to an even stronger cell."

The Welshman swallowed. He could still see the haunting lines cut into the rough stone walls of that second cell by some anonymous prisoner in times gone by.

"The new cell was even darker, and grimmer, and my imprisonment became miserable and I began to lose hope again. The walls of the cell were almost black with age, and there were seven little lines carved into them on one side, perhaps by some long-dead prisoner. I spent hours, whole days, wondering with dread whether those lines had been cut to mark the passing of days, or years." His voice and features had now become bleak, and he did not notice Tino's eyes widening, struck by a grim set to the Welshman's features that he had never seen before. "Had they been the seven days some poor soul had spent waiting to be executed?" The story continued. "Or seven years spent wasting slowly away into nothing but bones, there in the dark?"

The Welshman noticed Tino shuddering, and realised that he was frightening the child.

"Are you worried, Tino?" he touched the boy's shoulder reassuringly "I didn't stay there long."

"No, no, I'm not worried." Tino put on a brave face. "I know you're here now, so you escaped from the second castle, too."

The old man smiled. "It's true, I escaped from the second castle too. But it was a terrible experience. Are you sure you want to hear about it?"

Tino nodded, slowly. His curiosity was too great.

"In that castle there was one man, a mere servant, who was still loyal to me, though he did nothing to help me for a long time because he was terrified of my captors. But one day he was driven by events to take action on my behalf. It was almost dusk when knights came to the castle, sent by my wife's lover to kill me. The servant heard them discussing whether to suffocate me, strangle me, or stab me as they lingered, undecided, near the larder where he was working. He slipped away by an unseen door, and came swiftly to my cell to free me. 'Two knights have come to murder you.' He told me, as he pulled back the blocks. 'Come, take my cloak and wear it to disguise yourself.' I did as he bade me, and then together we stole through the corridors toward the gatehouse. There we found the porter sleeping, and the servant took his knife and slit his throat. Then we opened the postern, and were free at last." He shook his head with regret. "I believe that the two knights, upon finding my cell empty and the porter murdered, did not even deign to hunt for us. Their task was to bring back a heart as a bloody trophy, and they did not care to ride in haste and discomfit through the woods and fields by night. Therefore, they cut the heart from the chest of the dead porter and took it to my wife and her lover to gloat over." The Welshman sighed. If, at the time of his escape, he had been even a fraction of the man he was now, he would not have allowed murder to be committed on his behalf. But in those days he was so cowardly as to gladly accept any act of sacrifice or brutality for the sake of his own comfort and safety.

"Why were some people your enemies, and other people loyal to you, even in different castles around your country?" Tino asked the very question the Welshman had hoped to avoid. "Were you a very important man?"

"Yes," the Welshman admitted. "In a sense I was. Or rather... I was forced to wear the robes of a very important man."

"The robes? A mantle, a suit of armour?"

"Yes, but more than that, the face, the skin and the name. My father's face, and skin, and name. I am like him in many things. But... I never fit into his robes. And everybody around me, except for one person, cared far less about me than they did about the robes of my father that I wore."

"Was your father a baron?"

"No, he wasn't."

"A duke?"

"No, no... he was..." The Welshman made a decision. "He was a king." Tino's eyes widened, and he gasped with the pleasurable shock of the revelation. "Hush," the Welshman put a finger to his lips. "Not a word about that. It's not important at all. Let me finish the story."

From that point onwards, the story to tell became far less daunting, and an enormous weight was gradually lifted from the Welshman's heart by Tino's compassionate, comprehensive gaze as he listened. The tale now flew from the shores of Ireland to Normandy, from Avignon to Cologne, and from the Castle of Mulazzo to a hermitage near Cecima, just a few miles down valley from Pizzocorno, where he made his decision to leave the world and give his life to Christ.

"*'Filius meus, tu vis conversus Christo esse?'* The Abbot asked me. What did he say, Tino?" The Welshman remembered his promise to Signora Maria to help the boy's Latin come to the attention of Brother Demetrio. A little practice before the meal was in order.

The boy concentrated.

"'My son... do you want to be converted by Christ?'"

The Welshman nodded encouragingly.

"Almost. *'Conversus'* is not just 'converted', but also lay-brother. The meaning is both."

"Ah! And what did you reply?"

" *'Volo. Venio ad cenobium ut me de mundo separem, in Christo vivam.'*"

"I do." Tino translated. "I came to... What is *'cenobium'*?"

"Abbey."

"I came to the Abbey to... me... from the world, separate, and... live in Christ."

"*Optime!*" The Welshman was so pleased that he laughed aloud. But his joy was not only for the boy's swiftness to learn. It was for a new dignity he had found in Tino's eyes.

"When Brother Demetrio returns, and we break bread together, ask for your bread in the Latin. Do you remember the formula?"

"*Si vis, da panem a me.*" Tino replied so quickly and surely that it was clear he had been practicing, perhaps while weeding, or mucking out the animal runs.

"Good, good. Now, try not to be nervous. Brother Demetrio speaks much, much better than I do, but that just means that you and I are both in the same pair of shoes!"

As he said it the Welshman realized that, despite the forty-odd years, the thousand leagues of distance and the gulf of privilege that separated his birth from that of Tino, in that moment they really were walking in the same pair of shoes. Perhaps they had met each other by chance, travelling on Fortune's Wheel; Tino rising and the Welshman falling. But only Lady Fortune could say.

Chapter 18

Valley of the River Staffora, March 1338

The dolmen oak – the tavernkeeper's wife of Bagnaria – the blood spilled from the Holy Chalice

"Master John." I whispered urgently, pointing through the trees. "There's someone there in that hollow. Could it be the place we seek?" We stopped absolutely still, and reined in our mule beside us. It was late afternoon on our third day crossing the Apennines, and the twilight was descending rapidly. Through the dense beech trunks and branches I could just make out a cowled figure some fifty feet away, walking with the stately gait of the procession through the snow that still lay upon the slopes.

"I doubt it is the hermitage we are looking for. We should meet the river Ira long before. Perhaps there is a cell near here. Let's follow him, there may yet be warmth for us tonight."

I was more than willing. My feet were desperately numb from stepping in the snow, for we had now climbed high onto the ridges where the spring was slow to arrive.

"Master, shan't we call out to him?"

Master John shook his head. "We were warned that there are many bandits in these woods. I want to find out who else is in the vicinity before we reveal ourselves."

At a discreet distance we kept the stranger within sight as he wound among the leafless trees. It was nearly evening, and he must surely be returning toward his dwelling, whatever that might be. We were startled when, after ducking behind a twisted old black-barked holm oak, the stranger disappeared altogether.

"Could he have seen us, or heard us?" I murmured.

"Impossible." Master John shook his head. "We have given nothing away since we caught sight of him, I'm sure of it. Perhaps his cell is there, and we just can't see it from here. Let's take a closer look. Without being seen."

With the greatest of care to make no noise nor expose ourselves to view, we padded towards the old tree. As we neared, what had at first seemed to be the raised earthy knoll on top of which the tree stood, became the wattle-and-daub walls of the most curious little hut I had ever seen. A blend of bare, curving branches and packed dark earth formed a twisting, elongated dome that seemed to grow out of the base of the oak's trunk, merging with the tree-roots as they spread out, grasping the ground like a giant hand with forking wooden fingers. Somehow the builder of the hut had dug out the knoll the tree had grown on, leaving the roots intact as a part of the hut, or else the hut and the tree had grown together. From a small hole in the top of the dome, a thin trail of grey smoke snaked its way skywards.

"He must be a lone hermit." Master John mused, and then added "of the strangest kind. Perhaps he has pronounced a vow of silence."

"He will hold the obligation of hospitality as sacred as any other man, surely?" I protested. "I would gladly have a warm meal tonight."

"Against common sense, I say we should go and ask for hospitality. Warily."

We stepped into view of the odd hut's entrance, loudly greeting its occupant. "*Vale, Maria Jesusque sit tibi.*"

The reply did not come in the Latin, nor in any tongue we recognised. It had much of the ring of the Gaelic tongues, sisters of the Latin and the Greek, but many words of some forgotten Germanic dialect of the distant past. The speaker of this strange tongue emerged slowly from the shadow of the entrance, straightening up after standing bent beneath the low roof. To our astonishment we realised it was a woman.

"Good evening, Mary and her Son by your side." Master John repeated in the Occitan. We began to realise that the woman was every bit as strange as her house. She was dressed in a patchwork of every substance that could possibly be used to clothe a human frame that was so gaunt as to be nearly fleshless. Furs were tied to wool-cloth rags, to shreds of silk, strips of bark and pieces of matting made of woven Mediterranean heather.

"I don't speak your scholar's tongue." The woman replied in perfect Occitan, shaking her head. Her long, matted white hair raggedly topped her bizarre vestures like a hooded cape woven from old, mildewed straw. "The Romans never settled here until they were Romans only in name, and the barbarians swelled their ranks. And the Church is… ill at ease with the woods. I think it avoids anything that reminds it of Eden. The troubadours came here often, and sang their songs." She said, as though to explain her mastery of the common tongue in that part of the world.

"Are you a nun in hermitage?" Master John asked delicately. "We are sorry to disturb your prayer."

"A nun?" She raised an eyebrow, and for the first time I realised her eyes were as blue as Master John's. "Hardly. But I am in hermitage in many ways."

"May we beg hospitality of you tonight?" Master John asked for my sake. I am sure he would have preferred to sleep by the fireside again, with his back roasted and his belly freezing, rather than enter that woman's home.

"Of course you may." The woman smiled strangely. "And I may give it to you. Hospitality is sacred, but there is something about you I don't trust."

"Something about *us*?" Master John could not help but reply, looking down at his fine travelling gown of wool woven in Ghent and cut in Paris.

"Yes. Definitely. Let me ask a question of your young friend." And with that she stepped very close to me. She smelled, unsurprisingly, of musty forest litter. While Master John tensed beside me, she reached forward as though to caress my cheek, then her hand snaked behind my head and her long fingers entwining themselves in my hair. Had she been a pretty maiden I might have fancied she meant to pull my face to hers for a passionate kiss. For a moment her eyes lost focus, and she spoke a few soothing words in her strange language.

"Ow!" I jumped as her fingers painfully pinched, and she stepped backwards, smiling, something tiny and black wriggling between her fingertips. It was a flea. I felt embarrassed, and suddenly itchy, after two days of close proximity with a pack mule.

The woods-woman said nothing, but went to one side of her hut. For the first time I noticed that a wall of near-transparent, tangled white threads extended from the wood frame of the hut to the nearby bushes. There must have been a dozen spiders-webs there, some new, some old, some clean and others trapped fallen leaves, or the grizzly remains of past meals. Whilst Master John and I watched, speechless, she flung the flea into one of the smaller webs. A ripple in the ephemeral sheet of gossamer told us that the master of the web had claimed his meal. She waited a short while, and then reached into the web with a sudden, violent movement. She came away with a spider now wriggling between her fingertips. Master John and I shuddered, ghastly awestruck. Next the woman, who was beginning to terrify us, went to a small hole in the earth near the foot of the hut. She threw the spider, still struggling, deep inside. After a few moments, a delighted squeak told us that yet another denizen of this bizarre dwelling had claimed a meal. Now, the woman reached into the burrow with a rapid snatching motion, and dragged a field mouse out by the tail. It squirmed and fought until she unceremoniously beat it a few times against the ground, swinging it by the tail. Then she laid the stunned animal on its back on a flat rock by the entrance to her home, and drew something from her garments. With a gasp I saw that it was a blade made of flint, such as are sometimes found in the tumuli where the most ancient Britons buried their dead. It was a primitive knife, but effective. With one stroke she removed the head of the mouse and with a second slit its belly open. The entrails spilled from the warm stomach, and the woman bent low, scrutinizing them with great attention. It seemed to take her an age, and she must surely have traced every twist and turn in their course with her eyes. Finally, flinging the remains of the mouse into the underbrush, she straightened and turned to us.

"Your intentions are good. You mean no harm to me, and you have come to help someone. Please, enter my home."

I stepped forward eagerly, for my hunger at that age still won out over other emotions. Master John hung back, wearing a look of disgust.

"What have you done? This, this… soothsaying… has long been banned by the Church."

"Has it?" The woods-woman replied coolly. "I will gladly discuss the dictates of the Church when I may do so seated comfortably at a table with the Pope's hired assassins, his private bankers and his lovely mistresses. In the meantime, your young friend is hungry. Come in, there is a quarter of a goat stewing."

That was too much for me. I overcame my awe of the woods-woman and, without glancing back at Master John, for fear he would stop me, I entered the hut. Immediately a divine aroma engulfed my famished senses. I could see little or nothing in the gloom, but my nose effortlessly distinguished goat, mushroom and herb stew, roasted chestnuts and the most welcome smell of all creation: baking bread.

"Master," I called "come in. Don't be concerned, a woman who cooks this well must surely be a saint."

When our eyes finally grew accustomed to the light in the woodswoman's home, we realised that the interior was even more extraordinary than the outside. The walls were smooth baked earth, and the floor was comfortably paved with stone and covered with recently changed dried leaves. Here and there little pots filled with smouldering coals from the central hearth warmed the space. Near the fire an open-necked sack of taut cow hide was hanging just above a small cairn of stones. From time to time the woods-woman used a clay shovel to take a hot stone from the fire and place it at the top of the pile under the hide and took a stone from the bottom of the pile and placed it in the heart of the fire. From the sack came the sound of bubbling and the wonderful smells of cooking that had welcomed me to the hut shortly before. On the other side of the fire loaves of bread were baking on a broad ceramic plate lying directly on live coals removed from the flames.

The most surprising part of the dwelling, however, was to the rear of the hearth.

"Is that a dolmen?" Master John enquired, pointing. He had entered the hut with a suspicious air, and sat uneasily on a log-stool.

"It is." The woods-woman confirmed.

The back wall of the hut was the earth beneath the old holm oak, and the great roots of the tree were visible, some of them curving to form part of the roof and walls of the hut, and one of them even plunged vertically down through empty space from the roof to the floor. But what was most extraordinary was the fact that the roots below where the trunk must have been grew down and around an enormous horizontal stone slab, supported in turn by two vertical ones about half the height of a man, all of which were embedded in sweet-smelling earth.

"It has been there since the world was young. When the ancients forgot it, the leaves, and underbrush, filled the space beneath it and around it, and the wind brought dust and the dust and leaves became soil, and the dolmen became a knoll. The old tree grew upon it, and our home grew with it."

"*Our* home?" Master John asked.

"I am not the first, and not the only one." She mystically replied. "We are the ones who don't forget. But the young man is suffering. Here."

She scooped some hot roasted chestnuts into her hand from a large clay pot, and passed them to me. "Eat. The goat will soon be ready. There's a lot of it, because the villagers who gave it to me were very grateful. I cured their daughter. You'll need appetite, and appetite comes with eating."

I drew my knife to crack them open, but the woods-woman signalled me to put it away.

"Use your fingers. The shells are brittle and fall away easily. You can keep your knives, of course, but please don't use them. No metal may be used in this house."

For the first time I noticed that *none* of the objects surrounding us contained any form of metal. I put the knife hurriedly away. Fortunately, she was right and the chestnuts were easily shelled. Master John declined them, still wary of our host.

"You remind me of a monk at Sant'Alberto's Abbey." The woods-woman told him. "He does not trust my knowledge either. He always tells people that true knowledge comes from the study of the stars and planets and the spheres of heaven. He tries to convince the villagers all about not to come to me for help. Often-times they listen to him, and let him heal their children. Sometimes he is able." She admitted, a little grudgingly.

"The spheres of heaven are the only source we have of true knowledge." Master John confirmed, and I felt he must be repeating lessons learned at Paris and Oxford during his student days. "Is the world not imperfect?"

"It is." The woods-woman conceded.

"And are the heavens not perfect?"

She shrugged. "They are a part of the world, and so they must be imperfect."

"No, no," Master John shook his head "they are not a part of the world. They are apart, and perfect. They are the only perfection we mortals are permitted to see and study."

"How can you see the heavens, and study them, if they are not part of this world?" The woods-woman countered. "Consider a tree in the distance, a tree you will never walk up to in your life and touch, you know that tree exists because you see it. Is it not a part of the world?"

"Certainly." Master John agreed.

"And do we see the spirits, or the gods?"

"Certainly not."

"Of course not, they are not a part of our world. Perhaps I am simple, but I think that if you see something it is a part of our world. We see the heavens, they are a part of us, and as imperfect or perfect as we are."

There was a long, uncomfortable pause before Master John finally said with difficulty "Good woman, I think perhaps we should talk of something else. You are being very kind to us, and it is the worst of manners to disagree with one's host."

Starting to feel a little better with a fistful of hot chestnuts in my belly, I made my contribution.

"Did you mention that the troubadours came through these lands?"

Master John snorted just a little at my obsession with the troubadours and their chivalric songs, but I could tell he was pleased at the distraction.

"Yes, generations ago. They came to Auramala, the tower above Sant'Alberto's Abbey, to the court of the Malaspinas. They sang of love and honour to the Lords Malaspina, who knew nothing of either but adored song and poetry. They were beautiful, and their voices were sweeter than a blackbird's. Then they disappeared. The Church destroyed them. For a hundred years their like was not seen again, and then the Florentine came to Auramala. I met him, here in the woods. Like them, his words and song transcended all else."

With growing emotion I realised to whom she was referring.

"You... You met Dante Alighieri?" I was awestruck. She nodded.

"He was travelling much like you are now, with a few young servants and a mule. His mule, though, was laden with parchment and tools for writing. He had just left the court of Auramala, and was clearly very angry. I believe that man was indignant, for one reason or another, every single day of his life. Perhaps it was for the best, as it just seemed to sharpen the beauty of his voice. He accepted our hospitality…"

"Our? You were not alone?"

"At that time I was but an apprentice, and this house belonged to the woman who taught me how to live with the woods and the mountains. It was she who conversed with the poet. He spoke very little, but listened keenly, and seemed intent upon memorising every gesture she made and every expression upon her face. Perhaps her likeness is to be found today somewhere among his verses."

"Perhaps, yes, among…" I broke off, not wanting to risk offending our host by saying 'among the prophets or witches of Inferno.' The mere thought transported me to Dante's side in his wanderings through the other world among the legions of the damned in Inferno and Purgatory, and the blessed few in Paradise. I found myself thinking, a little blasphemously, that I would have been content even to find myself alongside the woods woman's predecessor in one of the circles of Hell, just for the honour of being written up in verse by Dante Alighieri. Master John, ever practical, broke the lengthening silence for the sake of our task.

"Good woman, we are travelling toward the Shrine of Saint Augustine in Pavia. But while we are here, I am seeking news of a countryman of mine from Ghent, in Flanders, who came to this part of the world, and never returned home, and we have had no news of him for many years. He was an old friend of my family's. His name is… William le Galeys." Master John's question was finely crafted to induce a helpful response. I was certain we were not tracking a man of Ghent, but a Welshman, but the name 'le Galeys', meaning Welshman, would make people think of the man we wanted if they had met him or heard of him. After all, there could not be many Welshmen around that part of the world.

The woods-woman raised her head abruptly, genuine surprise in her eyes. My heart started racing with anticipation, as surely Master John's was.

"Perhaps I have met him."

"Really? That is wonderful news. Where?"

"At Sant'Alberto's Abbey. There is a lay brother there whom they call 'lo Gallese', and he comes from a northern land, but told me himself he was not of Ireland, where the Gaelic speakers are. He may be your friend."

"The Abbey of Sant'Alberto? Are you sure? The last news we had of him, years ago, mentioned a place called Cecima."

It was the first time I had heard the name of Cecima. It was clearly another detail of our task that Master John had never mentioned, for safety's sake. The woods-woman shrugged.

"Cecima, too, is near here. But I met him as a lay-brother at the Abbey of Sant'Alberto."

"And is it far?"

"It is a day's hard walk away. You must cross the River Staffora, either over the bridge at Varzi or at the ford of Bagnaria."

I recognised the local name of the River Ira that Opicino had mentioned in Avignon. Everything was coming together, the 'Gallese', or Welshman, and the River Ira…

"I'm pleased." The woods-woman continued. "When I met him, lo Gallese was very lonely. Though you are sceptical of my means, I am quite certain your coming was for his good."

Master John's only reply was an expression so unreadable that I was certain our coming, as so often in the secret business, was a harbinger of great harm to this man.

"The goat is ready, judging by the smell." Our host informed us. "Let me serve you, and we shall break fresh baked bread together."

Following the woods-woman's directions the next morning, we soon emerged onto a ridge overlooking the valley of the River Staffora, with its brown woods still waiting for spring to paint them green, terraced vineyards, villages and towns and the silver river that snaked its way along at the mountains' feet. Far above, on a mountain peak, a large area was cleared of trees, leaving the crest bare. There, the last of the winter snows reflected the sun's rays upon the magnificent round tower of the Malaspinas, Auramala Castle, which seemed to leap skyward through that white glow like the head of an all-seeing eagle rising from its eyrie.

"Come," Master John beckoned "if we're lucky we'll have found our man by nightfall."

As we led our mule further and further down the slope, a rushing sound like wind in the trees grew ever stronger, and I realised it was the roaring of water. At last we stumbled onto the riverside. Not far from the opposite bank stood a large, grey-stone village, closed within its fortified wall on the hillside. We realised it must be Bagnaria, the town the woods-woman had mentioned.

The course of the river was broad, and violently swollen with rushing water from the melting snows in the mountains. The sound was now deafening, and I thought its name was appropriate, at least in the early spring, for this at last was the Ira, the 'Anger'. William Bateman's words in Avignon came ironically back to mind: one might find ruin even in the waters of smaller rivers, washing down from smaller mountains. Master John was evidently thinking the same thing, for he turned back from contemplating the river's course, shaking his head with doubt.

"The water is too fast and rough. Sensible men would turn east to Varzi, where there is a stone bridge, then double back."

I came forward to get a better look at the river myself, and shuddered at its vortices and eddies. Then a movement caught my eye, and I squinted against the sun to see better. There was a woman on the north bank among the reeds, a basket full of charcoal held steady on the top of her head with one hand. In the other hand she held a red scarf that she was waving to get our attention.

"Master John, look!" he followed my arm, and saw the woman, too. She started striding westwards along the river bank, beckoning us to follow along on our side. We followed her striding and waving figure, till she stopped abruptly at a point in which the rushing water was parted in the centre of its course by a large protruding rock, whose surface was stained by a rich colour somewhere between blood and rust. She pointed to the rushing water, and, never lowering the heavy basket from her head, made a comical imitation of wading. Master John and I looked at each other, and then at the surface of the water.

"There are less eddies here, Master." I bellowed into his ear.

"There must be a rock-ford down below that we can't see. But the water is devilishly fast, Will. Can we make it across?"

"Master, I have an idea." Since I had been obliged to hold our mule's rope reigns at every step over the Apennines, I knew how difficult it was to budge him. That would be a blessing for us now.

"Let's hear it."

"We each walk with our bellies against one of the mule's front shoulders, holding on to each other with one arm around his neck and the other over his back. I doubt the water will wash us away, with his leaden feet!"

Master John smiled, and agreed, so we both took our boots off and tied them to the pack on our poor mule's back. We then put one arm each over his broad back, and one around his neck, and clasped each other's wrists just as the sailor had shown me on the voyage from Great Yarmouth to Sluys. As we started walking into the water the woman on the far side gave encouraging waves of her red scarf.

After the shock of the ice cold water, like thousands of frozen pins driven against the skin by the current, I was surprised when my toes found flat stones beneath the surface. Obviously this was the ford the villagers used, just out of sight below the unusually high water. As we edged over the watercourse I gradually lost every sense of touch in my feet from the cold. As we came toward the centre of the river the mule continued to plod along, heedless of the great rock with its red stains. His path was flush with the rock, and he unwittingly pushed me up against the stone so hard I lost my grip on Master John's wrists. Master John and I were both washed violently against the rock, clambering desperately to find a hand hold against the red surface. Fortunately the mule stopped still when he felt our hold fail, and we were able to regain our grip on the beast. Before long, we were stomping through mud and reeds on the far side of the river, and the red-scarfed woman was gabbling away at us, half scolding and half teasing. Her tongue was too fast for us to follow, and the dialect too dense to comprehend.

"Good woman, we're thankful. Let God and Mary be always with you." Master John spoke to her wearily in slow Occitan, hoping she'd understand. To our surprise and gladness, she replied in the same tongue.

"And let Christ's saints be always with you."

After a promising beginning, speaking with the good woman of Bagnaria proved very difficult. She led us into the village, past curious onlookers, all the while gabbling at us in confused Occitan that was so heavily accented that we could only smile and nod our heads. We didn't want to offend her by asking her continually to repeat after she'd been so kind. She led us into the doorway of a kind of tavern, and switched to her impenetrable dialect to shout out in a commanding voice. Then she left us there, swinging down the street with her basket still on her head. In an instant a blonde, bearded landlord appeared, his tunic sleeves rolled up and his hands yellow with wet flour who spoke to us in thankfully intelligible Occitan.

"Good morning to you. You're lucky to have found the ford, with the river so high and fast. Or had you heard to cross where the blood of Christ stains the rock?"

"The blood of Christ?" Master John was startled.

"The great rock in the river where the ford lies. Did you notice the red upon it? That is the blood of Christ himself. When Saint Syrus came from the Holy Land he landed in Genoa, and converted the citizens to Christianity. He then decided to convert Pavia as well, and came north through these valleys. He crossed the River Staffora here at Bagnaria. He was carrying the blood of our Lord in the Holy Chalice, and as he crossed the river a great wave came down from the mountains and made him spill some of the blood on that rock. A thousand years of spring floods haven't been able to wash it away."

He looked curiously at us.

"Did you happen to touch the red on the rock with your hands?" The tavern-keeper asked.

"We did." Master John told him. "Why, what is the significance?"

"Ah, good, then. In these parts we say that if a traveller touches the Blood of Christ without knowing what it is, it is a sign that they are destined to do good."

We both looked at our hands with a mixture of fascination and awe, remembering the feel of the damp red rock against our palms.

"This is excellent news. We had no idea of the miracle of the rock, nor of the ford. A woman of the village helped us find it. A vigorous lady with green eyes, blonde hair and a red scarf."

Perhaps there were many such women in the village, for he scratched his chin through his bushy beard, thought over the description a little and then shrugged his perplexity.

"Who was that, I wonder? No matter, I'll bring you a bucket of water and some cloth to wash your feet. Have you eaten?"

So empty was my stomach after the morning's walk that it made me exclaim before Master John could even think: "Nothing at all!"

"Well, the mid-morning meal has passed, but don't worry, there are plenty of left-overs. You're a growing lad, but you won't starve in Bagnaria!"

Once he'd fetched us the bucket of water we washed the river-mud off our slowly thawing feet, and he set us down on benches near the fireplace to warm our toes.

When he arrived with the food I was pleasantly surprised. I had been expecting cabbage stew with beans, again, but instead we were brought a kind of red, uncooked sausage, very wide and long and covered with something white and powdery. Our host sliced it up finely and served it on platters with seasoned cheese, dripped over with honey, fine white bread and a vegetable that reminded me of fresh-water cress, boiled and tossed with salt and olive oil.

We were such experienced travellers, and so hungry, that we did not hesitate, not even when invited to eat an enormous, raw sausage with a white powdery skin. We were wolfing it down when our host, who had turned his back to fetch us more bread and wine, interrupted our enthusiastic chewing.

"Here, you take the skin off the slices before you eat them." He demonstrated.

"What is the white colour, good man?" Master John was ever curious. I was still too hungry to have cared.

"It's mould. It helps preserve the meat. We call this sausage salami, and nowhere is it made better than here. We marinate the chopped meat and fat with our strong red wine and garlic, then sack it in the clean guts. Then the salami is salted and smoked, and peppered if you are wealthy, and left to dry."

I believe that I would have eaten the mould itself that morning, if I'd been told it was a delicacy. We finished half the sausage and all of the hard, honey-dripped cheese, which our host told us was made of goat's milk. Finally the woman who'd helped us cross the river appeared in the doorway, holding our boots. At first we hardly recognized her without her basket on her head, and without the red scarf waving in her hand. We stood up hastily to greet her and thank her again, and the tavern-keeper laughed in his deep bass.

"But this is my wife, gentlemen!" he told us "and to think I didn't recognize her from your description..."

The woman understood, and promptly gave him an animated tongue-lashing in their native dialect. It was clear she had no qualms about using certain words, for her husband turned a little red, and shook his head ruefully. Perhaps he was recalling his wedding day.

The woman strode into the tavern, and helped herself to a slice of sausage. "You truly are kind, your hospitality is impeccable." Master John thanked them both, while I decided to keep the green-eyed woman company with another slice or two.

The tavern-keeper gratefully acknowledged with a half bow, while his wife settled down onto a bench.

"We are travelling towards the Abbey of Sant Alberto," Master John continued "to honour the Saint at his shrine and because there are some texts of interest there for us. We would, however, like to continue our journey in greater comfort. Do you think we can buy two horses here in the village?"

The tavernkeeper scratched his chin, thinking a while before answering. "Of course, we're on the salt roads here, and we trade horses as needs be with the merchants. We undercut the prices of Varzi, you know… But Sant Alberto's is a two hour walk away from here. Do you really need horses?"

Master John smiled. "Of course, after walking so far we can walk up the mountain to Sant Alberto's. But we do not plan to stay long, as we'll then be moving on. Since we've found such excellent hospitality here…" he indicated the man, his wife, and the tavern "we'd prefer to put our trust in your help for finding two good horses than gamble on finding such good people to deal with somewhere else along our road…"

The woman's green eyes lit up as she listened, and she slapped her thigh vigorously, then thumped her chest. "I will help you, friends. I will make it. My husband not good man for bargains like me, *I* come with you!" The tall blond man shook his head in exactly the same manner as before, and we were left wondering how much haggling he'd had to put up with every day since they'd tied the knot. Master John decided to accept.

"I was hoping you would make such a generous offer, good woman. We feel safe in your hands."

When we'd been left alone to finish our dinner in peace, we spoke in the Flemish a while.

"Master, why are we buying the horses here? Surely they will have some to trade up in the Abbey?"

"That's true," Master John was very serious "but I'm planning ahead in a different way. Listen to me carefully now.

"Today and tomorrow is our moment of greatest danger. We've been tracking this man because, when we find him, we must kill him." My suspicion was confirmed. "But to locate him we must seek hospitality in the monastery. It may take a day to find him if the place is big and populous. We will leave the two horses we buy in the woods along the road in a secret place, so we arrive at the monastery on foot. Once we're done and away the monks will *think* we are escaping on foot, and not realize that we're on horseback and escaping more quickly. With any luck, we shall find him this very evening, and by dawn be well away."

The tavern-keeper's wife led us, now fully fed and booted, to a smith's forge where there were also stables. We led our mule along with us.

"The smith be rich man in village" the woman confided to us "he trade horses too. Trade your mule in bargain, I make you best deal."

The blacksmith was found sipping wine from a pewter cup in a corner of the forge while two young men pounded away, sweating, over a plough-share. Our first impression of the man was not good, as he lazily watched the two boys slave over the hot iron. His chin was fresh-shaved, and his hair short and clean. I felt he spent more time grooming himself than working.

"Giosuè!" the woman shouted from the door-frame above the din, and the man turned to observe us. He came out to deal with us, wine-cup still in hand, but offered none to us. He and the tavern-keeper's wife spoke animatedly for a good while. She gesticulated wildly and he stood with the wine cup between both palms. To my surprise, he spoke no Occitan, and a complicated scene ensued in which our friend from the tavern had to translate for us as needed.

"This is Giosuè, the smith. He have two mares, one have five years, other young, have only two. He want four Genoese pound for old, five for young. Come, we see them."

Master John nodded, and we followed the smith around to his stables, where the horses thoughtfully chewed their oats and ignored us. The green-eyed woman slipped in alongside both horses, and thoroughly looked them over, even pinching their nostrils and inspecting their teeth. Like an actor in a mystery play, she made broad gestures and many an unnecessarily loud mutter as she found faults in our future steeds. Master John and I watched in admiration at the woman's theatrical talent.

She came out of the stalls with a face like a thunderclap, and began a tirade in her native tongue that made the smith pale. He did his best to answer back, and at one stage in the debate even managed to get three full syllables out before he was cut off. Finally, the smith looked more sorely beaten than the plough back in his forge.

The tavern keeper's wife turned to us triumphantly. "He take three pounds for old and four pounds for young, and one saddle he give you. Your mule is two pounds, and you keep saddle, so now you have two. Three and four, seven, less two is five. Is good with you?"

"Excellent." replied Master John, who'd enjoyed the show as much as I had, but wanted to get back on the road. He took out his purse without any further a-do, and counted out the silver pieces. Both the woman and the man looked at them hungrily, and I got the impression they were more accustomed to seeing coins of smaller weight in their village, even though merchants were a commonplace there. Master John paused as he handed the coins over to the smith. "Good woman, will you not take a commission for your hard work haggling?"

The woman snorted. "My commission from smith. My husband have debt with him. Now, no debt. Smith is fool. He have his money from lend money. Man must work, not lend. Stupid fool." Obviously, the man was the local money-lender, and therefore despised.

When our host had led us to the edge of the village and the road for the monastery, Master John asked the question he'd been nurturing since arriving in the village.

"Do you know the folk at the Abbey of Sant'Alberto at all?"

"Of course," she replied "I have cousin is lay-brother there. Sometimes I go visit. Also, in Pizzocorno they not have all things, and sometimes Brothers is come down here for buy things."

"Pizzocorno?"

"Is village near Abbey. Is little place." she sniffed, feeling herself very much a big-city woman, and I suppressed a smile. "You not pass Pizzocorno, is a road to left. You go always on. Is then two miles at Sant'Alberto. You there in sunlight, all good." She broadly gestured along the mountainside, where I fancied I saw the smoke of a village rising.

"Many years ago," explained Master John "a merchant-man of Ghent, my city in Flanders, left for this part of the world, and never came home. We later heard he'd taken up vows in a monastery north of Genoa. Might he be at Sant'Alberto?"

"A Flanders man... There is no Flanders man I know..."

Master John pressed a little. "Are there no foreigners from the north up at the abbey? This man's name is William le Galeys."

"There one north man, he call him *lo Gallese*. I think is from city of 'Galli', because is beautiful man!"

It took a long moment for me to get the joke. *Gallo* in the Romance tongues means 'rooster', or 'cock', and I guessed it was as much a synonym for masculinity in their country as it was in ours. She'd told us that the foreigner was so handsome he must come from Cock City.

"He is lay-brother of Brother Demetrio, the healer." She added helpfully, innocent of the harm she was doing the man.

"We haven't come all this way for nothing, Will," Master John exulted When we were safely on the road "He must be our man." Then he suddenly turned grim, and I understood why. Finding him meant murdering him. "Now let's keep our wits, Will, and be alert. After we pass the road to the left that leads to the other village we must look for a place to hide our horses. We will leave them in the woods below the Abbey, ready for our escape. In this way, we will arrive at the Abbey seemingly on foot, and the monks will believe that we are also escaping on foot, and that will give us an advantage if there is pursuit.

"If we don't find the Welsh pilgrim before the monks are sent to their cells, feign illness. That will bring us directly to the healer. Whatever happens, reason and reckon as if you were I, to predict what I will do from one moment to the next."

"Master," I asked, voicing a thought that had been weighing me down more and more as we approached our destination "may I know why this man is to die?"

"I understand, Will." Master John sighed. "It seems we are duty bound to defend our kingdom's honour with a dishonourable act. Rest assured that we are to kill a man whose actions have been so base as to put him forever beyond such considerations. We may 'weed out' this 'rose' in good conscience." In spite of the firmness of his words, he had the air of a man who was trying to convince himself as much as me. I was taken aback, though I hid it. Master John had never been subject to doubts.

"We have touched the blood of Christ today without knowing it," I observed, hoping to bolster his mood "and are destined to do good." I did not irk Master John by reminding him that the woodswoman had also said the same thing about our intentions.

"That is a great comfort." He agreed, though his gaze was still shaken by a trace of uncertainty.

"But what has this man, this Welsh pilgrim we have been tracking so long, actually done?" I felt the time had come to understand our task completely, and Master John smiled his acquiescence.

"You are right, Will, I must fill out your knowledge, now that we are on the verge of completing our orders. If, for some reason, I should be unable to carry out our duty, you will have to finish the task.

"The Earl of Lancaster's orders to us were as follows: 'Bateman. Welsh Pilgrim, Year III, Pope, Fieschi. Weed out the rose from the Fieschi garden of Pavia' " As ever, he looked at me expectantly, waiting for me to analyse the message and show myself worthy of the secret business.

" 'Bateman' meaning to go to Bateman in Avignon and consult with him." I mused aloud. " 'Welsh Pilgrim, year III, Pope, Fieschi' must refer to some event that happened in Avignon during the third year of the present king's reign. Naturally, Bateman, who knows everything that happens in Avignon at all times, could reveal to us what to do next. That is why we sent him those words in secret writing and arranged to meet him. He directed us to Opicinus, with sufficient hints to let us navigate this far, to these lands in the Diocese of Pavia where the House of Fieschi's influence is strong. The last part of the message, however, is new to me." I stopped, my eyes widening. "We are to remove someone who is pretending to be what they are not."

"Exactly, Will. 'Weed out the rose from the Fieschi garden of Pavia.' "

"To weed is to remove… naturally, to kill, in our case. But you do not weed roses, unless they are not roses. We are to remove… an impostor?"

"Precisely. Our victim is an impostor. He is pretending to be a member of our royal bloodline, a rose, in hiding as a lowly pilgrim in this Abbey. The House of Fieschi is using him to blackmail the King."

I felt at once indignant at such a crime and awed by the importance of the task that had been entrusted to us.

"They would blackmail the King himself? Master John, we have never been honoured by such a high-reaching task."

"It's true Will." he was most serious. "And now you understand why this man is beyond all redemption. This may be the most important day's work we ever do."

"But" I was not done reasoning "there is something else. The content of the second document Sir Thomas Aldcliffe delivered to you. There were two letters, not one, and you took a long time over memorizing them both. Am I to know what the other letter said?"

Master John was silent for a long while. The uncertainty that had plagued him earlier, when justifying the assassination we were planning to perform, returned to his eyes.

"I'm afraid not." He replied at last. "If I can, I will take that information with me to my grave, and may it remain there forever."

Chapter 19

Valley of the River Staffora, the same afternoon of March, 1338

*Natalino's doubts – toward the sunlight –
some wounds are natural*

That particular day, for a reason he himself could neither identify nor fathom, Brother Demetrio did not immediately return to his workshop after he left Tino with the Welshman. He paused at a short distance from the two, where the trunks and low branches obscured him but he could listen and watch their faces.

"I've remembered another story the old men tell in my land." The Welshman was saying. "It's about a unicorn." The Welshman smiled down at Tino's crown of curly brown hair. The boy's eyes were tracing the gnarls of a beech tree root that protruded from the snow that still covered much of the mountainside. He did not answer.

"What's wrong, Tino? Don't you want to hear the story? Yesterday you were begging me for a new one."

"Are *you* in the story?" Tino's tone was odd, and his eyes remained lowered. Both the Welshman and Brother Demetrio in his hiding place frowned. This was not like the cheerful young boy.

"No, it's not about me. Why?"

"Nothing."

"Would you like me to be in the story?"

Tino raised his head, his eyes strange, not meeting the Welshman's gaze.

"You'll change the story if I ask you to?"

"Of course. With a little imagination."

Tino finally looked up at the Welshman, his eyes flashing.

"You mean you make your stories up while you're telling them?"

"Well… sometimes." The Welshman admitted.

"I thought they were true stories." Tino was clearly wounded.

"Most of them are. The tale of the Red Dragon is very ancient. It's been told by all the great bards in my land, so it's particularly true."

"What about that story you told me, the one about you?" This was clearly what was worrying Tino, for his eyes dropped back down to the tree roots. Brother Demetrio, who had been on the verge of leaving to go about his business, was compelled to remain. Had the mysterious Welshman revealed his past to Tino?

"That was the truest of all. I was a part of everything that happened, and told it without inventing anything." He gently shook the boy by the shoulder. "I swear it to you, Tino. I never lie about myself. I am incapable of it." His young friend looked up at last in a mixture of trust and mistrust, gratitude and betrayal.

"Why this sudden concern for the truthfulness of tales?" The Welshman tried to make light, disturbed by those nascent tears. "You weren't so worried about that when all were saying my head would transform into a dog's head, or that I was a werewolf!" He twisted his lips into a playful mock snarl, and Tino couldn't help but giggle. Brother Demetrio, too, smiled silently in his concealment.

"It's Matteo, Gallese."

Brother Demetrio remembered Matteo. The oldest boy in the clutter of cousins in Tino's extended family, Matteo was on the cusp of manhood but not yet a man. He tried to make the other children obey him as though he were adult, but the more he tried the less they respected him, and his frustration grew.

"What has he said?" The Welshman gently enquired. "What has he done?"

"He says I'm a credulous baby, and that you and Nonno make everything up while you're storytelling. He says I need to grow up, and spend less time listening and more time working." Tino's words came out in a flood. "So I told him that once, long ago you were an important man – I didn't tell him what you told me, I kept it a secret – and he said I was gullible and silly, and he slapped me hard." Tino rubbed his cheek in recollection.

The Welshman smiled sadly.

"Tino… how can I explain…" He paused for a moment. "Do you see this great tree? Which way does it lean?" Tino was confused. The noble walnut stood on the edge of a small, snow-covered meadow that in the warmer seasons was a grassy nest of wild-flowers. The tree leant away from the shadowy woods toward the open sunlight.

"That way." Tino pointed.

"Why not that way?" The Welshman pointed into the dark woods.

"Because... because of the light. Here there's more light."

"And light is... good for the tree." Brother Demetrio felt the Welshman was struggling to find the right words. "You see... By nature, every being leans toward what it needs. A tree leans toward the light. What does *your* nature lean towards – Matteo's insults and abuse, or the stories your grandfather and I tell?"

Brother Demetrio realised that, in spite of his world-weary age, the Welshman's child-like simplicity led him to concepts and modes of expression that a bright peasant boy like Tino could share and feel a part of. Indeed, the youngster instantly smiled and replied:

"Toward you and my grandfather, of course." Then he pointed almost fearfully toward the gloomiest part of the wood. "But Gallese, what if a seed falls in there?"

"You're right, Tino." He frowned. "Sometimes a tree comes up where there is no light. Sometimes people do, too. There are sickly and twisted trees in the darkest woods, and men's souls can be the same."

"Why do some seeds fall in the darkness, and others near the light?"

"That's Lady Fortune's doing, I fear." The Welshman's tone was troubled. "I grew up... in the shadows cast by one mighty tree, my father. He was very different to your father. His shadow was so large, and strong, and so perfect, that I felt like nothing more than a shadow myself, not a sapling. And even when he was not there anymore, there were many other strong trees all about me, choking me of air and light." He paused, and then of a sudden smiled warmly at Tino. "But *you* are not growing in the darkness. Your father stands over you, protecting you from the wind, but letting the sunlight through. And when darkness touches you, you vie away immediately. You came to me here of your own will. Would you have come to meet your father here, or your grandfather, or grandmother?"

"Of course I would have come." Tino did not hesitate.

"And would you have come to meet Matteo here, if he had bid you come?"

"Never." Tino smiled, his eyes now tearless and sparkling. "He would love to get me alone for a beating, but he won't catch me."

The Welshman ruffled the boy's curls, fondly.

"I have met your father and grandparents, and know they are fine people. You naturally lean towards them like this tree leans toward the sun, and you naturally lean away from Matteo. If I am counted among the people you lean towards, I am deeply honoured. For me, you are like a grandson." The Welshman smiled warmly, happy to have said this at long last. "I know you are not my grandson, but I like to think of you that way. It's the way I humour… the old man inside me, the failed father and grandfather I left behind when I went away from the world. As for my stories, let your nature tell you their worth."

Tino smiled, not wholly understanding, but glad nevertheless.

"Now, Tino, our story-time has passed in chatter, and I think your nonna must be waiting for you to go to Pizzocorno. Don't worry any more about Matteo, he uses his fists because he has no wits to employ in their place!"

When Tino had gone, the old monk calmly emerged from behind a chestnut, his arms folded cryptically across his chest.

"Brother Demetrio," the Welshman rose quickly "were you looking for me for some work? I'm sorry, I was talking to Don Rogerio's boy."

"I know, I know. I heard." Brother Demetrio's face, normally lively with gruff kindness, was now thoughtful.

"I'm sorry if I have wasted time. How can I serve you?"

"Don't worry, *Gallese*, you haven't been wasting time. If I thought this were a waste of time, I would never have given you leave to accept the family's invitation, nor to meet the boy in free moments." Brother Demetrio was reassuring, but there was something unusual in his expression.

"Brother Demetrio, why…" The Welshman hesitated, wondering whether or not he really wanted to know. "Why *have* you let me spend so much free time for this friendship? The other lay-brothers work from dawn until dusk. You can't be doing this so I can teach him the Latin, for I'm hardly the best person for the task."

Now Brother Demetrio smiled. "You're a better teacher of the Latin than you are a speaker. The boy's progress has even been noted by some of my Brothers. He comes to confession more often than before, just for the pleasure of pronouncing the formulae.

"But I understand your question. I give you this time with Tino because I am a healer, and in this way I am helping to heal two people, a boy and a man."

The Welshman was perplexed, but content to be restored to the role of the pupil. "I don't understand. I'm aware of my wounds. But Tino? How is he wounded?"

"Tino is a bright boy, and a good soul, but his mother was denied to him at birth, and his father is so busy being a father to all, that often he is not a father to his son. Nothing so dreadful, and nothing that can't be said of hundreds of other boys in this world, but it is a wound nevertheless. And I am a healer."

The Welshman nodded.

"And *my* wound, Brother Demetrio?"

"Indeed." The strangeness in the monk's face deepened. "*Your* wound." The old man lowered himself onto the jutting tree-root, and scratched his chin. "Some wounds are difficult to see, because they are a natural part of any life. Just think of childbirth, and the wounds a mother receives giving life and light to her infant. They are natural, and right, but that doesn't mean they needn't be healed.

"I think your wound may come from something... unnatural. Something no man is normally called to experience. Of course, I cannot know what it is," Brother Demetrio carefully, delicately caught the Welshman's eyes with his "unless, of course, you tell me your story. Who you are, and what you have been through, that you should have chosen to come away from the world."

"I do not tell my story. I took a vow." The Welshman looked away.

"Confession is sacrosanct. You need not fear."

"I'm sorry, Brother Demetrio." The Welshman shook his head. "You have been kind to me. I just can't tell you."

The old healer nodded with a smile. "Of course, I understand."

There ensued a long silence, while the two men looked up to the sky through the waving branches, still skeletal after the winter but decorated with hundreds of tiny green buds ready to spring leaves. Finally the Welshman turned back to Brother Demetrio.

"Brother Demetrio, if you do not know the nature of my wound, how can you know that my friendship with Tino is healing it?"

"Gallese... since you made friends with Tino you no longer lose yourself in conversation with someone unseen." Brother Demetrio turned toward the Abbey. "Come, or we'll be late for vespers."

As they ambled back, the Welshman asked the healer "Isn't it foolish to give so much care to a peasant boy and a lay-brother? In the order of the world, we are so unimportant."

The old monk didn't think before replying. He didn't need to.

"Compassion can never be foolish. And, Gallese, do not mistake the world's order for the Lord's order. They are two very different matters. And I am a man who has taken vows. I observe the Lord's order."

Chapter 20

Valley of the River Staffora, March 1338

The Welshman's confession – a face once seen, long ago – rescuing one's own murder victim

It was an eerie feeling to prowl an Abbey, one of those bustling Citadels of the Lord, like two lionesses bristling with readiness for the kill. For the rest of the afternoon we kept our knives ready beneath our robes, even while we went to call upon the Abbot in his chapel, to pay our respects. As Master John would say, assassination is nine-tenths opportunity and one-tenth execution. We might chance upon our victim, whom we knew to be the healer's lay-brother, in one of the Abbey's winding stone corridors, under the carved arches of a cloister, exiting the kitchens, or drawing water from courtyard well. We made a point of stopping all the lay-brothers we encountered and asking them directions. 'Minister, are the Abbot's quarters on this floor?' or 'Minister, is the refectory near?' We hoped that the unique accent of the Welsh or of the English would betray our target. If so, and the place of that fortuitous meeting, by incredible luck, was deserted, we would make our kill there and then and begin our escape toward the horses in the woods. It was a remote chance, but a chance nonetheless.

None of the seven lay-brothers we met on the way to the Abbot's quarters spoke with a northern lilt. No sooner had we exchanged greetings with the saintly old leader of Sant'Alberto and taken our leave of him than, all alone in a narrow, windowless hall, we met a tall and greying lay-brother, with clear hazel eyes.

"Minister, is the library on this floor?" While Master John addressed him we both slipped our right hands beneath our gowns to our knife-hilts. When the man fixed Master John with a startled look, my heart skipped a beat and my fingers clasped my weapon. Was our victim acquainted with Master John of old? Surely I would have been informed?

"No, magister, it's on the floor below."

His thick accent left no doubt as to his origins: He was Sicilian. The man lived.

After more fruitless encounters with lay-brothers, we retired to our cell for ablutions before the evening meal.

"Master John, let me pretend to be ill. That's the surest way to find the healer's assistant."

My Master shook his head.

"Let's be patient. During the meal the entire population of the Abbey will be present. We will have all the time we need to look at faces. Afterwards, if we still haven't identified the 'rose to be weeded out', you will pretend to be sick, and we will go to meet the healer in the infirmary. In some way we will contrive to discover the whereabouts of his cell. Most probably idle chatter with him, or with the healer, will suffice. By sunrise he will be dead, silently and secretly."

The Welshman found great solace in the evening meals taken together with the community of Brothers in the refectory. After the meal, the lay-brothers left the hall first by tradition, but that evening his legs seemed loath to carry him to his cell. He lingered in the refectory hall while his peers filed out in silence.

Sharing bread and victuals with men of God while listening to a Bible reading, and then the singing of prayers before retiring to the cells, all instilled a sense of peace in his aging soul. Since coming to these hills, first to the hermitage of San Ponzo near Cecima and then to Sant'Alberto, he had discovered that Silence was the wisest of all rules in monastic life. He reflected that the Lord our Father, his Son and their Spirit were not to be found in any words other than the Word, which can only be heard if one is not talking.

Abruptly he realised that almost all of his fellow lay-brothers had gone, and he would have to hurry to avoid making the monks wait for him. As he stepped quickly to the stone archway, he came face to face with the Abbot's two guests, who had arrived that evening towards Vespers. According to tradition, they were the first to leave the hall after the lay-brothers.

The young pupil glanced at him for an instant, then looked away again. The older man, a worldly-looking cleric wearing fine Flemish woollens, caught his gaze with piercing blue eyes, and for the briefest moment the Welshman thought they might have met somewhere long before. He hoped he was mistaken. If they had met, it must have been during his worldly life. Shaken, he looked down and hurried through the archway.

That night in his cell, the Welshman found that the spiritual calm of the refectory hall had deserted him. Not only was he uncertain whether or not he had already met the Abbot's guest from Flanders, but he could not help wondering how much of his conversation with Tino had been overheard by old Brother Demetrio. In his anxiety he found himself, for the first time in months, slipping back into conversation with the unseen.

Did Brother Demetrio hear that I recounted our story to Tino? Will he try to interrogate Tino to find out more about us? But no, surely Brother Demetrio would not be cruel to the boy that way.

In his mind, the Welshman heard his own words to Tino, echoed by the very same words as he had pronounced them to Manuele Fieschi in confession at Cecima more than a year before.

"...And then a servant came to me, and he said 'My Lord, Sir Thomas de Gurney and Sir Simon de Bereford have come to kill you. If you please, I will give you my clothes, so that you can evade them.'..."

"*...Tunc cum dictis raubis, hora quasi noctis, exivit carcerem.*" Master John intoned, his face a mask of concentration. In our cell, I listened at long last, almost unbelieving, to the letter that my Master had memorized that night long before, at my home in Norwich, before we set out upon our journey. It was the letter Sir Thomas de Aldcliffe had brought, together with our orders. The two scribes in Avignon had paid with their lives for unwittingly copying that letter. It was the letter that had caused the Earl of Lancaster to engage our services.

"Then, wearing the guardian's clothes, at twilight, your father left his prison. When he had reached the last door without resistance, because he was not recognized, he found the porter sleeping, and immediately killed him. Taking the keys to the door, he left together with the servant. The knights who had come to kill him, seeing that he had escaped, feared the Queen's wrath upon their persons. They cut the heart from the porter and placed his body into a coffin, and maliciously presented to the Queen the heart and body of the porter as belonging to your father. This body was then buried in Gloucester as the body of the King. And after your father had escaped his prison, he was received by Lord Thomas in the castle of Corfe together with his servant, where he remained for a year and a half. Afterwards, having heard that the Earl of Kent had been beheaded for believing your father to be still alive, he took a ship with his servant and crossed into Ireland where he was for nine months.

"Fearing lest he be recognized there, having taken the habit of a hermit, he came back to England and proceeded to the port of Sandwich, and crossed the sea to Sluys. Afterwards he turned his steps to Normandy and from Normandy, as many do, going down through the Occitan, came to Avignon. There, having given a florin to the servant of the pope, he sent a document to Pope John. The Pope summoned him and held him secretly and honourably more than fifteen days. Finally he left for Paris, and from Paris to Brabant and from Brabant to Cologne so that out of devotion he might see the Three Kings, and leaving Cologne he crossed over Germany, that is to say, he headed for Milan in Lombardy, and from Milan he entered a certain hermitage of the Castle of Mulazzo, in which hermitage he stayed for two years and a half; and because war overran this castle, he moved to the Castle of Cecima in another hermitage of the diocese of Pavia in Lombardy, and he was in this last hermitage for two years, always the recluse, doing penance, and praying God for you and other sinners. In testimony of which I have caused my seal to be affixed for the consideration of Your Highness.

Manuele de Fieschi, notary of the lord Pope, your devoted servant."

By the time Master John had finished reciting the letter I was pacing the cell in agitation.

" 'your father', the letter says." I stopped and stared at Master John. "But the letter was addressed to the King… That means this lay-brother, the Gallese, the Welshman… Am I to believe that he is the father of the King? He is Edward of Caernarfon, King Edward the Second of England?"

"I am almost sure of it, Will." Master John's blue eyes were earnest. "I met the old King once, and I learned the important features of his face, the set of his eyes and mouth. He has changed, but not that much. And then, just look at him; Edward of Caernarfon always was a tall, handsome, athletic man. Yes, I'm sure it is him. The Earl of Kent did not give his life for a charade. They must have known the truth when they plotted to release him from imprisonment years after he was reported dead to the world. Edward of Caernarfon is alive." Even Master John, normally so calm and reasoning, had become agitated. And I understood why.

"Master, we have been told this man is a 'rose to be weeded', to be taken out. Until tonight you had thought that meant he was an impostor to be killed. And yet, now you are sure he is really the father of the King…"

"Will, I believe Bateman in Avignon uncovered a copy of this letter for the Earl of Lancaster. That is why we were sent to Avignon to speak with Bateman. But the Earl of Lancaster, after reading this letter, must have thought the man was an impostor placed here by the Fieschis as a ploy to blackmail our King. Or would he knowingly have ordered the assassination of a King of England?"

"It may be that he did, Master." I spoke slowly, incredulous at my own words. "Can you imagine the chaos that would break out if the old King were to return and attempt to reclaim his throne? I'm young, but I remember enough of his reign to realize how disastrous it was. How inept, how weak he was, how unlike a king, and how the barons despised him to the point of bringing war against him many times, tearing our England apart. The threat of restoring such a monarch to power really would be the perfect blackmail against the Ki… the present King. Lancaster may well have cold bloodedly ordered the assassination of a King of England to forestall that threat. And then, let us not forget that both Lancaster's uncle, Thomas, and his father, Henry, rebelled against the old King, who was their cousin, and had Piers Gaveston, his lover, executed."

Master John was silent. We found ourselves in a far land, alone in the depth of the night, faced by a decision far beyond our birth. Was this assassination really what the Earl of Lancaster had in mind? Our orders had been so… terse, and vague. Should we – *could we* - knowingly kill a king, no matter how despised?

"He's not King. He renounced his throne." Master John seemed almost to have heard my thought itself.

"He was forced to." I pointed out. "But a king is ordained by God before a crown ever touches his head. Can man undo what God has wrought?" Of the two of us, I was always the one who cared most for honour, and the divine law that imbued the nobility with its power. After all, my father was a Knight.

"No, man cannot. And yet, think of the consequences for England if he were to return. Perhaps... No!" He paused. "Or should we..."

"Master, please listen." I had never so openly sought to sway his mind. But then, I had never seen him so utterly at a loss for what to do. "How can we take it upon ourselves to make such a decision, out here, all alone, without sufficient information? Back when that candle was still burning tall," I gestured toward the stump by whose light we spoke "before we knew that the 'Gallese' was the King's father, if you had been asked what you thought of Roger Mortimer, wouldn't you have decried him as the greatest villain of our age?" Master John nodded, slowly. "And why? Because he seduced Isabella, who was then the old King's wife and Queen. Because he gathered rebels about him in Hainault and then took up arms against England, his motherland. But more than all these crimes, we loath the very memory of the man because he had the old King, Edward of Caernarfon, imprisoned and then killed. At least, we thought so. And that was a crime against God himself, even though Edward of Caernarfon had abdicated. It is true that he removed an incompetent king from power, but *nothing* can justify what he did. Or what we thought he had done. Are we now to do the same?"

Master John was silent for a long time, gazing at the candle. Then, quietly, choosing his words with great care, he began to reveal to me the greatest secret of his life.

"There's something I have never told you, Will. It happened in the last year of the old King's reign, more than ten years ago. The Earl of Pembroke, who oversaw the secret business in those days, had just died. With his death, the most powerful man in the country was now indisputably the old King's favourite, Hugh Despenser of Tewksbury. Orders and instructions had become sporadic and confusing. Sometimes our instructions even directly bore Hugh Despenser's seal, as though he were truly the lord of the land. Even when they did bear the royal seal itself, we were often unsure whether they expressed the King's will, or Despenser's. Some agents left the country, to sell their services to the highest bidder, but most, like myself, merely lay low until the situation improved."

"That was always the King's greatest weakness." I commented, thankful that the old King Edward's reign had come to a close when

I was still a boy. "How can a man who prefers the love of other men to that of the fairer sex be a leader of a nation?"

"And Richard the Lionheart?" Master John inquired. "Was his love for Blondel the minstrel really an obstacle between him and greatness? Certainly no one ever hesitated to follow him into battle, and perhaps his longing to accomplish deeds that could be sung by his lover pushed him to even greater heights of bravery. No, love is rarely destructive in and of itself, whatever its nature. It was the old King's inability to perceive that his favourites were manipulating him, and the ease with which he deferred decisions to his lovers, first Piers Gaveston and then Hugh Despenser, that brought us to ruin."

"Then Roger Mortimer escaped from the Tower of London, as you and I did from the castle of Genoa, and the shape of power within England was thrown upside down. He was the exact opposite of the old King Edward and his lovers. A successful, battle-hardened warlord, a promiscuous womanizer and a man of swift, firm decisions and steel will. When the rumour that he had seduced Queen Isabella started to spread, the fear in the Despenser camp was palpable, and the instructions to us, the royal agents, became more and more conflicting, confusing and panicky. Then, soon after the Battle of Boroughbridge, where I saved your father's life and forged the bond between me and your family, I received a summons I would dearly have loved to refuse, but could not. The old King himself, in person, wished to speak with me to give me a task.

"At court I was ushered into a room with the King and Hugh Despenser, and no one else. Despenser began by flattering me for my past service to the King, for the way in which I had saved your father's life, for my cool head in hot situations. Those who were unfortunate enough to have regular dealings with the man said he always started out by flattering, and finished by bullying. Fortunately, my acquaintance with him lasted just a few moments.

"When the King himself spoke, my impression was that he had rehearsed his speech to me many times, most likely with Despenser there to coach him.

" 'De Ulgham, I order you to go to Hainault and kill Roger Mortimer. He has seduced my wife, the Queen, and is holding my son Prince Edward against his will in their custody. The man is a traitor against his King, and therefore against God himself, and must be destroyed. I cannot afford to risk warfare by sending an expedition to capture him. I need you to remove him, invisibly and silently, for the Prince's sake and the good of all England.' "

"And that, Will, is exactly what I did... Or almost did. Unwillingly, I made my way alone to Hainault, travelling as a steelwright, an identity I have never used since. Then I broke into the palace of William of Hainault by night, and discovered the room where Queen Isabella and Mortimer were confabulating, planning the invasion of England and the deposition of the King. I had everything ready, my escape route was secure, and Mortimer's back was to me. All I had to do was step forward, cut his throat and then melt away again, before the Queen could so much as scream."

Master John fell silent. I had been tensely focused on the sound of his voice, not quite believing what I was hearing. Then the candle began to gutter and its glow to fade. I quickly lit another, and by the renewed light turned back to my Master.

"Roger Mortimer lived..."

"He did. Because I wanted him to." Master John's eyes held mine. "Because I realized that if I obeyed the King's orders, or Despenser's as they probably were, I would rob England of the one man still in a position to save our country from its own rightful ruler.

"You see, that was the paradox of the old King's reign. His behaviour upon the throne was so damaging that, one by one, all the nobles of the realm were forced to make a distinction for the first time between Crown and King. That was the root of the Ordinances that the Barons forced upon the King, the idea that the Crown was a separate entity to the man who wore it. The Crown represented the country itself and the Lord God's divine rule over it, and it was to the Crown that every Englishman owed his highest duty, including the King himself. For rebellious barons like Mortimer, this was the reasoning that allowed them to declare war upon their sovereign. For the King, of course, it was heresy. And for me? What did I believe?"

Master John sighed.

"Will, you can barely remember how dire the situation in England was toward the end of the old King's reign. The nation was nearly destitute, Scotland and Ireland nearly lost, and our heartland of England open to invasion should a foreign power have wished to conquer it. That night I found myself in the same position the great lords of the realm had found themselves in so many times before; faced with a choice between loyalty to the Crown and what it represented, and loyalty to the man who wore it. I chose the Crown. I chose England, in the hopes that Roger Mortimer might restore order to the land, and hand a strong kingdom over to the Prince."

"Master…" I hesitated "why are you telling me this now?"

I was surprised, and uncomfortable to perceive the puzzlement and uncertainty in his expression.

"I don't know. Perhaps… perhaps it is the fact that I once knowingly disobeyed this man when he was King that makes me want to give him a second chance now that he is a lowly lay-brother."

Master John shook his head, the set of his shoulders suddenly decisive. He rose from his seat, and looked me in the eye.

"Will, you are right. We cannot take this decision upon ourselves. We're going to take Edward of Caernarfon back to England, and deliver him to his son – alive."

The Welshman shivered, and drew his cloak tight about him. He had not expected such a penetrating, icy wind. But then, cloudless days always made for chilling nights.

He paused to gaze at the silver-specked canopy above. It stretched seamlessly from the jagged black horizon behind him, where the Alps threw their peaks up in vain toward the heavens, to the naked branches of chestnuts and beeches before him, grasping and groping at the fleeting stars. The milky-way was a wake of frozen sea spray, whipped from the crests of infinitely cold and distant waves by a gust of celestial wind.

The Abbey was already out of sight behind him, along the twisting road. He slowly resumed his journey.

The old healer picked his way carefully through his cluttered workshop. Mortars and pestles, knives with strangely shaped blades, bulbous glass vessels and little clay vases with many-coloured contents all crowded about him on the dusty shelves. Brother Demetrio carefully took down a vase containing a lumpy brown substance, and spooned a dose of it into a pewter cup filled with watered-down wine. He mixed it vigorously.

"Here, young master, this should make you feel a little better."

I started to sit up with difficulty, nauseously grimacing. I had been lying on the old healer's wooden bench. His young novice, Gilio, quickly put his arm around my shoulders to help me rise. My brow was spangled with cold sweat. It was a gift of mine, this ability to act so thoroughly ill when it suited me. I even let my ring finger tremble a little as I reached for the cup.

"Thank you, Brother."

"What did you eat today? This must be food poisoning." Brother Demetrio frowned at me as I sipped. I had the unnerving sensation that he was not taken in by my act. Master John answered for me.

"We ate in the town by the river, Bagnaria I think it's called. There was a kind of raw sausage. It was called… salom?"

"Salami?"

"Yes, that's what they called it. It was very strange, and it was covered with mould. They told us it was a delicacy."

"Hmmm." Brother Demetrio nodded, clearly doubtful that salami could possibly cause food poisoning. In other circumstances, Master John would have been more cautious in his probing, but we were dismayed to have arrived at the healer's workshop only to find that his lay-brother was not present. Our intention was to take him from the Abbey that very night. Where was Edward of Caernarfon?

"Brother Demetrio," Master John began "we were told in Bagnaria that there is a foreigner here, of the northern lands. Many years ago, a man of Ghent, my city, went shipping in the Mediterranean and never came home. Last year we heard that he had become a lay-brother in an Abbey near Genoa. Do you know if there is such a man here?"

I didn't look up from my cup of medicine, feigning disinterest in the subject. Brother Demetrio did not answer immediately. The novice, however, had none of his self-control.

"We have a lay-brother from the northern lands here, but he's not Flemish. He's *gallese*. He works with us. Well, he *tries* to work."

"Ah? What a shame he's not here." Master John had his next move ready. "Perhaps he is our fellow Ghentman. You know, his surname was Galéy, perhaps he just translated his name as *Gallese*."

The novice seemed taken aback.

"Really? Then it might be him…"

Brother Demetrio, however, remained impassively silent, watching me carefully. I cursed myself inwardly for my arrogance in presuming to fool such an experienced old healer.

"Can we meet him?" Master John's request seemed innocent enough, but Giglio shook his head.

"He's gone. A messenger came for him tonight, after the evening meal. He…"

"Giglio, *fave lingua!*" Brother Demetrio brusquely interrupted the youth. 'Shut up!'

Master John shot a glance in my direction. The old man hadn't swallowed our act. As one we rose, knives in hand. Before our hearts had beaten twice, my blade was pressed cruelly against Giglio's throat, and Master John's against Brother Demetrio's.

"Make no sound," Master John hissed "we don't want to kill you." He looked across into Giglio's eyes. "Yet." He had, correctly, identified the novice as the weak point to exploit.

I pushed the young man up against the work table, bending him over backwards till his head roughly struck a marble cutting board, my knife never leaving his neck. His breathing became spasmodic, and he began to whimper, his pupils wide with terror in the candle light.

"What happened to the Welshman? Where did they take him?" My voice was low, and my tone was implacable.

"I… He was… They… took him to Auramala. To… it's the castle…"

"How long ago?"

"Just… just now."

"Which road leads to the castle? How far is it?"

"To the right… of the gates. In the time… as long… as it takes to… to dine at mid-morning."

I felt something damp against my thigh, and pulled myself away slightly. He had wet himself in his fear.

Brother Demetrio was looking on, his grim face fearless.

"You mean to kill him, don't you?"

Master John did not answer.

"You are creatures of Satan." The old man grated, uncaring of the blade at his throat. "Life is God's gift. Healing is God's work. Killing is blasphemy."

"This morning" Master John murmured to him with earnest "we unknowingly touched the blood of Christ on the rock in the river. Believe me, we have come to do good." Then he carefully, measuredly clubbed Brother Demetrio on the back of his head with the butt of his knife. The healer slowly folded into unconsciousness in Master John's arms. As my Master gently laid him on the bench, I knocked the novice senseless much less tenderly, and left him sprawled on the table.

The Welshman halted once more where a curve in the path and a gap in the trees revealed the tower of Auramala, at once distant and awfully near, a bleak monolith of unearthly silver stone, bathed in the snow-reflected starlight and the first creeping rays of the rising moon. The sight of his destination seemed to petrify his feet against the icy road.

"I don't want to go." He told the Watcher.

The tall, black haired and black bearded man stopped, and turned slowly around to face his ward.

"You must." His eyes, as ever, were impenetrable save a hint of contempt. Not for the Welshman, but for everything he saw about him.

"I was two years at Mulazzo, and two more at Cecima. Why must I now move on so soon?

"You're too close to Cecima. The people of this valley have come to know you too well. The Malaspinas have many other castles, far from here, that guard hermitages in which you can hide."

"I don't want to go. Here I feel… I feel at home. The people are my friends."

The Watcher merely shrugged. "That's why you must go."

He turned back to the road ahead. The Welshman, however, did not move. After taking a few steps, the Watcher realized his ward was not following him, and stopped. Without even turning around, he spoke.

"You *will* come to Auramala with me." And he resumed his journey.

The Welshman felt strong hands gripping his shoulders and arms. He did not struggle with the Watcher's men-at-arms, for he knew it would achieve nothing. He knew that he was, and always had been, as much a prisoner of these men as he was protected by them.

The Watcher had first revealed himself when the Welshman had been the guest of Cardinal Luca Fieschi in Avignon, years before. At Avignon, Brabant, at Cologne, then at Milan and Mulazzo, and now here, the Watcher showed himself from time to time, as though to say that he had never been far away. When he saw the Watcher, the Welshman felt like a possession. It was an unpleasant feeling. He had felt that way throughout his childhood too, on those rare occasions in which his father had deigned to have his son by his side. He had felt like a possession, like one of his father's war-horses. Perhaps a little more prized, a little more valuable, a little more publicly vauntable, but a possession nevertheless.

After scaling the curtain wall and falling to the ground in the outer grounds of the Abbey, we skirted around to the gate. We identified the road to Auramala Castle. The road was still icy in many places, and the night was bitterly cold. We slipped our travelling boots off and, holding them under one arm, began to run barefoot. We could not afford to waste time slipping and sliding about in the dark. Would we reach the 'Welshman' in time?

In the silvery half-light of stars and moon, the trunks of trees, grey boulders and piles of snow seemed to whirl past us in dreamy silence. At one point we clearly saw Auramala in the distance, an eerie silhouette against the glow reflected off the snow. We wordlessly ran on. There was no need to speak. If we reached our quarry before it disappeared through the castle gates, we would do whatever was necessary.

They emerged once more from the woods just a few hundred paces from the castle of Auramala. The Welshman halted once more, unheeding of the hands that gripped him. He was appalled by the way the great stone tower, dizzying against the stars, froze the humors within him, and stopped his heart like a stone. Far up the slope, beyond the wall, the gate to the keep waited beneath its twin turrets, the portcullis a mouth ready to open. It would not just swallow him up. It would break the strings between him and the world in its great iron teeth, and spit out him towards another lonely, empty existence, somewhere among the mountains of the Malaspinas.

The Welshman promptly did something the Watcher's men-at-arms could never have expected. He sat down on the rock-like frozen mud of the road, cross-legged like a summer pilgrim in the shade of an oak.

"I can't go in."

The Watcher spun about, his eyes furious above his great black beard.

"Bring him! I don't care how he struggles. I don't care what you do, just bring him to the gate. I'm going to knock for the porter."

He started striding toward the gate in the curtain wall, scarcely two hundred paces away. One of the men-at-arms spoke roughly to the Welshman.

"Get up, or we'll kick you senseless before dragging you anywhere!"

"I won't go." The Welshman was far beyond the fear of mere injury or cruelty.

The man who had threatened him stripped off one long, mailed gauntlet, and slowly, carefully drew his arm back, ready to strike the his ward about the face. A sound behind the Welshman's back startled the man-at-arms, who paused. The next instant, the butt of a knife was protruding from the base of his neck, and he was reeling backwards. He slipped backwards on the ice, and fell to the ground, a gruesome sound gurgling from his mouth, and he clawed frantically, ineffectually at his throat, his eyes filled with the black knowledge of his own death. His companion, without knowing, had narrowly escaped the same fate as a similar knife sped unheard and unseen to skid in the snow by the side of the road.

The Welshman started, and craned about to see who had so violently torn the night asunder. Two figures were running, almost gliding above the frozen road, like incubi hurtling through a hellish dreamscape. The first leapt upon the second man-at-arms in a flurry of arms, legs and whirling cloaks, and the sound of his impact made it clear that he was no spirit, but a very solid presence. The two bodies crashed into the ground and rolled while the second figure swooped upon the Welshman, who thought he must surely be dead before his heart could race through another terrified, pounding beat. Instead of a knife plunging into his chest, he felt two strong arms clasped his shoulders and he was pulled half upright.

"Rise! Help me get you up, we have to go, there's a third man."

The Welshman was shocked to hear his native tongue, the court-French of England, spoken with the unmistakable intonation of a Northumbrian. He was so bewildered that his legs froze beneath him, though the stranger heaved with all his might to bring him to his feet.

"Your Majesty, stand, we have to go! We're here to take you away."

Take you away. Only one thought still registered in the Welshman's mind.

"I won't go." He brought his legs into a kneeling position, and even the stranger's powerful arms could not hold him up. Together the two men sank to the ground.

"You must!" The stranger heaved again with urgency. "We have to run, Forzet…"

The Welshman saw an arm come whipping out of the night, and a knife cutting viciously down at the stranger's back. Perhaps the Northumbrian saw the danger in the Welshman's eyes, or some fighter's intuition warned him. He seemed to melt away as the blade came bearing down, revealing the Watcher's snarling eyes and black beard behind him. The knife plunged into miraculously empty space between the Welshman and the mysterious Englishman, who was already bringing his open hand up in a savage chop at the Watcher's exposed neck. Now it was the Watcher who seemed to melt away from the blow, bringing the point of his knife up at the Englishman's belly. The Welshman had never seen two men move so swiftly.

The Watcher's knife-hand was seized in an iron grip as it rose, and he found himself being hauled bodily forward by the arm, over the Englishman's outstretched foot, which tripped him and hurled him to the ground. His wrist, though, had not been released, and now the Englishman bashed it with two hands against his own knee. The knife fell to the ground, but the Watcher was already twisting over to grasp it with his free hand, simultaneously kicking at the back of the Englishman's legs. The Englishman kicked the knife away, but couldn't stop himself being knocked down. He turned the impetus of his fall into a weapon, bringing his elbows down heavily on the Watcher's stomach. The Watcher was winded in spite of his mail undercoat, and could not prevent the Englishman rolling away far enough to come to his feet, his own knife in hand. The Watcher for his part rolled in the opposite direction, to give himself space to draw his sword as he rose. No sooner had the supple steel swept from its scabbard in a terrible, gleaming arc of reflected moonlight, than the Watcher's eyes widened, and he spun about and jumped from the shoulder of the road among the trees, and disappeared into the impenetrable murk of the forest.

The Welshman could not understand how an armour-clad man wielding a sword could have taken such fright from an opponent armed with a knife. Then he saw that the second of the Watcher's men-at-arms was lying prostrate and motionless on the road, and a tall young man stood above him, holding his fallen victim's sword in one hand and a dagger in the other. The Watcher had seen that he was outmatched, and had fled.

"Wait for me here, I'm going after him!" the Northumbrian cried loudly in the Occitan, but he did not so much as move.

"Master" the younger man whispered urgently "he'll get away!"

"I shouted that for the benefit of Forzetti, to keep him running."

"But we can't leave an enemy at our back."

"Will... He wounded me." The Northumbrian touched his right shoulder, where a tear was visible in his travelling cape. "And besides, we're two hundred paces from a hostile castle and we are the sole guardians of the King's father." He turned to the Welshman, who was still sitting on the road.

"Your Majesty, you will listen. I am John de Ulgham, an agent of the Crown of England, do you remember me? You sent me to kill Roger Mortimer many years ago, do you remember me?"

"You... Ulgham... who let Mortimer live?" The Welshman was in a state of shock.

"Yes, it is I, but none of that now. This is my pupil, William de Tels, whose father, Sir Henry de Tels was many times by your side in battle in Scotland and Ireland of old."

As he looked wonderingly at the two men, the Welshman realized that there was much in their faces that was familiar. Could it be true?

John de Ulgham continued.

"We are in the service of Bishop Richard de Bury, your son the King's secret-keeper. You *will* come with us, Your Majesty. The House of Fieschi is using you to blackmail your son. They're driving England toward bankruptcy by extorting your son, the King. If you come away with us, we will take you back to your son, who will be free of his blackmailers."

The Welshman stared from one man to the other, comprehending at last. He knew it must be true. This was why Cardinal Fieschi had been so generous with him. This was why the Watcher had been sent to move him on from place to place before he could become too familiar to the local folk. He was nothing more than a pawn in a game of blackmail.

The Welshman rose slowly to his feet.

"Tell me," he looked the Northumbrian in the eye "is my son a good king? Do the people love him?"

"He is the perfect king," answered John de Ulgham without hesitation "and we all love him dearly."

For a long moment the Welshman was silent. He looked up once more at the gaping maw of the gates of Auramala Castle, and the lofty tower now brightly moonlit against the black of night.

"Very well," he replied at last. "I am in your hands. I will come."

The heart-clenching tension that had gripped me since our arrival at the Abbey abruptly abated when the old King, our victim-turned-ward, agreed to rise and come with us. And yet the tension did not disappear altogether. We were forced to leave our most perilous enemy at our backs once again. Master John's fresh wound and the presence of an older man to protect forced us to abandon all thought of pursuing Forzetti. I quickly bound Master John's cut shoulder with torn strips of wool-cloth, then we set off immediately toward the place in the woods below the Abbey where our horses were tied up. We alternated spells of slow running with spells of brisk walking, to move as quickly as possible without tiring ourselves too much. The Welshman – as I would later learn to call him - was surprisingly swift on his feet, his frame old but long and lean. We were only too glad not to cast a single look behind us at the spectral keep of Auramala Castle.

"Master John," I murmured during a spell of walking "did Forzetti realize he wounded you? Do you think he will come directly after us, or will seek help from the castle first?"

"No, I'm sure he didn't notice. I gave him no reaction at all. He'll think both you and I are strong and whole. In any case, he knows that either of us alone is a match for him." I was warmed by the compliment. "He will fetch men-at-arms from the castle to help him before starting the chase." Master John thought for a moment. "By your reckoning, how long a lead will we have, Will?"

His tone was that of a teacher once more. I pondered the situation before replying. "If I were Forzetti I would wait until the castle gates are opened at dawn before showing myself. He should be afraid that we have not left at all, but are waiting in ambush to finish him off as soon as he approaches the castle for help. That's what we would have done, if you hadn't been wounded. I guess the chase will start at dawn, when the first guards emerge, discover the bodies of Forzetti's men on the road, and the alarm is raised. Then he will show himself, explain the situation, take a handful of men and start after us at a gallop."

"Good, Will, that's my reasoning too. And where shall we go now?"

Now the Welshman turned to listen, interested to know where our escape was leading us.

"We must strike north. Gherardo Spinola recommended we seek the hospitality of the Bottigella family, woad merchants at a place called Calvignano, a day's ride north of here, where the mountains become hills before meeting the plain. The head of the Bottigella family is married to Filippina Langosco, one of the daughters of Filippone Langosco whose lives were saved by Opicino de Canistris during the sack of Pavia. We can present them the letter in Opicino's hand that I forged, and also Messer Gherardo's letter of commendation, and ask them to hide us. The Bottigellas are kin of the House of Spinola, and should be happy to aid us against the House of Fieschi."

"Exactly, Will. The question is: did Forzetti discover that we were guests of the Spinolas in Genoa? He might have suspected that Henry Tideswell's dramatic escape was somehow linked with us. If so, did he investigate and discover that we received hospitality with that family? In that case he, too, will follow the same line of reasoning, and gallop toward Calvignano as fast as possible. And he probably knows the way, unlike us. Everything now depends on speed." He broke into a slow run again, wincing as the new gait jarred his wound.

As we quickened our pace the Welshman, who had been listening with attention, breathlessly commented "It seems you are both masters of the secret business. I'm utterly in your hands, but that's best. Whenever I have taken my life into my own hands, it has always led to ruin."

I was shocked, but said nothing. Could a man who had once held an entire nation in his hands, not want – not feel a burning need - to captain his own life? It was my first taste of that eerily childlike quality which seemed to pervade the Welshman's character.

The rose-gold glow of first light helped us find our way back through the woods to where our horses were tied. The Welshman mounted behind Master John on the sturdier mare, while I took the reins of the feistier young filly. Before long we were skirting the walls of Bagnaria while the town watchmen were still yawning over their breakfast, huddled in the gate tower. We took the road north along the River Staffora as the last of the night's gloom was coalescing into long morning shadows. We now had a number of problems. The first was to find the way to Calvignano without leaving Forzetti a trail of witnesses who had met three suspicious strangers hurrying along on two horses, asking the way to Calvignano. Not far from Bagnaria we caught site of another small town atop the river bank.

"Will, how shall we go about this?" Master John again let me work out the next step for myself, limiting himself to either approving or disapproving my plans.

"We can split up. His Majesty and I can calmly ride into town. I would look too suspicious if I went by myself. What well-to-do young man travels without a servant? You can go ahead through the fields to avoid our being sighted together. I will be Guiraut d'Orange, and enquire after woad merchants, being careful to name neither the Bottigellas nor Calvignano, until someone gives me the information I need."

"Good. Let's do it. Take my horse, and I'll slip by the town on foot. We'll meet again on the road after the town, at the first curve beyond the point where the town is no longer in sight."

Master John disappeared among the woods and fields, leaving the Welshman and me to approach the town on horseback. As we rode up, the townsfolk who owned fields nearby started to appear, walking away from the town gates with their tools slung over their shoulders.

"Let me do the talking." I warned the Welshman. "I will speak in the Occitan, and say I am a merchant's son from the town of Orange. You are my mute manservant. You can show that you understand the Occitan, but look blank if you hear anything in the local tongue or the Latin."

The Welshman considered this for a long moment, his eyes troubled, then he replied "These are lies."

Could he be so naïve, after all he had been through?

"You must have told lies before, Your Majesty. I'm sorry, but you will have to do so again."

He shook his head.

"No. I have never knowingly told a lie, neither with my tongue nor with a gesture."

I became exasperated.

"Forgive me, I am but the son of a knight and should not take this tone with you but... either you learn to lie today, or we will all die before sunset. If Forzetti catches up with us before we reach sanctuary, he will kill Master John and I, and we…" I swallowed hard "we will have to kill you rather than let you fall back into the custody of the Fieschis."

To my immense surprise and frustration, he merely shrugged, totally at ease.

"William, son of Sir Henry de Tels, I have put my life in your hands, and you are free to preserve it or to destroy it. Frankly, I care little. But I did not entrust you with my soul, and souls were not created to become twisted by lying."

I squirmed in the saddle. Such were the words you might expect to hear from a ten-year-old playing at being the village priest with his friends. I found myself in the awkwardly dangerous situation of having a ward who proceeded to reckon like a child, but whom I was bound by honour to obey. I realized that the great lords of England had felt the same way time and again during the Welshman's catastrophically incompetent reign. I sympathized with them acutely: could he not realize how much was at stake?

"Your Majesty…"

"Don't call me that. I'm not a king. After years of wandering like a bedraggled Ulisseys, I've found home in being lay-brother, which is far more than being a king."

I did not waste time finding this last statement outrageous or surprising, for an inspiration had struck me. I tore the wax from about the mouth of my water bottle, and roughly fashioned two little balls from it.

"Here, your Ma… Welshman. Take these and plug your ears. Hear nothing of what is said. Be a deaf and dumb servant, and this evening we will call you Ulisseys!"

Still he appeared dubious.

"It is not a lie," I told him, desperately "it is like… like two actors in a mystery play. You cannot hold storytelling on the same plane as lying."

Incredibly, and thankfully, the Welshman finally smiled and nodded. He took the wax and plugged his ears with it, and we were free to ride into town.

In the market place I stopped to speak with a man whose dress and bearing indicated a certain familiarity with the outside world. I addressed him in the lilting Occitan of Orange.

"God be with you, Sir, will you spare a moment for a traveller and merchant's son?"

"Of course, boy, God and Mary with you. My name is Musso da Saronno."

"And I am Guiraut d'Orange. What is the name of this town?"

"Godiasco, sir."

I nodded. The Welshman merely looked on serenely.

"Is it true, Musso, that there are hills nearby rich in the finest woad of all Lombardy?"

"Well," he chuckled, raising one eyebrow "it's certainly true that there are hills nearby where they grow woad, but I like to think the woad my wife's family grows in the foothills of the Alps is just as fine."

"Ah, I apologize, I was merely repeating hearsay." I managed to summon up a little blush to seem embarrassed, though inside I was aching to move on. "Unfortunately I cannot venture so far north, I have no time. Where exactly are the woad plantations hereabouts?"

"They're centred around a hamlet called Calvignano, but if you get lost you'd best ask for directions to Casteggio, the nearest town of consequence. In any case, your dealings will be with the Bottigella family, for they're the ones who control most, if not all, of the woad fields."

"Is the road long?"

He frowned, and glanced at his own shadow before answering.

"You may get there before sunset if you ride hard. And that would be wise, as there's little hospitality to be got between here and there. Cross Godiasco and take the road north along the river. When you see the mountains sweeten a little into rolling hills, the road splits. One way continues north, toward a town called Voghera, but the other skirts the hill flanks and turns east. Take this second road, which leads you through vineyards, and you will soon reach Casteggio, a large town on a hilltop overlooking the great plains. There you can ask for directions to Calvignano and go up into the hills."

I thanked the man profusely, and forced myself to stay and exchange banter with him for a short while. Though I knew that Forzetti might not be far behind, I did not want to leave anyone in the town with the impression that we were in a hurry. That would immediately arouse suspicion were Forzetti to question them. In my heart, though, I knew that all subterfuge was likely to be useless. Forzetti's formidable reputation hinted that nothing would fool him.

Beyond the north gates, the road stretched out toward the base of a low, green mountain, scarred in places by near-vertical, treeless scars where landslides had laid bare the rock. As the road curved around the base of this mountain, leaving Godiasco out of sight, Master John stepped from the bushes at the roadside to meet us.

"Did you get directions?" He asked as he mounted in front of the Welshman.

"We did, but most importantly we avoided the Sirens' song."

Master John looked confused, but spurred his horse forward without hesitation.

"You can explain that one to me as we ride, Will. We'll have to push the horses. We'll set a cycle of trotting for two hundred counts and walking for one hundred, as long as the horses can bear it."

I doubt I've ever looked over my shoulder in one day as many times as I did during the flight toward Calvignano. Forzetti would have one man to a horse, and no wounded shoulders. He might even ride his horses to exhaustion and then take fresh ones by force from some village with a warrant from the Malaspinas of Auramala. The worst of it was that the road wound quite a lot, and in many places the local folk had not cleared the shoulders on either side of the trail of trees and bushes as custom dictated. For this reason, we could not see far behind us, nor hear sounds from far away, until the road divided as Musso da Saronno had described, and we headed east along the flanks of the wine hills. There the road was a little elevated, and the woods gave way to low, neat vineyards, so we had more chance to see the road stretch out behind us. We now allowed the tiring, protesting horses to walk for two hundred counts and trot for one hundred, though it would have been best to let them stop altogether and drink, eat and rest.

The shadows had begun to lengthen again when a large hilltop town came into view ahead of us.

"That must be Casteggio, Master John. The Milanese man said there were no other towns of consequence on the area, and it is on a hill overlooking the plains, just as he said." Even as I spoke, I compulsively looked over my shoulder at the road behind us. Was that a flurry of movement among the vineyards at the edge of sight?

"Then at Casteggio we must ask for directions for Calvignano. We can use the same method as we did in Godiasco."

"I don't think so, Master." I was now staring hard at the road far behind us. "The chase is on in earnest. Can you see them? I make out four riders, and they're coming at a gallop." Master John craned around past the Welshman's shoulders, but his eyes were not as keen as mine.

"Are you sure, Will?"

I trained my eyes in earnest on those swimming black spots. I almost wished my eyes deceived me, but it was not so.

"I'm certain."

"Then let's gallop, if the horses can manage it. Your Majesty" he addressed the Welshman "dismount and get up behind William. His horse is less tired and might bear you better now."

Against groans of weary complaint, the horses were pushed into a gallop, though our speed was terribly limited by the fact that one of our steeds bore two men. Master John gasped in pain frequently as he rode, and I began to see blood speckling the edges of his bandage. My frequent glances over my shoulder confirmed what I feared. Forzetti and his new set of men were gaining on us.

"Will, stop looking behind us, there's something more important ahead." Master John soon shouted above the pounding of the hooves.

I turned to where he was pointing, and saw a train of pack mules and carts leaving Casteggio by a south gate.

"What is it, Master?"

"Look at the canopies over their carts, and the men's clothes. They are all bright woad blue. I will lay a bet that they're in the service of the Bottigella family, who publicize their wares this way. Actually, I'll bet our lives on it. Off the road, Will, across the fields, let's make for that train!"

Soon we were racing through long aisles of budding grape-vines, strung to their stakes, receiving startled and fearful glances from peasants who were busy among the vines. I was aching to see whether or not Forzetti had seen us leave the road, and was coming after us through the vineyards, but I could no longer look back over my shoulder. My tired, struggling horse needed constant guidance as it sped over uneven ground with two men on its back. At one point an angry, gesticulating man tried to halt us, perhaps the landowner. The Welshman turned in his saddle to shout an apology as we went, but the man can't have heard it over the noise of our passing. We were emerging from the vineyards on the south flank of the hill of

Casteggio, not far from where the train was winding into the hills. The men spun about at the noise, and the leader of the train, a great burly man, ran toward us pulling a heavy wooden club from his belt. Master John reined in his horse.

"In the name of the Pope, and lady Filippina Langosco, you must shelter us if you are loyal to the Bottigella family and the House of Langosco!"

The blue-clad man froze, taken utterly by surprise, speechless. Three strangers had burst from the fields at a gallop invoking the names of his liege-lady and the family to whom he owed his service.

"Good man" Master John continued "if you are true Guelphs, and if you love your master and his lady, hide us in one of your carts, for God's sake! We bear a letter commending all friends of Opicino de Canistris to give us help and refuge. Opicino was the tutor of Lady Filippina, and saved her life the night Pavia was sacked by the Viscontis. There's no time for the letter now, but if you know these names, I beg of you: hide us. In God's name take us in, four men-at-arms are coming at a gallop to kill us."

Even as Master John spoke these words, the sound of beating hooves became audible through the vineyards. The leader of the train evidently, and thankfully, knew enough of the history of his master's family to know that Master John might well be telling the truth. With barely a moment's hesitation he beckoned us to dismount, while he barked orders at one of the other men to unstring the canopy of one of the carts. As soon as our feet were on the ground Master slapped the flank of his horse sharply, shouting at her and snapping his fingers in front of her eyes. She sprang away through the vineyards in the direction opposite to Forzetti's approach. I did likewise with the filly, who was easily persuaded to follow the mare, and all three of us clambered breathlessly into the cart, murmuring our thanks to the men of the train. I noticed that there were eight of them, all quite large and muscular and armed with clubs. When the canopy was tied closed not a gap was left through which to look out, or in. I decided that the Bottigella family must also engage in smuggling, to take such precautions.

The noise of the hooves came rapidly closer, and we heard startled peasants' cries as galloping riders interrupted their work a second time. Soon we heard a voice calling loudly to halt. The Welshman breathed "The Watcher." It was Forzetti.

"God be with you, good man, I must inspect the contents of your carts." The voice continued in an authoritative tone. "I have a warrant signed by Marquis Alessandro Malaspina of Auramala."

"These are not Malaspina lands." Came the voice of the leader of the train.

"Are you refusing to let me inspect the carts? There could be grave consequences." I had no doubt that Forzetti's hand had come to rest threateningly on his sword hilt.

"Yes, I am." was the blunt reply. I imagined that the clubs of all eight men were at the ready.

"Whom do you serve, man?" Forzetti rudely demanded.

"Lady Filippina Langosco." The leader of the train cunningly referred not to Bottigella, a nobleman but of lesser rank in spite of his wealth, but to his higher-born wife. "Daughter of Filippone Langosco, Count of Lomello and Pavia." He added for good measure.

After a long pause. Forzetti decided to play the man at his own game.

"The House of Malaspina was granted rights over these lands by the Emperor Barbarossa himself."

"That was a long time ago." Was the unhesitating, unimpressed reply.

"Stand down, man. You will let us inspect those carts." We heard the sound of steel sliding out of a scabbard, and three other swords following suite.

"No, I won't." The leader's voice was astoundingly calm. How many times had he been in similar situations during his career as a carter and smuggler, I wondered?

A long pause again ensued. No doubt Forzetti was weighing the chances of four swords against eight clubs. Thankfully, he chose discretion over valour.

"It is well for you, man, that your Lady's high birth protects you, otherwise I would spit you like a pig." And we heard Forzetti sheath his sword.

In the darkness of the canopy all three of us went limp with relief. As we heard our pursuers ride away in the direction of Casteggio, muttering angrily amongst themselves, I noticed for the first time that we had all been holding our breaths throughout the exchange. Even the Welshman's breath had been restrained by some inner force of self-preservation. Now we breathed deeply once more, and our tensed muscles relaxed. The leader cried out "forwards!" and the cart lurched into motion. It was not until sometime later that we heard him beside us, speaking to us through the canopy.

"We're nearing Calvignano now, and the palace of Messer Matteo Bottigella, our master. He just happens to be here tonight. He will inspect this letter of Opicino that you speak of, and if what you say is false, I will personally beat all three of you to a pulp and feed you to our dogs. I did not enjoy that."

None of us replied, and he did not speak to us again, but something told me he had lied. In reality he had enjoyed facing down four armed bullies very much indeed.

Chapter 21

Castle Rising, Norfolk, July 1338

*The Fairy Queen's prisoner – the long life of oak trees –
for the sake of a girl*

"Her Majesty the Queen Mother will be here shortly." The steward, Thomalin, entered the inner hall. "She would have come to the gates to meet you directly, if Your Majesty had given us forewarning of your visit." Behind the stiff formality, there was just a hint of irony in the tall man's voice that took Edward back to their infancy.

"I apologise, steward, but with French pirates and warships reaving up and down the coasts, I felt it was safer to keep my presence here a secret. The North Sea is too close for comfort."

"I understand." Thomalin nodded. "But now, Your Majesty will have to wait." He gestured to a beautiful, high-backed chair by the window overlooking the lesser courtyard. Then, the irony returning to his voice, he added "Even older ladies prefer to put on their best faces before being seen in public, and mother is no exception."

Edward smiled at the word 'mother', happy it had been Thomalin who had mentioned their bond first. "Of course, steward." Then, deciding to set titles aside, he stepped a little closer and gently asked "Thomalin, is your life a little easier now that England is turning its attention to France and has stopped laying waste your homeland?"

Thomalin shook his head, and in turn abandoned formality, though he was not yet warm with the royal visitor. "Edward, I felt more ill at ease back when first your father, and then Baron Mortimer after him, were losing battle after battle against the Scots. Many of our old playmates turned their back on me, and derided mother behind her back for holding on to her 'Scottish pet', as they used to call me. And then, of course, Mortimer sent me away. Since your great victory at Halidon Hill, no one has bothered me with such nonsense."

Edward nodded. "I can imagine what it was like. We call them innocents, but little boys and girls can be very cruel at times. For my part, it's a welcome paradox that the King of England can have a Scotsman as a foster brother. I wish I saw you more often."

Thomalin smiled uncertainly, but the King approached him and the two men exchanged an awkward but fond embrace.

"I've sent you letters to this effect before now, Thomalin." Edward was earnest. "Now that we've met again after all these years, I can say it looking you in the eye. I'm sorry I didn't defend you when Mortimer banished you from our household ten years ago. I should have made a stand then, as on many other occasions during his tyranny. I'm sorry."

His foster brother smiled with relief. "Edward, think no more about it. You have other, greater things to turn your mind to now. But… thanks."

"You know Thomalin," the King changed the topic with good cheer "during my time in Scotland I discovered who your name-sake is." Ignoring the ornate chair he had been offered, Edward moved toward a long cushioned bench against the opposite wall where they could sit together.

"Really?" The Queen Mother's steward and foster son sat down beside his King.

"Yes, an old Scottish bard told us the story one evening. Thomalin is the way we English pronounce Tham-lin," he stumbled a little over the strange Gaelic syllables "the hero of an old legend. He was tall and handsome and red-haired, like you, and was in love with a Lord's daughter. But one day he went somewhere forbidden… a circle in the woods, or of stones, or some such thing… and the Queen of the Faeries was there, dancing with her court. When she saw him, she found him so fair that she captured him, to take him away to Faery-Land.

"Tham-lin's lady-love then went to a wise-woman for help, and the old woman told her to go to the forbidden place on a certain day, and wait for the Faery court to appear. Then she had to rush into the circle and take hold of her love, and not let go of him, no matter what happened. The lass did as she was told, and saw the Faery court appear before her, and there was Tham-lin, a prisoner at the Faery Queen's side. The girl rushed forward, and put her arms around her love. The Queen waved her wand and turned the boy into a ferocious lion, but he did not tear at the girl with his claws, and she did not let go for fear. Then the Queen transformed him into slippery eel, but he did not wriggle, and the girl did not lose her grip. The Queen turned him into one shape after another, I can't remember them all, but the girl never let go of him. Finally, he was changed into a red-hot poker, and the girl's hands burnt, but still she held onto him, ignoring the pain through the power of her love. Then the Queen realised she could do nothing against a power greater than hers, and transformed Tham-lin back into his human form and let him go back to his lover.

"The old bard told us that the girl was Scotland, and Tham-lin, her true love, was freedom, and no matter what we English do we'll always be like the Faery Queen, helpless in the face of a greater power, the Scots' love of freedom. He had come to my court to tell me so." Edward chuckled. "I could have had him whipped for his impertinence there and then, but I liked him. He was brave and honest."

"He was wrong." A commanding voice interjected from the entrance to the hall. Isabella, the Queen Mother, had arrived. Though she was not tall, the purple of her gown seemed to flow down from a great height as she strode austerely toward them. She wore the royal colour every single day, without fail. "*I* am the Faery Queen. And no one has ever managed to take my Thomalin away from me. Nor will they ever." Hearing these words, Thomalin's face became a battleground of pleasure and frustration. Edward realised that at his foster brother secretly dreamt of what life might be like outside his adoptive mother's thrall. His bond of gratitude to her, however, was too strong to let him admit such a thought, even to himself.

"I have always known that old story." Her hair had greyed, Edward noted, but the red flames of old still rippled in her voice and gaze. "I have never told anybody because I wanted to raise Thomalin as an Englishman, not a splinter of Scottish myth. And, my son…" her eyes never left Edward's "there is another story you only heard recently, that I have always known to be true."

Startled, Edward met her stare so intensely, and the silence brewed uncomfortably for so long, that Thomalin rose with a Steward's feeling for discretion. It was clear some grave matter was afoot, and he would soon be asked to leave mother and son in privacy.

"Thomalin, please make sure no one so much as enters the corridor outside, and no one approaches the courtyard." Isabella murmured. "Have wine and sweetmeats ready shortly in the great hall. We will not be long."

"Of course, mother."

Before Thomalin could leave, Edward stood and held him back a moment with a hand on his shoulder. "Thank you, Thomalin." His foster brother smiled at him briefly, then left. Edward now turned to his mother. He was a devoted son, but he was also King.

"What did you mean? Be clear with me. At once." He ordered.

"What Niccolò Fieschi tells you is the truth." She replied calmly. "They have your father, alive, somewhere on their lands. I've known it from the beginning."

"Niccolò Fieschi? My father?"

"Edward, there's no need to feign ignorance. I know exactly what is going on. Unfortunately, what he has told you is the truth."

"Really?" Edward's eyes did not waver as he considered her. He decided to play along. He might learn something interesting. "Then… why didn't you tell me years ago?"

"Old men die, Edward." She said, simply. "I hoped your father would, too, ridding us all of this problem. Even now, as we speak, he may be dead." She continued in a level tone. "He may have died recently, and Fieschi just isn't telling you…"

"Mother," Edward interrupted "enough self-justification. Just tell me what really happened."

She was silent for a long moment, her dark, fey eyes glinting in a way that had once been capable of inspiring terror, and her delicate, fine lips curled with a hint of cunning. Edward felt sure she had carefully prepared what she was about to say in advance. Indeed, she had learnt to twist people and events with carefully thought out words during her years at the side of Roger de Mortimer, the tyrant. When, seven years earlier, Edward had seized power with William de Montague's help, he had overthrown not one tyrant, but two. The second had been his mother. Since then, he had learned to listen to her with all the love a son cannot help but feel, but guarded by cold, sceptical detachment.

"To this day I don't really know how your father escaped, Edward. Roger ordered his murder without telling me anything." Her manner became almost apologetic, but he knew that was a charade. "He knew I would have opposed it. Killing your father for being the king he was... would have been like killing a mouse for being incapable of governing a land of cats. My husband couldn't help what he was; it was the birth that was mismatched to the man."

Edward refrained from commenting. He knew her assessment of his father was honest, but was sure the decision to rid the kingdom of him forever had been made by the two lovers, Roger de Mortimer and Isabella of France, in perfect accord. Indeed, the idea might well have originally come from his mother. He knew that perfectly well.

"Then that terrible night in September the two killers returned, saying that your father had escaped." she continued, subdued pain creeping into her tone, as though she could still not bear to think of those events. "A loyal servant had helped him flee just before they reached Berkeley Castle, and a porter had been killed during the flight. Roger was about to order his men to raise the hue and cry, when I persuaded him to follow a different path.

" 'Let these two knights ride back to Berkeley' I urged him 'and take the heart from the porter's body and case it in silver, as though it belonged to a king. Then have them place the corpse in a cool cellar to keep it until the royal funeral can be prepared.' 'Whose royal funeral?' Roger asked me. 'My husband's.' I replied. 'Let us stage his funeral with great pomp, and he will not show himself ever again, I'm sure of it. He has seen how the entire land rose as one against him during the recent war, and has understood that he can never again be King of England. I know my husband. He will find an Abbey in some secluded place where he can go away from the world and live among the monks. He always did like their company. He will find a more secure prison all by himself than we ever could for him, and he will be grateful to be dead to the world.' "

As he listened to her tale, Edward saw her again as she had been ten years earlier when she had supposedly uttered those words, her flowing hair rich brown, her eyes vivacious and captivating. He did not think for a moment that the events had played out simply and smoothly as she so glibly described them. Rather, he imagined the panic in the tyrants' rooms that night, and the hurried decision to stage a funeral, hoping all the while to track his father down and kill him as soon as possible.

"When Roger finally agreed, I sent orders arranging every detail of the funeral." The Queen Mother continued. "I sent no physician to embalm the body, for a court physician would have realised it was not your father. I had a common old wise-woman from a nearby farmstead do it. She had never seen your father in life, and could not know whose body she was embalming. Then I sent for her some time later, and she entered my service. She passed away recently, here in Castle Rising."

As he listened, Edward went to the arched window looking over the courtyard. The first drops of a fresh summer shower were glistening on the grass. There were some bulging straw targets at the far end, left standing on the lawn when Thomalin's order to leave the courtyard at once had broken up some youngster's archery lesson.

"Now I understand why he was given a funeral-mask for the procession." He muttered, as bleak as though the hearse were passing beneath the window in that moment.

"Yes, the mask. It was best for everybody, but first and foremost for you. You never wanted to see his face again. Do you remember saying that?" Edward remembered saying many things she had coached him to say, while Mortimer had been the hammer to Isabella's anvil, and his poor England the beaten iron in between. "And this way, you didn't see him. It would have been terrible for you. Imagine it, seeing his face, miserable and pathetic in death, and you unable to weep in public for lack of love. How awful you would have felt. It was for your good that I did it."

How her words writhed about the truth in oily coils, like an adder with its prey! Now the face beneath the mask had magically become his father's again, and the mask itself a concerned mother's attempt to protect him from the shame of not being able to grieve as a son should.

"I didn't even go to the procession." His voice was low. "That's why I didn't see him, not because of some mask. No one from court went, bar Mortimer."

"But for all I knew you might have gone. I wanted to spare you grief."

Edward remembered perfectly well that he had pleaded desperately to go to the funeral, but she had held him back. At that time he had just started to wear the crown, but not yet its power.

"How strange" he mused "that no one who was present insisted on lifting the mask and cerecloth."

"Many suspected the truth, and didn't dare lift it for fear of Mortimer. Other's simply didn't want to see his face, didn't want to be reminded of his reign. They hoped the troubles had ended. And the common people… they wouldn't have recognised him anyway, for the most part. For them, pomp and ceremony is the face of a king, not his nose and mouth, eyes and beard." Even now, ten years later, she was proud of her cunning.

"Pomp and ceremony…" Edward repeated "like the procession toward Gloucester? Ordering the Abbot to stop every mile for prayer, to let as many people see the hearse as possible? Having the villagers in Standish, where they stopped overnight, plant that avenue of oak trees to mark his passage?" Edward turned from the window to look at her, no longer seeing the beautiful, bewitching queen of a decade before. The hair beneath her wimple was steel-grey once more, and her face lined with age. "I've been to Standish and have seen the avenue there. The saplings grow well. When you ordered their planting were you hoping the lie would stand for hundreds of years, as those oak trees will?"

She blanched at the bitterness in his voice.

"You loathe deceit, just like your father." He said nothing. As a king he knew how often untruths were necessary. But, struggling to be a good king, he attempted to avoid them. "You are so like him. Not so tall, not so handsome" she smiled fondly "but his nose and chin, his eyes, his smile… and his generosity."

He turned away again.

"Edward… Listen to me. You must believe me." her expression now softened and Edward realised that, after a main course of concern for his best interests, she was preparing a dessert of motherly love mixed with self-pity. He hated it when she resorted to this. Her carefully crafted memories robbed him of his happy infancy, all rough and tumble games with Thomalin and sweet embraces with Nurse Margaret, and replaced it with a twisted world in which love was just another tool of power.

"Edward, I sought to spare your father out of piety and mercy. I know you think I didn't love him, but it's not true. I loved him dearly. However, you must understand that love and loyalty were wasted with him. I'm not saying he didn't return my love, for he did, no matter what anybody tells you. But there was always someone else who was nearer to his heart, some other love that was overruling and overpowering for him.

"At first I was too young to be his wife in anything but name. I was only twelve when we married, and he was a strong, athletic, beautiful man. Piers Gaveston was handsome to match him, and funny and kind. His mind was keen and he was accomplished in the art of combat. He made many an English knight and earl look like a fool on the tournament field. Your father adored him. I wanted so much to be in your father's heart that I jumped in at the only breach I could find: Piers. I lavished gifts and compliments on Piers for many months, and courted his affection until I was every bit as smitten by his charms as your father was. I even ignored all those acts that the world saw as insults to me. When Piers wore the purple at our crowning banquet." She looked down at her own gown of that same royal colour, which she never abandoned even for one day. In her eyes Edward could see the reflection of Gaveston's lavish brocades and silks that night "He sat at the high table all night with your father, as though he were the consort, while I was relegated to one side… And yet I just smiled, and gazed at them both infatuatedly, thinking myself lucky to have two such men to myself, not one. My relatives, however, raged, and Thomas of Lancaster in his jealousy swore to kill Gaveston." She paused, seeing another way to draw a reaction from her aloof son. "You know, that was the day rumours started to emerge about the nature of Thomas's own affection for your father, before they were estranged. Did you ever know such rumours circulated at the time?"

Edward smiled inwardly, realising he was meant to react with indignation or disbelief. He merely stayed at the window, looking at the grass below. It was now drenched.

"Thomas may have wanted your father for himself," she continued, her eyes boring into his back "who can say. I for one have never believed the notion." She paused, hoping he would speak, but soon understood that he was determined to remain silent.

"It wasn't until you were born, Edward, that I finally understood what your father had always known: how one love can overrule and overpower utterly, even though one's heart carried on loving others faithfully and genuinely. For your father, that love was Gaveston, an unnatural, ungodly love, and he paid the consequences. For me, that love was you: as natural a love as could ever be. But I never stopped loving your father, nor my brothers, nor my own father… It's just that, when you were born, they became like the faint moon that sometimes lingers in the sky, while the sun is climbing. And that is precisely what I was for your father; just a pale, mid-morning moon."

"You still loved him?" Edward's voice was hollow. A part of him wanted to continue 'even when you were with Mortimer?', but he held himself back. There was no point.

"I did. That is why I staged the funeral. I hoped he would live out the rest of his life far away, and in peace, and then one day just… die. And that's why I have never told you."

"Foolishness." Edward turned to face her, suddenly stern. "You had no right to hope such a thing. Hope exists to lift hearts and drive them to action, not as a substitute for action. The good of England may well be in the balance, and you knew it. You should have done more than hope, you should have told me."

"I never imagined" Isabella was almost pleading "that he might become a pawn in the hands of these treacherous Genoese. Are they blackmailing you? What price have they demanded for their silence?"

Edward did not answer. He finally understood why she had come to him speaking of Niccolò Fieschi. She had seen an opportunity in this affair to insinuate her way back into his council, and to influence the affairs of the kingdom once more. He calmed himself with an effort. He had no intention of letting an old tyrant back into his inner circle. Even if that tyrant was his mother. He said nothing, and merely raised an amused eyebrow.

"Edward? Are they blackmailing you? Won't you tell me?" Again there was no reply but a half-smile. "You came all this way to hear the truth, and now you are staying silent about the repercussions?"

"You think I came to hear that story, mother, but I never said so."

She was silent for a moment, genuinely mystified.

"Then why did you come?"

Edward chuckled at her expression. "To see my mother. I'm on my way to war with France, and I wanted your blessing before setting sail from Yarmouth. Though I admit, your tale… satisfied my curiosity."

"Then you didn't come to find out about your father?"

"No. I came for a kiss from you before going, and that is all." At first she was unbelieving, but when, with a mother's perception, she realised that he was telling the truth, her face paled to white. Edward, with a son's intuition, understood why.

As a young woman, her talents and intelligence had been ignored for decades by the sordid circus of favouritism that had thrived at court on his father's many weaknesses. When she had finally shaken off the last lingering traces of loyalty to her husband and had thrown her sharp mind and courage into the fray for her own cause, the result had been a fiery love affair, the deposition of the King, and three years of absolute rule at Mortimer's side. It had been the fulfilment of her lifetime. Edward, too young to govern in his own right at the time, had inadvertently been the source of her near infinite power. No mere tyrant's mistress, Isabella had been the King's royal mother and stewardess. Her presence at Mortimer's side, as the incarnation of her son's interests, had been the justification of the baron's power. She had acquired a regal aura of power and control that no one could have imagined while her husband was alive.

Reducing Isabella of France, who had once had the entire kingdom trembling at her feet, to a mere giver of royal kisses, was simply cruel. He had not the heart to close the matter there. He decided to let her have one more taste of the power games she had once dominated, one final satisfaction. He wanted the tears she would shed as he left her castle to be for his departure, and not for her own powerlessness.

"Mother," he looked at her shrewdly "it occurs to me that, if your last act concerning father had truly been staging his funeral, today you would not know anything about his whereabouts. I wonder why you are so sure that the House of Fieschi has him?"

The Queen Mother swallowed. "All England knows that Niccolò Fieschi has attained an unreasonable degree of intimacy with you since he arrived in England." Her tone was defensive, but colour was returning to her face.

"True, but there could be any number of other explanations for that. They could be bribing me with gold, not blackmailing me. Why should you have become convinced that the Fieschis are father's guardians, and are using him to blackmail me? If you had really never heard of him again since his escape, then for all you would know he might be in a monastery in northern Denmark, or in a hermitage on Malta, or else mouldering in a tomb in the Pyrenees. And yet, you came to me today quite certain that I was under the thumb of the House of Fieschi because they have father."

Now it was his mother who remained obstinately silent, giving nothing away.

Fieschi. Ever since she had uttered that word, all through her tale of his father's escape and false funeral, a part of his mind had been wondering how she could have known. Now he concluded that she still had spies in her service, and highly competent ones at that. In the years since the death of Mortimer, the years of her relegation to a role of mere formality at court and a peripheral residence at Castle Rising, she had somehow kept the deepest loyalty of some secret-keepers and secret-breakers.

"The more I think about it, mother, the more convinced I am that you have your own spies working in the world of the secret business. Perhaps at the Papal Court. Someone reported to you the letter I received from Manuele Fieschi, and now your sense of guilt has driven you to tell me the truth at long last."

"Manuele Fieschi? I thought the man's name was Niccolò." She lightly played the fool, but her son ignored it.

"Mother," Edward's eyes narrowed with a hint of slyness, as he understood what the finest gift he could bestow on his aging mother was, "hold on to these spies of yours. You never know, someday I may need you to use them on my behalf. Would you do that for me?"

After a long silence, during which she came to believe that her talents were still of use to her son, the Queen Mother said "Yes, Edward. I would." And then she finally gave her son a kiss and a blessing.

A short time later, court was convened in Castle Rising. While he sipped his wine and consumed sweetmeats in the great hall with his usual good appetite, Edward observed his mother playing the queen with her household. She insisted on almost absurd levels of formality at all times in her little domain, from her steward, Thomalin, from the wardens and their wives, from the captain of the garrison and his lady, from the knights and their damsels and their squires, and even the falconer and hunt master were present. Local landowners were there, for it seemed they came to pay homage to her almost daily, helping to populate the flourishing, gallant little court she had constructed around herself in her near-exile. All were obliged to speak not only in the French, but in the French of Paris that was Isabella's mother tongue. And in spite of the presence of their King, all seemed to defer the highest honour instinctively to his mother. Edward felt eerily that he was nothing but a guest of honour, a visiting dignitary, at the court of a sophisticated foreign power.

While he chatted with those few who politely broke off their adoration of his mother long enough to exchange pleasantries with their King, Edward never ceased to observe Thomalin discreetly. He had no wife, and no mother, but a Faery Queen who was both of these things and more. Isabella would never release him.

As Edward watched Thomalin he realised that his mother had been mutilated in her soul by the experience of life at his father's court. He tried to imagine his mother as a sixteen-year-old girl, adopting a Scottish orphan on whom to bestow her love, and from whom to earn love. For the sake of the innocent, despairingly lonely and spontaneously generous girl she had once been, Edward forgave his mother for having become first a tyrant, and then the pantomime Faery Queen and twister of truth that he now saw before him.

Chapter 22

Pavia, July 1338

Bianca Bottigella – the pear tree in the courtyard - God leaves the juciest fruit for the birds

Not long after the Bottigella family smuggled us from Calvignano to their palace in the heart of the city of Pavia, I met the beautiful Bianca. Unused to the labyrinthine building, I stumbled into an inner courtyard where guests were not meant to go. And there she was, seated beneath a pear tree, a great tome open in her hands, a frown of concentration on her brow.

Of course, I had already noticed her about the household. How could my eyes fail to dwell upon such a gracious creature? During meals I had discreetly gazed at her, seated at the ladies' end of the great table, and recognised her as a daughter of Lady Langosco, the wife of our host, Messer Matteo Bottigella. Her stately mother was one of the daughters of Lord Filippone Langosco that Opicino de Canistris had rescued from the sack of Pavia many years before, taking them to safety at the house of Messer Gherardo Spinola in Genoa. As I relived for a moment Canistris' dramatic narrative of those events, recounted to us in Avignon the previous autumn, I imagined the young Lady Langosco of that fiery night long ago exactly like her daughter now before me. Both shared long, perfectly straight and jet-black hair, olive skin and green-blue eyes.

I had last seen those eyes, her mother's eyes, the morning we had left Calvignano. Master John, the Welshman and I had been sitting in the bright blue Bottigella carts, embraced by the bitter-sweet smell of woad leaves. Messer Matteo and Lady Filippina had come to see us off, wish us well, and assure us that Master John would have the finest healer of all Pavia to look after his festering wound at their palace in the city. Bottigella had apologised for there not being a healer of the same stature in Calvignano, obliging us to make the secret journey to the plains. Lady Langosco, having read the letters of commendation we bore from both Opicino de Canistris (my forgery) and Messer Gherardo Spinola, felt a bond of affection and duty to us on behalf of her two old friends. Before the carters had closed the canopies of the woad carts to hide us, Lady Langosco had given us her blessing and kissed us on the cheeks, her gaze compassionate.

Now, two bright and dancing eyes of that same hue, but a generation younger, looked up arrestingly.

"Good afternoon, sir, may the Lord be with you." A barely suppressed ripple of playfulness underlay her courtesy.

"And with you, my Lady." I had intended to continue with some suave comment, but found my tongue unexpectedly clumsy. "You must… Um. I mean…" She looked at me with such amusement that I had to force myself to carry through. "You must be the daughter of Lady Filippina Langosco."

"I resemble her just a little, don't I?" She smiled, caressing her fine hair meaningfully.

Her confirmation merely worsened the knot my tongue was tied into. It is one thing to bed bony farmers' daughters or plump craftsmen's wives, and quite another to woo the granddaughter of a Palatine Count of the Holy Roman Empire. Her noble blood lent her beauty an aura that set her high above me, the mere younger son of a minor English knight.

"Yes, you do resemble your mother, but…" in that moment a line of Occitan poetry came unbidden to my mind, a lovely metaphor in which a damsel is likened to a white flower, and love to the apple, the flower's fruit. What a shame it was that my brains were addled! "You do indeed, but as a white apple in the spring…" I faltered, realising that I had said 'apple' in the place of 'flower'.

"Apple? In the spring?" Her expression was one of pleased confusion. Pleased, because she enjoyed her own power to be-muddle a young man's thoughts with beauty. "Do apples come forth in the spring time in your land? And are they white? Fascinating." She gave a peal of laughter, that fell upon my flaming, embarrassed ears both sweetly and cruelly.

"By the way," she looked at me with sudden intelligence "just where is this land of early white apples?"

I closed my mouth, unable to reveal any more of my identity than she might already know. After holding me with an unexpectedly intense gaze for a long moment, she smiled warmly.

"Don't feel beholden to answer me. I understand the need for secrecy. My mother told me that you three pilgrims are Guelphs, dedicated to the true church, like us. We are hiding you in our palace to protect you because the Ghibelline Beccarias and their ilk would clap you in irons, or worse, if they found you.

"But is it not already like living in a prison, being closed in our palace like this? For me, my father's palace is a prison." She frowned, and in those words I sensed years of forced seclusion in that building, in a city dominated by the faction that had slain her grandfather.

"But with you in it, Lady, it is a sweet prison to be captive in, just as my eyes are sweetly imprisoned by yours as we speak." There! I had finally managed to say something romantically poetic.

"Oh, I... Oh." She blushed ever so slightly, and it was now my turn to be satisfied at having achieved a little tongue-tying myself.

She was saved from having to find a reply by the sound of the latch on the courtyard's inner gate. The heavy wooden panels slowly swung half-way open, and the silhouette of an old, bearded man leaning on a stick was framed in them. He was speaking with someone unseen, standing behind him in the passage.

"First, Lady Bianca must have her lesson, and then I will assist you."

"But Master Ariperto, I must ask you…" The unseen person was a boy.

Lady Bianca – as I now knew her name to be - hissed at me urgently. "It is Master Ariperto. It is time for my lessons. He must not find you here, alone with me!"

"Then I must hide, but where?" I whispered.

"The old man is blind, slip past him to the gate."

Master Ariperto was still conversing with the boy at the half open gate. I could easily have done as she said, but I had no intention of leaving Lady Bianca's presence so soon.

"He would hear my footsteps. Look," I pointed to the pear tree's sturdy branches "I'll hide up there, and watch your lesson."

"Don't be ridiculous!"

"If I quit your company now, my eyes would wither like blossoms in the desert, for want of gazing on you." I retorted, satisfied that my gift of eloquence was fully restored. I had already swung a leg over the lowest branch, and was heaving myself up.

Fortunately, the old man was hard of hearing, as well as blind, for he had heard not a whisper of our conversation. As I settled into the branches, Lady Bianca sat down and opened her book.

"Good morning, dear lady." Master Ariperto noisily stomped toward the benches on his crutch. "Have you read on?"

"Yes, Master Ariperto." Glancing up at me with a mixture of amusement, for my secret presence, and anger at my disobedience, Lady Bianca flipped through her book to the page she had been studying when I had intruded on her solitude for the first time.

"Then read, Lady, and I will listen." The rasping old man settled slowly onto his bench, his milk-white eyes vacant.

"Sed hoc est quod recolentem vehementius coquit." Lady Bianca read slowly, tracing the line of text along the parchment with her finger. "Nam in omni aduersitate fortunae infelicissimum est genus infortunii fuisse felicem." At once I recognised Boethius.

"And have you understood this thought, Lady?" Master Ariperto spoke so slowly, it seemed he might fall asleep from one word to the next, and it was certain that his pupil would do so, before long.

"I... am not certain." She replied, uncertainly.

"Seek to interpret, and I will comment on your answer."

It was clear to me that Bianca had merely read the words aloud, without even attempting to understand them, for she rolled her eyes in irritation and re-read the phrase, frequently glancing up at me. I was grinning at her discomfort.

"Sed hoc est quod... but it is that which..." She hesitated, frowned, and rolled her eyes again "recolentem vehementius coquit... cooked the vehement memory...?"

I could have died from the effort not to burst out laughing. I am sure I was purple in the face from repressed guffaws, and I wagged my finger at Lady Bianca, mouthing *No, that's not it!*. She glared at me furiously.

Master Ariperto sighed, shaking his head.

"No, no, no, Lady. No. 'Recolentem' is is the participle... 'recollecting', 'not memory'. And 'cooked'? That was your translation!?" He was already exasperated. "How can you muddle poor Boethius so? You who live but a few paces from the place where he was martyred, here in this very city!"

"Forgive me, master Ariperto, forgive me. How must I translate it?"

"But it is this which vexes me most, recollecting it." He said, with the air of one who is reciting from memory. He must have been a formidable old scholar. "Now, go on." He instructed.

Lady Bianca scowled up at my smiling face, and lowered her finger to the next line.

"Nam in omni adversitate fortunae infelicissimum est genus infortunii fuisse felicem." As she read, her brow furrowed and she began to sweat, not from the summer heat but from the effort. She was attempting to comprehend even as she read.

"Child, translate for me." Master Ariperto leant forward on his crutch, his expression intense.

"In every… adverse…" glancing upwards, she saw me nodding vigorously. *That's it.* I mouthed. "In every adversity… of fortune… the gender…" I wagged my finger quickly. *No.* She corrected herself. "I mean, the type… most unhappy…" *That's it.* "of bad luck…" I made a *so-so* signal with my hand. "Um… The most unhappy type of misfortune… is… might have been happy?" She finished in confusion. I smiled down at her.

"Good, good, my child," Master Ariperto was pleasantly surprised, "that is closer to the true meaning. A Florentine poet I once met, by the name of Dante, would have said: 'There is no greater sorrow than to be mindful of the happy time in misery.'

"Now, if you will continue…"

Lady Bianca rolled her eyes again at the prospect, then flashed me a smile of sheer mischief.

"Master Ariperto, it is so hot, and I am terribly thirsty. Will you not reach up into the pear tree, for you know that I am too short, and pluck me a nice juicy pear?"

I'm sure my eyes fairly bulged at that. What game was she playing?

"Of course, of course, dear child." The old man, in spite of his rasping voice and dusty old lessons, was a gentleman. He rose creakily from his bench, and reached up into the branches. Blind as he was, he groped around among the branches for a long while.

"Further to your right, Master." Bianca directed his groping – towards me! What laughter there was in her eyes! "Further to your right, yes, there…" She told the old man. His hand came fumbling perilously close to my leg, which I was forced to swing precariously out of the way, hoping not to break any twigs noisily. Now it was Lady Bianca's turn to suppress laughter at my predicament.

Finally, old Master Ariperto's fingers brushed against a pear, and he plucked it and held it out for his pupil. Lady Bianca took it, and bit into it. It had the look of a fine, juicy pear, but she hadn't yet finished with her entertainment.

"Master Ariperto, this pear has worms in it. Won't you pick me another one?"

Once again, the old man reached up into the pear tree.

"Further to your right, again, Master." Oh how Bianca was enjoying this! Again I was forced to shift my weight in a hurry, lest his fingers brush up against my legs. I scampered up onto a higher branch for safety, trying not to make a sound.

"Reach higher, Master, there's a lovely firm-looking one just there. I'm sure it has the sweetest juices. Higher." Master Ariperto craned further and further upwards, and I was forced to arch out of his way, clinging for dear life to my branch. My foot slipped and I nearly fell, and Lady Bianca below bent over double in her struggle to keep her laughter silent. Master Ariperto clutched hold of a second pear, and held it out to his pupil.

"Is this one better, child?"

"Hardly." She replied a little tartly, taking it from him. "Master, why don't you help me climb up onto the branches, and I'll pick the pear myself?"

"But, Lady, you might hurt yourself…"

"I promise I'll be careful. I just want a pear."

"Perhaps I should call a servant to fetch some fruit." The old scholar was shaking his head.

"Please, Master, let me do it. You know I loved climbing this tree when I was little. It never did me any harm."

Master Ariperto thought hesitantly for a moment, then nodded. He was clearly a little soft with Bianca in matters non-grammatical.

"Very well, but be careful, Lady. My life is forfeit should you hurt yourself…"

"Don't worry. I'm a far better tree-climber than I am interpreter of Boethius."

And so, as I watched in admiration, she planted her right foot on the old man's knee, and he held her steady while she pulled herself up onto the lowest branch. As she climbed up towards me with mischief in her eyes, the old man cautioned her.

"Be careful, Lady, don't reach for the highest fruit! The highest fruits are the juciest, but the Good Lord leaves them for the birds, not for us."

I shifted myself onto the broadest, forked branch on the tree, and soon Lady Bianca slid onto the branch alongside me, her blue-green eyes sparkling. We were bound to silence by the presence of Master Ariperto below. I could feel her breath on my skin, her perfume in my nostrils, her hair smelling of rose-water. We looked at each other, smiling, for a long moment.

"Lady Bianca," Master Ariperto was warning her again "don't reach for the highest pears. God leaves the juciest fruit for the birds!"

Neither of us were listening. It was some time before Bianca returned to her lesson.

Chapter 23

Pavia, July 1338

Rhithmomachia – the trench digger and the Prince

When the Welshman came to the entrance of Master John's room, the Northumbrian spy was sitting up on the edge of his bed, closely scrutinizing a curious little table that had been drawn up before him. On the other side of the table sat blind old Master Ariperto, a mysterious smile on his face. The table-top was the most curious thing, formed of a great number of little ceramic tiles of many colours, inlaid into the wood in strange alignments. It was not until the Welshman came much closer that he made out the ceramic squares, triangles and circles scattered over the board, and understood what he was looking at.

"Ah, but it is a Rithmomachia set." He exclaimed.

Master John looked up, extricating himself with difficulty from his tactical contemplation of the game board.

"Come, come, Welshman." Master John greeted him in the Latin, respectfully allowing Master Ariperto to understand. "Are you any good with the game? Perhaps you can help me against this formidable old player. I'm in serious difficulty."

"I'll gladly help if I can, but I cannot believe that I can succeed where you, Master John, are failing. But tell me, Master Ariperto, how can you play if you cannot see the pieces?"

The old man chuckled through his great, bushy white beard.

"This set was made especially for me by a skilled ceramicist of the city. You see, the different numbers are cut deeply into the pieces, not merely painted on, and I feel them with my fingers. The black pieces have a little incision of a demon - in the bottom left, naturally - and the white pieces have a little angel incised into the top right, which I feel in the same way. And, as you see, board and pieces are made of ceramic. Should I ever play a dishonest man, he could not move a piece without making a little noise as the piece touched or scraped against the board, and I would notice the false move. Today I'm playing white, and am justly defeating the forces of darkness, represented by your friend here."

The Welshman had often played the game in his youth with abbots and priors throughout England, drinking chalices of opium-laced claret to help his concentration. He studied the situation, and marvelled at Master John's apparent ineptness.

"But look here, you have many opportunities to take Master Ariperto's pieces. Your triangle here bears an 8, and this circle a 4. The triangle can already jump, if it will, onto Ariperto's triangle with a 12. If you move the circle to the left, it too will be able to jump onto Ariperto's 12. 8 and 4 have a sum of 12, and you will have captured Ariperto's triangle. Or look at this square worth 4. Move it diagonally forward and right, and it will be three spaces from the same 12. 3 multiplied by four equals 12, and again you capture the piece."

Master John nodded ruefully.

"You are right, of course, Welshman. But unfortunately the situation is not so simple. We are not playing to merely take the most pieces, but by mutual agreement we must seek to formulate a mathematical progression by aligning pieces. It is a geometric progression of the third species…"

"Stop, stop, please." The Welshman raised his hands in a gesture of surrender. "I don't even know what these words mean, and I wouldn't know if you explained to me in our native tongue. If you are so bold, Master John, as to tackle such a task, you must do it alone. I am incapable of understanding such arithmetic."

Master Ariperto cocked his head, listening with curiosity.

"And yet, I hear that you are familiar with the game in its simpler forms. Where did you receive your learning, Gallese?"

"Well…" The Welshman was all too clearly embarrassed. Master Ariperto realised that he must have asked a question whose answer might be dangerously revealing for a political fugitive in the eternal conflict between Pope and Emperor, as the whole household knew Master John and his two companions to be.

"Never mind," the old man held up a hand "I understand. It was an indiscreet question. Do not jeopardize your safety for the sake of my curiosity. Indeed, it is time I went to young Arnaldo for his lesson. I take my leave of you. Master John, leave the board exactly as it is, and think over your next move. There's no hurry."

Master Ariperto rose stiffly to leave the room. The Welshman took his place opposite Master John, gazing at the eccentric Rithmomachia board with an expression of undecipherable complexity.

"Why so thoughtful, Your Majesty?" Master John enquired in the English tongue.

The Welshman answered after some time.

"I was thinking… I used to believe I was good at Rithmomachia."

"Pay no attention to two scholars playing a convoluted form of the game. It's no reflection of your skill at Rithmomachia if you're not familiar with mathematical progressions."

"No, that wasn't what I meant. A long time ago, back in England, I believed I was good at it. Then I started to doubt. I played it in Abbeys with monks and scholars. I always enjoyed their company, and loved to talk of the Saints as we did our sums over the gaming board and a glass of claret. I used to win. Almost always. And if I lost, it was always a hard fought victory for my opponent, after much tension and fist-clenching on my part. Sometimes I even had to hold back tears when I realised I would lose.

"Then my son Edward grew to adolescence, and took an interest in the game when his mother told him I played it. He never saw me play it in person; we hardly ever saw each other at all.

"At that time I was sometimes the guest of Tewkesbury Abbey, do you know it?"

"I once saw it from afar. I remember its magnificent tower. It benefited greatly from your… relationship with Hugh Despenser."

A fleeting hint of pain was swept from the Welshman's face by an expression of intense bitterness.

"He was false." He stated with simplicity. "He never loved me as I yearned to be loved. He wished only to use my nature against me, to his gain."

Master John nodded.

"I believe that is true. Most men learn with time to penetrate the fog love conjures up in our eyes. You never did, and it was your greatest fault."

"My vision was so contorted" the Welshman shook his head "that I saw the wealth of the kingdom and the lands of my subjects as little more than tokens of love, freely to be given and taken on Hugh's every whim, to glorify himself and his estates. The nation's finest craftsmen and masons were forced to abandon other, more urgent works to hurry to Tewkesbury because that was where Hugh intended to be buried. And I came there often, because I loved to bask in the reverence of Hugh's sycophants and hangers on. They were even falser than he, if that be possible."

"And Rithmomachia?"

"During a summer visit that was meant to be brief, the rains swelled the River Avon so much that the Abbey was cut off by the floodwaters. We were forced to wait there some days, and the Abbot and I played together at great length. Of course, I nearly always won.

"During one of these games he told me he had also played with my son during a visit to Westminster. I asked him if Edward were as talented as I. The Abbot smiled and said 'No, he lost dismally, and indeed says he has lost every single game he has ever played, and is resigned to it. It seems the Prince prefers chess, which he can play with barons and knights.'

"I was struck to the core by what the Abbot said. That same day I received news of fresh defeat in Scotland, but all I could think about was Rithmomachia. The great lords of the realm were debating strategy to regain our lost lands in the north, but their sovereign was preoccupied with Rithmomachia. Do you think I was distressed that my son was not capable of simple arithmetic? Not at all! While the court bustled with emissaries and messengers and the councillors took grave decisions, I was fretting over my own self.

"I knew my son was more gifted than I. He could do sums in a flash that I would struggle over for a long while, and his Latin was superior to mine before his twelfth birthday, I can now freely admit. How could he have lost where I had always won?

"That night I relived in my mind's eye every single game of Rithmomachia I had ever played: the dismayed expressions on my opponents' faces, the veiled comments of the onlookers, their warm congratulations for my victories. I suddenly realised that it had all been contrived. They had let me win, when really I was not at all good at the game. I became utterly furious. Now that time has passed and I can look back on these things objectively, I believe I chose Rithmomachia to play because I could not stomach the thought of playing chess with the barons or their knights. Unlike abbots and monks, they would not have hesitated to beat me soundly at a game; they would have delighted in it."

The Welshman paused. Master John had been listening carefully, a knowing smile slowly forming on his features.

"There was no way for you to become good at Rithmomachia. To learn well, one must suffer many defeats, and you never did. I remember that your son was often defeated by his companions in chess, and yet with good cheer he continued to challenge them, and slowly became a better player. Knowing your former self, Your Majesty, you probably flew into a tantrum as soon as you came close to losing the first time, and your opponent pretended to play badly and be defeated to appease you. Once it had happened that first time, word spread and it became a pattern that no other opponent dared break. You were never a sporting loser. Forgive me, I do not mean to offend, but I see that you have since come to view your own past in a more balanced way. No doubt your years of hermitage have given you ample time for these reflections."

The Welshman nodded, evidently not in the least offended.

"It's true. I became furious at the time, but did not yet realise that it was my own doing, as you saw immediately. Then, when I became a lay-brother, I started to look back over the events of my life as though through the eyes of another person, as though I had had a silent companion all along, who had seen everything I had done, and knew every motivation within my soul, and now could show me those events once more from the outside. And that was when I finally realised how pathetically laughable I must have seemed to my subjects on so many occasions.

"I saw myself defeating Abbots at the Rithmomachia board: a simpleton convinced he could beat scholars at their own game. In the same way, I saw myself digging ditches in the company of farmers: a Prince in silk gloves playing the peasant, not noticing how terrified the farmers were that they might not have loosened the soil enough beforehand with their harrows so that I might dig through it without earning myself a single blister."

Master John chuckled softly.

"I remember that particular eccentricity of yours, among the many others. It left the nobility of all the land scandalized. In many ways, your preference for the love of your fellow men was far more acceptable to them than affectations of commonness."

"And you, Master John? What did you think of me? Did you despise me, and look down upon me? Is that why you let Mortimer live when I sent you to Hainault to kill him?"

"I did not despise you at all. My feelings were... like those of many in the land. I *wanted* to love you, as subjects should love their king, but you made it very difficult. I think I, and most people, would have forgiven you any number of temper tantrums, male lovers and trenches dug, if only you had put England first, and not second to these passions and hobbies. Kings have done far worse, and been forgiven by people and by posterity."

The Welshman was bitter. "You should have despised me, then, I deserved it." But abruptly he smiled, and raised a hand as though to halt Master John's thoughts. "There! You see, that is the part of me which is petulant, and seeks the pity of others, and rails against any judgment of me... even now I struggle to contain it. But when it comes out, I recognize it."

Master John nodded. "You have come far indeed since you were King. I am truly sorry that we tore you from your hermitage, to bring you back to a world you never loved."

"It's not your fault, Master John." The Welshman's eyes were distant. "The Watcher was in the process of taking me away, in any case. And for once in my life, I can bow to the good of England, and not pursue my own fulfillment." He abruptly changed the topic of conversation. "But where is William? With the young Lady Bianca?"

"I imagine so." Ulgham grinned. "I've never seen him so profoundly struck by a woman before."

"I'm glad for him. At least something will have come of all this." The Welshman replied philosophically.

"I'm glad, too." Master John's grin was ever broader. "It was high time he discovered the sharpest weapons and deepest wounds on the face of God's Earth. Actually, I envy him."

Chapter 24

Pavia, July 1338

The witch of the towers – a lady is a kind of woman – a mother's tears

"William," Bianca whispered, reaching toward me with a conspiratorial smile, "come with me, there's something very special I want to show you. My cousin Luca has shifted the watch for me this evening. No one will disturb us." And she took my hand in hers. Our every touch sent a thrill running through me, and I could not have resisted her if I had wanted to as she pulled me toward an arched doorway I had never noticed before. It gave onto a steep, winding stairwell, and after many turns – each one punctuated by kisses that became more and more lingering the higher we climbed – we emerged onto a portico terrace at the top of a magnificent tower rising from the east wing of Bottigella Palace, and we were abruptly floating high above the rooftops of Pavia in the golden light of evening.

"At long last" Bianca cried "you see Pavia! I hope this may, in some small measure, make up for your being trapped inside father's palace, unable to visit the city."

"Oh Bianca, this is a magnificent gift…" I gazed all about me with breathless surprise "But… the city is a forest of towers!"

She smiled broadly. "Oh yes, it is. More than one-hundred and thirty, if you count father's." She patted the rich maroon terracotta of an arched window with pride. "But this tower is new, and more elegant. The old towers are very different. They barely have a window to look out of."

Indeed, the towers that rose at different heights and in different shades of brick red all about us, were mostly narrow, windowless tapering pinnacles that strove against one another with, it seemed, no other purpose than height.

"Your father's tower is the loveliest, and that's no false compliment. None of the others vaunt such a crown," the necessary poetic conclusion to my comment came unbidden to mind, and I did not take the reins of my tongue in time to stop it "of which you, Lady Bianca, are the noblest jewel."

In pure pleasure, Bianca tossed her long hair backwards with a long, sinuous movement that passed from the waist to her bosom and neck, and I imagined that an invisible hand had caressed her, and she had arched, cat-like, to the touch of unseen fingers. We were perilously alone on that terrace, and my notions of the chivalrous treatment of a lady would soon be put to an arduous test.

"Most of the towers are now two centuries old," she continued "but some are far more ancient. Look, you see how different to the others that one is?"

Bianca pointed to a most extraordinary sight; the sloping, conical roof of an octagonal stone tower that stood out among the square brick towers all about. The stonework just below the roof bore a ring of statues of the pagan gods and godesses that were so life-like, and their features so distinct even at such a distance, that they must surely be the work of the ancients, the 'hand of Rome' as Wiligelmo would have said.

"That is the old Roman tower, where Boethius was imprisoned by Theodoric the Ostrogoth, and where he wrote *The Consolation of Philosophy*, that you helped me translate for old Ariperto the other day."

"By all the Saints…" I breathed in awe "it is so beautiful, I feel I could touch it if I just stretched out my hand."

At the words 'touch' and 'stretched out my hand' it seemed to me that her body once more reacted, curving languorously toward me… as though obeying the same invisible force "…that bends the willow-wands by the riverside toward the rippling water below in the breeze…" I murmured aloud in my native tongue. She did not understand, but her eyes flashed sensually with the certainty that it had been another compliment.

"But why are there so many towers, Bianca?" I sought to distract myself. *'Bianca is a lady.'* I firmly told my nether regions.

"The old folk tell a legend, probably just a fable."

"Let me hear it, anyway." I didn't realise what a test of my resolve her story would be.

"Very well." Her expression became subtly teasing. "They say that two centuries ago there lived in Pavia a witch… a beguiling, fascinating witch, whose eyes and presence were irresistible, that no man could flee." She slowly stepped toward me as she spoke, in a slow dance, and my feet remained immobile, enchanted by her words just as the men of two centuries before. "And yet she was very wise, and all men were silent in her presence, the better to listen to her." My tongue was duly still as she stepped ever closer. "Indeed, so wise was she that often men came to her of their own will." She stopped moving, and waited. I knew I must bridge the small gap between us, and did not keep her waiting. Now we were standing less than an inch apart, and our bodies swayed toward one another of their own accord. "And the men" she continued in a whisper "would ask the witch 'How can I become the most powerful man in Pavia?' And to each she would give the same advice: 'Erect a strong, straight tower, taller than all the others," her voice had become husky "and all shall bend before you…" she lingered over each syllable. "But be careful! You may share this secret with no one, or the spell will be broken.' Then one day…" Bianca's pupils were broad, dark and compelling "the handsomest and gentlest of all men came before her… and on that occasion alone, she bade him seal their secret with a kiss…"

When, after a long interim of heavenly torture, our lips parted and I opened my eyes again, the evening light had turned scarlet and shone almost painfully against ice in the far distance. "What is that mountain, so high and bright?" I asked Bianca. My chin rested on her shoulder, and my face was half hidden by her scented black hair. Without ever letting a single inch of our bodies lose contact with one another, she turned about in my arms very, very slowly. At last her curving back came to fit flush and firm against my front. It was perhaps the sweetest sensation I had ever known.

"That is Monte Rosa. It lies to the north." She rested her head against my chest. "Your father's house is to the north, isn't it?"

"It is."

"And is your father a knight?"

"He is."

"I would dearly love to meet your father, and your brothers, and see your city as you have seen mine."

In that moment I wanted nothing more than to swear to her that I would bring her to my father's house as my bride. And yet, I knew that my duty would call me away soon, and there was no guarantee that I would be able to return. How could I make that vow? With my embrace and my lips I tried to silently convey that which my duty did not allow me to utter aloud.

When I entered our room I could still feel Bianca's warm breath on my cheeks, her bosom against my chest, her hips against mine. I slipped into bed as quietly as I could, for Master John was asleep. I squirmed a little on the old mattress, trying to ignore a part of me that was telling me very firmly to go back to Bianca and finish what we'd begun.

"Will… back so soon?" Master John's voice was drowsy.

"I'm sorry I woke you, Master. You need to rest."

"No, no, you did well. I was… having a horrible dream. I must be a little feverish. These damned mosquitoes keep biting the flesh around the wound."

"What did you dream?"

Master John slowly turned in the bed to face me, gasping twice with pain at his movements.

"I dreamt of the pauper at Sluys. The one whose ear you cut."

I was silent. I had come to feel guilty about my behaviour that day, just as Master John had hoped at the time. He continued.

"It was a strange dream. I saw him in a rainy, muddy village, in an alleyway, and there was Forzetti. He ran after the boy, and seized him, then cut his throat with my knife. The one I stuck in his shoulder that night in Avignon."

"That's awful." I murmured, disturbed.

Master John nodded in the mellow evening light.

"Yes, it was awful. But ridiculous. I feel a little feverish, that must be it. Forzetti would never have any interest in killing a beggar boy, and how unlikely is it that he could ever have met the same boy as us? And yet…"

"Master?"

"It had… the same feeling about it as those dreams you sometimes have, and later discover were significant."

I remained silent, not knowing what to think. Eventually, Master John shrugged with his good shoulder.

"Never mind. Time will tell. What were you doing this evening after dinner?"

"Oh, I was with Bianca." I tried to sound casual.

Master John chuckled softly.

"So, nature is following its course, Will?"

I felt a little heat come to my face. "We just walked up to the top of the tower. I wanted… to loosen my legs, Master."

He laughed again. "I've no doubt you were loosening legs, Will, I just don't think they were yours!" I was taken aback by his humour. Of course, I'd heard it before, and used it myself. We'd crossed paths with many young women during our travels, and often enough the inevitable had happened, for both of us. But this was different. Bianca was a lady, not the daughter of some peasant or shoemaker. She was the granddaughter of a Palatine Count, no matter how fatally her forebears might have stumbled in the sordid quagmire of Lombard politics. How could Master John make such coarse remarks about her?

"Master… Bianca is a lady!"

"Bianca is a woman" he retorted, though his tone was kind "and you're a man. Why should you not play love-games together?"

The ardour of my nether region had now deserted me, and in my embarrassment I was left cold in the bed despite the muggy summer heat. "Because a man of honour must not dishonour a lady, Master John." I answered, with youthful primness.

Master John chuckled again at this statement. He turned his lively eyes to mine and clapped my shoulder affectionately with his good hand.

"Why, Will, I'm surprised at you. Such an experienced lad as yourself, have you not yet learned there's more than one way to embrace a girl? You don't know what pleasure you've been missing.

"Trust me, Will, the realm of honor is open to all of love's little games bar one. I should think you can muster the self-control necessary to satisfy both this Lombard flower and your stiff English sapling without ever breaching anyone's honour."

I blushed even more deeply, but at the same time I was sure that I lit up the room with the shining of my eyes. Master John was right, there were ways and ways to play the game. I was at once fiercely grateful and keenly ashamed. But Master John's grip on my shoulder became suddenly vice-like.

"Take my warning, though, Will. She will tempt your self-control every way she knows, and in many ways she herself might not yet guess."

My gaze must have betrayed disbelief and confusion, for Master John added "It's not that Lombard ladies are loose with their virtue, for a Mediterranean milk-maid may be as proud, perhaps prouder than, an English queen. The point is that this family is desperate. Bianca's father can barely hold off their enemies in the city council, her grandfather is long dead in the dungeons of Milan and her mother is formidable, but aging. It's abundantly plain that you're a gentleman of family, probably also of land, and what's more your obsession with honour makes them think you'd make good your responsibilities, should you create them. You're the best chance they have in this world of finding a man who'll take Bianca away to a better place, and give them one less charge to worry over here in Pavia."

Still my denial of such a possibility showed in my face. Master John sighed, and made things plain. "I'm saying, Will, that she'll do her best to get with child from you and force you to marry her, and take her off to England. They think we're just politically persecuted goliards, Will; they have no idea of our business here, nor who the Welshman really is. They can't know that we're bound to vital duty and that we can't be off marrying and honey-mooning their daughters."

The red in my face had not gone away, though now it was there for anger. "Master John!" I whispered with as much fury as respect permitted "how can you think this of Bianca? She is the finest lady I ever met, and would never let such base reasoning…. She'd never…." I couldn't conclude for the rage.

To my surprise, my Master didn't argue the point. He could see that I was upset, and nodded. "You may well be right, Will, truly you may. She's as good a girl as I ever met, I'll give you that. But apply logic for a moment. A lady is just… one of many kinds of woman." He slowly settled down onto his back for greater comfort. I glanced at the bandage on his shoulder, but it didn't seem damp.

"A lady is just one type of woman, and the nature of woman is practical. Without them, Christendom would crumble within a year. It's only the way our loins keep us men bound to our women that holds us back from killing each other to the last man in pointless wars.

"The nature of women is practical, and little Bianca is most definitely a woman, as is her mother. Their best hope lies with you, Will, given their limited information. If she does try to get past your self-control, and play that game I suggested avoiding, it's only the kindest and sincerest of compliments to you, my good lad, that anyone could make." He looked away, upwards. "A compliment born of love, Will, make no mistake." His pupils started tracing the lines in the painted ceiling's flourishes. "God knows, I was never paid that compliment by such a fine lady."

I suddenly felt sorry for my Master, and though my faith in Bianca was still totally unshaken, I murmured a promise to that good, worldly man. "I'll be wary, Master, and keep my self-control." As I quietly slipped from the room I could feel my Master's eyes cease their ceiling-tracing and come to rest on my back, mirthful once more.

The evening of the next day, when I entered the dining hall, I schooled my expression as best as my craft allowed me. But Master John had the greater craft, and I'm sure he read the truth in the lines on my brow. And certainly he knew how to interpret the theatre that greeted us when we came to the supper table. The great lady of the Langosco family wept silently and forlornly into her bowl throughout the meal. The Welshman courteously asked her what the matter was, but she made no reply. She simply shifted her gaze to Bianca's seat which, strangely, remained empty that night.

The truth was that by that time I'd been wary, then tempted, then unwary, then tempted… and had lost my self-control no less than three times. And I'm happy I did, or I'd have no one to tell this story to.

Chapter 25

Great Yarmouth, July 15, 1338

The smuggler arrives – Henry Tideswell's demons – the tunnel beneath Nottingham Castle

"I have word from Ubaldo." Henry de Grosmont murmured over the sound of their footsteps. "Tideswell's ship is coming here, to Yarmouth itself. It may already be in the harbour. He will send us his seal-ring when Fieschi is aboard. It's time to spring the trap, William."

"We must speak with the King first, Henry." William de Montague was agitated as they swept into his chambers in Yarmouth town. "We still don't know if he is playing Fieschi for a fool or not, whether he wishes to see the man fall or not…"

"And when will we get the chance to do that, big brother?" Grosmont interjected. "We're in the middle of a war muster. He's surrounded in every instant by list-makers, inventory-writers and head-counters of every kind. The astrologers say the weather will improve tomorrow, and the fleet will set sail at last. In the meantime they have to load every single object that we might need to do battle against the French. Today and tomorrow there will be more confusion here than either of us has ever witnessed. This is no overland raid into Scotland, this is a war-fleet. Ubaldo is expecting Fieschi to meet Tideswell today, and we have to move as soon as he gives us the signal."

"We risk ruining something vital to the King." Montague was plagued by the need for certainty before acting.

"Maybe. But it may also be that Edward has no hidden agenda, and we will only pass up an opportunity to rid him of Fieschi's influence."

"We must be sure."

"William, if you don't order the inspection of that ship when the time comes, I will. We can't pass up this chance." Grosmont's eyes hardened with determination, just as someone pounded loudly on the door.

"Enter!" Montague called. His senior squire opened.

"My Lords, a page has come with the greatest urgency, speaking of a matter of importance to the Crown itself."

"Show him in." Montague and Grosmont exchanged a meaningful glance. It must be Ubaldo's signal. Indeed, the boy arrived, panting, clasping a golden seal-ring in his right hand.

"My Lords, Ubaldo de Fénis bade me bring you this." Then he bent double, gasping with exertion.

"William, I am going." Grosmont snatched the ring from the page boy's hand before Montague could. "The Genoese banker is on a traitor's ship, right under the King's nose as we speak. This is our chance." Montague was shaking his head with doubt. "No William, we can't hesitate. I'm going to make that inspection whether you're coming or not."

His gait purposeful, Grosmont strode from the room, Montague trailing behind with a scowl, knowing he could not dissuade his young friend. As they left the building, their squires fell in around them. At the corner of the market square Grosmont encountered a group of knights wearing the livery of Northampton, Suffolk, Salisbury and Lancaster.

"Sirs knights, Follow me. We go to arrest a traitor." Grosmont called to them. Montague's own men of Salisbury saw their liege-lord walking with Grosmont and fell in without question. The knights of Lancaster, among them Thomas de Aldcliffe, unhesitatingly followed their lord, and those of Northampton and Suffolk were caught up in the momentum. Soon a party of noble warriors was descending upon the port.

The harbour-masters not daring to halt the wealthiest lord in the land, and so many knights of renown, merely stepped back in awe as they passed. Soon Grosmont arrived at a shuttle boat tied to the wharf on the side nearest the ship he wanted to reach. The pilot was busy settling a barrel in the stern with his boy and had his back to the wharf. When Grosmont hailed him in the English of London, his accent was so natural that the man thought it was one of his peers speaking.

"Pilot, take us to that ship if you please."

"I'm bounden to take this here salte' beef o'er to Lancaster's ship." The man was a brash northerner. "If you wan' to ge' to a differen' boa', you can swim. Or woul' you rather tell Lancaster why he didn' ge' his beef?"

The party of knights and earls exchanged an amused glance, while Grosmont himself broke out into the wild grin he wore beneath his helmet whenever he hefted the weight of his lance in his gauntleted hand. Then he bellowed like a war-cry: "I am Lancaster!"

The poor pilot whirled about, his face as white as a Princess's bed-linen.

"My... my Lor'... I didn'... I mean..."

"Speak not, just row good man." The earl was aboard the boat with a laugh and a bound, motioning to Montague and the knights to follow suite. "I've taken no offence."

Among a great deal of tottering, man after man jumped into the shuttle boat. Soon the pilot and his boy were heaving at their oars with all their might against the morning breeze and the weight of their passengers. With every stroke the pilot mumbled under his breath "A grea' Lor' speakin the English like a comm'ner... when I's a boy them was always speakin' in their cour' French like's proper... You jus' don' know where you stan' anymore..."

The rotund cog was rocking at anchor not far into the bay, and the nobles were soon climbing the ladder to the bulwark while the sailors stood back in terror. Once on deck, Grosmont's beckoned to the knights to come and stand in a ring around the broad loading hatch.

"Lift." Grosmont ordered in a loud voice, and trembling sailors hurried forward to move the hatch covering aside, revealing Henry Tideswell below, panicking, darting to and fro at a crouch in the shallow hold like a hunch-backed hare cornered by a hungry tomcat. Niccolò Fieschi, half-obscured by shadows, leant impassively against the wall, his face a subtle mask of thin ice.

Grosmont cast Montague a look that invited him to do the talking.

"Henry Tideswell," the Earl of Salisbury began "do you know me?"

"My Lord," Tideswell stared at the earl's colours "you are William de Montague, Earl of Salisbury."

"And do you know the order of the King by which the twenty-thousand bales of English wool are forfeit to the Crown, to finance the King's expedition to Hainault?"

The smuggler nervously swallowed, his face swimming in sweat. "I do."

"And do you know that not even a quarter of those twenty-thousand bales has been collected?"

"I... do."

"And are you an Englishman, a subject of our King?"

Tideswell could only muster a cough in reply, so dry was his throat.

"Silence is assent." Montague quoted. He moved to the top of the ladder. "I am curious to see exactly what is in your hold."

As the burly Englishman began to descend, Fieschi stepped forward into the light.

"My Lord Earl, I am content to meet you here." His voice, as ever, was a model of calm and suavity. "I have single-handedly uncovered a move by this... scoundrel" he gestured toward Tideswell, whose expression was now frozen with fear "to cheat my dear friend, King Edward, of what is rightfully his. These" his hand swept about to indicate the entire contents of the hold "are bales of English wool!" His voice was delicately indignant at Tideswell's crime.

"Messer Fieschi" Montague began as he stepped down onto the floor of the hold "are you saying that you came here to investigate a case of suspected smuggling to the detriment of England?"

"Of course. After just two years in your land, my love and loyalty for my dear friend is absolute." The way he delicately repeated 'my dear friend' to remind them of his intimacy with the King grated with the Englishmen. "Surely that is why you're here, too?"

Montague glanced up at Grosmont, suddenly aware that their presence on the ship could seem just as inexplicable as Fieschi's. He was saved from answering when Henry Tideswell was so enraged by Fieschi's deception that he found his voice.

"That's a lie! He's here to check on his shipment. The House of Fieschi ordered these bails from the Black Friars of Gloucester through the Augustinians in Sluys and Clare. I'm just a go-between, I am innocent."

"The proposition that you are innocent" Grosmont spoke from the deck above "is as ridiculous as Messer Niccolò's claim that he is here to investigate your wrongdoings out of love for his 'dear friend'. You're both caught red-handed, the one exposed a traitor by his cargo, the other exposed a liar by his accomplice. Was this your idea of cleverness, Fieschi, bringing your dog to heel in Yarmouth bay, right in the middle of the King's war-muster?"

"My Lord," Fieschi replied without hesitation "how can you lend weight to the slander of a blatant miscreant? I am an ambassador of Genoa and a member of the King's Royal Council. Can you doubt my integrity on the strength of a known smuggler's word?"

Shadows in motion appeared over the loading hatch, making all turn toward the starboard bulwark. More knights were clambering aboard, this time wearing the livery of the King's own household. After them arrived first Richard de Bury and then King Edward himself. All present bowed and shifted so that their backs were not turned to the royal person, making way for Edward to come to the open loading hatch. At seeing his King above, Henry Tideswell's face twisted with the agony of seeing himself already hung, drawn and quartered.

"There is no time for this." Edward's voice easily carried to every soul aboard the cog. "I cannot be called away from the work of the muster except for matters of the greatest urgency."

"Your Majesty, I am sure the matter will be resolved forthwith." Said Richard de Bury, appearing at the King's side. "I am greatly reassured to see William, Earl of Salisbury here."

"Whose ship is this?" Edward asked, turning to his cousin Grosmont "What has its captain done?"

"The captain is one Henry Tideswell, Edward." Grosmont replied, with a natural familiarity borne of long friendship that Fieschi would never have been able to mimic. "William and I were warned by an informer that he was arriving in Yarmouth with a ship-full of contraband, and here he is. But wool is not the only suspicious thing we found on his ship." He gestured toward the Genoese.

"Messer Niccolò, are you here?" King Edward enquired startled, seeing who was in the hold together with William de Montague and the increasingly distraught Tideswell.

"Indeed, your majesty. I discovered the arrival of this smuggler before even the Earls of Salisbury and Lancaster, and was already on the ship with the intention of arresting him when they arrived."

"Alone?" Grosmont interrupted. "Salisbury and I, though we are warriors, brought these knights with us as witnesses and protection. You were very brave indeed, Messer Niccolò, to climb into a smuggler's cog, crawling with his crew, to arrest him all by yourself." He concluded with heavy irony.

"What are you insinuating, Henry?" The King's eyes were unreadable, his voice level.

"That Messer Niccolò was the man who commissioned this wool shipment, and came aboard ship alone to discreetly check his wares. The smuggler, Tideswell has said as much, seeking to exonerate himself."

"Your Majesty, my dear friend" Fieschi's tone was, as ever, tautly controlled "surely the word of a smuggler and traitor cannot be held against that of an ambassador and member of the Royal Council?"

The King's eyes opened wide, and he stared off into the grey sea-sky as though remembering something arresting.

"Tideswell… Henry Tideswell… Bishop Richard, isn't that the name mentioned in the letter that arrived from Genoa? The one concerning an escaped criminal?"

Niccolò Fieschi looked mystified at the mention of his city, while confusion began to blend with terror in Tideswell's features. Genoa? An escaped criminal?

"Yes, Your Majesty," Richard de Bury confirmed "I believe the 'Henricus Tidesvellus Anglicus' referred to in the letter must be this man."

"And would you remind me of the content of that letter?"

"Of course, Your Majesty," the old man replied readily "I just happen to have it with me." Bury drew the letter from his belt almost theatrically, surprising himself. Perhaps, he thought, he was coming under the influence of Grosmont's ebullient extroversion.

" 'Your Royal Highness, Edward the Third of England, from your loyal servant and friend Messer Simone Doria of Genoa, in the name of the Lord, Amen.' " He began to read. " 'The House of Doria despairs that it is unable to consign to the Crown of England one Henry Tideswell of England, a dangerous criminal who was arrested by a Doria sergeant-at-arms in the city of Genoa and imprisoned in the gaol of this city, due to the said prisoner's subsequent escape and unexplained disappearance from the Republic of Genoa.' " Tideswell, still crouching below in the hold of his ship between Fieschi and Montague, began to mutter "…never been to Genoa in all my life…", but Bury did not hear. " 'The criminal activities ascribed to the name of Tideswell are numerous and grave, both against the Crown of England, including treasonous smuggling to the detriment of Your Majesty's control of trade, and against the Republic of Genoa, including consorting with demonic forces in order to flee the gaol of this city, which all the world knows to be inescapable without supernatural aid, and…' " Bury paused, raising a quizzical eyebrow and glancing down at Tideswell " 'consorting with a male prostitute secretly and illegally introduced to the said gaol of the city of Genoa for sodomitic purposes.' "

"Male prostitute…? Sodomitic… demonic forces…" Tideswell was ranting in his bewilderment "but I wouldn't even know where to find Genoa, I've never been near the place…"

"My goodness," King Edward was highly amused "consorting with demons and male prostitutes, as well as smuggling? What a busy life you lead, Henry Tideswell."

"I swear before God and Mary, Your Majesty" Tideswell threw himself to his knees in desperation "it's not true! I've never been south of the Bay of Biscay in all my life… I can't possibly have…"

"Be silent." Montague cut him off. "The King speaks."

"Messer Niccolò," Edward resumed "is it true that escape from the prisons of Genoa is impossible without diabolic assistance?"

Fieschi smiled, looking at the King as though the two were sharing a private joke. "Perhaps the scribe elaborated the text, as scribes so often do, in his zeal to guard my city's fearsome reputation."

"Whatever the truth of the matter, it shall be settled by the court of Genoa, not here." He raised his voice to the tone he used when making decrees. "We shall forego the pleasure of having Henry Tideswell and his crew-members hanged, drawn and quartered," the smuggler closed his eyes, becoming limp with sheer relief "in favour of giving these wretches to the House of Doria to man their galley oars for the rest of their lives. This ship and its contents are forfeit to the Crown of England and its war effort."

Tideswell's eyes flew open again. He had heard horrific rumours about the lives of men enslaved by the Genoese in the Mediterranean.

"The House of Doria has no claim on me, Your Majesty, I've never even been to Genoa!"

"Then where have you been this last year?" Richard de Bury coldly asked him. "The last news the Crown had of you was last September, when you were fleeing the authorities of Sluys after the harbour woolhouse was burnt down, with your smuggled wool inside."

"Where have I been? Not to Genoa… I've been all over the north seas... working for him!" He jabbed a trembling hand at Niccolò Fieschi.

"For me?" Fieschi laughed lightly. "I have never seen this man before today, Your Majesty. I merely came to investigate information that had reached our agents that a wool-smuggler was going to arrive in this port today."

"You bloody bastard of a lying Genoese whore's son!" Tideswell railed against his disloyal partner in crime. "You mongrel son of..."

"Edward" Grosmont murmured quietly, coming to stand beside his royal cousin while Tideswell continued to fill the air with choice oaths "the same information about a smuggler came to our ears, too, but when we arrived Fieschi was already on the boat. Alone. That's hardly how you go about arresting a smuggler."

Again the King's dark eyes were fathomless. He raised his voice, cutting through Tideswell's expletives.

"Messer Niccolò, my dear friend, let us waste no further time listening to this criminal's wailings. My judgement here has been delivered, and if you will join me ashore I have ever need of your counsel for important matters of state."

"It will be my pleasure, Your Majesty." Fieschi smiled graciously, as though conceding a favour, and began to climb the ladder, leaving Montague in the hold, speechless beside the whimpering Tideswell, and Grosmont no less speechless on the deck above. As Fieschi and the King disappeared over the bulwark to board the royal boat, the circle of English knights burst into angry chatter.

"My Lord," Sir Thomas Aldcliffe summarised their feelings "that Genoese banker was surely deep in treacherous dealings with Tideswell when we arrived. The smuggler must be telling the truth."

"Of course I'm telling the truth..." Tideswell moaned below.

"That Genoese must be an enchanter" Aldcliffe continued "to have blinded the King so."

"... an enchanter" Tideswell's voice was becoming feverish "... an enchanter, I have seen him summon demons, it's the truth, I swear..."

"The King is no fool." Montague declared loudly. He had climbed up on deck, and the knights parted to allow him to join Grosmont at the centre of the group. "Nor is he under a spell. He is playing games with Fieschi, or I'll wager my lands and title." The knights fell silent.

"I fear My Lord of Salisbury is right." Bury intervened thoughtfully. "It is not the first time he has voiced this suspicion with me, and today's events would seem to confirm it." He turned to look at Grosmont. "Henry, you must admit that only a fool would not have doubted Fieschi's sincerity today, and the King is no fool. But neither did he seize upon the situation to rid himself of the Genoese. No matter how much we all loathe him," his gesture included the assembled knights, whose expressions clearly conveyed that he had grasped their sentiment "the King must want Fieschi at his side for reasons of his own. And we should trust him."

Montague nodded. "We may have jeopardized everything King Edward is planning today."

Grosmont eyes turned hard and rebellious, but he did not reply.

"Let us return ashore." Montague said tersely. "We have interfered enough."

As they boarded their shuttle boat and the old sailor and his boy began to row them ashore, more vessels laden with men-at-arms approached from all sides, to take custody of the smugglers cog, its cargo and its crew. From the ship still came Tideswell's voice, almost keening in its delirious self-pity, "…demons… Fieschi… I've never… innocent…"

Soon Richard de Bury and the noble company gratefully stepped onto the firm wood of the wharf. Montague recalled the knights' attention.

"Before you go, we will all take a vow of silence, witnessed by His Grace the Bishop of Durham, about what has befallen here today." He gazed meaningfully into each of their eyes in turn, and last of all into Grosmont's. One after another, the young men obediently swore themselves to silence.

"Now, about your business, sir knights, and be thanked." Montague dismissed them. Grosmont looked away. The young knights had all stood in awe of Montague since his heroic actions in aiding King Edward to capture Roger Mortimer and reclaim his kingdom eight years before. He wished he had been in the tunnel beneath Nottingham Castle that night.

"Pilot," he called out to the sailor in the boat below "have a care for my beef. Just because I'm in the middle of a war doesn't mean I want to eat gruel and drink water."

Montague turned away from the retreating backs of the knights and looked sharply at his young friend, but Grosmont's face seemed as jovial and carefree as usual.

Chapter 26

Pavia, July 1338

*The Iron Crown – the Arc of Augustine –
the arrow-pierced saint of Scotland*

The Welshman glanced at the mule driver, intent in his argument with Matteo Bottigella's warden, and then back at the forgotten service door, lying wide open.

"I tell you, there's a new man in Voghera now, and this is his mark." The mule driver was becoming angry. "His name is Bernaldo, and if he signed for seven mules full laden and one half laden leaving Voghera, that's all the mules you can expect to arrive in Pavia, and no fault of mine if you were looking for more."

"Word from Calvignano told us to expect ten, fully laden." The warden was wary of the wool that mule drivers often tried to pull over their clients' eyes. "What happened to all those woad leaves? Will you tell the dyers yourself?"

Their bickering faded into the background as the Welshman drew closer to the open door, irresistibly drawn by the glimpse of the outside world it offered. After months of protective captivity he was beginning to tire of even the luxurious interior of Palazzo Bottigella. Through the door a cobbled back street came into view, and two grimy city boys intent on a game of marbles.

The taller of the two knelt, his tumbling curls falling down to his brown eyes, as crystal-hard in the heat of competition as the glass balls he was attempting to capture.

If they were playing to the same rules as Winchester the Welshman considered the lay of the marbles on the road *he would try to break up the cluster and send all the marbles flying with a strong flick.* With an inward smile he remembered how ashamed of him his father had been when, in front of the whole court, he had asked Sir Guy Ferre, his tutor, for a set of marbles to play with. He had been very small at the time, and that was probably one of the first times he had displayed his passion for the pass-times of commoners to his horrified peers. As he had grown he had learned to row, swim, dig and even play football, indulging one by one in sports with ever more low-born connotations, until the lords of the realm had become convinced that he was making fun of them. The truth was, he simply loved those games, and desired to make fun of no one. He hadn't felt guilty about loving them then, nor did he now.

The boy cocked his middle finger against his thumb instead of his index finger, sure sign he would attempt a powerful flick. But in his zeal he miscalculated, and sent the cue marble flying over the cluster, not shuddering into it. The little globe skidded away over the round river cobbles, and the boy stood up with a groan, clenching his fists in anger.

Perhaps the rules are similar to the ones I learnt as a child. If so, the littler boy will try to nudge the Queen marble into the hole. If he takes all, that will mean they really are playing to Winchester rules.

The smaller of the two children, playful triumph in his eyes, swaggered up to the cluster. Victory was within reach, but the remaining marbles were crowded together, and the rule was that you could not touch any but the cue marble when you flicked, or the move was forfeit. With infinite delicacy he brought his cocked index finger to within a hairs-width of the Queen, and gave the lightest possible flick. She rolled obediently into the hole, and he jumped up, whooping with merriness.

"Omnia!" He cried, startling the Welshman with the same Latin word the boys in Winchester used to claim all the marbles in a game. Then he bent over and scooped up all of the marbles into his two scrawny hands.

Winchester rules indeed! The Welshman was astounded. He was about to back away from the forgotten service door, knowing he should never have wandered so far from the guests' quarters in the first place, let alone looked out into the world, when an act of injustice checked him. The taller street boy, angry at losing, churlishly struck at the smaller boy's marble-filled hands. The little fellow managed to hold on to all of his hard won treasures but one. The Queen marble flew across the street and came to a stop just inside the gates of Bottigella Palace. The two boys' eyes widened when they saw where it was. Neither of them dared even dart a few inches inside that door. What a beating it would earn them if they were caught!

The Welshman, knowing how precious a Queen marble was to a little boy, walked forward and picked it up to give it back to him. The two boys looked fearful. Perhaps their beating was already nigh. The Welshman smiled, though, and stepped out onto the street. He wordlessly held the marble out to the stunned victor. Startled by the movement, the older boy bolted. The younger held his ground, eyeing the marble and then the Welshman, who smiled again and dropped the marble into the youth's cupped hands. The little marble champion made off as fast as he could without scattering his prize all about him.

The Welshman hastily turned back to the door, and was dismayed to find it shut. The mule driver, or the warden, had shut it and locked it without so much as a glance outside. After a moment's thought, the Welshman spoke to his unseen companion.

This must be the manifestation of the Lord's Will. I have been drawn out into the city by a righteous act, not by falsehood. That means I'm out here for a reason. But where am I to go?

Master John had been fighting to keep his thoughts lucid all morning, but the confusion of fever kept rising, no matter how hard he concentrated. To sharpen his reasoning he had practiced encoding messages without the aid of pen and parchment. To his dismay he had found the numbers and letters aimlessly squirming about in his mind like so many flies trapped in treacle-water. Even fragments of the *Aeneid* that he had memorised as a child came back to him in a jumble, and he found the words stumbling on his tongue in the wrong case and order. In despair, he realised that the low fever he had been constantly aware of, and had been holding back ever since Forzetti had wounded him below Auramala, was flaring up.

"Master John, here I am." He heard Will enter the room, and rolled over, unable to hide the pain it caused him.

"Master, you look terrible…" His pupil's voice choked off.

"There's no time for that now, Will." He summoned a smile, but realised from Will's expression that the result was probably nearer to a grimace. "You have work to do. I cannot go. We'll talk about me later. Now it's time for work, and you're ready for the work Will, I know you are. I'm not at all worried about -" He closed his mouth, realising he was babbling.

"Must I leave the Palace?" His pupil replied, and Master John noticed a touch of eagerness in the young man's voice at the prospect of escaping into the city.

"Yes. The Welshman has got lost. He must be somewhere in Pavia. He can't have had time to leave. Where would he go? He must be in prayer somewhere, he is deeply religious. Who are the saints of Pavia? At which shrine might he be kneeling? Saint Syrus, Saint Augustine, Saint Juventius… there are saints and saints and saints…"

"Master, don't… don't you think he has decided to run?" Was the pain in Will's voice for the thought of losing the Welshman? Through the aching delirium Master John tried to cheer him.

"I don't think so, Will, don't worry. But I can't say why I don't think so. He might be in a church. But there are so many churches here, for every king of the Longobards had one built for his tomb, they tell me. But he would be looking for a saint, not a king. He doesn't like kings very much, does he? And you go to a church to pray to a Saint, you know."

"Yes Master," Will took his hand "I know."

"Then go, go to a church. There must be one nearby. There are so many in the city, you know they were tombs for the kings. Yes, yes, one is just near here, the church of the queens. Of course, the queens, not the kings, I shouldn't have said the kings, I meant the queens…"

"Master, I won't go until I've brought you help. You're so pale."

Ice shot through Master John's heart at these words, and for an instant he became lucid. He leaned half out of bed and tremblingly clasped William's hands in his own.

"It's time wasted, Will. These things happen. Go find him."

The young man averted his gaze, and looked down at his hands. His eyes widened with some new thought.

"Of course, Master. I'm going."

When the physician arrived a short while later, Master John was delirious once more.

The healing hands of a king… Master John's words the day I had threatened the pauper on the road south of Sluys came pressing back to mind. I raced from the building, straining to hold back tears of anxiety for my Master. I had never seen him look so weak, so vulnerable.

Near the gates of Bottigella Palace I met a scurrying priest and stopped him to ask of the church of the Queens.

"*Reginarum?*" he repeated, confused. "*Ah, Dominarum, intellego.* Go straight down the street and to the right."

From the outside the little church was almost indistinguishable, with a plain façade nestled between two larger buildings that hid the bell tower from view. I only realised it was a church thanks to the colourful ceramic bowls inlaid among the red brickwork to tell pilgrims they could find food and board there. Inside, the chapel was breathtaking, clothed entirely in the artwork of the ancient Longobards. But the Welshman was nowhere to be seen.

Next I sought out the church of the kings of Lombardy itself, San Michele, and my feet bruised as I hurried down the narrow streets, heedless of the round river cobbles. I still bear in my mind the image of its many-layered, many-colored façade, alive with sandstone serpents and griffins and harpies, as I emerged into the broad square in front of the church. I entered through the great, intricate portal, and I felt like I was stepping through a page of one of those miraculous gospel books that Irish monks painted long, long ago, with arts that have since been lost. Their infinitely complex, interweaving decorations here were made solid stone, the doorway to the House of the Lord. I raced past a dozen carven columns, where the heads of fantastical beasts glared down at me from every capital. I frantically traced the stone maze on the floor behind the altar with my eyes and trod the very stones on which Barbarossa had knelt to receive the Iron Crown as King of Lombardy. But I did not find the Welshman.

The healing hands… kings, kings…

Fighting back panic, I finally realized how foolish I had been. Of all people in the world, the Welshman was surely the one who cared least for kings and the churches they had graced. In his heart there was but one King, the King of Heaven, and one of the most devoted servants ever to have dedicated their life to Him lay some few paces from the city walls, in the Church of San Pietro in Ciel d'Oro. I would have to look for the Welshman at the Shrine of Saint Augustine.

"I am an Englishman." The Welshman told the youthful monk beside him. "I have seen many things, in my travels, that I thought were miraculous, but one of the most curious was what I saw this morning."

As he listened to the Welshman with curiosity, the young man frequently adjusted his black robes. He was newly ordained, and his habit still hung strangely about him.

"Two boys of Pavia were playing marbles. And the rules they used were the same as the boys of Winchester. Perhaps" the Welshman mused "a pilgrim's servant boy brought the rules with him. After all, the sister of King Alfred the Great died on the road, and was buried in this very city. Her retinue must have stayed in the city long enough to make friends among the Pavians, and teach them the rules of their game."

"Is Winchester your home, pilgrim? I have heard so much about it." The monk was curious.

"No, Brother Jacopo," the Welshman said hesitantly "I don't really have a home… I was born in Wales." He concluded with a more certain tone. His place of birth had, after all, come to define him in recent years.

"An Englishman born in Wales?" Brother Jacopo wondered. "Well… in prayer we are naked of our nationhood. The Lord our Father listens to the hearts of men, without regard for their birthplace, or other trappings."

The Welshman nodded, then proceeded to surprise the young monk with a clear, expressive voice as he began to intone the *Nunc dimitis*. Then the monk joined him in chorus, there before the sarcophagus of the saint.

"It is moving" the Welshman said when the echoes of their voices had died away in the crypt "to sing my prayer before Augustine, who taught us that to sing is to pray twice, once with words and once with music. Tell me" he continued "must the Father of the Church remain forever in this… grim old sarcophagus?" He nodded at the blackened old stone of the ancient Longobard casket. "Can they not build a more suitable monument to him?"

"Indeed," Brother Jacopo was eager "the city councillors and the Abbot are collecting treasure for this very purpose. They hope to bring Campionese master sculptors to the city to carve a great marble arc in the Saint's honour. They say a block of marble has already been chosen."

"Really? Then… are the councillors elderly? Normally barons and lords become pious only when they begin to notice that the Next World is not so far away." The Welshman's voice acquired an almost sour note.

"Barons and lords? The city councillors are mostly craftsmen and merchants."

The Welshman nodded. He had distant memories of courtiers

complaining that Lombards, Genoese, Venetians and Tuscans allowed common men to vote and receive votes in their city-states.

"In our northern lands, Brother Jacopo, it is said that you Lombards are barbarous because you elect commoners to elevated positions. But if they are promoting such works of devotion, I say your way of doing things must be wise. This city is to be jealously guarded, just as it jealously guards the relics of Saint Augustine."

Brother Jacopo had no chance to reply, for in that moment a young man came running down the steps into the crypt. When he glimpsed the sarcophagus he slowed to greater demeanour, but the urgency and agitation in his expression did not abate. The Welshman looked shocked by the pale anxiety in his face.

"Have you come…" The Welshman began in the French of the English court.

"Speak in English." William warned him in the obscure language of their island. "I have come to bring you back."

"But I haven't finished my prayers. When will I ever kneel before so great a Saint again? Author of the *Confessions*, and of *The City of God*…"

William knew that he was verging on sacrilege in tearing the Welshman away so abruptly, and crossed himself fearfully in the direction of the sarcophagus, but did not halt. He seized the Welshman by the shoulders.

"You must come, and immediately. Your old gaol-keeper may be in the city, and we would not know it. But there's worse. Master John is ill, desperately ill. If you are truly a king, come back with me and heal him, I beg of you! Please, you must come."

The Welshman blanched as though he had been struck a blow.

"I? Heal him? I'm, just a lay-brother, now, which is much more than I ever was as King, believe me."

"You're the crowned son of Longshanks!" as William almost shook him by the shoulders the pitch of his voice rose, and tears welled in his eyes. Brother Jacopo backed away, almost afraid of the newcomer. "You can heal him, you must."

The Welshman realised that his young friend was too distraught to reckon with, and nodded.

"I'm coming, William."

He crossed himself in the direction of the Saint one last time, and thanked Brother Jacopo. "*Gratias tibi.*"

Moments later, they hurried from the church in the direction of the city.

"Stop! William, you must stop, please don't-"
"No, let us through, we have to see him-"
"There's no point, William-"
"It's not true, the Welshman... the Welshman has to touch him-"
"William, Lady Langosco is right."
"Don't tell me this nonsense again. A king's hands..."
"No! William, listen to me, I am neither king, nor saint, nor the Son of God. What our Lord did for Lazarus, I cannot do."
"You.... you... please, just... Lady Langosco... please..."
"My poor William, I grieve for your grief, just as my daughter would, but Master John is... is gone."
"No... This morning he was healthy..."
"William, listen to me! I don't know why the three of you came, but I know it was for some high purpose. Men such as you do not travel abroad in great secrecy for matters of little account. And men of such good, strong hearts, must surely be doing the Lord's work. Now, William, *you* are responsible for finishing the task. And believe me, I would keep you here a while longer, for my daughter's sake, for she will be heart-broken when you go. But you cannot fall apart now. It is you who must finish this."

The silence which followed was so long that the Welshman and Lady Langosco began to fear that he might be going to faint. Finally, though, William drew a long breath, and for the first time lifted his eyes to the bed where Master John lay.

"I know."

The priest of the tiny, ancient chapel of Saint Gervasius and Saint Protasius was a confidant of the Bottigella family. He had arranged for Master John to be buried in his church in furtive secrecy by night, in a place no one would ever think to look: beneath the relics of Saint Guinifort of Scotland, who in Roman times had been martyred near Pavia, pierced by a dozen arrows.

The priest invoked Saint Guinifort's intervention with God in heaven on behalf of the John de Ulgham's soul. I imagined Master John's face among the seraphs and cherubs, and saw him smile. Master John would have thought it very ironic that he, a proud Northumbrian Scot-beater, was laid to his final rest beneath the sarcophagus of a Scottish Saint.

That imagined smile was the first sign I had that the hollow, aching pain of his passing was finite, and might one day lessen. I felt a little better.

When the death-mass had been sung, the priest turned to us, Matteo Bottigella, Lady Langosco his wife, Bianca their raven-haired daughter, the Welshman and I.

"There is no life without death, and no death without life. William, do you intend to wed Bianca Bottigella, daughter of Matteo Bottigella and Filippina Langosco tonight?"

"I do."

"Then come forward, both of you. I will marry you in God's sight.

Bianca's mother's eyes were already wet with tears after the funeral. Now the drops flowed down her cheeks. We were all emotionally exhausted.

The two of us stepped forward. Bianca, to my left, was dressed in her family's distinctive woad-blue. I wore the few Flemish woolens I still had. The priest, facing us, took my left hand in his left hand, and Bianca's right hand in his right hand.

"Will you love and obey one another?"

"Yes." We answered.

"Will you follow the Word of our Lord Jesus Christ?"

"Yes."

He joined our hands together.

"There's no time for more. You are man and wife. May God bless your union with many sons."

"Thank you, Father." I murmured, but the priest wasn't finished.

"Young man of the North," he looked at me severely "know that the laws of Rothar, the King of the Ancient Lombards still hold here in Pavia, where they were compiled. Tomorrow you are continuing on your journey. Should you not return within three years, Master Bottigella will be free to remarry his daughter. Return soon, son."

Bianca looked at me with desperation in her eyes. Three years…. The mere mention of so long a time was unbearable.

"I will return long before that. And I will take my wife to my father's household, where she will be cherished. I swear."

Chapter 27

Euskirchen, September 1338

Lady Fortune and the Pauper – Francesco Forzetti's hour – compassion can never be foolish

We arrived at Euskirchen after a month or more of walking in the guise of two English pilgrims. We were travelling north toward the Netherlands with all the other English pilgrims which, that summer, were avoiding the traditional pilgrim road, the Via Francigena through hostile France, by striking north from Pavia toward the Teutonic princedoms. The Welshman was content to do so, desiring for the third time in his life to visit the Shrine of the Three Kings at Cologne, where the prophecies stated his son, the King, was one day to be buried. I was Peter Westham, and the Welshman was, for lack of originality on our part, William le Galeys. Travelling as Englishmen also solved the problem of the Welshman's inability to tell a lie. As ever, he would speak as little as possible, and if asked his name would call himself 'le Galeys', which in any case meant 'the Welshman'. In spite of these precautions, we avoided other travellers where possible. The fewer people who noticed us the better.

The town of Euskirchen rather grandiosely proclaimed itself a 'city', though it had little to distinguish itself from a walled country borough but a marketplace and a stone guildhall, whose slate roofing had collapsed here and there and been patched up with shingles. The streets were packed earth, and the lesser buildings stood, or rather leaned against one another, in varying states of disrepair. This town was used to a certain number of pilgrims due to its proximity to Cologne, and the Shrine of the Three Kings, but now it was having to accommodate also the pilgrims who would normally have travelled the Via Francigena, and its little hospital was full to bursting. We were forced to choose our lodgings from among four inns, each one more rickety, seedier and smaller than the last.

We were English pilgrims of moderate good wealth, for the generous promissory notes Sir Thomas Aldcliffe had given us at the outset were still more than half intact. Thus we chose the comeliest looking inn at first, but the keeper was forced to send us away.

"I'm full up for the night. There's no bed here that's fit for gentlemen like you." For a fluent speaker of the Flemish such as me, the town's dialect was perfectly comprehensible. "You'd best get to the next inn. It's not as comfortable as my establishment, but they may have a mattress or two left."

At the next inn we were met with the same story, and yet again at the third. At the last, and definitely least, of the inns, the landlord shrugged, then scratched his enormous, gnarled beard in bemusement, scattering assorted fragments of his last few meals onto the rotting floor rushes of his hall.

"I'm sorry, I've no beds left. I've never seen so many pilgrims here." He said helplessly. "My cousin over in Rheinbach says it's the same there, too. He said the King of England himself passed through with his whole court, on the way to Koblenz to meet the Emperor. It seems all the world is coming through our land this year."

"Our King is near?"

"That's as my cousin told me."

I glanced across at the Welshman, but he looked on blankly, not understanding a word of any Germanic tongue but the English. Should I reveal to him that his son was so close by? I decided to make that decision later.

"With the war-tide rising in France" I told the tavernkeeper "Englishmen like ourselves are avoiding the Via Francigena through King Philip's lands by striking north from Pavia through Milan, and taking the northerly passes over the Alps. That leaves us in the Emperor's own realms, and he is on the best of terms with our King."

"Did you see the Veronica in Rome?" The bearded man asked, his eyes widening with awe. I assumed an expression of reverence and nodded slowly, drawing my crossed-keys pendant from under my tunic to show him. The Welshman, who did not understand a word of our conversation, took his out, too, following my lead.

The tavernkeeper crossed himself fearfully with one greasy, pudgy hand, and shook his head ruefully.

"I would willingly give such fine gentlemen a bed, but I have none left to spare, and trying to kick customers onto the street at this hour to make room would start a brawl. Particularly my customers."

He raised his eyebrows meaningfully, and that was that.

While we returned to the market square, I debated in the privacy of my mind whether the Welshman should know how close the King was. He might insist on changing course to meet his son, but I felt that was unwise until I knew just who had accompanied the King to the mainland. What if Niccolò Fieschi was with him, and Richard de Bury not? Would it be safe to deliver the old man to a court dominated by his one-time gaol-keeper? I knew it would be useless to try and explain these things to the Welshman. When he slipped away from us in Pavia he had proved himself too naïve to comprehend such dangers. I would tell him nothing, and avoid the risk of a second escapade.

"I think the best thing to do now is roll out our blankets in a corner of one of the churches, if the priest is a kind man. I'll ask a stall-holder where to find the friendliest priest in town. We may even get a meal before dark."

I approached a friendly looking butcher and his wife, gathering in their unsold sausages, to ask about charity in the local churches. Soon afterwards I was listening to the butcher, trying to understand his directions, interrupted at every turn by his wife who told him he was muddling things. The Welshman by my side looked more and more confused. While the poor butcher was protesting for the third time "I tell you, woman, it's *left* at the tannery" my gaze met two startled eyes looking at me.

Even at a distance of some sixty feet I had no doubt who it was, for his features had been engraved on my mind's eye since the day Master John and I had left Sluys. It was the pauper we had charged with our message, revealing that Henry Tideswell had been the ultimate cause of the fire in the wool-house. He was standing on the far side of the market square, looking in our direction, his face a mass of scars, scratches and pox-marks. I saw that one ear was missing a lobe, and the sense of shame Master John had instilled in me came flooding back.

Suddenly, a tall figure with black hair and beard stepped up behind the boy. With a chill I remembered Master John's dream, and the dread that it might have been prophetic took me. Was that tall man Forzetti? And was that a knife in his right hand?

I acted without conscious volition, as though under a spell, and launched myself headlong toward the boy to save him. He instantly took fright, and fled. As I followed, speeding past the point where he had been standing, I looked frantically about, but the tall dark figure seemed to have disappeared. The boy led me a frenetic chase through the market square of Euskirchen, dodging the townsfolk who were out and about to make the most of the last moments before the second curfew bell was rung. I had to stop him, to tell him I meant no harm to him this time, to tell him I was sorry.

At the edge of the square he made as though to dart into a side alley, but instead swerved and continued along the side of the square. By the time I realized what he was up to, I was already swerving into the alley, and as I corrected my course I knocked a red-crested cock off the shoulder of a stall-holder. The cock crowed indignantly, in a flurry of cropped wings and flying feathers, and its owner swore loudly after me. I was breaking every rule of the game of secrecy, but such a compulsion was upon me that I had no control of my own actions. As I pelted along the muddy streets, my mind was filled with the faces of Master John on his sick-bed, Forzetti in the moonlight below Auramala Castle, and the pauper as he had been that day outside Sluys.

Finally the boy turned off the square into the back-streets, and as I followed him around corner after crumbling, crooked corner, we both splashed mud onto passers-by. In spite of his desperation I was gaining on the boy, for poverty had denied him the sustenance that legs need to grow strong for running long and well. His breath now came raggedly, and he threw panicked glances back over his shoulders at me. Finally we were in a cul-de-sac, and when he realized that the pursuit was over, he turned about, his pathetically small hands bunched into fists, his eyes like those of a mouse in a barrel with a tomcat.

No words in the world could have banished that wild boy's belief in my ill will. Rather than speak, I sank to my knees like a sinner, my face a mask of un-feigned penitence. It was then that I bowed my head, trying to collect my thoughts. Why had I followed him? Certainly not to harm him. Why had this ragged beggar brought me to my knees? Surely mine was not the obeisance of a servant. Why was I still speechless? Perhaps because I knew well how to speak my mind, but not how to speak my heart.

My down-turned eyes focused on the muddy street surface, swimming with the rain that had just started falling.

"I beg of you," I began slowly in the Flemish "forgive me for my cruelty to you a year ago. I was foolish, then, and callous. But now…" In that moment the world darkened, and I lost my senses.

Rough, steel-toed kicks roused me to half-wakefulness. My head was split by pain, my eyes were unfocused and my wrists and ankles throbbed. I made out a blurred golden glow, perhaps a fireplace, and with the strain of trying to raise my head to see it clearly, I fainted again.

The second time I was awakened by cold water splashed on my face. The steel toes stung my ribs again, and I abruptly sat up, trying to reach for my knife. My torso was not yet upright when I was shaken by retching, and vomited what little I had in my stomach. Once more, my vision blackened, but this time I did not faint, and gradually spots of light appeared in the dark.

"*Vale, Magister Gandavensis.*" 'Greetings, Scholar of Ghent.'' The voice, laden with irony, switched effortlessly from the Latin to the English. "Or should I say, of Norwich?" Now it continued in the common Occitan. "Or should I say Guiraut d'Orange? Incidentally, what name were you travelling under just now? I hear you've been an Englishman again since you left Pavia. Not, I take it, William de Tels?"

The last shadows were clearing from my eyes, and I blearily cast about in the fire-lit room for my interrogator.

"How many names do you have, disciple of John de Ulgham?"

At first, only the man's profile was visible, his long black beard jutting forwards beneath a hawk-like, hooked nose. He turned to face me, and his features came into view in the brazen light. It was Forzetti.

"What… happened to the… boy?" My head still swam.

"The boy?"

"The beggar… you were about… to kill in the square… in the alley."

Forzetti's left eye involuntarily twitched, and a scar reddened on the cheek below.

"A boy in the square? In the alley?" He drew a knife from his belt, and tossed it into the air and caught it again deftly by the blade without even glancing at it. "I saw no boy in the square. And I wasn't in the alley when my men took you." He threw the knife and caught it again. "I was busy taking the Prince of Wales back into my charge. But don't be concerned, Master William. If there was a boy in the alley, I'm sure they killed him on the spot."

As he tossed the knife again I arched up with my legs and body in one movement. I meant to catch that knife and stab Forzetti there and then, but instead I fell flat on the rushes, my ankles and wrists on fire. Forzetti hadn't even moved. There was no need. In my confusion, I hadn't realized that I was manacled by the hands and legs. I stiffly rolled over on the floor to look up at his condescending smile. He hadn't interrupted his rhythmic throwing of the knife.

"Don't you recognize this blade, Master William?"

I focused on the knife, and realized that I had seen it literally hundreds of times.

"Apparently a simple eating knife, and yet perfectly balanced for throwing, and with a reinforced tip… I took it from my shoulder with a great deal of pain that night in Avignon." Forzetti continued. "I had intended to restore to its owner, but to the heart, not the shoulder."

"You'll have your chance before this night is over." I bluffed brashly, hoping news of Master John's death had not reached him. "But you've always been to slow and clumsy, and I'm sure you will be again when my Master arrives to kill you."

The knife effortlessly flew up once more, glittering in the fire light as it turned in the air.

"I'm sorry, Master William, but the Prince of Wales has already told me the truth. I sincerely regret not being able to prove myself against John de Ulgham."

Stung, I flung defiance back up at his infuriating face.

"You did prove yourself against Master John, Forzetti." I did not deign to give that vile creature a title. "Twice, you proved yourself an amateur."

He refused to allow himself to be distracted. He was too skilled a word-baiter to be hooked by word-bait.

"How ironic that such a man should die in his bed, like an elderly peasant…" he continued to taunt "leaving the Prince of Wales in the hands of a babe, who would only lose him for the sake, it seems, of a kerfuffle with a boy at the markets. And by the way, I am grateful for the promissory notes I took from your purse. Did Master John always travel so well provided for?"

Stifling a moan of frustration, I sought a less painful topic.

"Why do you call him the Prince of Wales?"

"Why, haven't you realized? That is my charge's true title. His father, Edward Longshanks, promised the Welsh after conquering their land that he would allow them to have their own Prince born in Wales, and who could speak no language that was not Welsh. So he had his wife give birth to their new son in Caernarfon Castle, and presented the baby to the Welsh clansmen saying 'Behold, a Welsh-born Prince who speaks no language that is not Welsh'. That was a man after my heart! And then, when Edward of Caernarfon was forced to abdicate by the Barons, the one title he would not renounce was that of Prince of Wales, and indeed that wild folk attempted to rescue him from imprisonment more than once, as loyal to him as he was to them. Courtesy constrains men of honour" his lips curled into a smile tainted by sarcasm "to call others by their rightful titles, Master William."

I opened my mouth to answer, and then closed it again. Nothing I might have said could have done any good. I would only have given Forzetti fresh opportunities to deride both me and, far worse, Master John's memory.

At dawn the next morning we left Euskirchen in a solemn train with Forzetti in the lead, followed by a Genoese man-at-arms, the Welshman and I, and two more men-at-arms who closed the column. Forzetti was clearly in a hurry to go somewhere. Even we, his prisoners, were mounted on horses. We left the town by the west-gate, and I felt Koblenz must be Forzetti's destination. If he had wanted to take us back to Genoese lands, he would have either gone south toward the Alpine passes or north toward the sea ports to meet up with a galley. I now felt sure that he was taking us to his master, Niccolò Fieschi, who was surely in the retinue of our King at Koblenz. The Welshman was once more to be a pawn in a great game of blackmail, and far from rescuing him from his fate I had become an added burden to our sovereign. And all because I had wanted to protect a nameless pauper from a shadow.

"Soldier" I murmured to one of the men-at-arms behind us in the Occitan, hoping he would understand "were you one of those who took me in the alley last night?"

He glanced forward at Forzetti's back a little nervously, then looked down at my bonds. Deciding I was harmless as long as I was in chains, he nodded confirmation.

"What happened to the boy I was chasing? Did you kill him?"

He shook his head, bewildered.

"No boy." He mumbled in the same tongue. "Nobody kill."

I turned to the Welshman in growing confusion.

"You know the boy I was chasing yesterday? Did you see him again, after they took me?"

The Welshman shook his head slowly.

"I saw no boy, William, neither before nor after. You simply ran away. I thought you were abandoning me." His tone was that of a man who'd been abandoned so many times that it neither surprised nor pained him anymore.

"You didn't see him? I chased him all over the market."

He shook his head, helplessly.

"You must have seen him." I was almost plaintive.

"William, who is this boy? Why did you chase him?"

"He… He's a pauper I once mistreated. I thought he was going to die. Master John once dreamt of Forzetti killing him, and yesterday I thought I saw… But Forzetti wasn't there, and then I chased him because I wanted to tell him I was sorry."

"Why?" The Welshman's eyes deepened in a way that surprised me. "Why should you, the son of a Knight, apologise to a landless pauper?"

As though I were in a confessional, my tongue began to tell truths of its own free will, and my reasoning mind listened with growing understanding.

"Because Master John said we are all alike, born of woman's womb just as our Lord Jesus was, and that Fortune lifts us up and throws us down all alike. And then I met you, who are the living proof of Fortune's fickleness, and I saw the way your hands were happily worn by the work of a lay-brother, and I understood that Master John was right, and when I saw the boy I wanted to redeem myself with him, and show him that I had changed…"

"William" the Welshman raised his chained hands to silence me "I understand." For a moment he was silent, then he continued, speaking slowly and choosing his words carefully. "The knowledge that Fortune can raise the lowest high, and throw the highest low, might make some people look to their betters, to cardinals and kings, and say 'one day I might be like them, I am not so different to them after all'. But you took that knowledge and looked to a poor boy, and said 'one day I might be like him, I am not so different to him after all'."

"I didn't want to apologise to him just because I realized I might one day be reduced to poverty. I really wanted to apologize because… because…"

"Because you feel for him." The Welshman finished. "To whom are you most alike, William? Your father? Your brother? And whom do you love the most? The answer is the same. After years in his company and service you became very like Master John, and indeed you loved him dearly. When you understood that you are not so different to the pauper, that you are like him in some way, you began to love him. That" he sighed "is something I myself only learnt a short time ago. Lady Fortune makes us realize how alike we all are, if we pay attention to her. Most don't. I didn't, until it was almost too late."

I mulled over those words for a long time. The Welshman's childlike philosophy had finally managed to unravel my feelings. Nevertheless, a sensation of guilt remained.

"But I'm not even sure the boy was really there. No one else saw him. Maybe I threw our freedom away for nothing but…" I struggled to find the right word "a vision."

"You were the only one to see him, because you were the only one who *needed* to see him." The Welshman spoke earnestly. "Why should anyone else have seen him? The test was for you, not us. Do you think you passed it?"

"If it was a test, I… Yes. I think so. But it brought about our capture. When I chased the boy and caused a stir Forzetti and his men noticed us. Otherwise, I might have seen them first, and been able to avoid them."

"I have never understood… I have no learning to match the mystery of why Destiny pushes and pulls us so roughly to and fro." Answered the Welshman, troubled "But a good man once told me compassion can never be foolish. As long as we are bound in chains, we can do nothing but hope he was right."

Chapter 28

Koblenz, September 1338

The Earl of Lancaster tells the truth – the old and the new – the Earl of Lancaster lies

"Books, books!" Henry de Grosmont exclaimed, as he and William de Montague stepped into Richard de Bury's chambers. "More than I possess in all my homes!"

Richard de Bury's had brought little with him to Flanders. Many of the English lords had brought draperies and carved wooden chairs with them on campaign. The wily Bishop of Durham preferred austerity, and had brought almost nothing with him – except books. Most of the volumes were magnificently bound and decorated, like the many Irish gospels. One manuscript caught Montague's attention for its plain binding, in places falling apart. He squinted in the half-light of the candles, but the title was in a strange language.

"It's a treatise on the poetic art by Snorri Sturluson of Reikjavik." Bury arrived at their shoulders. "It's a remarkable work. The sophistication of the Vikings' *ars rhetorica* was second only to that of ancient Rome." The old man sighed. "If only my agents were poets, we might use their array of figures of speech to encrypt messages. It would make a most elegant form of secret writing."

"I understand" Montague feigned nonchalance, "that John de Ulgham's young pupil, William de Tels, is a lover of poetry." Grosmont looked up sharply at these names.

"William de Tels…" Bury murmured, stroking his white bearded chin. "Thank you for mentioning him so quickly. William de Tels is precisely the reason I asked both of you to call on me here. But come, let's be seated, to speak more comfortably."

Montague and Grosmont took their places on stools by the hearth.

"David." Bury called, and his chamberlain appeared with cups and a pitcher. He laid them on the hearthstone and discreetly withdrew again.

"Tels" began the old Bishop and bibliophile, pouring claret into the cups "Is here in Koblenz."

Grosmont shot up on his stool, his customary boyish demeanour hardening into adult alertness. Montague, too, stiffened with tension.

"What? Tels… and what of John de Ulgham? Is Tels here alone?"

"No, unfortunately he is not." Bury's was as urbane as ever, but his eyes chilled with pain. "Ulgham is dead. He died of a fever in Pavia earlier this summer."

"Dead?" Grosmont leaned forward, searching Bury's face. "But then… who is with Tels?"

"My dear Henry, you could easily guess the name of the man who arrived here with him."

Montague, listening with growing excitement, realized that he was on the verge of finally understanding Grosmont's secret. Tels must have brought the mystery with him to Koblenz. "Who is the man with Tels, Henry, and how is it that you can guess at his identity?"

Grosmont opened his mouth and half rose, his face suddenly pale, but checked himself immediately with a coy little smile. He sank back into his chair with a flourish, as though he had risen simply in order to bow.

"My dear Richard, like William that day at the London ale-house, you very nearly had me falling into your trap. Here you are claiming that Ulgham is dead and Tels is here in the company of someone whose name I can guess. And yet, I have not seen him, and cannot know he is really here." Bury started to reply, but Grosmont held up his hand. "And even supposing you let me see him, I cannot know it is the real Tels, and not an impostor, for I have never met the man. I might unwittingly reveal what you do not know – what I rightfully keep secret - believing that you know it all anyway. Is that what you were hoping for?"

"Not at all, though I compliment you. That is a trick we sometimes use, and in that case you would not have fallen for it. However, Tels really *is* here in Koblenz, and Ulgham, may his soul rest in peace in the bosom of Our Lord, really is dead. And unfortunately, Tels and his companion are here in the custody of Niccolò Fieschi. They are being held securely in a secret place that I have been unable to discover."

When Grosmont, unbelieving, disdained to answer, Bury continued.

"I think I have understood the pattern of events, Henry. I will recount everything to you both from the start, as I have reconstructed it, so that William, too, will see the complete picture.

"Henry, you quite understandably became suspicious of the ease and rapidity with which Messer Niccolò Fieschi penetrated the echelons of the King's council, in his first weeks in England. You quite rightly also wondered why the Florentines should suddenly be so generous with their loans to the Crown, when a short time ago they refused our King even the smallest line of credit for fear it would not be repaid. You asked me the favour of lending you some agents for a matter of urgency and in the higher interests of England. Knowing that you are far more cunning and sophisticated than you let the world perceive, I gladly did you this favour. I hoped it might be the first signs that you were maturing into the high role that your bloodline has carved out for you.

"You soon discovered evidence that Niccolò Fieschi was acting behind the scenes as the King's mediator with the Florentine bankers. It was clear to you that Fieschi's mediation hid some secret. Indeed, conspicuous sums of money seemed to disappear in the transactions, never reaching England nor Florence, and you felt that they probably stopped in Genoese bank vaults. Is this all correct, so far?"

Grosmont nodded slowly, his gaze indecipherable.

"At this point" Bury continued "one of the agents I had lent you stumbled upon evidence that Messer Niccolò Fieschi was holding something dire as a threat over the King's head. Something so terrible that Fieschi was able to use it to convince the Florentine bankers to lend all that money, secure in the knowledge that the House of Fieschi would be able to force the King to repay it by threatening to reveal their secret. Now that Tels has arrived, I know what that secret was.

"The House of Fieschi held none other than the Prince of Wales himself in their custody."

The picture of events had gradually been crystallising in Montague's mind as Bury spoke, but when the older man mentioned the Prince of Wales, he was thrown into confusion.

"You mean, some Welsh rabble-rousers have elected a new Prince? What should Edward care, he could crush them with one hand."

"No, no," Bury assured him smoothly "this is not a *new* Prince of Wales, and it is not a Welshman. It is the first English Prince of Wales himself."

After another moment of confusion, the truth dawned on Montague. He stood up in agitation.

"The King's father!" And he set himself to pacing before the hearth.

"Yes," Bury confirmed "it is the King's father. Half, perhaps more than half of the nation has long suspected that he was not dead, that the traitor Roger Mortimer had made a show of burying him in a death-mask to hide the fact that he did not possess the man's true corpse. The Bishop of York is still convinced to this day. Poor Edmund, Earl of Kent, gave up his life in this belief, and we all thought he was a madman for raising armed rebellion in the name of freeing a dead man from prison. And now I discover that York and Kent were right all along.

"Tels took the Prince of Wales from custody in the region of the Castle of Auramala, and had arrived safely into the protection of a Guelph family at a place called Calvignano. From there he, his pupil and the Prince continued northwards towards Pavia under this family's protection, but were forced to stop there for some time, due to an injury Ulgham sustained while liberating the Prince. Unfortunately, while we were sailing for Flanders with the King's muster, Master John was dying in his sickbed in Pavia. Tels departed once more, now under the disguise of English pilgrims, Tels calling himself Peter Westham and the Prince calling himself William le Galeys. They travelled directly north toward the Germanic lands with the other English pilgrims who decided to avoid the Via Francigena, in order not to pass through France in times of war. Now they have been recaptured by Fieschi agents and brought here. This very afternoon the King will meet his father in a place of Fieschi's choosing."

Grosmont had been listening attentively, his expression slowly changing from anger to despair. "But have you seen the man who claims to be the old King, Richard?" He interjected.

"I have not. However, late this morning Niccolò Fieschi called upon Edward and me to tell us that he has the old King in his custody here in Koblenz, in a secret location. He brought William de Tels along, bound in irons, as proof of his claims. Tels did not deny what Fieschi told us. Before he was taken back to imprisonment in that secret place, I gleaned enough details from him to reconstruct events."

"The man in Fieschi's custody is not the old King at all, but an impostor, I am certain of it." Grosmont was almost too earnest. "Ulgham and Tels made an awful mistake. I ordered them to kill that man as an impostor, not rescue him."

Bury studied him closely for a long moment before replying.

"An impostor? That is highly unlikely. Ulgham clearly felt confident of his identification if he rescued him. Ulgham, like myself, saw the old king on many occasions, and is skilled in memorizing faces. This was Ulgham's profession, and none perform it better than he did. Would he have made such a mistake?"

"Think, Richard, that's not necessarily so." Grosmont had become suddenly very earnest. "The Fieschis must have known - for all the world must have known - the chatter among the people that the old King wasn't dead. They must have known about Edmund of Kent's uprising to free him, long after he was dead and buried. The legend must have inspired them to create an impostor in the image of Edward of Caernarfon, and use him as a weapon of blackmail against our King, to manoeuvre Messer Niccolò into the Royal Council so he could whisper in the King's ear."

William de Montague interrupted.

"Something puzzles me in all this. If this really is the King's father, Richard, why did the House of Fieschi wait so long before making a bid for a place in the Council? Nearly ten years had passed before Niccolò arrived in London to lord it over us all. Why didn't they start the blackmail earlier?"

Bury nodded. "Indeed. I asked myself the same question. Messer Niccolò came to England just a few months after old Cardinal Luca Fieschi, the undisputed leader of the House of Fieschi, died. Evidently, Cardinal Luca had sought to protect Edward from blackmail, perhaps out of sympathy for his cause against the French, or perhaps because of his bonds of kinship and friendship with our royal family. Or, more likely, to ensure the support of the English cardinals at a later date in an eventual bid for the papacy. Then Cardinal Luca died, his dream of becoming Pope unfulfilled, and this vicious, conniving Niccolò took the reins of the family affairs. His ambitions do not lie in the direction of the papacy, but revolve around money, and money alone.

"With his blackmail of our King, Messer Niccolò guarantees Florentine loans to England, and for every loan granted, the House of

Fieschi receives commission fees both from our Crown and from Florence. But even more importantly, with these loans, the Genoese have also allowed England to go to war. Soon both the French and the English will be hiring Genoese mercenaries with their galleys and crossbows. And for every war company that sets sail, the Boccanegras and Grimaldis, and even the Dorias and Spinolas who are the Fieschis' enemies, will surely pay them a commission fee, because business is business, and war means business for these carrion-feeders.

"Now, commission fees are paid in ready cash. Interest is repaid far in the future, and if the royal treasury is emptied in the meantime it may not be repaid at all. The Genoese are not financial risk-takers. Fieschi has been pocketing vast sums of ready cash for the last two years. The Florentines run the risk of never seeing their capital or their interest payments again. Indeed, they are only taking this risk because they feel sure the Fieschis can enforce repayment from England by blackmail, having the King's father tucked away."

Montague was disgusted by these machinations. "I'm beginning to see just how brilliant Niccolò Fieschi's strategy has been. He has no doubt maintained the veneer of goodwill from the start. 'Don't worry, Your Majesty' he must have said 'we have your father on our lands, and we are taking good care of him out of ancestral affection for the English crown. In fact, we are *so* fond of England, that we want to help you finance any war you care to wage… shall we say, for example, against France? We can organise loans for you from the Florentine banking houses. There will just be a small commission for our trouble, but not too much.' Fieschi has made a fortune from this, without investing any money of his own and without threatening the King directly."

Montague sat down heavily, his expression deeply troubled.

"Now I understand why Fieschi felt so sure of himself, why he was so arrogant with me when I warned him not to carry out further murders at the King's court after his agent, Forzetti, had flayed a youngster of the Spinola family alive, and thrown him into the Thames."

"Such murders are common practice among rival families, south of the Alps." Bury sighed. "And you have just mentioned the blackest of the black pieces in this great game of chess: Forzetti. Tels told me that he and Ulgham had closed with Forzetti in combat on two occasions already. But Forzetti was still alive, and hot on their heels.

In a market town not far from here Tels and the old King were recaptured by Forzetti, and taken into Fieschi custody. They remain hidden away in Fieschi's custody even now, and there is nothing we can do about it. I have tried to uncover their hiding place, but have so far failed."

"But why" Grosmont was exasperated "do you insist on speaking of this man as the old King? I tell you, I swear to you, I am certain that he is an impostor!"

Bury leaned forward intensely.

"Will you tell us how you can be so certain?"

Grosmont did not open his mouth, but his eyes smouldered with unknown emotion.

"This is the second time you have refused to bare all to us." Bury was becoming angry "This is a matter of such great importance, for ourselves, for our King, for the land of England itself, that you *must* reveal what you know."

When Grosmont remained silent, Bury spread his hands in a gesture of stalemate.

"In that case, Henry, I will instruct Tels that from now on he must answer only to myself, or to the King in person. I cannot trust you any further in this affair."

"No, Richard, you will do no such thing!"

"What? Do you think to order me about as though I were one of your serfs?" Bury rose from his stool, his knuckles white about his wine cup, the beginnings of fury in his eyes.

"I am the foremost Lord of all England, and I will do as I please unless the King himself bar me."

"These affairs are *my* bailiwick and you must bow to my decisions. *I* am the overseer of the King's secret business."

"You are the Bishop of Durham and an old school master." Grosmont retorted. "You couldn't force me to study when I was a boy, and you can't force me to do your bidding now I'm a man! Officially there is no such person as 'overseer of the King's secret business'. How do you intend to overrule me? Will you come to parliament parading a title no king has ever openly acknowledged?"

"Enough." Montague spoke more loudly than either of them without even raising his voice. "Both of you trust me, even if you no longer trust each other, which is a grave pity. Richard, I beg of you, leave us alone now. Henry and I are brothers in arms, and as such I wish to speak with him. Forgive me, Richard, but I think it is for the best."

Such was the respect in which William de Montague was held that even Richard de Bury, Bishop of Durham and overseer of the King's secret business, put his wrath in check, breathed deeply three times, and quit the room. Grosmont turned away as the Bishop left.

"Henry, I will have the truth." Montague began in a level tone. "Richard and I have played your game. We've given you our help. We've run your risks with you, side by side. Now you owe it to us – you owe it to *me*, Henry, or do you call me 'big brother' no longer? – to speak the truth. What were your orders to Ulgham and Tels, and what motivated them?"

Grosmont's back stiffened, at first with displeasure, and then with resolve. Slowly, he turned about to face his friend.

"The agents in my employ discovered a letter, from Manuele Fieschi, cousin of Niccolò and a cleric in the Pope's service, to Edward. In the letter Manuele Fieschi told the story of the old King's escape from Berkeley Castle, and that he had found hospitality in a hermitage in the Diocese of Pavia, where he was doing penitence. It was clear that it was a blackmail letter. That was when I wrote my orders to Ulgham. Just a few simple words." He spoke slowly, his voice low but calm. His eyes were like jet in the candle light, his hair the exposed, flowing grain of polished ebony. "So few words, but they were enough. The first was 'Bateman' – the agent in Avignon who discovered the letter. Then I wrote: Welsh Pilgrim, Year III, Pope, Fieschi', then under I wrote a complete phrase: 'Weed out the rose from the Fieschi garden of Pavia'. I sent these orders to Ulgham with a complete copy of Manuele Fieschi's letter.

"I knew Bateman would confirm their destination without saying anything explicitly; he knows how to talk in subtle riddles. Then the weed… In the secret business, 'to weed a garden' is to remove one or more people from a situation forever, by assassinating them. I called it the Fieschi garden of Pavia, because the letter mentioned the old King being held in the diocese of Pavia. It was clear, was it not?"

"Too clear." Montague approached him with five unhurried steps, and laid two thick hands on his shoulders, bringing their faces close. "You were so sure he was an impostor that you used that expression, 'weed out the rose from the Fieschi garden', knowing full well they would kill him? What if you had been wrong, what if he was the real Edward of Caernarfon? You would have been responsible for regicide."

So long was it before Grosmont replied, that the quivering shadows seemed to lengthen as the candles burned lower.

"Can you kill a man that all the world knows to be dead?" He mused quietly. Then he raised his eyes to Montague's. "I knew he was not an impostor. I knew he was the King's father." He suddenly smiled, his curving lips like beaten bronze in the flame-light. "Ulgham was right, he is the old King, the Prince of Wales, as Bury calls him. That was the one title he refused to abjure when he was deposed." He sighed. "Yes, I knew it was he."

"Then for God's love why?" Montague was horrified. "Why did you write orders that would have him killed? Who are we, you or I, to decide that a king anointed by Heaven should live or die?" His incredulity made him exclaim one sentence too far. "It's a blessing Ulgham recognized him. Would you have put yourself among the ranks of those men who would kill a king, like…" He broke off, staring with abrupt realisation.

Grosmont nodded, wisely.

"Like my uncle and father, you were going to say?" There was a note in his voice that was almost triumphant. "Like Thomas of Lancaster, my uncle, and Henry of Lancaster, my father, the old King's estranged cousins? The men who put whole counties to the torch and split the kingdom in two, in order to bring to the gallows first Piers Gaveston and then Hugh Despenser?" As he spoke, images of those far off events seemed to be seared into his dilated pupils, though he had been a small child, and could not have witnessed them.

"*This* is why, William. This is why I wanted him dead. That… that man… the old King" His voice almost shook with emotion "nearly ran the country to ruin in his blind affection for one pet lover after another. Gaveston and Despenser bled the land for their comforts and ambitions, laughing down their noses at the barons and earls, because the old King didn't have the character, wisdom or gumption to refuse them anything, anything at all! My uncle and my father had the courage to do what was *needed*. Yes, they rent the country in two to achieve it, but they were *right*. Damn the chroniclers, they were right! And our country's thanks? My uncle quartered beneath his own castle, and his head on a spit over Monk Bar in York, where the ravens could peck out his eyes and the people would cross themselves for fear of the Devil as they passed beneath his rotting flesh.

"And can you imagine, William, what it has meant for me among my peers, though I have always been the foremost in wealth and title save Edward himself, to be the nephew and son of would-be regicides? How much crowing, how much derision, how much riling and ridicule?"

"I never held you to blame for your uncle's actions." Montague affirmed, holding Grosmont's gaze steadfastly. "And your father, in spite of his rebellion against the King's father, was also the first to move against the traitor, Mortimer, and all acknowledge he was just and courageous in doing so. For all his age and infirmity, he is still held by all among the great lords of England today." The younger man's eyes flared into dark fire.

"Blame, did you say? There's no blame to be allotted for just actions, only merit. You couldn't have held me to blame. What they did was right!" With visible effort of will, he calmed himself, and smiled at his old friend. "I know, William. I know you never taunted me for what occurred in the old King's time, but many have. You have no idea how often I have heard phrases like 'blood runs true', and 'like father, like son', whispered behind my back. Tell me, what is a man, what is a family, if not fame? How could I let my bloodline's destruction in posterity go unpunished?

"It all started as an honest attempt to find out what was behind Niccolò Fieschi's sudden influence at court, I swear. But when I found Manuele Fieschi's letter, I realised that the time had come to set things to right, at least privately, at least between myself and the old King. If he really was alive – and I felt strongly it might be so, after all the rumours there have been – then I would have avenged my family without fear of inflaming the country or dividing it as happened in the old days. Who can rise up against the killing of a dead man? If, on the other hand, it was merely an impostor, I would have freed Edward from a thorn in his side in this most delicate moment, standing on the precipice of war." His tone became abruptly rueful. "I thought I could not possibly stand to lose."

Montague nodded. "You had no way of knowing that Ulgham would recognise the old King, and remove him, alive, from the Fieschis' grip."

Grosmont shook his head. "How could I have foreseen it? And

now, here he is: alive, unpunished, but still held by the House of Fieschi and so a greater thorn in Edward's side than ever. Had he been killed the day Ulgham met him in the Apennines…"

"Whether certain or not of his identity, the murder of a king is a crime neither you nor Ulgham would have wanted to stain your souls."

At first Grosmont did not reply. He slowly unclasped Montague's hands from his shoulders, and stood taller than ever, as though to give authority to what he was about to say.

"Is the life of a king so different to the life of any other man? The old King had my uncle, an earl, executed. What made *his* life less important? If old Edward Longshanks had lost all his sons, as many kings have, my uncle would have inherited the throne, as the sovereign's oldest nephew. The very same man who was executed for treason, with the same humours, sinews, bones and – remember this! – the same soul; would have been King. He would then have been inviolable to your way of thinking. What makes it so? Surely the mortal stuff of Thomas of Lancaster was identical, whether king or earl?"

"Fortune makes it so. Fortune saw him die an earl, not a king."

"Lady Fortune!" the words exploded through Grosmont's clenched teeth. "Lady Fortune did not see in my uncle, a man of strong character, those qualities that make a man fit for kingship, which instead she saw in the weakling, indecisive Edward of Caernarfon? She is no judge of man."

"You know it's not that simple. There is also free will, and God's will, and…" Montague broke off. He was no man of philosophy, and the finer mechanisms of fate were an enigma to him.

"And?" Grosmont shook his head, a sudden weariness evident in his head and shoulders, which now slumped. "This is useless. Neither of us is a man of the Word, neither of us can comprehend these matters. We should go from this place, and talk of other things. What's done is done, big brother, and now the old King's destiny is back in the hands of the House of Fieschi. How I pity William de Tels." With an effortless touch, like a master painter's finishing brush-stroke, Grosmont the actor raised his face suddenly, as though a thought had just occurred to him. "The poor man must be desolate now. He has a right to know… that his good Master John did not die for nothing. That they really did rescue Edward of

Caernarfon, and not some impostor. I will petition Niccolò Fieschi to let me see him."

"You know, beneath your showy, and sometimes raging exterior" Montague smiled with genuine affection for Grosmont "You are a kind soul."

The Welshman was completely unconscious of the chains about his wrists as Fieschi's men-at-arms led him into the room. For more than a decade now he had thought of himself as constantly wearing bonds, whether his hands happened to be free or in irons in any given moment. Then his son turned around to face him, and those eyes, so similar to his own, widened as they fell upon the chains. The Welshman held up his wrists with a smile.

"They're nothing, Son. Don't worry about me."

His son's eyes now rose to meet his, and he saw that they were bright with emotion. The Welshman now forgot the presence of Forzetti's men-at-arms, though two held him firmly by the shoulders. The rest of the world seemed to have vanished, and only he and his son remained.

"Have you done penance, father?"

"No. Well... yes. I've done... what would have been penance for a king. But for me it was wholesome. Actually, it is the life I would have chosen over being a king. I've done a lot of digging." He laughed, and his merriness seemed out of place in that solemn hall.

"They used to damn you for that pastime of yours."

"As a king. As a hermit it's applauded. You know, if you want to eat you have to dig. It's interesting. I had never really understood that, when I sat on the throne."

His son shook his head in wonder.

"I understand that, father, and I sit on the throne. It's obvious that you have to dig if you want to eat."

"No. It's not obvious to a bad king. You are a good king. You follow your people so that they will follow you, and you understand them while remaining above them. You're their fellow, but also their Lord, and you know digging's worth, what digging is for and who must dig.

"I used to dig for sport, not knowing its real value, and the people thought I was mocking them, and I was less their fellow than ever, though all I longed for was to be a common man with calloused hands."

His son stared for a moment, realising the truth of this, then shook his head, as though to rid himself of a spell. "Father... Why are two kings, past and present, talking about digging? What would the chroniclers say if they heard us? How disappointed they would be!"

They both laughed tensely, from their opposite ends of the hall, and again the sound felt alien. In that moment, the Welshman wanted to embrace his son more than any other thing he could imagine. There had been a time when he would not have dared say so, lest he suffer refusal and injury.

Now, a different man, he said "Embrace me, Son. The chroniclers would expect you to do that."

"Or to kill you to protect my throne." His son replied without hesitation.

The Welshman nodded calmly. It was true, after all.

"It's probably a shame for England you cannot kill me here, with Fieschi's men all about me to keep me as his pawn in this game of blackmail. If you wanted to kill me though, I would understand it, and wouldn't try to change your mind. But" and he smiled wryly "think of the poor chroniclers... Before trying to kill me, embrace me at least. That would be the perfect story for them. You would be safe, and I... happy."

"No, father" his son did not step forward, though moisture welled up to give his blue pupils the misty-watery quality of a mirage over the morning sea. "You are not in my power to be killed. And you are not in my heart to be embraced."

"And these tears?"

"These tears... What son who has always lived without a father would not wish to have had one? Even before you were deposed by mother, you and I never knew each other."

"What you say is true. There is a peasant boy in Lombardy that I know better than I ever got to know you. I am sorry for that."

"Father, these tears are for the embrace there might have been, that I *do* long for, but an honest embrace, not a fiction. I... I want to be an honest king, and to be that, I must first be an honest person."

"Then you are right not to embrace me. But believe me, on my side, there is that embrace, and it is an honest one."

This young man, so much a mirror of himself and his queen, allowed a drop of salt water to roll down his cheek, and nodded. "I believe you, father."

In the silence that followed, they both realised that their short conversation had exhausted everything that was, that had been, and that could be, between them. Nothing else of moment existed to be said. It was the Welshman himself who turned to his guard and, with a last look over his shoulder at the one true gift he'd given his country, its new King, he bade them take him back to the secret cell Fieschi had arranged for him. His journey back to Auramala would soon begin.

There came two sharp knocks on the door. One of Forzetti's men went to open it, and the other stayed behind to guard me, the light touch of his hand on my shoulder a leaden presence. The door swung inwards, and beyond was a tall man, his athletic frame clad in clothes that were at once as fine as a king's and too flamboyant to be the attire of a monarch. His brown eyes looked straight into mine as he strode into the room, sparing no attention for the space or its occupants. I knew at once who he must be. He was the most powerful man in England beneath the King. With his more than a hundred manors, his retinue was an army to match that of many a small realm, and his gaze left no doubt that he knew it well.

"William de Tels." He addressed me without pleasantries.

"My Lord Henry of Lancaster, my service to you." I leaned forward to bow, but the restraining hand of Forzetti's man held me firm.

"My condolences for the loss of your Master. He was the finest of all."

I nodded my acknowledgement. The earl came forward, his expression consoling. So close, I could see he was just a few years older than I, though we were worlds apart in character and importance.

"Perhaps it's for the best that he is not here now," he continued "to see how this sad affair is coming to its close."

Far from consoling me, his words only ripped further open the wound in my pride, that I should have failed just as soon as Master John was no longer there to guide me. He spoke again.

"Yes, it's a sad affair indeed, William de Tels. So much time and trouble and sorrow, for a mere…" He stopped, suddenly, and a look of indecision came into his face. He spun from me, and strode halfway to the door, where he stopped again. "Forgive me, Tels." I could only see his back. "I shouldn't have come. I shouldn't be telling you these things."

"My Lord? I don't understand."

He turned to face me once more, and I saw that his face was wracked by some powerful emotion I could not grasp. Was it guilt?

"I'm sorry, Tels, I'm truly sorry. I shouldn't…"

"Time and trouble and sorrow for a mere… what, my Lord? I don't understand."

"For a mere impostor. That man is not the old King, he's an impostor."

Without my bidding, my body was wracked by a convulsion as though I were seized by a fit, and the second guard quickly came to help grip me tighter. My mind could not accept what I had just heard. Could Master John have died for nothing? Could I have abandoned my beloved Bianca in Pavia in the name of my duty toward a king, who was in truth nothing but an impostor?

"I know, I know." the earl murmured, his expression less tortured now. He stepped close to me once more. "It is too awful to contemplate. We are letting the rumour spread a little that he is the King's father, but we know that is not the case. This morning Fieschi allowed us to come here, to this secret place, blindfolded, just as I was brought to you now. We smuggled a bible in with us, and we put the man to the Trial of the Holy Word. He opened the Book himself, and his finger came to rest upon Timothy: *mali autem homines et seductores proficient in peius errantes et in errorem mittentes…* 'wicked men and impostors will go forth, ever worse and worse, deceiving and being deceived'.

"When confronted with this, the wretch broke down in terror of God, and confessed all. He is the Fieschis' man, trained up to play his role of the King's father with the greatest care, but in truth he's the disowned son of a Nottingham burgher." I thought I saw tears in his eyes.

"I understand that the Fieschis are going to send you and the impostor back Lombardy," Grosmont continued "pretending to the world that he is the real Edward of Caernarfon. The King will play along with the fiction to keep the Florentine bankers happy, and keep the loans coming. You are the son of a Knight, William." his mentioning father only made me feel even more ashamed "Men like you and I are born to chivalry, not politics and scheming. I have done what I could, but now the matter is no longer in my hands. So here I am, to wish you luck. I'm sure you will one day prove the man you are. In the meantime, try to settle these events, and forget them. God and Mary by your side, William, and may the road rise with you."

He slowly turned and left the room, while I remained speechless, half standing and half born in my captors' arms.

Chapter 29

The road south, September 1338

The shame of failure – the boy who heard the story – the many hues of love

As I unwillingly journeyed south, my habitual place was the rear of the train. Thinking back on it later, I recognised that I should have befriended one of the Genoese guards. I would have improved my knowledge of their tongue, and it might have led to an opportunity to turn my situation around. I was, however, so young that my rancour got the better of my astuteness, and rather than have someone to speak to on the road I sullenly followed behind the escorts with a permanent black scowl. To pass the time, I sang aloud fragments of old songs of chivalry, but no longer the passages in which the heroes set forth, their armour splendid in the shining sun, but the darker moments in which the knights of Charlemagne were killed by treachery.

After some time, Forzetti seemed to tire of my woeful singing. Somewhere south of Strasbourg, he reigned in his horse, signalling to the others to continue, and waited to the left of the road until I came alongside. Then he spurred his mount into step with mine, and he laid a falsely companionable hand on my shoulder.

"Young Master Tels, why so glum?" I shrank away from his grasp. "Two men are lonely because one is sulking." He continued. "The Prince of Wales is riding all by himself at the front. Why don't you keep him company?"

"Shouldn't you be afraid that I might concoct some plan to free, or even kill the impostor, if we're allowed to speak together?" I asked him sourly. "That's not clever thinking."

Forzetti drew Master John's knife from his belt and, as was his habit when wanted to irk me, started throwing it up, again and again.

Each time the steel blade flashed high in the sunlight, twisting in the air, he effortlessly caught it again by the hilt without looking.

"William," he sighed condescendingly "a good jailor must keep his wards as content as he may. Poorly treated and lonely prisoners are far more likely to seek escape than well-fed, talkative ones. As for killing the Prince, Messer Niccolò permitted you to live and accompany His Majesty to his place of imprisonment so that you will later report what has been done to the King of England. Leaving the bones of your Prince in the bushes by some German high-road will serve no one's purpose."

"How I guard England's honour is my business, not yours."

"Of course, of course," he said, as though soothing an errant child "but the road is long. Come, don't make it a sufferance for you both. Ride on with me to the Prince's side."

He sheathed the stolen knife, and seized my horse's reins. Spurring his horse forward, he brought me up beside the Welshman, who was clearly glad of the company. He turned his grey head to me.

"William, God and Mary by your side. How is the road for you this morning? You know, the first time I came this way it was on foot with a pilgrim's staff and scallop shell - tougher on my legs, but easier on my wrists." He held up his bound hands and rattled the chains with a rueful smile.

"The young man found the road solitary." Forzetti told him. "I brought him forward so you could keep each other company, and spare us all the miserable songs."

I silently cursed both the Welshman and Forzetti, the one for his light heart and the other for his heavy malice.

Fortunately, the years have now softened the double-blow I received when Forzetti arrested us near Koblenz, and I later 'discovered' that the Welshman was an impostor. The gift of hindsight tells me that what I really hated was being the loser. Never before had I been the loser in the secret business, for Master John had always found a way to gain the upper hand in any strife. Now, without him to guide me, I had failed. And that was what I grieved for above all: shaming my Master after his death.

"Impostor," I grated "Forzetti brought me forward with some end of his own in mind. The truth is that you and I have nothing to say to each other."

The Welshman was, as ever, completely unpredictable. In complete contrast to his simple, boyish tone just a few moments before, his face became intensely serious.

"I understand, William." Worldly sympathy welled in his eyes. "You have become convinced that I'm nothing but an impostor, and the thought of Master John de Ulgham's sacrifice having been made for nothing rends your heart in two. Is it not true?"

I didn't, I couldn't reply. It was true; profoundly and intensely true.

The Welshman drew a deep breath.

"I *am* the Prince of Wales, the father of the King of England. How I long to convince you of the truth! Not because who I may be has one whit of importance. I would do it for John de Ulgham and Bianca Bottigella. You, who earned such love from them, have the right to know the truth about why you were forced to part with those who love you. Who I am is a part of that truth.

"For the first time in my life I truly feel sorry about how little like a king I am; because now I cannot convince you that your Master did not die for nothing, and that you had to leave your Bianca behind in Pavia for a purpose. Otherwise, I would not care at all about being kingly."

The long silence that followed was broken by Francesco Forzetti.

"Surely the young man has heard your story in full, Your Majesty?" He turned to me. "Master Tels, how can you doubt that my prisoner is the Prince of Wales? Who else could tell that extraordinary story so fully?"

"Any silver-tongued liar can tell stories!" I snapped.

The Welshman was visibly hurt. "I see. I realize that I *should* have told you my story. John de Ulgham accepted who I am. You weren't there during our conversations," he smiled at me, trying to regain our former rapport "because you had a lovelier distraction in Pavia than an old man's memories."

"You mean," Forzetti raised a dark eyebrow "in all the world you have told the full story to no one other than my cousin, Manuele Fieschi?"

In that moment, the Welshman made his great mistake, but I was still too immersed in my own frustration to notice the imminent danger and silence him.

"Not just your cousin. I also told one other person, but… no one of moment. In your eyes."

Forzetti suddenly looked very intensely at the Welshman, his eyes alive with a rapid succession of thoughts, and then I saw realization suffuse his features. I shouted with alarm at the Welshman "Stop! Say no more!"

At my outburst he shut his mouth abruptly, looking wildly back and forth between me and Forzetti. I could feel my face flushed with emotion, but Forzetti just gazed at me with a thin smile that was perhaps a mix of triumph, and pleasure at the thought of the murder I realized he was soon to commit.

"Forzetti will kill the person you told, whoever he is!" In my mind's eye could see Wiligelmo's terrified face in Avignon, and Forzetti's black form in the dark, and that cursed knife of his hurtling through the gloom towards Miquel.

The Welshman was genuinely greatly alarmed at this, and looked at the Lombard for confirmation. The man's expression didn't alter, and he resumed toying with his knife, tossing it up, tumbling into the air and catching it without ever taking his eyes from mine.

"Kill him? Why?" The Welshman seemed dizzy with bewilderment.

"You are a fool." I told him, all decorum forgotten. Why should I pay respect to an impostor? "At least two young men have already died because you told this ridiculous tale of yours. They were just scribes, who had mistakenly copied Manuele Fieschi's letter for the King, without ever knowing its significance. Forzetti hunted them down, in Avignon. I was there. He butchered them. No one can know your story and live. What will this brute care if a little more blood is spilt?"

"Even if this is true," the Welshman objected "no one knows who else heard the tale but I."

"Forzetti knows, I can see it in his eyes."

Forzetti's smile deepened at this, and the Welshman became as pale as ever I saw a man, and a protruding purple vein pulsed violently at his temple. He looked searchingly again at Forzetti, but our captor made no attempt to deny the truth of my words.

"But how?"

Forzetti casually took out Master John's knife once more, and started tossing it again.

" 'No one of moment', you said just now." He replied calmly. "And when you met your son in Koblenz, you told him that you are close to a peasant boy in Lombardy. My men-at-arms were present, and reported every word of the conversation to me. A peasant boy... he must live somewhere in the vicinity of Auramala. I won't have much trouble finding him."

Both the Welshman and I realized we were powerless to stop him killing that boy when the time came. Forzetti addressed me ironically.

"Why, surely John de Ulgham's apprentice can't possibly have a soul unstained by blood-letting. How many men have you slain? Do tell us."

To this day I don't know why I answered him, when I could have kept my tongue still. What business did this brute have in the intimacy of my conscience?

"Six men?" He laughed brightly at my reply. "Six? And you are, what... twenty-one, twenty-two?"

The Welshman was now regarding me with an expression of reappraisal and not, as I had expected, with horror.

Forzetti mused. "Now I no longer marvel at Ulgham's fame among the practitioners of our profession. What a wonderful achievement for a teacher. At your age I had yet to discover the joys of killing. Nevertheless, you look at me with that holier-than-thou expression. Why? Is your England a sound reason for murder where the gold of the House of Fieschi is not? I wouldn't say so.

"Young man, whenever you're ready to work for men who can pay you with gold, not honour, my door is always open. You might enjoy yourself."

I made no reply, and Forzetti just looked at me and laughed, and tossed Master John's knife up again.

By the time the trees' shadows had lengthened another hour, Forzetti, having discovered what he had wanted to know, had ridden back to the head of our little train. I stayed in the centre with the Welshman. I couldn't draw myself away, for I knew I must speak with him about the boy who was soon to die. We spoke softly in the English tongue.

"Welshman, who is this boy you told?"

"Why?" His expression became almost penetrating, surprising me again. "Do you wish to kill him yourself? Aren't you an assassin, too?"

"No... Yes."

He chuckled, leaving me disconcerted. At the prospect of his young friend's death he had become deathly pale, yet now he laughed cynically about murder. Would I ever understand this man?

"Doesn't that bother you, that I've killed men?" I asked him.

"If your knife is to be pressed against little Tino's neck, yes. Otherwise, no."

I stared, not knowing what to say. Who was this man? What meanderings did his mysterious mind perform?

"Perhaps for you all deaths are equal." He continued. "For me, they are not. I've had my own cousin's rotting head set in front of me, and felt no more tenderness than I would for a spit pig. Actually, far less." His eyes were so expressive that I could see the grizzly scene reflected in them. "You remember Grosmont, that man you met in Koblenz?" This made me question my conviction that he was an impostor. Only a king could call the foremost earl in the land 'that man'.

"You remember him? The handsome, gallant earl? His uncle, Thomas, was my cousin. When we were boys we adored one another. But he showed me no loyalty when we were men, and he killed…" His throat suddenly choked up, but he continued. "He killed my love, my one love. He was enraged to the point of insanity… before I met Piers, we were the closest of friends, and though I preferred his company to that of anyone else, I believe his love for me was even greater, even deeper, and more intense. When father died, and I was free at last to make my own choices, I let Piers declare our companionship to the world at my coronation, with his coat of arms and mine entwined above the high table at the feast. Thomas became wild with rage, and swore to kill Piers." He turned tearful eyes to mine.

"I've played my part in hundreds… perhaps thousands of deaths. I've led my share of battles, parading about in the sunshine in my armour, as though the heads of the Scots and the Irish were so many bloodied balls to beat about from horseback for sport. There were also crushing, cruel battles in the rain and mud. Once, you know, an impostor who claimed to be me left his entrails at the foot of the White Tower. When I was imprisoned, loyal Welshmen, who sought to free me, died in the attempt. Hugh Despenser, who used my nature against myself and our country, he died also. Even my dear half-brother, Edmund… He died to rescue me, believing me a prisoner in Corfe Castle.

"Perhaps you will think me a monster, but I played my part in all those deaths. I couldn't help it. Whoever I turned to, whichever way I looked, the counsels they gave me clashed against one another, and all I ever wanted was the good of those I loved. Is this so very strange to you, who have both killed and loved?"

A plaintive, almost boyish note had entered his voice, and I suddenly saw a vision of him as King after the death of Piers Gaveston. There he was, seated on a bare throne in an enormous echoing hall, dwarfed by his own crown, pleading his lonely cause to distant councillors, who leant against the far off walls, just-visible in the gloom of the palace in attitudes of cold, self-serving cynicism.

"You allowed others to govern in your stead." I replied, and as soon as I had pronounced the words I realized I'd spoken as though the Welshman were, in fact, Edward II. I hastily corrected myself. "Our present King's father sat back and did nothing while first Gaveston and then the Younger Despenser ridiculed our nation and its nobles. It led to two civil wars."

The Welshman sighed heavily, nodding.

"You're right, of course you're right." The King with a boy's heart I had glimpsed in the vision was gone, replaced by the old man again. "I know I was wrong to let Hugh Despenser pronounce judgment in my place, as though he was the cock of the run. King John Lackland won even fewer battles than I, and blackened hearts against him across the whole of England, and yet has never been as loathed as I am."

His voice was so naked in its exhaustion and emotion in that moment that I could scarcely keep my scepticism alive. To protect my grief and childish indignation, I tore the conversation away from Edward of Caernarfon, that strange un-dead Prince of Wales.

"You didn't tell me about the boy, the child you've sentenced to death. Who is he? If I can, I will prevent his death."

The Welshman nodded, still trusting in me, perhaps for Master John's sake.

"Don Rogerio's son. He is an innocent, and I love him as a grandfather loves his grandson. When I told him my story it was just as any grandfather will tell his little boy a fairy-tale. For his pleasure, to pass the time…"

I was startled by the deep emotion that engulfed me at these words, as the image of my own father telling fairy-stories to my little nephew Robert sprang before my mind's eye. What wouldn't I have given to return to that peaceful night! To be back before this deadly journey had begun, warmed by the great fire, laughing with father and with Master John over our ale-cups, with my father's servant, and Madge, looking on disapprovingly.

Chapter 30

Antwerp, October 1338

The laughing earl cries – the Knight of Lancaster – the wings of an eagle

For the hundredth time since the dream had first come to him, Henry de Grosmont began proceeding along the street toward the great doors of Westminster Abbey, though he knew that it was hopeless, and this time it would end the same way it always had. Behind him, and on both sides, the voices of his subjects rose like an angry tide. The crown and his royal regalia began to weigh him down and, as always happened, each step he took became increasingly difficult. The voices became louder, and louder, and the doors of the Abbey seemed to retreat from him, even as he walked toward them.

"There goes the King of Folly," some common man in the crowd insolently cried out in the English "wearing the crown his uncle stole from the rightful King Edward."

"And what a spitting image of his uncle he is," A rough-voiced woman replied scathingly "From the skin right through to the heart. All swagger and bluster in tournaments, but hesitant and skittish when there's war afoot!"

"Behold, Londoners," a third voice struck up "the ablest general to wear the crown in living memory. It took old King Edward months of hard riding in the north to lose at Bannockburn, and he had to take the field himself. King Henry was able to lose Newcastle to the Scots with hardly any effort at all. He didn't even have to get up from his throne, and never so much as saw the battlefield!"

As the crowds on either side of the road broke out into coarse laughter, Henry de Grosmont saw the great doors of Westminster Abbey now terribly, terribly far away, and felt the animosity of the people crash over him in waves of scorn that slowed him ever more. He had to reach the Abbey... he was not safe in the street. But the people laughed, and laughed... He stopped proceeding, and turned from side to side at the crowding, grotesque faces of his subjects.

"You don't understand..." he wanted to speak to his people in their native English, but his words came inexorably in the French of court "Lady Fortune has frowned upon me ever since I took the crown..."

"We've endured one of Fortune's dunces after another, we have," a burly merchant bellowed through his beard "what good was your uncle's taking the Crown if his heirs are no better than King Edward was?"

"I... I have lost many castles, it is true" Henry de Grosmont stammered, his voice sounding small against a sea of loud muttering "but I share none of King Edward's other faults."

"Hah! Your uncle did, or so they say." An old woman shrilly piped. "I've heard tell he hated King Edward with the passion of a jilted lover!" The multitudes roared with venomous laughter at this. "And don't the same blood run in your veins?"

Henry de Grosmont realised with rising panic that he could never persuade his people of his worth. He must get into the Abbey, he was not safe there in the street. He turned back to the Abbey doors, but they were no longer visible. On all sides the faces of the poor folk pressed in on him, with their scabs, their dirt, their matted hair and their pawing, calloused hands. Suddenly he felt cold steel strike through his back like fire, and he was overwhelmed by convulsing waves of pain. He tried to turn about to see who his attacker was, but could only fall forward on his face, paralysed, as the rage in the voices of the people became a roar of savage approval. Even as the life bled from him, he felt a rough toe roll him over ignominiously, and the crown fell from his head to the cobblestones with a clatter. At last he looked up into the face of his attacker.

"William..." the hoarse and bitter word struggled from his throat "you..."

Montague looked down at him with a mixture of revulsion and regret, crimson tears of blood dripping from the tip of the dagger he held.

"Damn you, Henry, for making me do this." His face writhed with rage and remorse. "If only you had put the kingdom before yourself... your vanity... your greed." The burly, greying Earl of Salisbury stooped and collected the fallen crown, then turned toward the crowd. All fell respectfully silent.

"It is done." he cried with a great voice, brandishing the bloody dagger "King Henry the Fifth is dead. His sins against the English have been avenged." He held the crown aloft. "Long live the King!"

"...William, now do you understand why I wanted you to be present at my confession?" Montague looked into Grosmont's eyes, and for the first time saw genuine tears there. "Please, William, Edward," he turned to his cousin, the King "witness my act of contrition. And you, Your Grace, Bishop of Durham," his eyes met those of Bishop Richard de Bury, who was taken aback by Grosmont's sudden obeisance after the harsh words they had exchanged earlier in the campaign "perform for me the sacrament of confession and penance."

"But what is your sin, Henry?" Bury asked him. "Dreaming that you were a sinning king is not a sin itself. We may as well ask William here to do penance for murdering you in your dream."

"No, no... that is not my sin..." Grosmont, still feeling the dagger-point between his shoulder blades, dropped his gaze to the floor.

"I am not guilty of one sin, but of many. So many, I don't know where to start telling you."

"Begin, then, with the oldest sin, and finish with the most recent." The old Bishop suggested.

"I have shunned the memory of my father and uncle." Grosmont began slowly. "All my life I have sought to distance myself from them in the public eye, behaving so unlike them that no one might recognise their blood in me. No son or nephew should deny his ancestors in this way, no matter what crimes they committed."

Bury allowed the slightest hint of a smile to play at his lips, while the King raised one eyebrow in surprise at his cousin's behaviour. Montague, however, spoke earnestly.

"But Henry, you told me you felt obliged to behave that way from an early age by the rumours, the teasing and the scorn of your companions."

"Is that any justification? I should have ignored them."

Bury considered for a moment. "This is a very slight sin, Henry. Do not be too concerned, it should not be difficult to expiate it."

Grosmont shook his head, miserably. "No, that is not the whole of it. I believed, or at least a part of me believed the rumours about my uncle..." he continued speaking with difficulty "the rumours that he felt unnatural love for the old King Edward when they were boys. I felt ashamed of him, and even of my father who followed him in all things."

"And so you felt the need to deny your uncle and father. I see." Bury mused, while Montague and King Edward nodded, at last beginning to fathom Grosmont's confused sentiments.

"No, no, it's not so simple." Grosmont struggled to make clear the mixed feelings of a lifetime. "Only a part of me felt ashamed of them, and in public I cowardly crafted for myself a personality that was the opposite of theirs. But another part of me, whilst shying away from the thought that my uncle may have loved the old King in a sinful manner, justified him and my father for their rebellions during his reign. They were right, I thought, to rebel against the old King, because he was disastrous and inept. And as a child I came to covet the Crown," he looked into his cousin's eyes "for I thought that if my uncle had been successful in his first rebellion he would have worn that Crown, and then my father after him, and it would sooner or later have come to me. And I was convinced that we would have been worthier of the Crown than the old King. I'm sorry, Edward, for the Crown is yours alone."

King Edward only smiled.

"Mine? Not at all. It is England's crown. But this is a moment to speak of you, Henry, and not of the Crown. You coveted it as a child, no doubt seeing the continued disasters of Roger Mortimer's three years of tyranny. But since his fall, since you and I have been allowed to become companions, have you still coveted the Crown?"

"No." Grosmont's reply was so firm there was no doubting its truth. "Never. How could I? No sane man could wish to see it on another head after seeing it on yours, cousin."

"Richard, William," the King turned to the others "do you believe Henry in this?"

"Completely." Bury confirmed, and Montague nodded agreement.

"Well, I am no priest, but I imagine that the loyalty you have shown me in the last eight years has more than expiated your sin of desiring the Crown." King Edward concluded.

"Indeed." Bury inclined his head approvingly.

Grosmont almost smiled, but then his face fell again.

"Edward, twice I have sought to bring about the death of your father."

After a long moment of silence, King Edward merely spread his hands with a soft smile.

"It's a Lancaster family tradition, Henry. Why should you break it?"

"I beg of you, Edward," his voice was strained, and none of them had ever seen Grosmont so ill at ease with himself "don't make light of my words."

"I understand, Henry." Edward leaned forward earnestly. "Richard has told me everything. But it seems you were convinced that the man in Fieschi custody was an impostor." Montague looked away at these words, remembering his conversation with Grosmont the day the King's father had been brought in chains to Koblenz. "You wanted to do the right thing, and I appreciate that."

"It's… not true, cousin. I knew he was not an impostor. Or rather… I hoped he was not. I truly hoped he was not, and that Ulgham would kill the true Edward of Caernarfon."

"Edward, Richard" Montague intervened "Henry told me as much the very day your father was brought to you. I listened to his motivations, all of which are comprehensible, for all that they are sinful. I genuinely believe he repents."

"No," Grosmont's face was white "at least, that day in Koblenz I did not repent."

"Henry" Bury spoke "why did you say that you had *twice* sought the death of the old King? Surely only once, when you sent out Ulgham and Tels?"

"Because… that day in Koblenz I managed to convince Fieschi to let me speak with William de Tels. I told Tels that the man he and John de Ulgham had rescued really was an impostor. I even invoked the Bible in doing so, may God forgive me, for I told him we had put the man to the test and he had opened the Holy Book at Timothy, *mali autem homines et seductores proficient in peius errantes et in errorem mittentes…*"

"But how did you explain the fact that Fieschi so carefully kept the old King and Tels in his power, keeping them prisoner, and then sent the old King back to his place of custody in Lombardy, with Tels to witness the act for the Crown?"

"I told him that we had all agreed to pretend that the impostor really was the old King, in order to let the Florentines believe that the House of Fieschi still had the means to blackmail Edward. In that way, the bank loans we need for the war would keep coming."

"Henry," Bury was grave "Tels is very young, and his heart is full of chivalry. He was wracked by shame for his failure to deliver the

King's father into our hands when I spoke to him that day. I have no doubt that, after what you told him, he will kill the old King mercilessly as an impostor if ever he has the opportunity. He is a formidable young man, Ulgham's finest disciple, and could well make opportunities arise from nothing."

Montague nodded severely. "You may well have sentenced the old King to death. And this time the sin is unforgiveable, Henry, no matter how many nightmares it brings you. You knowingly repeated the attempt to have him killed."

Grosmont's tears now filled his eyes.

"I know... I know. By day I am cold blooded, and carry out my deceits with a firm hand and a bold face, but by night I am plagued by guilt, and I dream..."

To their surprise, King Edward began to chuckle quietly to himself. When Montague looked at him enquiringly, he said "Why, Henry, how astute of you. That is precisely what I would have done, if he had been an impostor and we had unmasked him. I would have pretended he was father, because that was precisely what I needed."

William de Montague nodded, thoughtfully.

"I imagined as much, myself. Tell me Edward, and we will finally have the truth of this: have you been using Fieschi for your own ends all along?"

"Of course I have. I thought you would have realised that. How could I be so foolish as to follow the council of such a viper?"

"We did realise that," Bury assured him "especially the day we caught Fieschi *in flagrante delicto* on the smuggler's ship. But tell me, as you might have told me from the start," there was reprimand in the old man's tone "what game have you been playing?"

"I have been procuring myself a war that I can win." The King replied simply. "This has just been one of many stratagems I have used to make sure that war between England and France is profitable to all the powers of Europe bar France itself. The Emperor stands to gain everything: the weakening of the only monarch in the West that is comparable to him, and taxes on every transaction involving warships and mercenaries that are setting out to war even as we speak. Of course, the Genoese are making money out of commissions and selling their services as mariners and mercenaries. King Robert of Naples is delighted that the French will be tied up with the English and will not think of invading Sicily for decades, and I..." he leaned forward, his eyes ablaze with intense joy "I am sure that I can win this war, with men like you at my side."

"Fieschi is not manipulating you?" Montague wanted to be sure.

"Niccolò Fieschi? Well," he laughed heartily now "he thinks he is. Cardinal Luca was twice the man that Niccolò is. If Manuele Fieschi's letter is true, it is clear it was the Cardinal who first gave father sanctuary, and yet he never tried to use him against me. Niccolò Fieschi is just a fool who thinks he is crafty and subtle. I have always had Niccolò Fieschi exactly where I wanted him. Everything he has done has been a boon to me. Thanks to his machinations, the Florentines are lending me the money I need for the war. That would have been impossible, otherwise."

"And how do you plan to pay it back?" Montague asked, voicing Bury's own thoughts.

"I won't." Edward replied simply. His listeners gasped, but the young King continued. "What can the Florentines do? Invade England? Even if they did, not enough coin has been minted in England in the last hundred years to cover the loans they have made to me. They are hoping that I will soon control the marketplaces of Ghent and Paris, but even if I do, I shan't repay them. They can go bankrupt for all I care. The only result might be a war between Florence and Genoa, but I expect the Florentines won't even have enough money for that."

"Your Majesty," Bury's eyes had slowly been widening as he listened "you will throw the finance of all Europe into grave disorder…"

"And England shall benefit. We have not built our edifice around promissory notes that may or may not be paid off with silver. We have been considered backwards for decades because we built our land up with stones, mortar, farmland and hard silver coin. But if the banks of Florence collapse, all shall be affected bar us. I will not even be excommunicated, because the Pope is a Frenchman and loathes the Florentines." He concluded.

Montague smiled broadly. "Edward," his voice was warm with affection "what a lion England has unleashed upon the world! I am proud of you."

The King basked in Montague's admiration, but Grosmont shook his head. "If you are a lion, what am I after today? A stoat?"

The conversation was interrupted by knocking from without.

"Your Majesty, my lords earls, I beg leave to intrude." It was a squire bound to Montague.

"Open, if it is important." Edward replied.

The door opened and the squire stood on the threshold, a tall hooded man behind him.

"It is Ubaldo de Fénis, sirs. I would not have interrupted you, but I remembered his face from the Round Table Tournament, and knowing that he has sent important messages to my Lord of Lancaster and my lord of Salisbury before now, I thought it wise to bring him to you."

The tall figure hesitantly came forward, pushing back his hood to reveal the familiar face of the knight of Savoy, though far gaunter and more careworn than before.

"Your Majesty, Your Grace," he bowed deeply before the King and Richard de Bury "my brothers," he stressed the word Montague and Grosmont had used to describe their relationship the day they had met at the Sign of the Laughing Earl "I come before you a desperate man. Since I fulfilled my word to you, and signalled the arrival of the traitor and smuggler Henry Tideswell in Yarmouth Bay, I have been pursued across England, France, the Occitan and the Savoy by vicious assassins." His face was alive with a patchwork of nervous twitches, and it was easy to believe that the man had been living on the edge of the abyss for months. "I finally resolved to come and seek you out, knowing you were in Flanders, and throw myself at your feet." Like all truly chivalrous men, he made his word his deed, for he threw himself onto the floor in the centre of the four nobles. "I beg your aid, for I no longer have the strength to run," he spoke into the tiles at their feet "and the knife in the dark is waiting for me every night. In God's name, help me."

With the King, Montague and Grosmont startled into silence by the sudden apparition, Richard de Bury was the first to regain his tongue.

"Excellent." He declared with the triumph of an old schoolmaster who has finally found a way to make a delinquent pupil study. "This is where your penitence begins, Henry. Enough moping about feeling like a stoat, boy. Get up and do justice to the lion I know is in you, just as surely as it is in Edward. But first," he raised an admonishing finger "you must reach peace with your conscience through acts of charity. Your first donation to our Saviour shall be the life of this miserable but worthy knight. He is your liegeman, now, your ward. You must shield him from Fieschi's thugs, give him land from your lands, armour from your armoury, a pension from your treasury and above all every opportunity to fulfil his chivalrous vows."

Grosmont had lifted his face, his eyes shining through glistening moisture. "Then I say, this is the most joyful penance I could have hoped for. Gladly, most gladly will I do this. Rise, Ubaldo de Fénis, Knight of Lancaster."

Ubaldo rose, tears now in his eyes too, and the two men embraced each other.

"Remember, Henry" Bury intoned "your duty to Ubaldo is every bit as profound as his duty to you."

"Of course. And that is the greatest delight of all." Grosmont laughed, but then his face straightened and he became suddenly serious once more. "My dear brother Ubaldo, go with the Earl of Salisbury's squire now, who will take you to my household, where you shall receive plentiful food, wine, and new clothes. There is still something I must discuss with the King, the Bishop of Durham, and our brother the Earl of Salisbury."

"Of course, dear brother." Ubaldo, upon hearing that food, wine and fresh clothes were waiting for him, was glad to withdraw. As the door closed behind knight and squire, Grosmont turned back to his fellows.

"My penance has begun, but my sin is still at large. Can we not send a messenger to find William de Tels and reveal the truth?"

"How?" Montague asked. "They left weeks ago. The messenger would need the wings of an eagle."

"It's true," Bury confirmed "it would be impossible now. We can only wait, and hope that the Lord's design will unfold in a way that leaves you with as few feelings of guilt as possible. And in the meantime, you can do penance."

"You said, Richard, that taking Ubaldo into my protection was my first act of charity. What else must I do in order to be absolved? Must I have a chapel built? A hospital?"

"I don't want to build a hospital or a chapel, Henry. I want to build a great lord. I think the most valuable thing you could do is give up enough of your life from fighting in tournaments to become a scholar and... write a treatise. Shall we say, a book about redemption for the sin-sick soul?"

Grosmont swallowed hard. This was indeed bitter news. "I... study? Write?"

"Indeed. And since there is no guarantee that you will be a good scholar, you can also make life easier for those who are. My friends at Cambridge tell me there is dire need of more space for lessons and lodgings for the students. You are immensely rich, Henry. Found a college or two."

This was far easier penance for a man like Grosmont, and he regained his smile.

"Will this suffice, Your Grace?" He asked.

"Perhaps." The Bishop of Durham was noncommittal. "For now."

"Then I solemnly swear that I shall compose a philosophical treatise on medicine for the sin-sick soul, and I shall found a college..."

"Or two."

"...or two, for the scholars of Cambridge University."

Like Montague and King Edward, Richard de Bury smiled.

"*Ego te absolvo...*"

Chapter 31

Valley of the River Staffora, November 1338

Forzetti and the candlesticks – a landslide has blocked the road – for the sake of a boy

As we journeyed south we seemed to race against the oncoming of autumn. The leaves had been yellowing near Koblenz when we had left, and though a month had passed, it seemed that everywhere we went the leaves had just begun yellowing. Surely, by now, those leaves in the northern lands of the Emperor had fallen to the ground, leaving their trees bare. Yet here, south of the Alps, the process had just begun.

It had been a torture for me to revisit, one by one, the cities we had so carefully negotiated on our way north. The Welshman remained sympathetic, but Forzetti played with me. Every time we stopped for the night, he would say something like "Finally, we're in Como. Just a few days to Pavia. Won't it be difficult for you, to pass the city and never see little Bianca?" And then again "Milan, how I love this city! Can't you feel the beating of the hammers, the spinning wheels clicking, the needles sewing? They're all so busy making money, ripe gold and silver for bankers to hoard. If we ride hard in the morning, we'll be at the gates of Pavia by sunset. But it's better for you if we don't enter the city, it would be such a shame to let Bianca see your wrists shackled together like a common thief's."

Indeed, we did not even enter the city where my young wife was waiting for her husband to return, not knowing I was so close. Rather, we lodged in a hospital just west of the city walls, at the Church of Saint Lanfranc of Pavia. While the Welshman and I crouched in a bare corner, without even straw to warm the stones, one of the Brothers proudly told Forzetti "This is the church of that Lanfranc who guided the hand of the William the Conqueror when he invaded

England, and became the Archbishop of Canterbury and built there a great cathedral."

I lifted my head with interest, but the Welshman's reaction was one of deep emotion.

"Saint Lanfranc... Saint Thomas... So many times have I knelt before the shrines of these two saints in Canterbury, my feet sore from the pilgrimage. And now my pilgrimage seems complete. Or nearly."

As we were led through the church nave to receive grace, I saw a fresco depicting the murder of a bishop in his cathedral by four armed knights. "This must be Saint Thomas Becket." I murmured to the Welshman, whose eyes became immediately moist. Forzetti, though, found this an opportunity to tease us again.

"How ironic! Was it your great, great, great grandfather who accidentally had him murdered?" He addressed the Welshman. "Your family has a gift for inadvertently causing the death of innocents." The next day we resumed our miserable journey, skirting the city walls toward the bridge. I remember staring so hard at the red bricks of the great walls that I would have pierced them with my eyes: Bianca was somewhere inside. She could even be with child.

We had then made our way south to the sweet rolling hills that rise in leisurely waves from the plain, their vineyards newly bared by the harvest. Everywhere there was the strong, cloying smell of must and fast fermenting wine. At times we passed so close to farmhouses that we could literally hear the rich dark liquid fizzing in the great barrels. Wherever we stopped for the evening, Forzetti and the three guards were offered many ladle-fulls of the previous year's vintage, always with the same phrase "Drink up, travellers, the new wine will soon be ready for pouring, and it would be criminal to throw away last year's wine." Forzetti's men gulped the rich liquid down with obvious pleasure, barely even pausing for mouthfuls of the chestnut cake the locals offered them. Of course, the Welshman and I were scarcely given a glance, and neither wine nor meal was forthcoming for us.

As we climbed higher into the hills the next day, the vineyards gave way to yellowing chestnut woods, and to our left and right the valleys were dotted with stone watch-towers and castles. That evening, while the guards lit the fire, Forzetti rolled out his blankets and took a finely wrapped package from his saddle bag.

"How curious I am." He turned the parcel over in his hands, examining it. "Niccolò Fieschi bade me take this to the Abbot of

Sant'Alberto. It seems that King Edward begged Messer Niccolò incessantly until he agreed to send it with me. Here, is this the seal of the King of England?" He showed us the impression in the wax, and there was no denying that it was our royal seal. "At this hour tomorrow we shall probably be at the gates of Sant'Alberto's Abbey, and I will be giving this package to the Abbot. I hope I'm not giving him anything worth keeping. That would be a pity." He casually took out Master John's knife, its thin blade gleaming as he thrust it into the red flames of the newly lit fire. He then let it cool slightly, testing it constantly with his fingertips until it was just the right temperature, before deftly slipping it under the seal. He was skilled in seal-breaking, and the package fell open with the seal intact, ready to be set back in place.

The Welshman gasped.

"The King's seal is made inviolable by God's will."

"Really?" Forzetti's voice was amused. "Is that what they told you when you were King? They misrepresented the matter. It's made inviolable by men's fear of the King. We are far from England's sphere of influence, here in these hills, and very close to Genoa's. I wouldn't like to deny my masters a treat for fear of some distant monarch whose lands will probably be gobbled up by the French within a year. Shall we see what his gift to the Abbot is?"

He delicately drew forth from the silk wrapping two candlesticks. In the dim twilight their beauty made even the rough men-at-arms turn and stare. They were intricately decorated with such fine enamelwork that they could only have come from the famous workshops of Limoges. Each was supported by three lion-paw feet, above which running lionesses alternated with ornate flowers. The colours of the enamel were of an intensity that only the most precious materials could create. These candle-sticks were a gift of royalty.

"Wrap them back up, thief." I commanded Forzetti, knowing the authority in my voice was hollow. "You shall rob neither the King nor the Abbot."

He calmly continued to turn them over in his hands for a while, his face inscrutable, then he looked up at me with his usual ironic expressing.

"Rob? Why would I bother stealing these?" He dropped the candle-sticks roughly back into their wrappings with disdain. "Only you backwards islanders from the north could possibly think such old-fashioned clutter was treasure. Don't you know that tastes have changed? These are the sort of trifles Cardinal Luca's grandfather might have bought as a youth on a whim, and since forgotten in some dusty corner of his house."

The Welshman's eyes hardened with injured pride.

"I know these candlesticks. They were among those used to light the feasting halls of our court when I was a child. They were purchased by Richard the Lionheart on the occasion of his marriage to Berengaria of Navarre. They were the work of the finest craftsmen of Limoges, in my ancestors' land of Acquitaine. Do not mistake them for objects of passing fashion."

Forzetti merely smirked. "How marvellous, Your Majesty," he drawled with sarcasm "the great King of England's gift." He dropped the candlesticks back into their wrapping with an air of disdain.

"Don't worry, Master William, it's not worth my while stealing them. I might as well give them to the Abbot as requested."

He began to heat Master John's knife once more to reseal the package.

Throughout the following morning, my anxiety mounted. I was sure we must be in the vicinity of Auramala, and the knowledge that our journey would finally come to its ignominious close was hard to bear. As soon as the Welshman was returned to the custody of the Malaspinas I would be freed to return to England and report to the King. I passed the time looking down at the earth of the trail as it slowly jolted by with every step of my mule, reciting in my mind what I would say to the King and Richard de Bury when I returned to England. And then, around midday, I heard alarmed shouting far ahead of me in the Genoese, and abruptly looked up.

"The road... blocked... rocks... fallen..." It was Forzetti, calling back to his men, and I could barely make sense of what I heard. He was beyond a bend in the road, and I could not yet see what the matter was. Two of the three soldiers hurried around the bend one by one, while the third stayed close to the Welshman and me. More animated chatter mixed with expletives told us that the situation was serious.

As we ourselves turned the bend at a steady pace, what I saw stole my breath from me. The mountain side opened out, as though torn asunder by some immense hand, and our path, some twenty feet ahead, came to a jagged and rocky end on a new-born precipice. A vast landslide had broken away from the slope, tearing with it a piece of the road. On the far side of the gap left by the landslide, the road continued as though nothing were amiss.

The trees around the great rip in the mountainside jutted precariously with half their roots in the air, and the slope underneath us was an unsteady jumble of jagged boulders and smaller rubble. There, on the edge of the cliff, Forzetti and the two guards were dismounted and testing the ground for a stable enough point to begin edging across. As their feet found loose gravel every time, they burst into ever more colourful oaths.

A full view of the valley now spread out in front of me. There were columns of smoke from hamlets and farmhouses rising tantalizingly here and there in little cleared meadows among the chestnut woods. The scene made me ache within, for the woods, the nature of the slopes, the style of building and the sky itself all told me we had nearly arrived. All about us on the slopes were visible great vertical, bare patches of crumbling grey rock, where landslides had torn away the mountainsides.

"Thank you, thank you, I can manage, now." It was the Welshman's unmistakeable voice behind me.

I started about to see him dismounting from his mule with the remaining guard's help, his wrists still chained together. He felt my eyes on him, and looked up.

"A call of nature, William." He smiled, and started ambling toward a tree. The man-at-arms folded his arms and stood, watching impassively. The Welshman started softly singing a song in an English tongue, while he searched for a discreet spot to relieve himself. At first I did not follow the words of his song, but after two or three repetitions, I realised he was singing *distract him, my friend, distract him.*

My heart nearly skipped a beat. Was the Welshman just singing some half-forgotten rhyme, or did he mean it as an instruction to me? The Genoese had not noticed anything. Among them probably only Forzetti understood some of the common man's tongue of England, but he was too busy venting his anger at the landslide to hear. Should I distract our guard? What could the Welshman, an old man, want to do, what with both of us still in irons?

"Can I, too, dismount? When the Welshman has finished, I'll go, if I may." I spoke courteously to the guard. He nodded without even thinking twice, and came forward to hold my right forearm steady while I swung my left foot from the stirrup. As I brought first one foot to the ground and then another, I heard a rustling sound to my right. I pretended to overbalance, and clutched at the guard's wrist, holding it firm for a moment so he could not turn around to look. Over his shoulder I saw the Welshman, his head low, running with surprising speed. His long legs were catapulting him not away from our captors for escape, but towards Forzetti, still standing on the edge of the precipice. It was not until a fraction of a moment before the impact that Forzetti, some dreadful sense having warned him of the danger, turned around with his cruel knife in hand.

"*Let us die together!*" The Welshman screamed as he collided with Forzetti, and the two were hurled over the brink into nothing.

My guard rushed to join his fellows at the edge of the landslide, allowing me to dart unseen to his horse. Though my wrists were bound, I was able to slip his eating-knife from his saddle pack. It was not much of a weapon against mailed, sword bearing men-at-arms, but it was something.

At the end of the road, the three guards were swearing, jumping to and fro, uncertain of what to do, while screams of agony came from below.

"Help… help me, quickly!" it was Forzetti. One of the men-at-arms obeyed, kneeling on the edge of the slide and starting downwards on all fours. The other two also knelt, watching his progress.

Hiding the little knife behind one wrist, I slowly approached, carefully assuming an expression of fear and wonder. The remaining two men-at-arms saw me, and remembered their duty. One stayed by the cliff, the other rose to take custody of me once more. It was the same man who'd helped me dismount. As he stepped up to me, too close, I whipped my wrists around, his own knife in my palm, and stuck him hard through the eye. He had had no time to react, and simply dropped to the ground, dead, for there is no swifter or surer way to kill a man.

As his body curled up, limp, the other man-at-arms realised what was happening and started to rise to his feet, even as I was coming for him at a run. He was an intelligent man, and went for his dagger, not his sword. He would not have had time to draw the longer blade, and the tip would have caught in the sheath as I closed on him. As with the other guard, my only hope lay in striking at the eyes or neck, for the rest of his body was too well protected. His dagger was now up in front of his face, and I could not lunge without taking a cut on my un-armoured arms. I accepted the injury without hesitation. In combat, hesitation is death.

I deliberately thrust his blade aside with my right forearm, taking a long and deep cut that did not, however, check my momentum. Then we collided, falling together to the ground, my little knife hacking at the veins at the base of his neck. Hot blood sprayed over my face, and I rolled away, but not before his panicked convulsions of self-preservation cost me another small cut to my side. Leaping to my feet I kicked the dagger from his weakening grip, just as he began to shriek and writhe in agony, a shocking sound that pierced the blue sky and the dark woods. The man's blood violently spurted out to the rhythm of his pounding heart. Soon, he broke into great shudders that wracked his entire body, and crimson froth came gurgling from his throat. I turned away from the macabre spectacle, toward the edge of the precipice. A human figure was hoisting itself bodily up onto the road. In a moment he was over the edge in a flurry of flying dust. Across two dozen paces, I was staring into the eyes of Francesco Forzetti. He had not perished in the fall, nor even been badly maimed. Battered but not broken, he was wild with rage.

With my two hands bound at the wrist, I struggled to take my last victim's sword from its sheath as he thrashed about in his death throes. In the space of four heartbeats it was firmly in my grip, and I spun about to meet Forzetti's onslaught.

My enemy was determined to end his young opponent once and for all. I was appalled by my weak position as Forzetti snarled triumph through his black beard. He had the greater build, he was wearing light armour, and he held a small buckler-shield in one hand, to deflect blows while his sword was free to lash at me. And what a sword! From the moment I saw it I realised it was a Spanish masterpiece that might splinter the inferior, common soldier's blade I held as though it were wood. I had but one advantage: Forzetti was enraged by his fall, and might be induced to err.

Forzetti advanced with such fury that he seemed to be surrounded by an aura of fire. Feigning myself daunted, I gave a few steps of ground, letting my enemy close in, and saw the hope of a quick victory in his eyes. Like a boxer leading with his left, Forzetti punched my blade aside with his buckler and lunged with his sword for my face. I sprang beneath the blow and used the one advantage my predicament gave me: greater strength behind my sword. My parry forced his sword arm wide out across his body, and as I danced back out of reach I pulled through in a long slice-off across his body. My poor-man's sword was so blunt it failed to cut through even his hauberk. Dismayed, I realised that only a lunge might wound him.

As Forzetti twisted about I drive home two further strokes, graceless thrusts that he beat away with his buckler and served no purpose but to prevent him regaining his poise. My two-handed strength made him stagger, though, and give ground behind him, toward the edge of the precipice. Panicked by the thought of being backed up against the abyss, Forzetti swung violently at my head to distract me. I made as if to parry but at the last instant swerved my blade aside, and ducked instead. He had counted upon the force of my parry to counterbalance his blow, and when it did not arrive he was overdrawn, and stepped forward within my reach. Before he could cover himself with the buckler, I punched the tip of my blade with all my might into his chest. As horror turned the flame in Forzetti's eyes cold my blade snapped, but the tip was left behind, buried deep in his bosom.

With what was left of my sword I clubbed his own weapon from his hand. Frantically he retreated, clutching at his wounded breast, trying to keep me at bay with the buckler. With a flurry of blows I drove him toward the landslide. At the last he found himself trapped between the steel and the fall. He was relieved of deciding his own doom by the cliff-edge, which crumbled beneath his right foot and sent him scrabbling and tumbling over the precipice.

Warily, I lowered myself to my hands and knees and peered down. The third man-at-arms had earlier crawled to the bottom of the grey shingle slope that was left behind the landslide. Beside him lay the Welshman, alive, but clearly weak, as blood oozed from several wounds. He must have taken the brunt of the first fall, sparing Forzetti.

My enemy, a few yards away from the Welshman, was a twisted heap of cloak, legs, arms and bloodied, rent flesh. Nevertheless, he still had the strength to howl to the surviving man-at-arms "Help me, you fool, help!" His voice was barely recognisable, garbled and mangled by sheer pain into something more akin to a wild animal's bleating.

The man-at-arms looked up and saw me, my face a mask of battle-fury, my arm bloodied, standing alone on the jagged edge of the collapsed road. He realised that if I was standing there alone it was because I had already slain the other two men-at-arms. He swiftly decided not to join them in the afterlife, and began scrambling away downwards as fast as he could, slipping and sliding.

"Go back up, kill him you coward, go!" Forzetti, unable to move, screamed at the fleeing mercenary, but the man had already disappeared. Forzetti ceased screaming, and looked up at me with mortal fear, though the pain from his wounds was so great that he could not suppress moans and gasps.

"William de Tels" he called to me through clenched teeth "have you reconsidered my offer? Will you join me? Last year alone the House of Fieschi paid me 100 gold florins… Have you ever held that much gold in your hands? Would you like to?"

By way of answer I dropped the broken sword and moved to where Forzetti's horse stood, tied to a tree-branch. Hooked to his saddle bag was his crossbow, its goat's foot and quiver. I drew the weapon and loaded it slowly, leaning it against the ground at my feet, pausing twice because blood on my hands made me lose my grip on the goat's foot lever. Finally the string was drawn. I fitted a bolt and returned to the precipice.

"Don't be foolish, your Master is dead… You need my help now…" Forzetti was almost delirious in his fear. "I can introduce you to the richest men in Europe! I can protect you, I can…" I let fly the bolt.

The Genoese make the finest of all crossbows, and the steel plate on his chest might as well have been silk cloth as the bolt crushed through his breastbone and destroyed his heart. Forzetti opened his mouth as though to speak once more, but his face froze into a mask of death, and no sound came.

Laying the crossbow down, I began to lower myself cautiously toward the Welshman. I slipped in several places, but each time I managed to recover stance and balance. The wound to my arm was painful, and my vision swam more than once, but finally I came to the Welshman's side. His eyes blurred and cleared again and again as he looked up at me, and his breathing was ragged.

"William… Is Forzetti dead?"

"Yes, he's dead. Wait… His keys." I carefully crossed to where

Forzetti was lying, and set my shoulder against the dead man's waist to turn him over. The key to our bonds hung from his belt. I was forced to painfully twist my wrists in order to fit the key, and the lock did not turn easily, but finally I was free. I slipped the key from the belt and turned back to the Welshman.

"Hold up your wrists, Welshman, I have the key."

He smiled weakly, and raised his hands. When his shackles fell, he sighed deeply and stretched his arms out.

"Aahh... Do you think... this is freedom?"

I didn't answer, not knowing what to say. His eyes came into focus on my bloody forearm. "You're hurt." He reached forward and clasped the wounded limb.

"It's not serious. I can manage. It's you I'm afraid for."

"Afraid... for an impostor?"

I spoke then without thinking, and it was for the best, as I realised that my tongue knew the truth better than my mind.

"You may be a false king, but you are a true saviour. For what you did today, Tino will live."

"That is far..." He tried to laugh, but it became a seizure of pain. "... far more important to me." He ruefully looked across at the corpse of Forzetti. "The other men? One... I saw flee."

"I killed them. Thanks to the distraction you gave me."

The Welshman laughed painfully, and blood foamed slightly at the corners of his mouth.

"My dear... young William... Surrounded by... fallen foe, like... Roland, with... a broken sword like... our Curtana."

In spite of my weariness, I felt a hint of warming pleasure. He had heard me singing of Charlemagne's heroes, and knew precisely which compliment to offer me.

The Welshman fumbled inside his tunic with his free hand, and took out a strange object. "Here, this... is for you."

I made as if to take the object, then snatched my hand quickly away. It was a curled snake.

"No, no... it is petrified... stone."

Slowly, I took it in my hand, feeling its weight, searching fruitlessly for the head or tail in amongst the granitic coils.

"Thank you." I said, mystified.

"It is magical... It gives the gift... of story-telling. It will help... you tell... this story."

I took the stone snake, though I was bewildered by this gift. As I tucked it into my clothes, I realised the pain had disappeared from the cut to my forearm where the Welshman's fingers gripped. It is a bad sign when a wound turns completely numb.

"Welshman, I must look at my arm, it has gone numb."

"Of course, William."

He weakly removed his hand, and I stripped back my sleeve to examine the injury. I wiped away the cloying blood, but could not find the deep cut which had caused me such agony until a moment earlier. My heart quickened. The wound was gone... I gazed at the Welshman in wonder.

"Then it is true" I breathed softly "you are a king. The hands of a King heal."

He looked at my arm in confusion, and his eyes widened as he realised the skin was unbroken.

"I... have healed... you?"

"Yes." I answered in wonder.

"Today..." he continued "I helped save Tino's life..." his words slowed as his soul gathered itself to leave his body "Today... for the first time... in my life... I really felt... a king."

Those were the last words he said aloud. His eyes clouded, and seemed not to focus on the world around him anymore. Soon, his lips resumed their movement, but in soundless speech directed at someone only he could see. As he formed silent phrases, his expression mirrored the feeling in those words I could not hear, and there were pauses in which he seemed to be listening to an answer, and that which he heard brought tears to his eyes. Gradually his movements slowed and his breathing waned towards one last, endless sigh. My eyes, too, filled with tears.

Though whole once more, I realised I had no way of carrying the old King's body back up to the road. If I could not give him a Christian burial myself, nearby were those who could. Before climbing back up the slope, I retrieved Master John's knife from Forzetti's belt. That was the first act of closure I performed. The second was to use that knife to cut into Forzetti's forehead the mark of the House of Spinola. After his corpse was discovered, sooner or later word would spread that he had been slain in the name of the House of Spinola. Messer Gherardo would know that our promise had been fulfilled.

I took Forzetti's crossbow, sword and buckler-shield, I dressed myself in the fine clothes I found in his saddle bags, and mounted his beautiful horse. I decided that I would travel from then on under my own identity, the younger son of a Knight. Leaving the carnage I had wrought, the dead and the blood strewn about, I turned back the way we had come, searching for a safer route to the mountain of Auramala, the Abbey and the village. There was another act of closure waiting for me there.

Chapter 32

Valley of the River Staffora, November 1338

The boy who mattered – the Abbot's gift – a Lady is waiting

It was on a sloping, wooded path much like the one where I had fought Forzetti that I encountered the pair. One was very old, with an imposing bald head and flowing white beard, his black Benedictine hood thrown back in spite of the chill wind. The other was a young boy, between seven and nine years of age, a wealth of curly brown hair about his head as he walked self-consciously in the robes of a child-oblate. They both turned as they heard hoofbeats. I recognised Brother Demetrio, the old healer, immediately, and he soon recognised me, though my clothes were very different, and my appearance that of an armed squire and not a cleric, with Forzetti's sword at my belt and his crossbow hanging from the saddle. The healer's eyes widened, and he stepped in front of the little boy.

"I know you." Brother Demetrio told me, resolute.

I reined in my horse a dozen paces away, not to frighten them unduly, and dismounted.

"God and Mary be with you both. I mean you no harm, Brother, and I sorely regret that when we first met, back in the spring, my Master and I were forced to do you harm."

Brother Demetrio remained wary. "Men such as you live by lies and violence. You pretended to be a man of the Word when we first met, but you proved yourself a man of the sword and the fist. Why should I accept your apologies and good manners as genuine now?"

I nodded. "You are right, and now words can convince you. If you please I shall not come any closer. But first, look." I untied my scabbard from my belt, hooked my sword to the saddle bag. I led my horse to the side of the path and tied the reins to a tree branch, then stepped away.

"That is the best I can do as a sign that I mean no harm. I swear that I am not carrying any hidden blades, but I cannot make you believe that." I could see the child novice peeking out from behind Brother Demetrio, his curiosity triumphing over the fear he must have felt seeing the old man so apprehensive.

"No, you cannot make me believe you." Brother Demetrio was steadfast. "But a plausible explanation may help convince me. What has happened to… the man who disappeared the same night as you? And what has happened to the man travelling with you, whom you just called your master?"

I felt a chill at the prospect of reliving and describing the Welshman's death, and above all my first duty was to the boy, Tino. I suspected, but could not be sure, that he might be the very novice Brother Demetrio was now shielding. If that was the case, I must choose my words carefully.

"I would gladly tell you, but there is one who should be the first to know. Even though I will soon come back to the Abbey, bearing an important gift for the Abbot, first I must find the village of Pizzocorno now. That is where this person lives."

"In Pizzocorno." Brother Demetrio repeated thoughtfully, and I saw his robes about his legs move, as though shaken from behind by little hands. He stretched one strong arm backward and stilled the boy behind him.

"That is an odd place to seek. Surely the Abbot has the right to be the first to know the fate of his own lay-brother?"

"That would be true. But…" I paused, searching for the right words "his lay-brother's fate came about… in honour of this person in Pizzocorno. His fate was a sacrifice made for this person. And so I think, by some higher order, it is best to go to the village first, and not the Abbey."

Brother Demetrio's tough old eyes took on a hint of sadness, as he realised that the Welshman must be dead. For the first time he looked down, no longer challenging me with his gaze.

"I know of only one person in the village" Brother Demetrio spoke slowly "for whom that lay-brother might have made such a sacrifice. Is he a boy?"

I nodded, impulsively glancing down at the robes about the healer's legs, which were now still.

"Forward, Tino." Brother Demetrio led the boy out. "I believe this man is looking for you."

"The person I must speak with is a boy called Tino." I confirmed.

The youngster came forward hesitantly, his face a little fearful, sensing the sadness in his old protector. Though I was still many paces away from the two, I dropped onto one knee, feeling more comfortable speaking with the boy at his own eye-level. Brother Demetrio, his knees too stiff to let him kneel down too, put a comforting arm around Tino's shoulders.

"Tino, I'm very sorry, but I must give you bad news about a friend of yours. The lay-brother who disappeared from the Abbey in the spring."

"Lo Gallese?" Tino asked, his voice so small it barely carried to me.

"Yes. I'm… truly sorry. But he has passed on to the next life." I drew a breath of cold, autumn air. "He is dead."

"Lo Gallese… is dead?" He stammered, his eyes wide with shock.

"Yes, he is."

"He's not coming back?"

"No." I shook my head.

Tino, like any peasant boy, surely knew death well, having seen cousins, aunts and uncles taken to the next world before their time. His face became distraught with realisation and his eyes suddenly filled with tears. The old monk embraced him as best he could, and the boy hid his face in the healer's robes, sobs beginning to overcome him.

"I'm sorry, Tino, I'm sorry…" Brother Demetrio soothed the boy. "I'm sorry… these things happen… weep, weep boy, but know that lo Gallese loved you."

Little Tino wept, and Brother Demetrio looked up at me, half questioningly, half accusingly. I stood up straight.

"I understand what you are thinking, Brother. But he is not dead by my hand, and not that night in spring. He is but a few hours dead. He lies amongst the rubble of a landslide not far from here. He… fell."

For a long moment the old monk seemed determined not to trust me, even after seeing how delicately I had sought to tell Tino of what had happened. Then his expression softened a little.

"Brother Demetrio, may I approach?" I asked courteously

"There's something I must tell Tino, and I would prefer to be face to face with him."

Brother Demetrio nodded, and I stepped forward and knelt down again, just in front of the boy, whose face was still hidden in the healer's black robes.

"Tino, I know it is hard, but please look at me." The little face, tear-streaked and red, emerged from the folds of wool. "Before he passed to the Lord's Kingdom, lo Gallese said that you and he were very good friends, and he had told you the story of how he came to be a lay-brother."

Tino nodded, his wide eyes looking into mine, but he did not speak, and the old monk still held him firmly about the shoulders.

"Tino, it's very important for me, in memory of lo Gallese, that you should know something. He used to be a very, very important man. So important, that many people wanted to use him, and some people wanted to kill him. He escaped them all, to come here, but he was forced to live in secret as a lay-brother. Do you understand?"

Tino did not nod immediately, his gaze searching.

"Lo Gallese was very important, and had many enemies. He escaped them, and came here, but to be safe here he had to live in secret, and tell no-one his story. But he loved you so much that he wanted to tell it to you. You, the only person in the whole world. Do you understand?"

Tino nodded, holding back a sob.

"Then one of his enemies found out that he told you the story. This man, the enemy of lo Gallese, and of me, wanted no-one to know the story. No-one at all. So he wanted to come here, and find you, and… hurt you. Lo Gallese wanted to stop that enemy from hurting you, because for him, you were like a grandson. Do you understand?" Again, he nodded, his eyes now brightening with this knowledge. "So lo Gallese fought with him, and he died in the fight. But you must always remember he died for you."

Tino remained silent, but it was clear he had understood.

"Do you remember lo Gallese's story?" I asked him.

"Yes, I remember."

"Listen to me now, this is very, very important. Someday, a long time from now, you may tell his story. Many people will doubt it, many will say it was a lie, something he invented. Many will say it was impossible, and say you are a fool for believing it. But I want you to know that his story was true. It really was true. Tino, The man you called Lo Gallese was once King of England. England is my land, far, far to the north." I rolled up my sleeve. "Here, I was badly cut in the fight when he died, but when he touched my arm, the wound was gone. In England, we say that the hands of the King heal. By the flesh of my arm, you know that his story was true."

Tino broke into a tearful, relieved smile, and he leaned toward me against Brother Demetrio's arms. Soon the old healer let him go, and he stepped forward to embrace me. I held him hard and long, and when our embrace was over I stood up again. The old monk looked me in the eye.

"And what of your Master?"

"A fever took him." I smiled sadly. He just nodded. "Are you going to the Abbey?" I asked.

"We are."

"Then, with your permission, I will walk with you. I have a gift for the Abbot from the King of England."

"Come with us. You shall take the most trusted of my brothers to where the Welshman lies, so they can bring him back to the Abbey for proper burial. And then you can rest within the Abbey walls for a time."

I nodded, grateful, and at the word 'rest' suddenly felt upon me the fatigue of the last weeks. I returned to my horse, freed its reins, then the three of us started up the mountainside toward the Abbey of Sant'Alberto.

That night, after retrieving the Welshman's mortal remains, I would dine with the Abbot, and give him the beautiful, precious candlesticks the King had sent. And then... the road. And along the road there was Bianca Bottigella, waiting for me in Pavia. I prayed to the Lord that my father would still be alive when I returned home, to meet my wife and know that the story would continue.

And as you know, continue it did, and continue it shall, through light and shadow. I lost your grandmother to the Black Death, and one of your uncles and one of your aunts. And yet, here you are, as strapping and able as I was the day I left Norwich with Master John. And where is Master Geoffrey Chaucer taking you, I wonder? Hush, hush... I know you can't tell me.

Epilogue

Sluys, 24 and 25 June, 1340

Among the councillors all eyes were now turned toward the right wing of the harbour, where the huge and swift Genoese galleys were patrolling the straits beside the French ships. While the French ships were chained together, deck to deck, in lines blocking most of the harbour mouth, the galleys commanded by Egidio Boccanegra and his captains remained free to maneuver by both sail and oar. Agility and speed was where their strength lay, despite their greater size.

At the start of the day there had been no less than three parallel lines of French ships. Early in the morning the first line had been raided, ravaged and reduced to mere wreckage bobbing in the waves. In the fighting the French admiral had been killed. The English fleet's second assault had been repelled when the King had been struck in the shoulder by a crossbowman. Now they were attacking for the third time, hoping to break the second French line.

On the flagship, the great lords of the kingdom maintained their tense silence, straining their eyes to make out the movements of the galleys. All hoped that Boccanegra would be true to the unchivalrous pact he'd made with the English King through Fieschi's mediation. Fieschi unconsciously half rose to see the better over the bulwark. His eyes seemed to grow darker, ever darker; with his stare he was willing his countryman to act. Finally, the galleys started changing course. Time seemed almost to stand still. Were their prows swinging toward the open sea? Or were they turning toward the English to meet the fresh attack? Should those fearsome galleys clash against Edward's slow, wallowing cogs, the loss of English life would be horrendous, and a French victory a certainty.

All held their breath, except Morestede the surgeon and his apprentice, George, who were fitting the King's shoulder plate back on over the bandaging.

Time passed with aching slowness. The galleys swung about on their keels, then one by one settled on a new course. Yes, there could be no doubt, the prows of Boccanegra's galleys were now turned as one toward the North Sea! The oars were working quickly, and all the sails of the three masts had been deployed, billowing in the southwesterly. Their speed was almost shocking compared to that of the English fleet. Their graceful hulls seemed to skim the surface of the wave as they passed away, far from the battle and their French 'allies'.

"Boccanegra is true to his word." cried Niccolò Fieschi, turning and rising in triumph to face the King and his councillor, defying Montague with his burning eyes.

"Not as far as the French are concerned." Laughed Edward. "He gave his word to them, also."

Montague stepped forward "Our naïve cousins of France simply failed to secure it with enough gold."

Fieschi was becoming angry with the bearded Earl of Salisbury. What did the man want?

"You know nothing of us Genoese, Montague. You know nothing of Boccanegra's motivations. The King alone knows the whole truth. Leave these matters to your betters."

"Do you dare reprimand my friend and councillor?" Edward interrupted sharply, the laughter fleeing his face, his voice lowering to growl. "Do you presume to instruct an earl of England?"

Fieschi took a hesitant step backward. The King had never spoken to him in that manner before now. All the oddities of the last half hour crowded in on his thoughts. What had happened? Why was Montague so forward and public in his loathing? Why had the King spoken of his late father in front of everyone? And why did he now adopt a harsh tone with Fieschi? What had happened here?

"The time for your lording arrogance is passed, Fieschi." Montague stepped closer to him. "I *do* know about you Genoese, I *do* know of Boccanegra's motivations. Just as I know of yours."

"What do you want? What is the meaning of this?" Fieschi stepped sideways, giving himself space and moving away from Montague.

"Now that Boccanegra's well on his way to the open sea" Edward began dryly "what was the fee again? 2,000 marks for Boccanegra's betrayal, and that's fair. But as for those 3,000 marks you demand for your family's services in procuring this desertion… I rather think that's too much."

"Your Majesty," Fieschi was shocked, his eyes bulged, his face darted from side to side, taking in the stunned faces of the men of the Council. "not in front of these men! These are our private matters."

"Why not in front of us all?" Montagu replied, savouring his enemy's discomfort. "What would you like the King to hide?"

Edward was implacable. "I see no reason why I should pay you so much as a single silver piece for your services."

Fieschi's jaw dropped. "How… … How can you…? How dare you….?"

"How dare I? Because I know that which you do not, Master Fieschi." He paused in triumph. "William de Tels is alive!" He took another, inexorable step closer to Fieschi. "William de Tels is alive, and his task completed. For the better."

Though he didn't say it, both men knew that with those words he also declared: I know what happened to my father.

Fieschi wasted not one moment more, but leapt aside and around the two approaching Englishmen. Angling his gait effortlessly with the ship's rocking motion, he dashed to the King's admiral and sought to wrench the signalling flag from his grip. The admiral, taken by surprise, nearly let go. He managed to hold on to the wooden handle with his left hand, but was near to stumbling, and Fieschi now possessed the demonic strength of desperation. "Let me have it you swine!" he all but screamed through clenched teeth in his native Genoese tongue. He had to signal Boccanegra, he had to bring those galleys back.

Before he could wrest the flag from the English admiral's grip, Montague was on him. What the earl had done many times in his secret day-dreams, now he could do in the real world. He brought his mailed fist smashing down on Fieschi's jaw with all the strength of his arm and shoulder and all the weight of his sudden charge. Fieschi was catapulted, reeling into the bulwark, and fell flat upon the decking.

Montague looked over to where Henry de Grosmont was watching the scene from the forecastle of his ship, threatening to overtake the *Thomas* in the rush toward the battle. The two men exchanged a smile of sheer contentment.

Fieschi slowly propped himself up on his forearms, dazed and dizzy, blood gushing from his mouth. He struggled to raise his head to look the King in the eye.

Edward calmly spoke. "You know, I expect your family can even search in its own bank-vaults to find the money it now owes to Boccanegra." With his right hand he indicated the departing galleys, never taking his eyes of the dark Genoese. "England shall pay for none of it."

The door closed behind the two men. For a long moment there was no sound but the distant dripping of water. Sluys, like London, was a dank, mouldy city where it seemed to rain perpetually.

"My Lord Earl, I beg forgiveness." The Genoese knelt low onto the stone floor, his head bowed. He was taking the trouble to speak in his best English court-French. His humble opening met with a raised eyebrow in the fair, northern face, nothing more. The blue eyes let only a hint of satisfaction show.

"I find myself caught between the hammer and the anvil... Should I tell my brothers, my cousins, my uncles that they must pay Boccanegra his fee, they will exile me to the humblest, dirtiest place in Europe... Perhaps they will kill me outright. But if we do not settle our account with him, Egidio Boccanegra will go to the Patricians of Genoa and sue the House of Fieschi for treason..." His dark eyes flickered over Montague's features, vainly looking for a sign of clemency.

"I understand that my behaviour has been... reprehensible in the extreme... but I can still be of service to His Majesty the King! No one in Europe knows of my humiliation yesterday... I can still carry out England's secret business abroad. You know my talents in this work!"

Still no reaction. Montague's eyes moved about naturally from the speaker's face to small objects around the room, as though he were wholly at ease.

"In God's name, I beg of you..."

There was another long moment of silence. When finally the Earl of Salisbury spoke, it was in a soft, delicate tone, measuring every word and every pause. His reply was calculated to make abundantly plain the enormity of the concession.

"All of the nobles who witnessed your humiliation yesterday, and all of the commoners, have been instructed to keep the strictest silence about what they saw. They are all loyal men. Your position as ambassador and negotiator will not be compromised. You will hereafter take orders first and foremost from the King of England, even at the cost of the wellbeing of your family, or of your city. If, by dint of truly excellent service, you demonstrate your worthiness to the King, you may yet be released to return to your lands and kin. Until such time, you are utterly in the power of the Crown of England.

"His Majesty is a just man, and will pay both Boccanegra's fee and a modicum to your family."

Fieschi sighed in naked gratitude. He bowed his head once more and spoke, his eyes upon the grey stone of the floor.

"I've learnt that the power of the Crown of England is… a power that runs very deep, my Lord Earl."

The Englishman inclined his head ever so slightly. He had known this from the very beginning.

A note on the sources

Only now do I realize that I have spent more time reading than writing in order to create *Auramala*. Research is already exhausting when one is writing about the present. When the story concerns the past, however, it becomes even more vital. Much of the information I have used came from historian friends and colleagues. Thanks to their vast knowledge I was able to orient myself in the world of the 14th century. Giovanni Acciai, Stefano Castagneto, Elena Corbellini, Luciano Maffi, Tomaso Perani, Christopher Wellington, and many others.

Many scholars have written about Edward II, his reign and the mystery of his death. In particular, I wish to mention Ian Mortimer, Mark Ormrod, Seymour Philips and Kathryn Warner. I also drew upon the work of Pierre Antonetti, Franco Cardini, Giovanni Cherubini, Bronislaw Geremek, Paolo Grillo, Jacuqes le Goff, Giovanni Miccoli, Jacques Rossiaud, Aldo Settia and many others in order to recreate the atmosphere and the context of medieval Europe. However, the source documents I made the most use of were original texts written in the 14th century. No historical study, however detailed and accurate it might be, can possibly bring that lost world to life like Boccaccio's *Decameron*, Chaucer's *Canterbury Tales*, Dante's *Divina Commedia*, Petrarch's letters, the writings of Opicino de Canistris, or the medieval statutes of the Lombard *comuni*, such as Voghera and Varzi. An exhaustive explanation of everything that lies behind this novel will unfold on *theauramalaproject.wordpress.com*

I am also profoundly grateful to Alessandro Balossini-Volpe, Diego, Peppe and Roberto Battaglia, Tiziano Bozzarelli, Marcella

Bricchi, nonna Gina Calissano, Simonetta Castronovo, Gianmarco Centinaio, Lucrezia Chiofalo, Eleni Corbellini Papapithagora, Riccardo Corbetta, Anna Corbi, Craig Foster, Simone Giugno, Sue and Christopher Gordon, Obizzo and Currado Malaspina, Lorena Mangiavacca, Raffaele Manni, Celestina Martinello, Monica Masanta, Sonia and Steve O'Hehir, Luigi Panigazzi, Ugo Perego, Chris Polatch and the English Naturally staff in Winchester, Serena and Oscar Ragni, Martin Richards, Alessio Rombolotti, Augusta Silvana Santachiara-Benerecetti, Ornella Semino, Annamaria and Claudia Soligno, our friends at Associazione Spino Fiorito, Christopher and Liisa Springham, Antonio Torroni, don Vincenzo, the monks of Sant'Alberto monastery and the Order of don Orione.

A note for the purists: certain errors or cases of imprecision found in Latin expressions are deliberate; the Welshman himself admits to being a poor Latin speaker… Indeed, as is common knowledge, medieval Latin was a far cry from the Latin of Cicero!

The Auramala Project

1327. Was the man found dead in Berkeley Castle really King Edward II of England? Or, as certain contemporary documents claim, did he escape to live the life of a hermit among the Apennines of Pavia? This is the mystery of the king who lived twice.

This is a medieval detective story, a tale of international intrigue whose resolution still lies buried in a secluded valley. Old men who live on the green hills and mountains of the Staffora Valley still recall their grandfathers telling them about "a king who escaped, otherwise they would have killed him…"

The Auramala Project has three goals: 1) to bring the mystery of the fate of Edward II to the attention of the general public by means of the historical novel *Auramala*; 2) to explore the archives of northern Italy, and not only, in search of hitherto unknown documents that may shed light on these events; 3) to use forensic techniques to ascertain exactly where, today, the remains of Edward II lie.

Auramala is not just a novel. It is a challenge to traditional history, written by the winners. It is a way to arouse attention concerning the life and death of Edward II, involving scientists, historians and lay people in an interdisciplinary research project designed to illuminate history, from the grassroots.

One of the most interesting aspects of *The Auramala Project* is the way in which the reader is involved in the mystery. It is an invitation to explore your own origins, and take part in the genealogical research.

Are you the king's descendant?

Index

XI   Acknowledgements

 3   Fabulae personae

 7   Prologue

13   Chapter 1

24   Chapter 2

34   Chapter 3

46   Chapter 4

51   Chapter 5

66   Chapter 6

75   Chapter 7

85   Chapter 8

92   Chapter 9

105	Chapter 10
120	Chapter 11
130	Chapter 12
140	Chapter 13
152	Chapter 14
162	Chapter 15
175	Chapter 16
195	Chapter 17
203	Chapter 18
222	Chapter 19
228	Chapter 20
254	Chapter 21
266	Chapter 22
273	Chapter 23
279	Chapter 24
286	Chapter 25
295	Chapter 26
304	Chapter 27
313	Chapter 28
329	Chapter 29
337	Chapter 30

347	Chapter 31
359	Chapter 32
364	Epilogue

| 369 | A note on the sources |
| 371 | The Auramala Project |

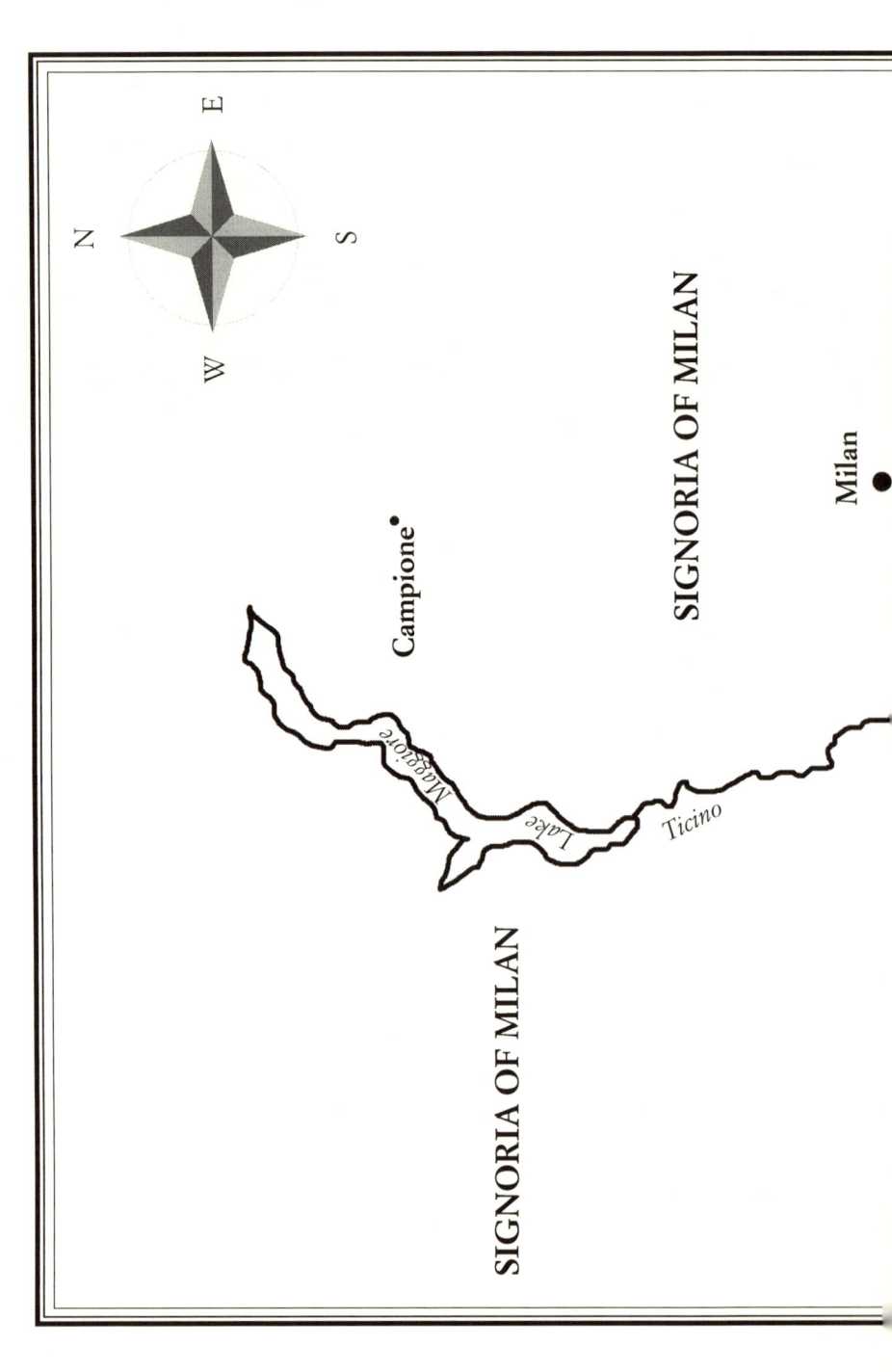

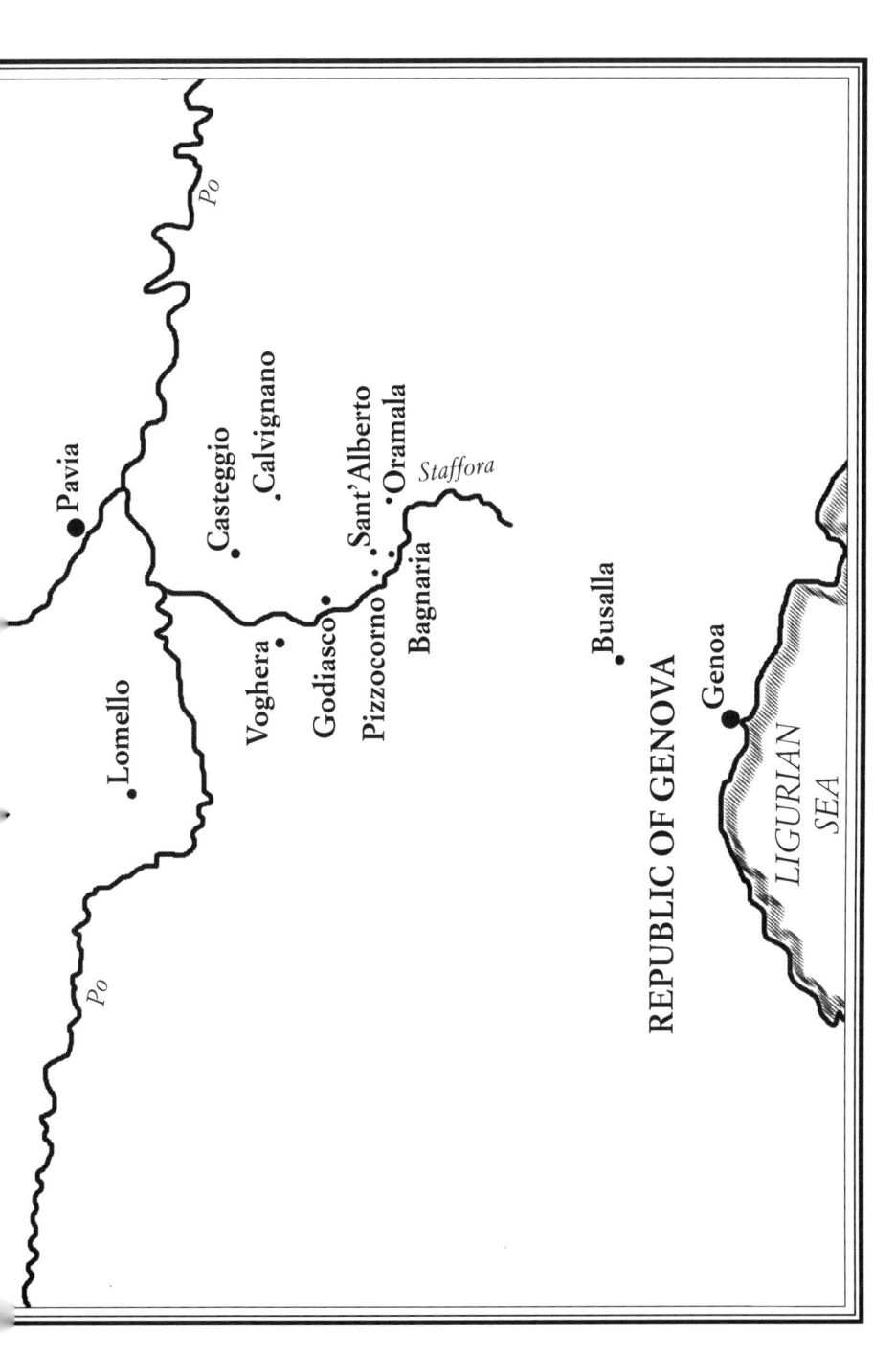